# Wilder

## The Halversons: Book #7

By

# KIMBERLY RAE
# JORDAN

# THREE**STRAND**
## P R E S S

A CORD OF THREE STRANDS IS NOT EASILY BROKEN.

*A man, a woman & their God.*
*Three Strand Press publishes Christian Romance stories*
*that intertwine love, faith and family. Always clean.*
*Always heartwarming. Always uplifting.*

Scripture taken from the New King James Version®. Copyright © 1982 by Thomas Nelson, Inc. Used by permission. All rights are reserved.

**Wilder/ Kimberly Rae Jordan**. -- 1st ed.
ISBN-13: 978-1-988409-80-1

*Teach me to do Your will,*
*For You are my God;*
*Your Spirit is good.*
*Lead me in the land of uprightness.*

Psalm 143:10

# CHAPTER ONE

Wilder Halverson shifted in his seat, grateful that, for whatever reason, the airline had upgraded him from economy to first class for his flight from Reykjavik, Iceland to Spokane, Washington. He'd traveled enough in economy, with his knees bumping the seat in front of him, to appreciate the times he was blessed with an upgrade.

"Heading home?"

He looked at the older woman seated beside him. She was probably about his parents' age. But while his mom tended to choose more comfortable clothes when she traveled, this woman was dressed in a dark blue pantsuit with a paisley scarf. Her short silver hair was styled elegantly, and she wore several pieces of jewelry that Wilder was sure cost a fortune.

When he traveled, he opted for comfort over style, like his mom. Which meant he was dressed in a pair of black joggers, a long sleeve T-shirt, and a pair of Converse sneakers.

At first, he'd assumed the woman was a bit of a snob, because she'd spent most of the flight working on her laptop. Wilder had also spent his time working, though he'd been on his tablet.

"Yes. My family lives in northern Idaho." He smiled at her. "And you?"

"I'm meeting some friends for a girls' weekend near Serenity Point. Do you know the place?"

"I do," Wilder said with a nod. "It's my hometown."

"I've never been to this part of the US before," she said. "What's it like?"

Wilder had no problem giving her the run-down on the area. After all, he knew it very well, plus he was used to sharing the highlights of a place when he did his travel videos. It was a nice reminder of all the things he loved about his hometown, and why he was eager to get back to Serenity.

When the announcement came that they were beginning their descent into Spokane International Airport, Wilder turned to look out the window. The sun had set about an hour earlier, so there wasn't much to see beyond a scattering of lights across the dark landscape.

But they were lights that represented home.

His time away from Serenity seemed longer than it had in the past, though that hadn't actually been the case. In fact, he was coming home a little earlier in the year than he usually did. He wasn't usually so glad to be back, but he was.

In the past, he'd always been happy to be back in Serenity and to see his family, but this time, it felt like more than that. It was a sense of relief that he hadn't ever experienced before, which made no sense. Especially since he'd seen his parents only two weeks earlier.

His parents had been with him at the orphanage in Thailand until they'd had headed home while he'd flown to Iceland to film a collaboration that he'd had scheduled with a travel company there. He'd enjoyed spending time with his parents in a ministry setting, and he'd been proud of how they'd thrown themselves into the work there.

Once the plane was on the ground, the woman next to him exhaled audibly. "Flying is not my favorite thing."

"It is always good to get back on land," Wilder agreed, though he didn't really mind flying. If he did, he wouldn't be able to live life the way he wanted.

Because they were in first class, they were among the first to disembark. Wilder thought the woman might walk with him, but she took off, walking quickly up the jetway.

Wilder followed at a more leisurely pace, knowing that he'd still have to wait for his luggage at the baggage claim. As he neared the area, he looked around, curious to see who was there to pick him up.

Once he'd had his flight information, he'd dropped it in the family chat and trusted that someone would be there to pick him up. It was how he'd done it the last few years whenever he'd returned to Serenity Point.

He grinned when he spotted his brother, Lee. "Did you draw the short straw?"

Lee pulled him in for a hug, pounding him lightly on the back. "Nah. I volunteered."

Wilder hadn't seen much of his older brother in the last few years, since Lee hadn't lived in Serenity. They'd usually seen each other for Christmas, and that was about it.

"So, I hear you're settling down," Wilder said as they stood at the baggage claim conveyor.

A smile grew on Lee's face as he crossed his arms. "You heard right. New job. New love. It's been a bit of a journey, but I'm happy here."

"Never thought I'd see the day, honestly," Wilder said as he thumped him on the shoulder. "You seemed very happy in Chicago."

"I was," Lee agreed. "But circumstances change, you know."

"Your breakup?"

"No. I would have stayed there after that, but then I was laid off."

"Did they just happen to be hiring at the vet clinic in Serenity?"

"Dr. Carl had been trying to handle it all on his own since it's not a super busy clinic, but his wife told him he needed to hire someone to help now that he was getting older."

"Perfect timing."

"God's timing," Lee said.

Wilder wasn't surprised by Lee's response. In his family, God's timing was definitely an accepted belief. Even he had experienced moments when it seemed that God had guided him to just the right place at just the right time.

"You didn't bring your new girlfriend with you?" Wilder asked as he eyed the suitcases that were tumbling down onto the conveyor belt. "Afraid she might decide she likes me better?"

Lee's laughter was immediate. "Yeah. No. That's never going to happen."

As he spotted his suitcase, Wilder took a step closer to the conveyor belt. "You seem pretty sure of that."

"I'm not just *pretty* sure," Lee said. "I'm one hundred percent certain."

Wilder grabbed the suitcase's handle and hefted it off the belt. "I'm wondering if I should take offense to that."

"It has nothing to do with the sort of man you are," Lee said. "I would be as certain about her meeting Chris Hemsworth."

After pulling the handle of the suitcase up, Wilder set his backpack on it. "That kind of makes me feel better, I guess."

"Rori's an amazing woman, and I know she is as devoted to me as I am to her."

As they walked away from the baggage claim area, Wilder's thoughts went to the woman he'd gotten to know during his stay in Thailand. Miriam was the daughter of the couple running the orphanage. She'd grown up there and had returned to the US to study nursing. Once she'd graduated, she'd gone back to Thailand to work alongside her parents.

Since they were close to the same age, and their parents had gotten along well, they'd ended up spending a lot of time together. For the first time, Wilder had seriously considered how a relationship might fit into his life.

Unfortunately, despite the connection they had as friends, the relationship hadn't gone any further. There had been no romantic connection. Wilder had left Thailand with the promise that they'd keep in touch, but only as friends.

"Are you ready for the ski season?" Lee asked as he guided his car out of the airport parking lot.

"As ready as I ever am." After spending several months in the heat and humidity of the tropics, he was looking forward to winter. His brief stop in Iceland had been a nice re-introduction to cooler temps.

"Kayleigh said they've built a big indoor ice rink at the resort."

"Yeah. She mentioned that in one of our chats."

"She didn't seem one hundred percent sold on its necessity."

"Neither am I. I don't know that it's going to get a lot of use, but it was Alexander's call, and he was adamant."

"I get the feeling that one doesn't argue with Alexander," Lee said.

"You've met him, right?"

"Yes. At Kayleigh and Hudson's wedding. He appears to have a forceful personality."

Wilder gave a huff of laughter. "That's one way of putting it."

"Kayleigh did mention that someone would be hired to work there with people like you do on the slopes. She might even give figure skating lessons, which works out well because the woman that's been teaching Layla and Amelia has recently moved away."

Wilder was looking forward to seeing his nieces and nephews. He viewed them and the lives they lived in a different light after his experiences of the past couple of years with the orphanages. He'd gotten a good hard look at how their lives could have been, had they been born under different circumstances.

It also helped him view his adopted brothers and sister in a new light. He'd never really questioned why his parents had adopted kids when they had so many of their own. However, Wilder had seen firsthand where kids who lost their parents or who were abandoned could end up.

"You could give skating lessons," Lee said. "If I recall, you enjoyed ice skating."

"Well, not figure skating. If I'd done any on ice sport, it probably would have been hockey or maybe speed skating."

"Does the same group of people come back every year to work the ski season?"

"Not usually. I'm the only one who's been a regular for the last several years. But there will probably be one or two people who are back from last year."

"You don't keep in contact with your co-workers?"

"Not really. The only one I talk to periodically is the sport shop manager, who is my supervisor when I'm here."

Given how he'd chosen to live his life, he had a lot of friends in a lot of different places, but those friendships weren't necessarily close. There were a few people who also had a nomadic lifestyle that he hung out with if their paths happened to cross when he was traveling.

"Are you okay staying at Charli and Janessa's?" Lee asked.

"Yep. All I need is a decent bed, and I'm happy."

Before they'd left, his parents had let him know that they had some friends coming to visit them for a few weeks. He probably could have stayed there anyway, but hanging out with his siblings and their families wouldn't be a hardship.

"You still living there too?"

"Yep. Eventually, I'll probably get a place of my own, but I'm in no rush."

"You don't mind having the kids around?"

"Nope. They're good kids, and I think Charli appreciates having several other adults around to help with them."

Wilder let out a long breath as he relaxed back into his seat. It had been a long day of travel, and he was ready to get to where he was going to call home for the next little while. Give him a shower, a comfortable bed, and no need to be up, and he'd sleep like the dead for twelve plus hours.

He was hungry though, so he asked Lee to pull into a fast food place so that he could eat something that wasn't a bag of peanuts or didn't cost the earth. Airport restaurants and the food offered on the plane was always well above his budget.

For the rest of the trip home, they chatted about what was going on with the family, and Wilder shared a bit about what he'd been up to. A lot had already gone on that year, what with Charli and Blake getting married on New Year's Eve, then adopting a baby girl.

He hadn't met the baby yet, but his mom and dad had shown him a ton of pictures. Every day Charli sent them pictures of baby Shiloh and the older girls. Though there was a big focus on the baby.

It was nearly nine by the time they made it to the house, but as he and Lee approached the front door, it was flung open to reveal his oldest niece.

"Uncle Wilder!" Layla greeted him with a grin and a tight hug.

She'd grown since he'd last seen her. He was sure that was true for all his nieces and nephews. Being away from them was one of the downsides since it meant he was missing those changes in them.

"Hey, princess," he said as he hugged her back. "How's life?"

"Good!"

"It's good to have you back home," Charli said, hurrying over to hug him.

With each hug—or back slap—that he shared with the members of his family who were there, Wilder felt a piece of his heart settle into place. It wasn't a foreign feeling—he got it every time he returned home—but this time, the feeling was stronger than ever.

Though he loved traveling around the world, meeting new people and seeing new places, that lifestyle came with some stresses. There were language barriers, cultural differences, and unfamiliar foods. None of that had ever been detrimental enough to tempt him away from the nomadic life. Still, it was a bit of a relief when those stresses slipped away as soon as he stepped foot back in Serenity.

There really was something to be said for coming home.

# CHAPTER TWO

Wilder climbed out of his car—the one he left parked at his parents' house whenever he was away from Serenity—and headed for the ski shop.

On his drive there, he'd swung by the newly constructed ice rink, which fit right in with the resort's look with its large glass windows and timber supports. He was going to have to check it out some day.

He wasn't due to start work as a ski instructor officially until there was snow on the slopes, which could still be three or four weeks away. But when he'd called Trev, he'd invited Wilder to come in for the recreational department weekly staff meeting.

The department included the people who took care of all the recreational areas, the instructors, the lifeguards for the hotel's pools, and the people who worked in the shop. It was usually a good group of people, and Wilder looked forward to seeing a few familiar faces among the news ones.

"Wilder!"

He smiled at the man striding toward him. "Hey there, Trev. How's it going?"

Trevor clapped him on the shoulder as he grinned back at him. "It's going great. You showing up means it's almost my favorite time of year."

"What? My arrival isn't your favorite time of the year?"

Trevor laughed. "Nope. Sorry, it's not. But it heralds it."

Chatting about the upcoming ski season, they made their way to the staff room at the back of the building.

"So is the skating rink under your supervision too?"

Trevor nodded as he took a seat at one of the tables. "Yep. Although, at the moment, there are only two skating instructors and a guy who takes care of skate sharpening, rentals, and the ice. There's a café there as well, but those employees don't fall under this department."

"Hey, Wilder!"

Wilder lifted his hand for a high five from the young man who'd joined them in the staff room. "How are you doing, Anthony?"

"I'm doing great!" He dropped down beside Wilder. "How are things out there in the big, wide world?"

Wilder thought of the orphanages he'd spent time at. "Some good. Some bad."

"So kind of like life in Serenity."

"Yep."

"Did Trev tell you we have some new employees?"

"We always have new employees."

"Yeah, but these ones." Anthony's eyes widened. "They are... wow."

Wilder lifted his brows, but then gave a shake of his head. "You certainly haven't changed in the months since I've been gone."

"Why would I change?" Anthony leaned back in his chair, stretching his legs out under the table they sat at, and laced his fingers behind his head. "I'm perfect."

"And humble to boot."

"Humility is overrated."

Wilder didn't happen to agree, but he also didn't plan to waste his breath trying to convince the guy of that. He'd learn that lesson soon enough. Perhaps at the hands of one of the new employees.

A few more people joined them, and Anthony took it upon himself to introduce the new employees to Wilder. The young man's grin grew as he interacted with a couple of the girls who worked as lifeguards with him. They were—of course—very fit, and both had long blond hair pulled back into braids.

"Nice to meet you, Wilder," one of them said with a flirty smile. "Anthony has told us about you."

"Only good things, I hope," Wilder replied.

Both girls giggled. "Of course."

Wilder could see why these girls appealed to Anthony. They were beautiful, engaging, and because they worked the same job, they already had something in common.

Amy, the taller of the two, kept her attention on Wilder while the other young woman chatted with Anthony and another guy who'd come in with them. "Do you ever swim here?"

"Not usually. I pretty much stick to the slopes when I'm at the resort."

"That's too bad," she said, coming around the table to sit next to him. "You should reconsider. They've redone a couple of the pools. One is saltwater, which a lot of people really like, and the other has a rock bottom."

If he was going to swim in saltwater, Wilder much preferred the ocean. And sometimes that also came with a rock bottom, depending which beach he was at.

Another woman showed up as they talked, glancing around for a moment before sliding her way between people to take a seat in the back of the room. Anthony didn't introduce her, though his gaze followed her.

It was the next woman who arrived that captured Wilder's attention in a way the other women hadn't.

The new arrival was small in build and stature, but as soon as she stepped into the room, she commanded attention. Her dark brown hair was pulled back, leaving just a light sweep of long bangs across her forehead. It was her eyes that stood out most to Wilder. They were a pale icy blue, framed by long dark lashes.

Coming to a stop just inside the door, her frosty gaze swept the room. She stood with her chin lifted and her shoulders back. The confidence with which she carried herself, even in stillness, fascinated Wilder.

It was like everyone was holding their breath, waiting to see what she would do.

Her gaze met Wilder's for a moment, just long enough for him to give her a smile—which she didn't return—before moving on to the woman beside him. When she did move again, it was to head toward the woman who'd arrived just before her.

Once she'd taken her seat, Trev got to his feet.

"Thanks for coming, everyone," he said. "I won't keep you too long. However, we've started to move into a new season, which means we have some new people joining our team. I thought it would be a good time to introduce everyone and to answer any questions you might have.

"First, introductions. I'm Trevor White, the recreational supervisor." He motioned to Anthony, giving his name as he introduced the aquatic employees before moving on. "Wilder is our head ski instructor. He's worked here the longest, so if you have any ski related questions, talk to him. Most of the ski crew will be starting in a few weeks, depending on the snow situation."

Wilder nodded in acknowledgement. He knew from past years that Trev tended to be fairly hands off when it came to the ski instructors because he trusted Wilder to keep them in line.

"We have three new employees who've been hired to work at the skating rink." Motioning to a middle-aged man who stood near the door, Trev said, "George is in charge of skate sharpening and rentals, along with ice maintenance. Alexandra is in charge of the rink and helping to people who need it on the ice. Talya is part-time, working the two days that Alexandra is off to supervise the rink's use."

*Alexandra.* The name held a regalness that matched the way the woman held herself. It made Wilder very curious about her.

Maybe he would see what Kayleigh could tell him about the newest resort employee.

Although, asking any of his siblings about a woman was a sure way to crank their matchmaking attempts up to maximum. He wasn't ready for that.

Alexandra kept her gaze on Trev as he finished his introductions and moved onto his expectations for staff members of the recreation department. Trev might come across as easy-going and laid back, but he ran the department with a tight fist. There was no way he would have kept his job at the resort if he didn't.

There had been a few employees over the years who had mistakenly thought he'd cut them slack when it came to timeliness or the tidiness of their uniforms. They were now working elsewhere.

"Any questions?" Trev asked once he was done. "None? Okay. Just remember that you can always come and speak to me about any questions or concerns you have. I like to keep the lines of communication open."

When no one else spoke up, Trev dismissed them. Anthony flashed Wilder a peace sign as he left the room with the other lifeguards. Wilder stayed in his seat, watching as Alexandra spoke to Talya. The other woman seemed a bit uncomfortable, which didn't surprise Wilder too much.

Some people probably found the confidence that Alexandra carried to be intense. They didn't know how to react to it.

In some ways, Alexandra reminded Wilder of Kayleigh. His sister also carried a very confident air and had always been focused and determined. She'd worked hard to earn—and keep—her position as manager of the resort. Sure, she was now married to the son of the owner, but she had earned the position well before she'd met Hudson.

Trev headed over to the two women. "Is everything okay at the rink, Alexandra? No concerns with the schedule or the building?"

"No. Everything is fine, though it seems to be rather dead most days."

"I think it will be like that for a little while longer," Trev said. "It's something new at the resort, so it might take some time for it to garner more interest. Are you able to fill your time when there's no one skating?"

Alexandra nodded. "I spend most of my time on the ice, whether or not people are there."

Wilder wondered what sort of skater she was. He imagined they would want to make sure they had people who had some knowledge about skating. Even on the slopes, they didn't just hire people who liked to ski. They had to have enough knowledge of the sport to be able to coach others—especially those who were skiing for the first time.

He'd wager it was easier to teach someone to ski than to ice skate. Back when he'd been learning both sports, he'd definitely found that he picked up skiing faster than skating. But that could just be him. He enjoyed his time on skis more than on skates.

However, he might make the time to do some skating at the new ice rink.

"I have a couple of girls coming for a lesson on Saturday morning," Alexandra said.

"Are they guests of the hotel or from Serenity?"

"From Serenity. Apparently, their previous teacher quit."

Wilder's brows rose at that. Was she talking about Layla and Amelia? He knew Charli had spoken to Kayleigh about the girls getting some coaching from the new employees at the rink.

He might just have to tag along.

Wilder watched as Alexandra got to her feet. The top of her head barely reached Trev's shoulder, but she seemed to stand taller.

"I'd better get back to the rink. I got a call from the front desk saying they'd had people ask about rink availability today, so I want to be there when we open."

"Sounds good." Trev turned to Talya. "Thanks for coming out for the meeting. I hope you remembered to log in. You'll be paid for your time."

"I did. Thanks." She gave him a quick smile, then followed Alexandra out of the room.

Trev stared after them for a moment before turning to face Wilder. It was just the two of them in the room once again.

"I'm never sure how to deal with her." Chuckling, Trev sank down in a nearby chair. "She actually intimidates me."

"I can see why." Wilder didn't think he'd be intimated by her, but that was probably because he was used to dealing with confident women. Alexandra did seem to take it to a whole new level, however. "Is she local?"

Trev shook his head. "She's a top-hire. Alexander Remington sent her to us."

"Really?" Wilder wasn't surprised that the man had involved himself in the staffing at the resort. He'd been instrumental in the positions Wilder and Kayleigh held, though most didn't know the connection. "Do you think the rink is going to be popular?"

Trev shrugged. "I think we're going to need to make it a bit gimmicky, at least at first, which isn't something I ever thought we'd want here at the resort."

"Gimmicky?"

"You know. Have theme nights. Stuff like that."

Wilder remembered that the old roller rink in town had been like that. It made sense to utilize something similar at the resort, but he wasn't sure that Kayleigh or Alexandra would agree. They both looked like they didn't buy into gimmicky stuff.

"Well, I'm due to grab some lunch with Kayleigh," Wilder said as he got to his feet. "I'll probably be around, but I won't show up to officially work the slopes until the snow is here. However, if you need me for anything, you know you can call me."

"I do. I appreciate your willingness to help out." He held out his hand for Wilder to shake. "I think we're good for now."

Wilder walked through the front of the building, where people could come to buy or rent ski equipment or just hang out near the fireplace. It was quiet at the moment, but once the slopes were open, that would change.

Cool air greeted Wilder as he stepped outside. He glanced around as he strode to his car, checking to see if Alexandra was still in the vicinity. There was no sign of her, so Wilder climbed into his car and set off for the hotel.

A few minutes later, he was greeting the hostess at The Steak-house. She was someone he knew from his time working there, so he chatted with her for a couple of minutes before she left him at the table Kayleigh had reserved for them.

Wilder spent some time looking through his social media while he waited for his sister to appear. He didn't have much to respond to since he hadn't posted a video in a few weeks. He still had to finish editing his sponsored video from Iceland, along with a couple of other videos he'd taken while in Asia.

In addition to his videos, he also did some digital marketing. His degree was in business with a focus on marketing, and he'd slowly been building up a portfolio. He was a digital nomad, which meant that he could do his work from anywhere as long as he had an internet connection.

He knew his family thought he was just about traveling and posting videos of the places he visited, and then working as a ski instructor in the winter. Both of which were true, but he was also building another business. He knew that he shouldn't put all his eggs into one basket, which was why he had several streams of income.

"Hey."

Wilder looked up to see Kayleigh settling into the seat across from him. "Hi."

"It's good to have you back," she said with a smile. "I must say I breathe a sigh of relief whenever you and Mom and Dad come back home."

"You worry about us?"

Kayleigh shrugged. "I think that's natural given the places you visit sometimes. They're not always safe for foreigners."

"Sometimes they're not safe for their own citizens either," Wilder said, thinking about the street kids he'd seen.

"True. But you're the ones I love."

Wilder hadn't been especially close to Kayleigh growing up since she was a few years older than him. He'd been closer to Lee, Charli, and Janessa. But since they'd begun working at the same place, they'd grown closer.

"Is Hudson around?"

Kayleigh shook her head. "He's off in New York meeting with Alexander. He'll be home later this afternoon."

It had been a surprise when Kayleigh had gotten involved with Hudson, but now that Wilder had gotten to know the man, he could see how perfect they were for each other. He also appreciated how Hudson had fit so well into their family.

"How did your meeting with Trev go?" Kayleigh asked.

"It went well. He introduced some of the new employees for the season." Wilder paused before adding, "He mentioned that he was intimidated by one of the new employees for the ice rink."

Kayleigh laughed. "Alexandra?"

Wilder nodded.

"Yep. I think she intimidates most people."

"Kind of like how they are of you."

Pressing a hand to her chest, Kayleigh batted her eyelashes. "Intimidated by little ol' me?"

"You both might come in small packages, but you sure pack a wallop in personality."

"What did you think of her?"

"She seems very confident," he said. "Which could make her intimidating, I suppose."

"Alexander hired her."

"Is she a hidden daughter?"

"Ha. No. He told Hudson that she's his goddaughter."

"Does Hudson know her?"

Kayleigh shook her head. "Nope. All Alexander said was that she was the daughter of an old friend of Candace's, and that he was her godfather. I don't know much about that kind of relationship, so I have no clue how close they really are."

"What type of skating experience does she have? She comes across as a performer."

Kayleigh didn't have a chance to answer before their server approached the table. Since they both knew the menu well enough, they went ahead and placed their orders.

Once the young man had left them, Wilder prodded Kayleigh for the information again. "Experience?"

"I don't know if it's supposed to be confidential, but since she skated under her real name and she's still using it here, I can't imagine it's a big secret."

"Well, that sounds ominous." And definitely ramped up Wilder's curiosity about the woman.

"It's not the best of situations," Kayleigh said. "Bottom line is that her father got involved in some illegal activities and will probably have to spend the rest of his life in prison. He defrauded a bunch of people, including her skating partner and his parents, and their coaches. Her partner dropped her, and she was basically shunned by the figure skating community."

Wilder would never have guessed that by the woman's demeanor. "So she's not skating competitively anymore?"

"She has no partner, and it seems that people thought she'd had knowledge of what her father did. Kind of hard to get a partner and coaches without trust and money."

"That must be tough."

"Definitely." Kayleigh thanked the server when he returned with their drinks. "Part of me thinks that Alexander built that ice rink just to give her somewhere to go."

"Alexander... Alexandra... Was she named for him?"

"It's possible. Alexander didn't say."

"What type of career did she have competing?"

"Pretty illustrious. They were national champions for a few years and had several medals at world championships and an Olympic gold. She and her partner had been favorites for the gold at the upcoming Olympics, which are next year, when everything fell apart."

"So she wasn't just a pretty face with lots of money. She had the talent."

Kayleigh smiled at him. "You think she's pretty?"

"You don't?"

"Well, yes, I suppose she *is* beautiful."

"I think anyone with eyes could see that. I'm sure it helped her career. Beauty and talent are always a deadly combination." Recalling the comment Alexandra had made, Wilder asked, "Is she going to be giving the girls lessons?"

"Yep. Their first one is tomorrow. They're very excited. Well, Layla is excited. Amelia's a little nervous."

"How do you think Charli and Blake are doing with all the changes in their lives?"

Kayleigh's expression turned contemplative. "I think they're doing okay. Charli's struggling with being back to teaching full-time and away from the baby."

"Yeah, she mentioned that."

"But other than that, I think she and Blake have really stepped up and done what is necessary for their family. The girls seem to be thriving as well."

Over the past couple of days, Wilder had enjoyed hanging out with Layla and Amelia. The latter was still a bit shy around him. Considering he hadn't had much time to spend with her before he'd left in April, it wasn't a surprise. Hopefully she followed Layla's lead and warmed up to him because even though there was no blood tie between them, Wilder considered her a niece as much as Layla was.

"Are you coming to pizza night tonight?" Wilder asked.

Kayleigh shook her head. "With Hudson just getting home, I'll be hanging out with him."

"I think there's a game at the high school this evening too, so some of us will probably be going to that."

As much as Wilder enjoyed the freedom of navigating the world on his own, he also enjoyed the traditions and familiarity of being in Serenity. Hanging out with his family and going to the basketball games that Jay coached were definitely at the top of the list of things he liked to do.

He wondered what Alexandra did with her time. Did she have any friends who had stayed with her after everything that had happened with her dad? Wilder hoped so, but he knew that not everyone was a friend who stuck with a person through the rough patches in life.

It was possible that with her intimidating personality, she didn't have an easy time making friends. Or keeping them.

Good thing for Alexandra, if she needed a friend, Wilder would be happy to be one.

If he could just get past the walls it seemed like she'd erected with her intimidating personality.

# CHAPTER THREE

Alexandra Corbyn stood with her arms on the top of the boards of the ice rink. Well, they weren't really boards. They were nothing like she'd ever seen at any rink she'd been at.

The half wall encircling the rink was something transparent, though she didn't think it was glass. Topping the transparent part were rustic looking pieces of wood that had been polished and matched end to end to form an oval. It really was a beautiful-looking place.

Most rinks she'd skated in had bleachers surrounding the ice, but this one had round tables with chairs ringing it. The walls of the building itself were made up of floor to ceiling windows with opaque blinds that could be lowered, depending on the position of the sun.

This rink—like many—had a place to get drinks and food. Only the menu didn't offer hotdogs or bags of chips. No, it had complicated sandwiches, fancy soups, and pastry items.

It was definitely over-the-top for what a skating rink usually offered. But this skating rink catered to the rich who might want to grab a bite to eat in between laps around the rink. Or a parent who brought their kids to the rink but didn't want to skate themselves.

And here she was, in charge of the place. Oh, how the mighty had fallen.

At one point in her life, if they'd come to the resort, Lexi would have been out on the ice, and her mom would have been sitting at one of the tables with an expensive coffee in hand.

Right then, however, she would have given it all up for the more practical rink she'd practiced in for years. Or a rink with ads on the boards and an audience who loved figure skating competitions, screaming and waving posters with her and Mikhail's faces on them.

Lexi's stomach tightened as a familiar anger flickered inside her. She took a deep breath, held it, then exhaled heavily.

Would she ever not feel angry and betrayed?

For sure, it wasn't that day.

She pulled her phone out of the pocket of her jacket and checked the time. Seeing it was nearly six in the morning, she tapped the screen to pull up her mom's contact information.

Every day at that time, she called her mom, since she was in the south of France, so nine hours ahead of where Lexi was in Idaho.

"Hello, Lexi, my darling." Her mom's face filled the screen of her phone. "How are you doing?"

"I'm fine, Momma," Lexi said, unwilling to ever tell her anything to the contrary. "How are you?"

"I'm doing well." The luminous smile on her mom's face seemed to back up her words. "Leland is off checking on the yacht. They're supposed to be finishing up the interior this week, and we're going to go out for a few days once it's done."

Lexi smiled, though it wasn't how she really felt in the moment. A small part of the anger she held inside was directed at her mom. Even though she loved her beyond words, Lexi struggled with how easily her mom had moved on.

That was probably because she hadn't lost her career the way Lexi had, along with the betrayal they'd both been dealt. She might have lost her first marriage, but she'd already moved on to her second.

The moment Eileen Corbyn had gotten a whiff of the fact that her husband was under investigation for fraud, embezzlement and a bunch of other white-collar crimes, she'd filed for divorce. She'd put distance between herself and her husband as quickly as possible.

The man she'd married afterward was nice enough, but it hurt that her mom had been able to put everything behind her so quickly while Lexi still struggled.

Lexi hadn't been able to escape the impact of her father's actions as easily. The past year and a half had been a struggle, as she'd lost her career due to her father's notoriety. And his recent trial had been a horribly difficult time for her.

Obviously, it had been difficult for her father too, but Lexi didn't particularly care what he felt because he'd made his own bed. He could lie in it.

The punishment she'd been dealt for his actions felt particularly harsh, but she hadn't been able to mitigate any of it.

The only reason she'd finally found a place for herself on the other side of the country in small town Idaho after her mom had left New York City for France was that her godfather—a man she hadn't even known—had stepped in and offered her a job at the new ice rink he'd had built at one of his resort properties.

She was grateful that Alexander Remington hadn't abandoned them like so many friends had, but she supposed it helped that his wife had been a friend of her mother's, not her father's.

"Do you think you'll come visit soon, darling?" her mom asked, interrupting her rabbiting thoughts. "I miss you so much."

"I've only just started here, Momma. I don't think I can ask for time off so soon."

Her mom wrinkled her nose. "Maybe I should have a word with Alexander. Surely he'd understand."

Lexi wasn't so sure that her namesake was going to cut her any slack. From what she'd learned about him recently, he was a fair, but firm, businessman.

He didn't have any involvement in her job there beyond hiring her. The manager at the resort was a woman named Kayleigh St. James, who Lexi had discovered was married to a high-level employee in Remington Properties.

"No, Momma," Lexi said firmly. "Don't bother Alexander about it. For now, we'll just have to be happy with this way of communicating."

Her mom's shoulders slumped as she gave a little pout. It was a pout she'd never grown out of, apparently, since Lexi had seen her doing it all of her life. While it might have worked on her husbands, both current and ex, it didn't work on Lexi.

She was immune to her mom's attempts to get her way. For as much as she loved her, Lexi didn't like how she moved through life, usually manipulating in subtle ways to get what she wanted. She had a super sweet disposition, which helped make people want to give her what she wanted. That just wasn't Lexi's personality.

From a young age, Lexi had learned that if she wanted to reach her goal of winning gold medals for her skating, she was going to have to work hard. No coy smiles or pouty looks were going to get her what she wanted.

It was a weird way for her mom to operate, considering she was also a Christian. Her dad had claimed to be a Christian, too, but that admission hadn't been borne out by his actions. It was probably because of that claim that he'd been able to swindle so many people behind the scenes.

"You and Leland can always come visit me here," Lexi said. "The resort would definitely meet your standards as a vacation destination. Lots of luxuries. Great views."

Her mom wrinkled her nose. "You know I don't want to go back to the US just yet."

Lexi did know that, and part of her understood her mom's reasoning, but she wished she'd still be willing to come back in order to see her only child.

"We'll just have to see how things go for now," Lexi said.

"You better be here for Christmas."

"I make no promises, Momma. But I'll try."

Another pout told Lexi that her mom wasn't happy with that response, but there was no other one that she could give her.

"Are you going to skate this morning?"

"Yep. Want to watch for a bit?"

Her mom had been at most of her practices over the years. Since her dad had built a practice rink on their property in Maine, it had been convenient for her mom to attend the practices.

"Of course, darling."

Lexi set up her phone, carefully situating the tripod for her mom's optimal viewing of the ice. Bending over into the frame, she said, "If you need to go before I'm done, I'll talk to you later. Love you, Momma."

"Love you too, darling." She blew Lexi a kiss. "Now off you go."

Lexi used the Bluetooth connection on her tablet to bring up her playlist and start it. She went to the entrance of the ice and slipped the guards off her blades. Setting them aside, she stepped onto the ice and took a few strokes toward the center of the ice.

She closed her eyes for a moment, relishing the feeling of gliding across the ice.

This was her home. Her special place. Her source of joy and comfort. Her past, her present, and, at one time, her future.

It had been her everything... until her life had imploded thanks to her dad.

Opening her eyes, Lexi clenched her hands, then shook them out. She was trying to keep her anger off the ice. Especially when she was alone, able to do all her favorite jumps and spins.

If she'd been a singles skater, she would have had programs she could skate through. Unfortunately, she was a pairs skater without a partner.

That was okay, though. She had adapted some of the programs, and she'd also developed her own choreography to some of her favorite songs.

She'd done some stretches when she'd first arrived at the arena, but now she stretched some more as she moved across the ice.

Soon, the last vestiges of her anger evaporated, and she forgot where the ice she skated on was located. She forgot that her mom was watching from her phone.

Lexi forgot everything and let herself become one with the ice.

Calm flowed over her as she completed jump after jump. The spins took her apart and put her back together again.

Halfway through the length of time she usually skated in the morning, she took a break to drink some water and catch her breath. When she skated over to her phone, she saw that her mom had gone, which was fine and not out of the ordinary.

When her playlist ended, Lexi stroked to the edge of the ice and stepped off. She bent over to put her guards on her blades, then once again leaned against the boards, staring out at the ice.

Though she'd skated to other music that she and Mikhail had used in previous years, she still hadn't been able to listen to the compilation of Ed Sheeran songs that they'd been preparing to use at the Olympics, which was now just months away.

It had been her favorite program to date, and the romance of the music had reflected their off-ice relationship. After seriously dating for a couple of years, they'd gotten engaged in the off-season.

Pushing away from the boards, Lexi sat down on a nearby padded bench and unlaced her skates. Once off, she removed the guards to make sure the blades were dry before putting them back in place.

She slid her feet into her favorite pair of sneakers, then picked up the skates and carried them to the small office she'd been assigned. Since she'd only been there a couple of weeks, she hadn't really personalized the space yet.

Lexi was still trying to figure out her position there. When he'd hired her, Alexander had been sort of vague in what he wanted her to do, which seemed out of the ordinary for a businessman of his stature.

The rink was open from one until seven on weekdays and eleven to nine on weekends. Her current schedule was from Thursday to Monday. Although, if they'd asked her to work seven days a week, she would have happily done that.

In addition to her time spent at the rink for her job, Alexander had also told her she could take on private students if she wanted. Lexi wasn't sure yet if she wanted to do that, beyond the two girls she was meeting with the next morning.

At one time, her focus had been on her future. Every win she and Mikhail had achieved was another step up the staircase of coaching respectability. Every win gave them the ability to command more exclusivity and pay. They would be able to choose who they wanted to coach.

A career as a figure skater had to be as much about the present as the future. People couldn't maintain a highly competitive level of performance until the conventional retirement age.

Some people went on to perform in skating shows, and while Lexi hadn't been opposed to that, eventually, even that would end. So she and Mikhail had been looking past even that.

It was why they'd both worked so hard on their craft. They'd been known for being great pairs skaters, but beyond that, they'd been great singles skaters too. They'd practiced their singles elements almost as much as their pairs ones. And when they weren't on the ice, they were working out and taking ballet lessons.

They'd been very involved in the choosing of their music and choreography, while Lexi had also focused on their costumes, working with designers to create the perfect outfits that reflected them and the music they skated to.

Now it was all gone.

The early morning practices. The workouts. The hectic travel schedules. The fierce competitions. The injuries. The recoveries.

None of it was left except for the practices and workouts that she'd continued with, even a year and a half after she'd last competed. But they were without real purpose now.

Still, she couldn't get away from the habits of a lifetime. Which was why she was headed home to spend time working out in the gym at her apartment building before returning for the staff meeting a little later and her shift at one.

# CHAPTER FOUR

Lexi made the short drive from the ice rink to the main part of the resort, planning to grab a bite to eat before her shift started. She still didn't like to cook for herself, so she tried to eat at least one good meal at the resort each day.

Previously, her dad had hired someone to do meal prep for her and Mik. All of it had been nutritiously sound and scientifically balanced, prepared to give them the energy they needed for their intense training.

Food had never been a thing of enjoyment for her. She ate to fuel her body and for no other reason, and she'd always been careful to eat at specific times. Now that she was on her own, though, it was sometimes hard to remember to eat. She should probably set alarms on her phone to remind herself, like she had in the past.

She usually grabbed a piece of fruit and some yoghurt for breakfast, followed by lunch at the resort. Supper was a salad or more fruit and yoghurt. Something easy to prepare.

It wouldn't have been enough to fuel her body previously. But now, even though she was still skating and working out, her skating routine wasn't anywhere near the intensity of before.

The hostess at The Steakhouse greeted her with a friendly smile when she walked in. She showed her to a small table near the back of the restaurant. It was where Lexi preferred to sit, and now the woman took her there without her having to ask.

After she sat down, she glanced around. It was fairly busy, but that wasn't unusual since they were gearing up for the weekend. She'd learned that the resort was busiest from Thursday to Monday, which was why her work hours were scheduled like they were.

Her gaze lit on Kayleigh St. James, where she sat in a booth a couple of tables away. It wasn't the first time Lexi had seen the woman in the restaurant, but if she was there, it was usually with her husband. The tall, handsome man many described as Alexander's right-hand man.

Today, however, Kayleigh sat with one of the men who'd been present at the meeting earlier. Lexi recalled that Trev had introduced him as Wilder, a ski instructor.

Wilder had dark hair and a short beard, and, if she remembered correctly from earlier, dark eyes. Unlike Kayleigh, who was dressed professionally in a dark green pantsuit, he wore a pair of jeans and a long-sleeved T-shirt.

While Kayleigh sat with her spine straight and shoulders squared, Wilder definitely had a more relaxed posture, leaning back against his side of the booth.

It was clear they knew each other well. Their smiles and laughter came easily as they talked while they ate.

Lexi's first thought was that they had some sort of relationship, but then she dismissed that idea. There was no way that someone as successful as Kayleigh would meet a boyfriend at a place where her husband was as well known as she was.

And Lexi didn't think it would go well for Kayleigh if she was, in fact, cheating on her boss's right-hand man.

"What can I get for you?"

Lexi looked up at the young man standing beside her table, realizing she hadn't even looked over the menu. Not that she really needed to. She'd basically ordered the same thing every time she came.

"I'd like the grilled steak salad, please."

"And to drink?"

"Water with lemon. No ice."

"I'll be right back with that," the man said, then he left the table.

Lexi resisted the urge to keep watching Kayleigh and the ski instructor. Instead, she did something far worse. She looked up the results for the first senior figure skating competition of the season.

It had started the night before, but she hadn't had the nerve to check the results. She wasn't even sure that Mik and his new partner had qualified. It was possible that they'd been given assignments based on Mik's previous track record, even though that track record had been with Lexi.

However, he and his new partner weren't doing all that great. Mik hadn't found a partner that could elevate him to the status that partnering with Lexi had. That wasn't her pride talking. It was a fact.

She and Mik had been partners since they were children. They'd learned the art of pairs skating together, so their styles meshed perfectly. And they'd shared a work ethic that included total devotion to the sport.

She'd given up much of her life to become the best skater possible. Her dad had told her that he'd earn the money to pay her bills, she just had to work hard to make it worthwhile.

Other skaters had jobs or went to school, so their focus was split. Their time was split. That hadn't been the case for her and Mikhail. It was why her career goal had been to coach. After the path she'd chosen to take with Mik, she wouldn't have had any other skill to fall back on when she retired from competition.

Two years ago, this was one of the competitions she and Mik had won. And if they'd still been skating together and had been assigned to the competition, they'd no doubt have won it again.

Sadly for Mik, he was no longer skating with her. After the short program, he and Amberlyn were sitting in seventh. And there were only eight teams there.

Lexi knew she shouldn't feel happy about that. But seeing him struggle was a balm to the wounds Mik had inflicted on her after finding out what her father had done.

She was innocent in everything, but that hadn't mattered to Mik.

It had made her wonder if he'd truly loved her, or if he'd pursued a relationship with her because it was guaranteed to keep them together in a way a partnership might not.

With some distance from everything, she'd come to think that the answer was that he hadn't loved her. If he had, he wouldn't have been able to say those words to her. He would have stuck by her side while they tried to figure out how to move forward.

The price she'd paid had been her whole career. And now low marks were Mik's price.

She fitted her earbuds into her ears, then found the video of the performance on YouTube. But then, deciding that she didn't want to be interrupted, Lexi closed that out and spent the time while she waited for her meal looking over the headlines and her social media.

Her *new* social media. She'd had to abandon her old accounts because the vitriol thrown her way had been horrific.

Now, she had a generic social media profile where she posted simple pictures of food and flowers. Nothing she was truly passionate about. However, it allowed her to follow the accounts she was most interested in without revealing who she was.

Among those accounts were figure skating costume designers. She didn't follow any skaters. She hadn't done that even before everything went south, and she didn't plan to do it now.

Many of the other skaters had been friends, or at least friendly, with people they competed against. Some of that was because they trained at the same place or were trained by the same coaches.

Since that wasn't the case for her and Mik, Lexi hadn't seen the sense in trying to cultivate friendships with people who stood between her and the top of the podium. She knew she hadn't been well-liked by her competitors, but they could hate her for all Lexi cared. All she'd cared about was that the judges loved them.

Once she had her salad in front of her, Lexi went back to the video, then tapped the screen to start it. It was definitely a form of self-torture watching Mik and Amberlyn circle the center of the ice before they took their starting positions, Mik's hand gripping Amberlyn's hip the way he used to grip Lexi's.

When the music started, Lexi wrinkled her nose at the very basic classic piece that they'd chosen. It took a bit of effort, but Lexi forced herself to switch out of ex-fiancée/partner mode and into coach mode.

She and Mik had been fairly even in their physicality on the ice, but of this pairing, he was definitely stronger. It showed in Amberlyn's shaky landings on throws and jumps. Even falling twice. Her positions would be more precise if she was strong enough to hold them. She needed a stronger core.

By the end of the program, Amberlyn's shoulders were drooping, and the smile she'd sported at the beginning was gone. There were no hugs and high fives as the music faded away. Instead, just murmured conversation as they skated back to the center of the ice.

Lexi felt a pulse of pain as she listened to the applause for them, watching Mik take Amberlyn's hand as they acknowledged the crowd with bows. He spun her around like he used to do with Lexi.

She missed that moment. When the crowd gathered there to watch them shared their appreciation of the program the skaters had performed—good or bad. There would sometimes be a shower of stuffed animals, and Lexi had always made sure to pick one up and wave appreciatively at the people who'd shown up that day.

Following Mik and Amberlyn's program, there was nothing but polite applause that ended quickly as the pair made their way to the boards. And there stood her former coaches. The husband and wife team who had worked day in and day out with her and Mik.

They greeted them with hugs, but Lexi could see how displeased they were by the firm set of Irina's lips and the crease between Lev's heavy brows.

Mik slumped down on the bench and took the bottle of water offered to him. When Amberlyn sat down beside him, her shoulders were curled forward, and after taking a drink from the bottle of water she'd been handed, she picked at the label while Mik and the coaches held a conversation around her.

Lexi felt a bit sorry for Amberlyn. It was never easy to face the lens of the camera after a skate when your mistakes were many and very noticeable.

Mik had had a few as well. He had looked more winded than he usually did following a performance. Maybe he wasn't working out enough to keep his stamina and strength at the level where they should be.

Lexi closed out the video before the scores were posted.

It didn't matter. None of it mattered to her anymore. It wasn't her responsibility to keep Mik motivated to stay strong. And it certainly wasn't her responsibility to help Amberlyn.

She wasn't a partner. She wasn't a coach. She was nothing.

Trying to shake off the melancholy that wanted to blanket her, Lexi opened her eBook app and, while she finished her meal, she read. Occasionally, she glanced at the table where Kayleigh sat with Wilder.

At one point, they both got up. Kayleigh held out her arms to the man. Wilder bent down and lifted Kayleigh off her feet, making her slap his shoulders. Laughing, Wilder set her down, then pressed a kiss to her forehead.

When she strode away, Wilder sat back down in the booth. Lexi quickly averted her gaze so that he didn't discover her staring.

The whole interchange was weird, but honestly, it was none of her business. Lexi doubted that Alexander would really be that interested in the personal life of his employees. And why would she cause trouble in someone else's life when she had enough in her own?

The next morning, after a workout at the apartment, Lexi arrived at the rink by seven. Her day was going to be long and busy, but she was ready for it. Looking forward to it, in fact. Anything was better than sitting in her apartment all alone.

She called her mom again, but they didn't chat too long because her mom was going out for the evening with Leland and needed to get ready. In the quiet of the empty rink, she spent her time once again going through all her jumps and spins.

Deciding not to skate any of the old routines, Lexi put on a song that she'd begun to create some choreography for. Not that she needed a choreographed piece of music. It was more of a mental need. A creative outlet for her. Much like the skating costumes she designed in her sketchbook that would never become reality.

As nine o'clock neared, Lexi went into her office to change into her fitted workout pants and jacket. When she skated on her own, she often just wore leggings and a sweatshirt. But if she was going to be showing the girls any jumps or spins, she wanted them to be able to see her body lines clearly.

She'd just returned to where she'd left her skates when the door to the rink opened. Turning, she spotted Kayleigh and Hudson coming toward her hand-in-hand.

"Good morning, Alexandra," Kayleigh said with a smile. "Thank you so much for being willing to coach my nieces. They're very excited."

"I'm looking forward to it."

"How are you finding Serenity and the resort?" Hudson asked, his gaze intent on her.

"It's nice. This is especially spectacular," she said with a wave of her hand at the rink.

"Yep. Still not sure what Alexander was thinking, but once that man sets his mind on something, there's no stopping him."

"It might take a bit to find its footing," Kayleigh said. "But I'm hoping that we'll get to where it's an integral part of the resort, just like the slopes are."

Hudson chuckled. "I think your dreams might be a little lofty, darling. Personally, I think Alexander had it built to give Candace and Sabrina something to do while he and the boys are off skiing."

"You're probably right."

When the door swung open again, they all turned toward it. This time, a whole group of people walked in. A couple of girls—one with dark hair, the other blonde—followed by a woman with dark hair like Kayleigh's. A tall man came behind her carrying a car seat.

Bringing up the rear was a familiar face. Wilder stepped into the rink, letting the door close behind him.

Lexi looked over at Kayleigh and Hudson, trying to puzzle out the situation, but she didn't have long to do that as Kayleigh motioned for the girls to join them.

The wide eyes and excited expression on the oldest girl's face hinted at her knowing who Lexi was. Did she know everything that had gone down?

"This is my sister, Charli, her husband, Blake, and their girls." Kayleigh rested her hand on the shoulder of the tallest girl. "Layla, Amelia, and baby Shiloh. Also, this is my brother, Wilder, who tagged along for whatever reason."

"Boredom?" Wilder suggested, a teasing smile on his face.

"Are you going to skate with us, Uncle Wilder?" Layla asked.

"I don't know. I'll probably just watch." He lowered a large bag that he had slung over his shoulder. "But first, you need your skates."

Lexi watched as the girls scrambled to pull their skates from the bag. She wasn't sure why she hadn't even considered that Kayleigh and Wilder might be siblings. Perhaps the fact that she had none of her own meant it wasn't the first relationship she reached for as an explanation.

"Thank you for being willing to take the girls on," Charli said. "They both really love skating, and I would have hated for them to have to stop lessons."

"What happened to their other teacher?"

Charli's expression saddened. "Her husband's mom was diagnosed with cancer, and they moved to be closer to her."

"I'm sorry to hear that."

"We were too."

"How long have they been skating?" Lexi wanted a bit more background before they began their first lessons.

She already knew that she was going to have to approach her time with these two differently than she might have if she'd picked her own students. Her plan had always been to coach up-and-coming competitive skaters. It wasn't likely that these two were aiming that high.

Just like not every person who took piano lessons went on to play at Carnegie Hall, not every person who took skating lessons went on to compete at Worlds or the Olympics.

Once the girls had their skates on, Lexi sent them onto the ice to do a couple of laps while she put hers on. It didn't take long, and soon she was stepping onto the ice herself.

Blocking out the audience leaning against the boards, Lexi called for the girls to join her. They same to a stop just a few feet from where she stood.

"Why don't you each show me your favorite jump and spin?" she said.

Layla quickly volunteered to go first, leaving Amelia with Lexi as she stroked away from them. Lexi could already see areas where Layla would need more work, but she did a passable job on the spin and jump that she'd chosen.

"I haven't been skating as long as Layla," Amelia said when Layla was done. "So I'm not very good."

Lexi knew how her coach would have responded to that, but she took a gentler approach, even though it felt a bit foreign to her. "We all have to start somewhere, and Layla is also older than you. Don't measure yourself against her. Just do your best."

Amelia gave a single nod before she set off to do what Lexi had asked of them. It was clear that she was more of a beginner than Layla, but Lexi could see a natural talent in her that didn't appear as strong in the older girl.

"Good job, both of you."

For the next hour, Lexi focused on helping them improve the jump they'd each chosen. Though she'd had relatively low expectations of the girls, they both showed that they were there to do the work and not just goof off. She appreciated that they weren't wasting her—or their—time.

"Do you have any questions about what we've done here today?" Lexi asked at the end of the hour.

Both girls shook their head, but then Layla said, "Can you skate for us?"

"Skate for you?"

"I know you can do better jumps than the singles you showed us today," Layla said.

That was definitely true, as she'd stuck to doing single jumps to illustrate positions and speed to the girls. "I don't know..."

"Please?" Layla gripped her gloved hands in front of her chest. "You're my favorite pairs skater."

"I'm not a pairs skater anymore," Lexi said, trying to ignore the hurt saying those words caused her.

"I know, but you're still one of the best skaters."

Lexi sighed. "What do you want me to do?"

Grinning, Layla said, "We did our favorite jumps and spins for you. How about you do your favorites?"

"Okay. Stand over by the boards."

# CHAPTER FIVE

The girls hurried to do what she asked of them, then Lexi began to skate around the rink. It was a full-size rink, so there was plenty of room for her to build up the speed necessary for the jump combination she wanted to perform.

The triple Axel-triple loop combination was one of the more difficult combinations she did, but she'd practiced hard to get it to where it was reliable. It wasn't just a combination they put into a program and then she'd cross her fingers and hope she'd land both. She landed them with a high level of consistency.

In reality, her favorite jump was a throw triple loop. Flying through the air was an amazing feeling. And landing was even better. But that wasn't an option that day.

After taking enough strokes to get up to the speed she needed, Lexi launched herself into the air, spinning the three and half rotations required for the Axel. Then, after landing on one foot, she immediately jumped up into a triple loop.

When she landed, she held the glide, then she skated toward center ice and shifted into position to begin her spin. She decided on the Biellmann spin, which wasn't one she did very often as a pairs skater, but she loved it, so she'd worked to perfect it. Grabbing the blade, she lifted her leg behind her into the air. The stretch felt good, as did the freedom of the motion.

She did the required eight rotations, then releasing the blade, she shifted into an upright spin, the speed increasing as she raised her arms above her head. When she lowered them after a few rotations, her speed slowed and finally, she came to a stop.

Applause quickly reminded her that it wasn't just her and the girls at the rink. There was a temptation to bow to the people at the edge of the rink who were clapping. Instead, she just nodded in recognition of it as she skated to the girls.

"That was amazing," Layla said. "I wish I could skate like that."

"I skate like that because I've devoted a lot of time and energy to it," Lexi told her. "When I was your age, I spent eight hours at the rink and at the gym. Some days I had ballet lessons."

"Didn't you go to school?" Amelia asked.

Lexi shook her head. "I had a tutor who worked with me for two or three hours a day. The rest of my time was spent training."

"Did you like it?" Layla asked.

"Some days I did. Other days, it was hard. But just like with anything you want in life, you have to work for it."

"Thank you for showing us your jumps and spins," Layla said. "And for teaching us."

The three of them moved to the opening in the boards, and Lexi watched as Blake helped both girls to the bench, then knelt to take off their skates.

"That was great," Wilder said from where he leaned against the boards. "You're super talented."

"Thanks." Lexi wasn't sure what more to say.

"The girls are never going to stop talking about this," Kayleigh said as she joined them. "It's not every day they get to take lessons from an Olympian."

Lexi schooled her expression to keep from grimacing. As far as she was concerned, the fewer people who knew that about her, the better.

"Are you finding that the people coming to the rink are experienced skaters?" Hudson asked.

"Several have had enough experience that they were able to stay up on their blades. Others have needed more help. Especially the kids."

"Are you open to more coaching?" Kayleigh asked. "I know you kind of did this as a favor to me."

"The hours here at the rink make it a bit difficult. If it's kids wanting lessons, I would only have Saturday and Sunday mornings available, since they'd be in school during the week."

"Well, if it becomes too much to give the girls lessons, just let us know," Charli said. She held an adorable baby facing out on her hip. The little girl looked at Lexi with big brown eyes while she chewed on her fist. "We really appreciate your willingness to do this much."

"I think it'll be fine. Do they have a place to practice during the week?" Lexi asked.

"We have a local rink that we can go to. Although, since both Blake and I work, we are limited in the time we have to take them there."

Lexi remembered all the times her mom had gotten up early with her to go sit in the cold rink and watch Lexi work with Mik and the coaches. She had to remember that these girls weren't able to devote the time or energy to skating like she had at their age.

"Any practice they get is good. Have they entered any competitions?"

Charli shook her head. "They've really just been learning the basics. Their other teacher wasn't a choreographer."

"Let me know if you're interested in them competing," Lexi said. "I could come up with programs for them."

Charli glanced to where Blake was still down on one knee in front of the girls. They had their skates off and were listening to whatever he was saying.

"I'll talk to Blake first and then the girls."

"Competition could be good for them," Wilder said.

"What do you mean?" Charli asked.

"I think Jay and Cole benefited from being on the basketball team in high school."

"But they were aiming for the NBA," Charli said with a frown. "I don't think either of the girls plans to be in the Olympics."

"Not everyone who competes has the Olympics as a goal," Lexi said. "There are lower-level competitions that they can enter. Competing can help them learn to accept the good and the bad. To understand that some days they're better able to stay on their blades than others."

"I just don't want them to get upset if they don't win."

"Let them get upset," Wilder said with a shrug. "It will either make them buck up and work harder or they'll decide that skating isn't for them. Even among the best, there can be only one winner. Right, Alexandra?"

Lexi gave a nod. "And the ones who don't win aren't losers, especially if they've skated to the best of their abilities."

Wilder grinned at her. "How many times did you lose if you skated to the best of your ability?"

"Once we reached seniors? Never. If our program was flawless, we won."

"That's amazing," Charli said. "I can't imagine the work it took to get to that level."

"A lot. Skating was my life."

"It still is, isn't it?" Kayleigh asked.

Kayleigh truly had no idea how ludicrous that statement was, but Lexi couldn't fault the woman for it. Unless someone was a high-level athlete or was involved with one, they would be unaware of how different her current life was from before. This version of skating was one she never would have wanted.

"I'm still very involved in skating," Lexi said in lieu of letting Kayleigh know how this current chapter of her life differed from her competing chapter.

Layla and Amelia came over to the boards with Blake trailing them. When he joined them, he slid his arm around Charli.

"Thank you for the lesson," Layla said.

Lexi gave her a smile. "You're very welcome."

"Will you give us more lessons?" Layla asked. "Mom said that we would see what you said after our first one."

Lexi hadn't thought to turn down doing the lessons. It wasn't how she'd imagined coaching, but it was something to help fill her time, and the lesson had gone as well as she could have hoped. There was no reason not to continue with the lessons.

"Sure. I'm fine with that."

Layla's smile was beaming. "And I want to learn a program."

"We can work on that too," Lexi assured her. "But maybe not right away. Let's get used to each other first, then we'll start looking at putting together a program for each of you."

Shiloh let out a wail, distracting everyone as they all turned to look at her.

"Guess that's our cue to head for home," Charli said. "We've missed her morning nap."

"Maybe next time you don't all have to come," Kayleigh said.

"I know. But we enjoy watching the girls skate."

Blake took the fussing baby from Charli and carried her to where the car seat sat on the bench. He bent to strap her in while Charli talked to Lexi about payment for the lessons.

Lexi had no idea what to charge. If she'd been coaching someone with high level competitive goals, she could have charged more. But that wasn't the case with these girls.

After hearing what their previous teacher had charged them, Lexi wasn't sure what to say. Thankfully, Kayleigh stepped in. "Charli, I'll talk it over with Alexandra and let you know."

Frowning, Charli said, "Just remember that... well..."

Kayleigh reached out and put a hand on her sister's arm. "I know. Trust me."

Charli stared at her for a long moment before nodding. "Let me know what we owe you, and I'll pay right away."

"Okay."

When everyone had their jackets on, they said goodbye and left the building. Everyone except Wilder.

"Are you waiting for a lesson too?" Lexi asked.

Wilder's eyebrows rose as he grinned, making his eyes sparkle with humor. "Would you give me one?"

"I've never coached adults."

"I'm pretty good at following instructions."

"Have you ever skated before?"

"Yep. Hockey."

Lexi rolled her eyes, not sure why she wasn't sending this guy on his way. "That's not going to help you."

"At least I know how to stay on the blade."

"Did you bring skates?" she asked, curious if he had planned to skate all along.

"Yep. My hockey skates."

"No toe picks, but I guess you're not going to be picking into jumps just yet."

Wilder's grin grew. "Be right back."

As he went to the bench where his duffle bag waited, Lexi wondered if she'd lost her mind. She didn't exactly trust the easygoing smiles and attitude that Wilder displayed.

And why would he want to spend time with her? Did he want the inside scoop on her past?

That wasn't going to happen. She spoke to *no one* about the details of what had happened to her family. A lot of it had been paraded out for public consumption during her dad's trial, but there had been plenty of stuff going on behind the scenes with her life as a result of everything that she'd never shared with anyone.

As she waited for Wilder to join her on the ice, Lexi moved away from the boards and circled the ice, crossing over her skates with ease as she circled around the far end.

When Wilder stepped onto the ice, she came to a stop a couple of yards from him.

"Show me what you can do," she told him.

Another flash of his grin and he was off. The man might not have jumps and spins, but he certainly had speed. He had spent more than a little time on skates at some point in his life.

After he'd done a couple of laps around the ice, he called out, "Wanna race?"

Lexi stared at him for a moment, trying to figure out if she had a chance. He had several inches on her, so his strokes would be longer and more powerful. She wasn't slow on her skates, however.

"Our size difference gives you a definite advantage," she pointed out. "How do you think a race could be fair? I'm not a speedskater."

Wilder seemed to give her question serious consideration. "I'm not just out to prove I can beat a woman. How about we do spins, then skate?"

"You know how to spin?"

"I think so."

"Okay."

Lexi wasn't sure why she was even entertaining his suggestions. He was a complete stranger to her. She should have just said she didn't have the time and gone to her office.

Apparently, she was missing interaction with others more than she had realized. She'd just assumed because she'd had no friends beyond Mik and her coaches that she didn't need friendships. Maybe what she *didn't* need was *a lot* of friends, and what she *did* need was a small circle of close friendships.

Not that she planned to start up a friendship with someone like Wilder. She'd heard about Wilder even before meeting him, since Trev had mentioned him when he told her about the members of the recreation department.

He was only in Serenity for the winter ski season, then he was off flitting around the world for the rest of the year. Definitely not what she needed in a friend.

After discussing the number of rotations needed before they could skate, she and Wilder took up their positions. At his prompt, they began to spin.

Lexi quickly finished her rotations and set off down the ice. She'd rounded the short end of the ice just as Wilder finished his spin. He definitely looked a little wobbly as he tried to pick up some speed. She lapped him, then turned backwards, watching as he finally found his footing.

They had only planned on one lap, so she'd already won, but she could tell by the gleam in his eyes that he wasn't going to stop after just a single lap. Turning, she put on a burst of speed, her thigh muscles burning with the sudden demand.

Unfortunately, Wilder had regained his equilibrium and made quick work of passing her. He beat her back to their starting point and was waiting with yet another broad grin on his face.

"I won," she announced, because she really couldn't bear to lose at anything.

"That you did," Wilder agreed between deep breaths. "I think we should call it a draw, however."

"Why?" she demanded. "The race parameters were spin, then skate a lap. You can't change things at the last minute."

"You're right." Wilder crossed his arms as he skated backward and forward, crossing and uncrossing his skates on the ice. "My fragile ego, though..."

She rolled her eyes at him. "I have a feeling your ego is just fine. After all, you did prove that in a straight race, you'd win."

"I just don't understand how you figure skaters can spin like that and then still skate in a straight line."

"It takes practice," Lexi said.

"Are you planning to stick around Serenity long-term?" Wilder asked, taking her off-guard with the switch of subject.

It wasn't something she'd thought a lot about. The plan she'd had for her life was gone, and she hadn't figured out what her new one should be.

Could she be happy coaching kids in a small town like Serenity? Or would she be forever discontent because she couldn't be involved with the sport at the high level she wanted to be?

She'd already accepted that it was unlikely that anyone with Olympic aspirations would ever hire her. Her past meant she came with a lot of baggage and distractions.

"I haven't decided yet." That was at least halfway true, although it made it sound like she had options, which, unfortunately, she didn't feel she did. "I'm here for now."

Wilder's smile widened. "That you are."

She really didn't know what to make of Wilder. Most of the men who had been in her life had been very intense. Her dad. Mikhail. Her coach. They'd all been men who focused intently on things and were never lighthearted the way Wilder seemed to be.

Did that mean he didn't take anything seriously?

Even if she'd wanted to be more relaxed, Lexi had no idea how to be that way. All her life, everything was serious. Her fitness. Her health. Her diet. Her outfits. Her skating. She would have never done with Mik what she'd just done with Wilder.

She and Mik had never been ones to skate to lighthearted music. The closest they'd come was the program they'd been preparing for the Olympics. It had been a selection of songs that, at the time, Lexi had thought represented their romance.

They'd had programs that focused on love before, but they'd been dramatic and often had tragic endings. That new program had been the one where it would have ended happily for once. Only she wasn't destined for her happily ever after. On the ice or off.

Wilder stopped his figure eights at the point closest to Lexi. "Hope we didn't overwhelm you today with all of us showing up."

"It was fine." If she could skate in front of crowds of thousands or tens of thousands, she could handle a small family group.

"We Halversons can be a lot for some people," he said. "Particularly when there are more than one or two of us."

"That wasn't all of you today?"

"Nope. This wasn't even half of us."

Lexi felt her brows lift before she could stop them. "Big family."

"Yep. There are ten of us kids, but the family is growing as spouses and children come into the picture."

"I bet reunions are a blast."

"Most of them are," Wilder agreed. "We're mainly all together for weddings or Christmas, and since my mom has put her foot down that there will be no squabbling at any of those events, we're forced to get along."

Lexi was blown away at the idea of so many people in one family. Like, *why* would people want that many children? She was pretty sure that had her parents had more than her, she wouldn't have had the chance to skate competitively the way she had.

"You don't have to worry about us all showing up here, however," Wilder said. "Three of the ten don't even live in Serenity at the moment."

Which meant that *seven* of them could still arrive to watch the girls' lessons. Seven plus spouses and children.

Whatever. It still wasn't an arena full of people.

"They need to come when the rink is officially open. Then they could have coffee and food."

"Trying to drum up business for the resort." Wilder nodded his head. "Kayleigh would definitely appreciate that."

"Are you always this way?" Lexi asked.

Wilder tilted his head. "Which way?"

"Kind of flippant about everything?"

"I'm not flippant," he protested. "Just because I don't take everything seriously doesn't mean that I dismiss everything, either. In this case, that was a little poke at my sister. She can be too serious about stuff sometimes, so I try to lighten things up for her."

"So you think she can be too focused or too intense?" If he thought Kayleigh was that way, he was definitely going to think Lexi was that way, too.

Wilder waggled his hand back and forth in front of him. "Kayleigh has always been very determined. She knew what she wanted in her life from a pretty young age, and she's worked hard to accomplish it. We're very proud of her, but we also know she needs a little balance in her life. She's learned to accept that we're going to help her out with that on occasion. Now that she's married Hudson, though, she's a little more likely to leave work at the door and let her hair down and have some fun."

Lexi would have thought that talking more to the man would help her understand him, but it seemed the opposite was happening. The more he talked, the less she could make of his personality, even though he didn't appear to be holding any part of himself back.

Her smart watch buzzed, forcing her to put her musings on hold. She glanced down to see a reminder that the rink would be opening in twenty minutes since they opened at eleven on Saturdays and Sundays. It wasn't like she'd lose track of time, but just in case she did...

"The rink is going to open soon." She pushed off with one foot in the direction of the exit off the ice. "I need to get ready."

Wilder followed her, then went to the bench. Lexi slipped the guards on her blades since she would keep them on for the time being. Taking her skates off when she didn't need to, and then having to put them on again was a waste of time.

"Thanks for letting me hang out for a bit," Wilder said as he put his skates in the duffle bag. "I enjoyed a reason to get back on the ice."

"I'm sure Trev would let you use the rink whenever you wanted," Lexi said.

"Probably. But this was more fun." He headed toward the door, walking backwards. "I'll see you around."

Lexi knew that was true. She just wasn't sure she knew how to handle having even a tiny bit of his upbeat lightheartedness in her life.

# CHAPTER SIX

The following Saturday, Wilder held the door open for everyone, then followed them into the rink. Blake carried Shiloh's car seat to the bench they used for putting on their skates, while the girls headed straight for Alexandra.

She greeted them with a smile. But even from a distance, Wilder could tell that it was a polite, cursory thing. This woman might be confident, but she was also aloof and somewhat prickly.

"Good morning, Alexandra," Charli said as she joined them. "How are you?"

"I'm fine, thank you." Alexandra's smile briefly reappeared for Charli. "How are you?"

"We're good. The girls are very excited about the lesson today. They've been practicing through the week."

"Uncle Wilder took us to the rink four times so we could practice the stuff you showed us," Amelia informed her.

Alexandra's gaze landed on Wilder briefly before she addressed the girls. "That was nice of him."

Wilder had figured that with Blake and Charli both working, it would be a help for them. Plus, it wasn't like he had a ton of stuff to do. He was just biding his time until the slopes were ready for skiers.

When the girls went to the bench, Wilder and Blake helped them lace up their skates. Once done, the girls walked over to the ice, where they removed their guards and joined Alexandra on the ice.

They'd only been skating for a couple of minutes when the door to the rink opened again. Wilder glanced over to see Lee and Rori walking toward them.

Since arriving home, Wilder had enjoyed getting to know his brother's girlfriend. Rori was sweet and had a sense of humor that he really appreciated. He could see that Lee absolutely doted on her, and he was more protective of her than Wilder ever remembered Lee being of previous girlfriends.

"Oh, I'm glad we're not too late," Rori said as she came to stand beside Wilder at the boards.

"Yep. They just went out on the ice."

"I wish I could have taken skating lessons when I was a kid," she said.

"It's never too late," Wilder told her. "I'm sure you could learn enough to enjoy skating."

"She looks so at ease on such a thin blade," Rori stated after watching the girls and Alexandra for a few minutes. "It's like she's walking on the ground."

"I'm sure she spends a lot of time in her skates." Lee slipped his arm around Rori's shoulders. "Skating is probably like walking for her."

Wilder hadn't attended the girls' lessons with their previous teacher, so he wasn't sure how she'd been with them. Alexandra looked to be a firm, but also demanding, coach.

"Try it again," Alexandra said when Layla landed her jump on two feet. "You want to flow out of the jump with your foot and leg leading the way."

Layla headed off to circle around and try it again. While she was doing that, Amelia was working on a spin. Alexandra switched effortlessly between the two, never making it seem like she was ignoring one while working with the other.

The next jump was much better, but it didn't appear to be good enough for Alexandra.

"You did a good job of keeping your foot off the ice, but we need more flow." Alexandra did the jump herself, not needing nearly as much ice coverage to pop up and spin into the air before landing, her leg positioned higher and straighter than Layla's had been. "You need more leg extension. Both of you come here."

Once Layla was in front of her, Alexandra had her get into the position she should aim for at the end of her jumps. "Hold that and make a note of how it feels."

She had them both get into the position, then hold it for several seconds before lowering their leg and doing it again. After having them do that a few times, she sent Layla off to do her jump again. Then she had Amelia try the jump she'd been working on that week.

Wilder wondered if this coaching thing was a good fit for the girls. He knew from talking to Layla that she had no desire to go to the Olympics or anything like that. She just wanted to be able to do a few programs in pretty costumes and to be better than her friends.

Amelia, for all that she was the shyer of the two, seemed more interested in pursuing competitions. But even there, Alexandra seemed better suited as a coach to skaters who definitely wanted to compete at elite levels.

He wasn't going to share his thoughts with anyone, however.

"She's so beautiful and elegant," Rori said as they continued to watch Alexandra show the girls jumps and spins.

Wilder had done some research on Alexandra over the past week. While Layla had known a lot about her skating record with her pairs partner, what Wilder found was more gossipy.

From what he'd read, Alexandra might have been a favorite of some because of her skill, but she wasn't a favorite among fellow skaters and even some skating fans. She'd been nicknamed the Ice Queen, and it hadn't seemed to have anything to do with her mastery of skating.

He'd watched some videos of her and her partner competing, and even with his limited knowledge of the sport, Wilder had been able to see how talented the pair were. They were beautiful on the ice, athletically skilled but yet also dramatic artistically.

Several articles had touched on the fact that Alexandra and Mikhail had been engaged, so after everything had transpired with her dad, she'd lost more than just her career as an elite athlete, she'd also lost the man she'd planned to marry. That had to be devastating.

"Do you know how to skate?" Rori asked as she looked up at Lee.

"Yep. Like Wilder, I played some hockey. I was never going to be a pro player, but I got pretty good at staying upright on the ice."

"Maybe we should go skating some time, and you can teach me."

Lee smiled at her. "I'd love to do that."

"You should come to the rink when I take the girls for practice," Wilder said. "It's usually not too busy."

"Are you going to be able to keep taking them once you start working?"

"Yep. I'm usually done by five in the winter. Earlier even when the days are at their shortest."

Rori smiled at him. "That's so good of you to help out like that."

Wilder hadn't spent a lot of time with his nieces and nephews over the years, but as he'd gotten more involved with the orphanages, he'd realized what he was missing out on. If he could spend time with kids he didn't have a connection to, he should be able to do it with the ones in his family.

"I've enjoyed it because I go skating as well. I don't just leave it to them."

Wilder glanced down the boards to where Charli and Blake stood. Shiloh must have been sleeping in her car seat on the bench because she wasn't with them.

It never failed to surprise him to see Charli with Blake. Over the years, she'd kept pretty much every man at arm's length. Now, though, if Blake was nearby, she was next to him.

At that moment, Charli was watching the girls with a frown, her hands clasping the top of the boards.

Wilder wondered if she regretted her decision to bring the girls to Alexandra for coaching. Charli had always loved children and was protective of her own. Even Amelia and Shiloh, who weren't hers by blood. If she thought working with Alexandra would harm the girls on some level, she would put a stop to it for sure.

At the end of the lesson, Layla once again asked Alexandra to do some jumps and spins. He wondered how long it would before Layla tried to talk the woman into skating one of her old programs for them. Modified, of course, since she no longer had a partner to skate with.

"Goodness," Rori exclaimed as Alexandra did one of her jumps. "She jumped so high, and she skates so fast."

Wilder thought of their race the previous week, and he wondered if she'd get mad if he hung around again. He was intrigued by her, but he was also thinking that if he could get a read on her, he might be able to help Charli feel more comfortable about her coaching the girls.

"How long until I can do a program?" Layla asked as the three of them skated to where Wilder and the others stood watching them.

Alexandra paused before she asked, "What do you know about programs?"

"Not too much."

"Okay. So here's some homework for you," Alexandra said. "I want you to do research into what the requirements are for programs at your level. Once you can tell me what's needed, then we'll talk about doing a program."

"Do I need to do that too?" Amelia asked.

Alexandra looked down at her and nodded. "Yep. You can work together to get the information and get your mom or dad to help too if you need it."

"We'll do that," Layla promised. "I can't wait to have a program."

"Keep working on your elements. You've done well this week."

"Will you take us to the rink again, Uncle Wilder?" Layla asked as she stepped off the ice.

"I think I probably could," Wilder said. "For a fee."

Layla's brows rose. "What sort of fee?"

"Brownies would work. Or double chocolate chip cookies."

That brought a smile to Layla's face as she laughed. "I can make those for you."

Wilder held out his hand for her to shake. "Consider it a deal."

Alexandra stayed on the ice while the girls headed to the bench with Blake and Charli.

"You're a very beautiful skater," Rori said to Alexandra with a friendly smile. "How long have you been skating?"

"Thank you. My folks put me on skates when I was two or three. I ended up having a natural talent for it, so they got me official lessons with a coach."

"That's amazing. I'd love to see you skate a program."

Wilder held his breath, hoping Alexandra wouldn't lash out at her for bringing up something that was probably pretty painful.

"I don't really perform anymore," Alexandra said, her expression unreadable. "But I'm sure you could find videos online of me skating."

"I can send you the links to a few," Wilder volunteered.

Alexandra turned her icy blue gaze on him, and her eyes narrowed slightly as she regarded him. "You've looked up videos of me skating?"

Wilder shrugged. "You're working with my nieces. I don't think me being a little curious is unexpected."

She stared at him for a moment before she nodded. "Look up the long program from the World Figure Skating Championships two years ago. It was my favorite program, and we skated it flawlessly that day."

"I think I watched that one," Wilder said. "It definitely deserved the gold."

"It did." A small smile tugged at the corners of her mouth, but it was fleeting. "Which was why we won."

The statement could come across as prideful, except that he'd watched the program, and it had been stellar. She and her partner had obviously worked hard at it. She was merely stating a fact.

After watching those videos, Wilder had a bit more understanding and sympathy for the magnitude of the loss she must be dealing with now that she was no longer skating competitively. Especially since stopping hadn't been her choice.

"We're heading out," Charli said, then turned to Alexandra. "Thank you again for your time."

The girls chimed in with their thanks, then the family headed for the door.

"We're going to the church for worship practice," Lee said. "See you at home later."

"Are you skating today?" Alexandra asked once it was just the two of them.

"I don't know. I feel like I don't rate sharing the same ice as you."

Alexandra let out a huff. "Flattery won't get you anywhere, I'm afraid."

Wilder was sure that was true. How could you flatter someone who had already been showered with gold? There was nothing he could say that she hadn't heard before.

"Unfortunately, I'm not really up for learning how to jump or spin," Wilder said. "And I doubt you're interested in hockey tips."

Her nose wrinkled as Alexandra shook her head. "Not really, no."

"Do you still watch the competitions?" Wilder asked.

Alexandra rested her arm along the top of the boards. "I shouldn't because it probably isn't healthy, but to be honest, I just can't help myself."

"I suppose when it's been your world for so long, cutting yourself off from it is nearly impossible."

"It's what I should have done." Alexandra plucked at the cuff of the fitted workout jacket she wore. "But it's the second season since I... quit, and I still haven't managed to not watch at least some of the programs."

"Does being here doing this make it worse?" Wilder asked, gesturing to the rink.

"Maybe." She shrugged. "But I don't have any other skills that aren't tied to skating. I probably should have taken some college courses or something."

"I have one brother who could have played basketball professionally and another who's still hoping that will be his future, but my parents insisted they each get a degree in something unrelated to the sport in case something happened to prevent them from playing."

"And did something happen?" Alexandra asked.

"Well, Cole is still hoping he'll make it, but Jay decided not to follow that path. He ended up back here in Serenity, working at the medical clinic my family runs."

"Do you all work there? I mean, except for Kayleigh?"

Wilder let her guide the conversation away from herself, knowing that they'd been mired in a difficult subject. "Nope. Most of us don't, actually. My oldest brother is a doctor there, along with Jay's wife. Jay is in charge of the office, and our sister, Janessa, is the nurse. My other sister-in-law is also a part-time nurse/receptionist there."

"Was that a brother or sister?" Alexandra asked, gesturing toward the door.

"Oh. I forgot to introduce you to them. I'm sorry. That was my brother, Lee, and his girlfriend, Rori. He's a vet, and Rori works as a receptionist at the same clinic."

"I can't imagine having that many siblings."

"How many do you have?"

"None. I'm an only child."

"Well, to be honest, I couldn't imagine that."

"I was so focused on my skating that I didn't really miss not having a sibling."

Wilder wondered if that also applied to friends. Just because she hadn't been friendly with her competitors didn't mean she hadn't had friends off-ice.

"Say, Kayleigh mentioned that you and her were discussing having a themed night here soon."

Alexandra nodded. "I'm not sure what else to do to encourage people to spend some time at the rink. That sort of thing is not my forte. I wasn't responsible for bringing people into the events I was a part of."

"And yet a lot of people came because of you. I saw the posters with your name and face on them in the crowds where you competed."

Alexandra's shoulders stiffened. "I'm not using my fame—or notoriety—to bring people in. I already told Kayleigh I wasn't willing to do that."

"You don't think people will recognize you?" Wilder asked.

"It's possible that some might, but I don't want my name to be what attracts people. Those aren't the type of patrons we want."

Wilder understood what she was saying and agreed with it. "So what theme are you thinking?"

"An 80's night."

"You want people to come dressed in 80's fashions?"

"If they want, but we'd also play all 80's music to skate to."

"That would include some great tunes," Wilder said. "I like the hair bands of that era."

"But I'm not sure how to get the word out. I am not the right person to design posters or social media posts."

"I can help with that. I have some experience in marketing and digital design."

"Really? I thought you were a ski instructor."

"I am, but as I said earlier, my parents insisted that we all get a useful degree, though they didn't force us to use it. I'm the only one with a degree who doesn't have a full-time job in their field."

"So you could design posters for the event?"

"I can, yep."

A relieved smile crossed Alexandra's face. "I want the event to be a success, but had no idea how to make that happen. Are you sure you don't mind helping?"

"I don't mind at all. We'll have to run it by Kayleigh, just to be sure, but I doubt she'd have a problem with it."

"Oh, that would be great."

"I know it's not convenient right now, but if there's a time that would work for you to meet and go over details, just let me know."

"I guess I should get your phone number," Alexandra said as she slipped her guards on her blades. "My phone is in the office."

Wilder waited by the boards while she retrieved her phone. When she returned, he gave her his number to input into her contacts. His phone chimed with a text alert, and he pulled it out and checked to make sure it was from her.

"Got it." He quickly added her to his contacts. "If you have any ideas, be sure to jot them down."

"Will it be a problem if I don't?"

"Nope. We can brainstorm together."

"Kayleigh also said that Alexander spoke to her about us putting on some sort of Christmas skating program. Do you think there are enough skaters in the area who might be interested in being part of that?"

"Possibly. As long as you don't want them to do anything too tricky. Even I can skate in a straight line."

"Maybe you could be Santa."

That made Wilder laugh. "I don't know about that. Would you be Mrs. Claus?"

As soon as the question was out of his mouth, he realized that she might take it the wrong way.

Alexandra shrugged. "The girls would probably like to be elves."

"I'm sure they would."

"I don't normally work with children," Alexandra said. "I might need some help coming up with a creative idea for a Christmas program."

"Charli's an elementary teacher, so maybe she'd be able to help. I'm pretty sure that she creates programs for her class at Christmas."

"I hate to impose on you all."

"No imposition," Wilder assured her. "I can't promise that Charli will be able to get involved, but there's no harm in asking. My help, however, you can count on."

"I appreciate that, as I don't have the connections that would be necessary to pull off something like this."

"Be honest with Kayleigh about stuff like that, because she might just not be thinking of what'll be necessary. She's very business-minded and is used to delegating."

Alexandra nodded. "I'll talk to her."

"Excellent." Wilder smiled at her, hoping she might give him a truly genuine smile back. Unfortunately, it was just a fleeting moment across her face. "I'm going to head off and let you get on with your day."

After they said goodbye, Wilder left the building and got into his car, but he didn't start it up. He sat for a moment, wondering if he should move out to his folks' place since their company had left.

The idea didn't hold a whole lot of appeal now that he'd experienced living at Charli and Janessa's. He enjoyed being surrounded by his siblings and their children. It was more lively, and he liked that.

He doubted his parents would be upset with him over the decision, so he just needed to talk to Charli and Janessa to see if they minded. If they had any reservations, he'd move back to his parents without hesitation.

Resolved to talk to them, Wilder backed out of the parking spot and headed for home. As he drove, he couldn't help but wonder if Alexandra struggled with what most likely was a lonely life in Serenity.

Even if she hadn't had lots of friends or a large family to support her, she had had a group of people—her partner, her coaches, and her parents—who were always around her. Losing all of that must have been a real blow to her.

Wilder wasn't sure that there was anything he could do about that for her, aside from inviting her to things with his family. He didn't know how Kayleigh and Hudson would feel about that, though, since she was technically their employee. Any invitation should probably come from one of them—preferably Kayleigh.

At the very least, he could talk to Kayleigh and see what she thought. Apparently, conversations with his sisters were on the agenda for the afternoon.

# CHAPTER SEVEN

Lexi was certain she must be in a dream. Or maybe it was a nightmare. Whatever it was, it was her living a life she'd never dreamed of or even wanted.

Though she'd managed to not sound like she hated the idea when she'd told Wilder about it, she, without a doubt, one hundred percent, hated the idea.

An 80s themed night?

While ice dancers had to stick to a theme for their short programs—and she thought 80s had been one of them—that was not a part of Lexi's skating experience. The only constraints put on the music she and Mik had used were for time, permission to use songs, and their own desires.

And choreographing a Christmas program? No thanks.

Her choreography had always centered on making sure the required elements flowed and got them the maximum points through where they were placed in the program. It took skill and time.

Christmas wasn't that far away. How on earth was she going to organize a program when she didn't even have skaters? All while she put together an 80s themed night...

It was utterly ridiculous, and she hated all of it.

"So, how difficult do you think it will be?" Kayleigh asked.

They were currently sitting at one of the tables in the rink, drinking coffee. It was during their open hours, so there was some noise around them, but the rink wasn't too busy.

"Challenging, I think, is the word I would use. Choreographing a program for people around Layla and Amelia's skill level isn't difficult. The challenge comes in rounding up the skaters who are willing to participate and then figuring out costumes for them all."

Kayleigh looked contemplative but undeterred as she lifted her mug and took a sip of her coffee. "We could probably spread the need for younger skaters through Charli at the school. If we need older kids, my brother-in-law, Will, could probably help spread the word since he teaches at the high school. We could also post information at the local rink in town. And I can put out feelers at our church to see if anyone wants to participate."

"You do know that this rink isn't really set up well for good viewing, right?"

Kayleigh glanced over toward the ice, frowning as she realized that she couldn't see past the couple of people who were standing at the board watching what was happening on the ice. "We would need bleacher style seating."

Lexi nodded. "Is there anything like that around here?"

"Well, yes. The local rink has that since they host hockey games. But since we want this event to focus on the rink here at the resort, I'd rather not use that one."

"What other options do you have, though?"

"I wonder if we could do an outdoor rink." Kayleigh picked up her phone and tapped the screen rapidly. "I'm going to ask Wilder if he could take care of getting some information on whether or not that would be feasible."

"Still doesn't solve the issue of the bleacher seating," Lexi pointed out.

"True, but if we can get a good rink area set up, we could possibly rent bleachers to put around it."

"This seems like... a lot of work."

Kayleigh sighed. "I agree, but Alexander was the one to suggest it. And by suggest, I mean, demand it. He said—and I quote—we're coming for Christmas, and I'd like to see a Christmas ice program."

Did her godfather actually hate her? Was he trying to make her pay by throwing a nearly impossible task at her?

"Okay." She could hardly let down the man who had given her the space to retreat from the scandal, all the while letting her continue to skate and earn a living. "First, we need to figure out if the outdoor rink is possible. If so, then we have to make sure we can get the bleachers."

Kayleigh nodded as she tapped the screen of her phone. She didn't seem upset that Lexi had taken control and was rattling off a list of what they needed to do. Lexi was used to being methodical when faced with a task. Even a task that she hated. Though such tasks had, fortunately, been few and far between.

Over the next few minutes, they hashed out a plan, then Kayleigh said, "I want to get Wilder involved in all this too."

"Why?" Lexi asked. It wasn't that she objected, really, but she was curious about what he brought to the table.

Kayleigh glanced at her. "Well, he's familiar with the area and what's available, plus he knows lots of people. He can connect you with many who can help out with the event."

Lexi thought of the handsome man with friendly brown eyes and an easy-going personality. Would they be able to work together? She wasn't going to be pleased if he dragged his feet on things when she was trying to work her way through the list that she'd set up with Kayleigh.

"He'll be a big help," Kayleigh said. "I promise you."

"I guess as long as he doesn't mind giving up his time to help."

"Right now, he's not working since the slopes aren't open, so he has the time. Once he starts work, he'll have to do anything we need him to do outside his hours on the slopes because they count on him for instructing during the ski season. He's very popular with the guests."

Lexi could understand why that might be. "Do you have a lot of regulars here?"

"Yep. We have people who return yearly. Some even more frequently than that." Kayleigh frowned, then said, "By the way, Wilder wanted me to make sure that you are aware that if any guest bothers you, you should speak to me or the HR manager right away."

"Bothers me?" Lexi asked. So far, the people she'd come in contact with had mainly been young men and women who traveled in groups. None of them had paid her much attention.

"We've had some guests over the years who've felt that since they've paid for an employee's time that they are entitled to more."

"Really?"

"Yes. And that applies to both genders. Wilder has dealt with it from wealthy women who thought he'd be flattered if they wanted more than just ski instruction from him. He's had to change his phone number at least once after a guest got hold of it and started to harass him. We have a strict policy about not giving out the phone numbers of our employees. And I would suggest you not give anyone your number either. If they want to book a slot of time with you, tell them to do it through the main desk at the hotel."

"I never even considered something like that happening."

"I hope it never does, but just know that it's something we take seriously. Don't think you have to tolerate any kind of behavior that crosses the professional line."

Lexi had never been the sort of person to accept someone behaving in an untoward way to her. It hadn't occurred to her that she might run into that at the resort, but she supposed it made sense. Some people with money assumed those without would be at their mercy or would be appreciative of the attention.

"Anyway, Wilder just wanted to make sure that you knew how we handle situations like that here."

She had a moment of awe. A guy who barely knew her wanted to make sure that she knew how to keep herself safe. And as she considered it, Lexi realized that not once had he made her feel unsafe around him.

It wasn't something she thought a lot about since her life had been fairly insular, and it was rare that a man who she didn't know well had access to her. And for the ones she didn't know well, she'd never been left alone with them.

"Thank you for letting me know," Lexi said. "I appreciate it."

"You're welcome." Kayleigh smiled at her, and for a moment, Lexi had a glimpse of Wilder in her features. "I need to get back to my office, but do you have any questions before I go?"

"Will you speak to Wilder about us meeting together, or do you want me to do it?"

Kayleigh picked up her phone and tablet and got to her feet. "I'll talk to him about it, then he'll probably contact you to set something up. Since the slopes still aren't open, his schedule is more flexible than yours."

Lexi walked with her to the door of the rink, then returned to her office once Kayleigh was gone. She sat down behind her desk and leaned back in her chair as she thought back over their meeting.

This was all so far out of her comfort zone, and it made her want to just run away. The possibility of failure was high, which wasn't something that Lexi was comfortable with.

The unfortunate part was that there was no way she could impose her high standards on a group of casual skaters. And yet, the idea of putting out something that wasn't perfect made her feel a little sick.

A skating program with a crowd of people—many of them children—was just asking for trouble. All she could envision was all the ways something could go wrong.

On Friday morning, Lexi was at the rink early to meet with Wilder. He'd called her the day after her meeting with Kayleigh, enthusiastically on board with what his sister wanted.

Lexi had hoped that he would tell Kayleigh that what she wanted was impossible, but nope. The man had sounded so excited on their call that Lexi knew that the event was going to go forward, regardless of her apprehensions.

Taking a seat at a table near the corner, she relished the warmth coming from the nearby fireplace. Outside the rink, it was a gray day, and light snowflakes drifted down. November was off to a cold start, though they weren't forecasting too much snow just yet.

It wasn't too long before Wilder stepped through the door, pausing to stamp the snow from his boots on the large mat in front of the doors.

Glancing around, he smiled when his gaze found her. Lexi gave him a quick smile in return, then watched as he walked toward her with something in his hands. He had an easy gait, his long legs quickly eating up the distance between them.

"Good morning," he said when he reached the table.

He set down a container and a tray with two cups on it, then unzipped his jacket and took it off, revealing a sweatshirt with a college logo on the front. After hanging it on the back of the chair, he sat down across from her.

"I didn't know if you drank coffee," he said as he worked one of the cups free, then set it in front of her. "But I brought you a cup. I also brought some sugar, sweeteners, and cream."

"Why didn't you just get coffee here?" Lexi asked as he reached into the pocket of his jacket, pulling out a bunch of stuff that he put on the table.

Wilder grinned at her. "To be honest, I forgot about the cafe."

"Well, thank you." Lexi wrapped her hands around the cup, enjoying the warmth that seeped into her fingers. "I'm not much of a coffee drinker, but I do indulge once in a while."

"Indulge?" Wilder asked. "You think coffee is an indulgence? Personally, I find it's a necessity."

"It had to be an indulgence since I don't like to drink it black."

Wilder frowned. "So because you added cream and sugar, you couldn't have it every day."

It didn't surprise Lexi that he couldn't grasp how things had been in her life when she'd been performing. Few could. "When you demand a lot of your body, you have to make sure that what you intake is the best fuel possible. Sugar was a definite no-no."

"Hmmm. Well, if you're still watching sugar intake, you're really going to hate me when I open this." He tapped the lid of the container he'd also brought with him.

"Why's that?"

"My brother's mother-in-law made fresh cinnamon buns." He peeled open the lid, then tilted it so Lexi could see. "They're to die for."

Lexi stared at the baked goods in the container, convinced that she could feel herself gaining weight just by looking at them. "Uh... they do look delicious."

"I don't know if you want some, but I'm going to have one." Wilder proceeded to produce some napkins and a knife from the other pocket of his jacket.

"Did you bring everything but the kitchen sink?" Lexi asked as she watched him use the knife to cut one of the cinnamon buns and lift it out to place it on the napkin.

"Yep. But I'm gonna wish I had the kitchen sink to wash my fingers off in a minute here. These are sticky, sticky."

He ripped off a piece from the pastry and popped it into his mouth, closing his eyes and humming in appreciation as he chewed. It was so, so tempting to indulge with him. But after she'd doctored the coffee to her satisfaction, she wasn't sure further indulgence was good for her.

On the other hand, she wasn't competing anymore, so she didn't need to keep her body in top physical condition. However, if she ever returned to competing, she couldn't have let herself go because the climb back to the top would be even harder.

But what was the likelihood of that happening?

"I didn't realize it would be this difficult a decision for you to make," Wilder said. "I don't want to tempt you to do something you'd rather not."

When he reached for the lid to put it back on the container, Lexi put her hand on his to stop him. For a moment, she stared at the contrast between their hands.

His large and strong. Hers smaller but no less strong. His skin was tanned, while hers was pretty much as fair as a person could get without being completely white. Her mom had drilled into her the necessity of sunscreen whenever she went outside, in order to keep her skin looking young.

"Change your mind?" Wilder asked.

"I..." Lexi moved her hand from his, for some reason feeling like she was standing on a precipice. It was ridiculous to feel that way over a cinnamon roll, and yet, there she was. "Yes. Yes, I have."

Wilder grinned at her, almost as if he was proud of her decision. "You won't regret it. I promise you.

Lexi wasn't so sure about that. In the past, when she'd eaten things not part of her plan, guilt had come swiftly, chasing away any pleasure she might have gained from it. Would that be the case for this? Or would it be different because she was no longer training? No longer under the strict eye of her dad, Mik, and her coaches.

"Here you go," Wilder said, holding the knife out to her. "Cut yourself however big of a piece you want. I'll eat whatever you don't."

Lexi wanted to throw caution to the wind and claim a whole bun, but in the end, she took half of the half that Wilder had left.

She waited for Wilder to make a comment about it, but he just kept smiling as he ate.

Her fingers sank into the soft bread as she lifted it to take a small bite. She expected it to be super sweet, but she discovered that it was the perfect blend of buttery, sweet, and spicy.

"Good, right?" Wilder said, making Lexi realize that she'd made an audible sound of appreciation, much like he had.

"Very good."

Wilder cut the remaining cinnamon roll into four sections, then took another piece. When Lexi finished her piece, she picked up her coffee and took a sip. She thought Wilder might encourage her to eat more, but he didn't. And he didn't say anything when she caved and indulged in another piece.

"So I hear we're planning a Christmas skating program," he said after he'd finished his third piece. "Is it all Kayleigh's idea?"

"I don't think so. Apparently Alexander told her they were coming for Christmas, and he wanted to see a skating program. Maybe we could blame him."

Wilder chuckled. "I'm on board with that. So, how are we going to make that happen without you losing your mind?"

"What makes you think I'll lose my mind?"

"The Christmas programs at the school usually do that to Charli, so I thought this would probably be comparable."

Lexi gave a small nod. "I'm not sure how to pull it off with so little time to practice. And if I have to judge every person's skating level beforehand..."

"You could just say that it's impossible and refuse to do it."

That would be the ideal response, but there was a part of her that didn't want to let Alexander or Kayleigh down. They'd given her a chance when she'd been floundering for a new direction in her life.

This direction, however, seemed fraught with rough ice. She really had no idea how she was going to make it work.

"I can't refuse to do it," she said, which felt like admitting a weakness. If he forced an explanation from her about that, she'd have to admit that she needed this job. To help her out financially, but also to help her mentally. She needed to move past her competitive skating career, and this job was the first step to doing that.

Wilder regarded her for a moment as he took another sip of coffee, then he said, "Okay. Refusal is off the table. What are we left with?"

*We?*

A knot she hadn't even known existed loosened inside Lexi. She'd missed being part of a team. Because she was a pairs skater, she hadn't even gone on the ice alone like single skaters had. She'd taken her best friend—the man she loved—out there with her.

When everyone had abandoned her, she'd felt very adrift and alone. Even her mom had moved on with her life, leaving Lexi behind.

It wasn't until that moment, when she realized she wouldn't have to deal with this program on her own, that Lexi felt like maybe she had found a place where she could plug in again.

"I guess we're left with checking the feasibility of where to have the program and planning the program itself."

"I can definitely help with the former," Wilder said. "Not too sure about the latter."

For the next little while, Lexi laid out for him everything that she and Kayleigh had discussed. After she was done, he turned in his seat to survey the rink.

When he got to his feet, she stood up as well, curious what was going through his mind.

"I don't know about doing an outdoor rink," he said. "My biggest concern is weather. We have no way of knowing how cold it might be, or if we get a lot of snow, creating and keeping the ice in good skating condition might be an issue."

"Yeah. I didn't think about that."

Wilder flashed her a grin. "You're used to doing your winter sport indoors. Because I'm outdoors for a good chunk of time, I'm more aware of how the weather can impact things."

"So, what other options do we have?"

"If we moved all the furniture that's currently in here out, I think we could bring in small sets of bleachers to put around the entire rink."

"You think so?" Lexi tried to picture that but had a difficult time.

"Depending on the dimensions of the bleachers and how portable they are, I'd say that's our best option. Unless Alexander wants to build *another* rink more suited to performances."

That got a huff of laughter from Lexi. Given how rich the man was, he could probably do it if he had the time. Unfortunately, she wasn't sure that even *he* could get it together in the time they had until Christmas.

"I'll phone around and see what I can find out about bleacher rentals. Once we have that, we'll know exactly what we're working with."

"Kayleigh said you could also help me figure out how to recruit skaters."

"Let's sit back down," Wilder said, then led her back to the table.

The more she and Wilder discussed the details, the less Lexi felt like it was an impossible task. He broke it down in ways that her brain could handle, and he was more than willing to take on the responsibility for several things.

Maybe... just maybe... this wouldn't be the catastrophe she'd thought it would be. All thanks to this man who had unexpectedly stepped into her life and offered the support that she'd been so desperately missing.

# CHAPTER EIGHT

Wilder climbed from his car and headed for the entrance to the rink. He was running a bit late, but he hadn't let that stop him from coming.

The first two times he'd come for the girls' skating lesson had been mainly curiosity. This time, however... it was something more.

The times he'd spent with Alexandra so far had intrigued him, drawing him to want to learn even more about her, because every detail felt important.

And now they'd broken bread—quite literally—which felt like a milestone. He hadn't thought through bringing cinnamon rolls and coffee to someone who had been an elite athlete. Which was why he hadn't pressured her to accept any of what he offered.

He'd given a tiny internal dance of victory when she'd chosen to indulge of her own accord. Though he understood why she wouldn't want to eat like that on a consistent basis, surely, once in a while would be okay. When it came to food, Wilder tended to have the *everything in moderation* mindset.

Reaching out, Wilder grabbed the wooden handle and pulled the heavy door open. While it was definitely warmer inside the rink, the temperature shift between inside and out wasn't as great as it might be in another building. He knew they kept the rink cool for the sake of the ice.

It was too bad the café wasn't open. A coffee wouldn't go amiss. He could have stopped for one, but since he was already running late, he hadn't wanted to delay further.

This time around, Janessa and Will had come along. Will was currently helping Layla with her skates, while Blake did Amelia's. Janessa was standing with Charli, peering at Shiloh in her car seat.

Wilder spotted Alexandra on the ice near the boards, so he went to her. "Hey."

"Hi." Her smile lingered a bit longer than it previously had, which Wilder hoped meant she was warming up to him. "Come to watch the lessons again, huh?"

"Yep. It helps me know how to help the girls when we go to the rink during the week."

"That's good that you're doing that for them."

Her gaze flicked past him just as he felt an arm go around his waist. Shifting, he spotted Janessa next to him. He lifted his arm, then put it around her shoulders.

"Did Charli introduce you?"

"Nope," Janessa said with a shake of her head.

"I forgot to introduce Lee and Rori when they were here, so I don't want to do that again." He looked back at Alexandra. "This is Janessa, another of my sisters. And that's her husband, Will, helping Blake with the skates. Nessa, this is Alexandra."

He could see the curiosity in Alexandra's gaze as she skated closer to the boards and held out her hand. However, she didn't remark on the fact that Wilder and Janessa looked nothing alike.

"Nice to meet you," she said with what he'd come to think of as her performance smile.

After having watched a bunch of videos of her competing, Wilder had realized that the smile she wore when acknowledging the crowd was the same every single time. It was the same after a perfect performance as it was after a flawed one.

It seemed like she kept herself tightly controlled, and that smile didn't offer any glimpses into the depth of her emotions.

"Nice to meet you too," Janessa said. "I've heard a lot about you from the girls. They think you're amazing."

Alexandra's eyes widened briefly, then she said, "That's sweet of them. I think they're pretty amazing, too."

Wilder had no idea if she was being sincere in her response, but he hoped that if she wasn't, that at some point in the future, she'd realize that the girls really were, in fact, amazing.

"And yes, I'm adopted," Janessa said, a grin spreading across her face. "People are always a bit confused when we first introduce ourselves."

"I suspected that was the case," Alexandra said. "But I thought it might be rude to remark on it."

"Nope. Not rude. Our family is very open about the fact that four of us are adopted."

Before the conversation could continue, the girls approached them, now wearing their skates.

"Ready to go?" Alexandra asked, shifting her attention to Layla and Amelia.

"Yep." Layla stepped out on the ice and took a couple of strokes before turning back around to wait for Amelia.

"We're going to warm up first, so follow me."

When Will joined them at the boards, Wilder dropped his arm from Janessa's shoulders, and she moved closer to her husband.

As he watched Alexandra with the girls, Wilder wondered if she would be able to handle more kids at a time. Because if this Christmas program really came together, she'd be dealing with more than just two kids.

"Why are you here?" Janessa asked.

"Why are you?" Wilder shot back.

"We've gone to a lot of the girls' lessons," Janessa told him. "So this is normal for us."

"Since I take them to the rink during the week, I figured it was a good idea to see what she was working on with them. Plus, I'm working with Alexandra on a project."

He told them about the program, not surprised when Janessa expressed some skepticism.

"You don't have much time."

"I know." Sighing, Wilder leaned more heavily against the boards, resting his arms on the top of them. "It's going to be a minor miracle if we can pull it off. I feel like Alexander and Kayleigh are asking a lot of Alexandra when she's barely got her feet wet in this job."

"It does seem like a lot. If we can help in any way, let us know."

"Hopefully you mean that, because I may have to prevail upon a few of you to give us a hand."

"As long as I don't have to get on skates, I'm there for you," Will said. "And I won't dress up as Santa or an elf."

Janessa grinned at her husband. "Ah. Come on! I would pay big bucks to see you in an elf costume."

Will just rolled his eyes, then pressed a kiss to her forehead. "Sorry to disappoint you, my love, but that's not happening."

"You're not going to get Jay on skates either," Janessa said. "He definitely does not like the ice."

"Well, we need more than skaters. Once we've had a chance to sit down and really flesh it out, I'll have a better idea of where you guys can help us."

Janessa smirked at him. "I'm sure you're not objecting to spending more time with the beautiful figure skater."

Wilder couldn't deny that there was a part of him that was drawn to Alexandra. Why, he wasn't sure. It wasn't that he had a certain type of woman that he was attracted to. But usually, he found himself drawn to women who shared a similar outlook on life as him. Easy going, laid back, willing to take risks and explore the world.

Alexandra didn't seem to have any of those qualities. But still, he wanted to spend more time with her. Perhaps it was the "duck out of water" vibe he got from her that made him want to help her out.

"Wow. I can already see that the girls have improved," Janessa said as she watched them on the ice. "That's incredible."

"She's spent a lot of time teaching them correct positioning," Wilder told her. "And that seems to have helped them perform their spins and jumps better."

"I guess that's what happens when you have a coach who is a gold medal Olympian. She's probably undergone some pretty rigorous training."

"I wasn't sure it would make that much of a difference," Charli said, having joined them at the boards with Blake and Shiloh. "But I can see I was wrong."

Wilder was glad that they saw the value in Alexandra's skill and talent. And though he wasn't sure either of the girls would make the Olympics one day, they'd definitely be better skaters for having been under the coaching of Alexandra.

When the hour drew to a close, Alexandra once again performed a bunch of jumps and spins that Layla and Amelia requested of her.

"One day I'm gonna know how to do that," Amelia announced after Alexandra did what looked to be a particularly difficult jump.

"You keep practicing, and I'm sure you will," Charli told her as she reached out to smooth back a wisp of hair that had come free from her ponytail. Amelia glanced up at Charli, her eyes wide.

Wilder knew that Amelia was still finding her way in her new family with a new maternal figure, just as Layla was doing the same with Blake.

When she was done, Alexandra skated toward them, coming to a stop not far from the boards.

"They're doing really well," she told Charli. "I can see that they're practicing in between lessons."

"Yep. Wilder has been helping us out with that by taking the girls to the rink in town throughout the week."

Alexandra gave Wilder a quick smile. "It's paying off, for sure." She turned her attention back to the girls. "I know you want to do programs right away, but I'm afraid it's going to have to wait."

"Why?" Layla asked, her brow furrowed.

"I have to work on a Christmas program here at the rink, and that's going to take up a lot of my time. Come January, we'll focus on your programs, and hopefully by the fall, when the next season starts, you'll be ready to tackle some competitions."

"I'm sure you can wait until after Christmas," Charli told Layla, who looked the most disappointed by the news. "And in the meantime, you can be part of the Christmas program."

Layla looked at Alexandra. "I can?"

"Yep. We're going to need a bunch of skaters. I haven't got it all figured out yet, but we'll start doing some practices for it soon. We might have to reschedule your lessons for a few weeks to fit in those practices." She turned to Charli. "Will that be okay?"

"I'm sure it will be fine. We can figure it out once you know the schedule better."

Shiloh let out a squawk and then started crying. She was generally a pretty chill baby, but when she got upset about something, it took a bit to settle her down.

"Let me help you get your skates off," Will said as he held out his hand to Amelia.

The girls followed him and Blake to the bench, while Charli tried to settle the baby.

"I think she might be teething," Charli said. "All she wants to do is chew on her fingers."

"That doesn't sound like fun," Janessa cooed at Shiloh, reaching out to tickle her belly. "Our little sunshine has turned into a thundercloud. It's a good thing we all like storms."

Wilder glanced at Alexandra and saw that she was focused on Janessa and Shiloh. Had she ever contemplated having a family? He imagined that it wasn't easy for professional athletes—especially women—to fit having children into their lives. A woman couldn't exactly compete while heavily pregnant.

When the girls were done with their skates, Charli and Blake packed everything up, said goodbye to Alexandra, and left the rink with Will and Janessa.

"You're a great coach," Wilder said once it was just the two of them. "We're all seeing that despite you not having many lessons with them, the girls are much improved."

Alexandra skated close to the boards, then rested her arm on the top of them but kept her gaze out on the ice. "I had always planned to coach one day. I just hadn't thought it would be this soon."

"And I imagine you planned to work with highly skilled skaters."

She glanced at him, her lips tightening before she nodded. "I did, but I guess that... God had other plans for me."

"Do you really think you can't go back to your career?"

Her gaze hardened, making her blue eyes even more icy. "My dad didn't just screw over strangers, he stole money from my partner, his parents, my coaches, and other parents of skaters. He took their cash and told them he was going to invest it, but instead, he pocketed it. That was just one of the awful things he did. So no, I'm not sure how I can go back to competing when I don't have money to pay for coaches, even if they were interested in working with me."

"Could you compete without a coach?"

"I don't know. Some have tried, but it's hard not having a support team with you."

"Coaching might not be out of the question, though, right? I mean, there's no questioning the skill and experience you have."

"Maybe." Alexandra shrugged. "But for now, this is where I'm at."

"It's not such a bad place to be," Wilder said.

"So why do you only spend the winter season here?"

Well, wasn't that a good question? "It's not because I don't like it here. It's just that there wasn't anything here I wanted to do in the off-season. Unlike this ice rink that can run in the summer, if there's no snow on the slopes, I have no one to instruct."

"What exactly do you do for the rest of the year?"

It had been a while since he'd talked about his time away from Serenity with anyone outside his family. "I have a travel channel on YouTube where I upload videos of places I've been, giving people tips on traveling to those places. Right before I came here, I went to Reykjavik, Iceland. I was collaborating with a travel company there to highlight what they had to offer people wanting to visit Iceland. So, once I have that video edited, I'll upload it onto my channel."

"I've traveled to lots of places, but I haven't really played tourist while I've been there."

"So, what do you do for fun?"

Alexandra once again looked away from him to focus on the ice. "I don't know. Something I've always enjoyed doing was designing costumes. I used to work with a designer to create our costumes."

"But you don't do anything else?"

"Like what?" Alexandra asked, her brow furrowed.

"Rock wall climbing? Baking? Cooking? Reading? Doing crossword puzzles? Needlepoint? Pouring candles?"

Alexandra's eyes widened as he recited his list. "No. None of that."

"So when you're not at work, what do you do?"

"I practice. I work out. Honestly, I spend most of my time here, even when the rink is closed. It's what I know. It's where I feel most at home."

Wilder felt a pang of sympathy for her. He couldn't imagine what it must be like to be so focused on one thing that everything else in one's life just faded away. Even Kayleigh, who was the most focused and determined of all of them, had found a hobby in cooking.

"Have you thought of developing a hobby?"

"I would have *no* idea what that might be." She skated a little ways away, then came back. "What are your hobbies?"

"Well, skiing, but I also enjoy traveling, videography, and I do some digital design as well. That's kind of part of my job, but I still really enjoy it. I also read a lot, which is a good hobby to have when I'm traveling."

It was too bad that Alexandra worked on Friday evenings to give her a break from the rink. If she didn't, Wilder would have invited her to the pizza nights at Charli and Janessa's. They had apparently been having outdoor pizza dinners during the summer, when the weather was nicer. But now they were back inside. The night before, they'd ended up playing games after they ate, and it had been a lot of fun.

Once he started work, he'd be on the same schedule as Alexandra as far as days off went, but his day on the slopes would end with the sunset, which came fairly early in winter.

When her watch chimed, Wilder smiled. "Guess that's my cue. I'll let you get on with your day."

"Do you think you'd be available tomorrow morning to go over some things?"

"Not tomorrow," he told her. "I attend church in the morning, but I could do Monday morning."

She hesitated a moment before nodding. "That would work."

"Perfect. I'll see you then."

As he neared the door, Wilder glanced back to see that Alexandra was still watching him. She lifted a hand, and after returning her wave, he stepped out into the crisp autumn day.

It had snowed the day before, but with temperatures hovering just above freezing, the snow had melted almost as soon as it had hit the ground. That wouldn't be the case for much longer, however.

Soon, he'd be back to work on the slopes, and he was really looking forward to it.

The following Tuesday, Wilder drove to the address Alexandra had given him the previous day. They'd decided that it was time to invite others into the planning to see how they could pull the program together.

Kayleigh had offered to spring for supper for everyone since it was a meeting pertaining to something at the resort. Alexandra hadn't been entirely sold on having the meeting at Charli and Janessa's, but since they wanted Charli's help, it was the best place. She had responsibilities at home, so it made sense for them to go to her, instead of her having to leave everything to Blake to come to them.

The apartment building he pulled up in front of was familiar, since it was where Jay had lived prior to marrying Misha and moving into the home they'd bought together. It was one of the nicer buildings in Serenity, and it had great security, which was good since Alexandra was on her own.

Once he'd parked at the curb in front of the building, Wilder sent a text to Alexandra to let her know he was there. It was only a couple of minutes later when she appeared, and for a moment, Wilder just stared.

He was so used to seeing her in her workout clothes with her hair up. That evening, she had on a black cropped jacket over a purple shirt and slim-fitting jeans tucked into a pair of knee-high boots. Her hair lay in loose waves over her shoulders, glossy in the fading daylight.

Wilder got out and went around the car to open the door for her. "Ready for some chaos?"

Alexandra lifted her brows. "Chaos?"

"Well, there will be quite a few of us there, besides the girls and the baby." He smiled as she slid into the seat. "You'll see."

Sure enough, the minute they walked into the house, they were greeted by loud conversation and a crying baby, along with aroma of rich spicy food.

"I hope you like Indian food," Wilder said. "I didn't think to ask you ahead of time. I'm sorry."

"I can't say I've had it very often, but I'm sure it will be fine."

Wilder hoped so. Since he knew how restrictive her diet was, he should have checked with her first.

"Hey there, Alexandra," Kayleigh said as they walked into the kitchen. She stood at the counter with several bags in front of her, and she and Janessa were pulling containers of food out of them and putting them on the counter. "Hope you're hungry."

Wilder guided Alexandra over to his sisters, then searched out Charli. She was by the pantry, taking paper plates out of a large plastic bag.

"What can I do?" he asked as Kayleigh engaged Alexandra in conversation.

"Do you think these are sturdy enough to use buffet style?" she asked as she handed him one of the paper plates. "They usually work for pizza, but I'm not sure about this. We don't need a repeat of the bean incident."

Wilder grinned, remembering the time his mom had used paper plates for a barbecue that weren't quite sturdy enough. More than one of them had ended up with the plates bending and spilling baked beans, potato salad, and burgers on the ground. Jay had been standing behind their dad when his plate had folded, dumping beans all down the back of the man.

It had been hilarious for everyone but Jay and their parents.

"These will be fine," he said.

"I hope so. We don't need Alexandra thinking we're complete idiots for serving food on weak plates."

"I don't think you have to worry about that."

He had no idea what Alexandra thought about their family, and he was fairly certain she wouldn't tell him the truth if he asked. Especially if that truth was that they were too noisy and overwhelming for her.

He wouldn't want his family to change, however. Their gatherings were always lively and fun, and he hoped Alexandra would come to appreciate that, since they were probably going to be spending a bunch of time together over the next few weeks.

## CHAPTER NINE

Lexi didn't know if she was supposed to offer to help, but it seemed that everyone had things under control. The food smelled delicious, so she hoped she liked it.

She hadn't been altogether truthful when she'd told Wilder she hadn't had much Indian food in her life. The fact was, she'd never had any, so she was about to get her first introduction to it.

"Hi, Lexi." The soft voice had her turning to see that Lee and his girlfriend, Rori, had joined them in the kitchen.

Lexi smiled, hoping it disguised how out of place she felt. "Hi. How are you?"

Rori's smile grew. "I'm good. How about you?"

"I'm fine."

"How are you finding life in Serenity?" Lee asked. "Is it different from where you lived before?"

"Not really. I lived rurally in Maine, so it wasn't like I came from a big city."

Lexi heard barking and watched as a little dog came bounding into the kitchen with Amelia hot on its tail. Its ears flopped forward as it came to a stop, looking around. As soon as it saw Lee, it ran over to him and sat at his feet.

"She wants a treat, Uncle Lee," Amelia said, then smiled when she spotted Lexi. She gestured to the dog. "This is Elsa. She's Uncle Lee's dog, but we all love her."

Lexi could see why. The dog was really adorable.

"Can I give her a treat?" Amelia asked, looking up at her uncle. "She's sitting pretty."

Lee chuckled. "Of course she is. Maybe put some foot in her bowl so she can eat while we do."

Amelia hurried off toward a doorway in the kitchen, then disappeared inside. After a moment, she popped back out with a cup full of dog food in her hand.

Elsa hurried over to where Amelia was emptying it into a small bowl. She immediately sat, her tail sweeping the floor while she watched Amelia closely.

"What type of dog is she?" Lexi asked.

"Cavalier King Charles Spaniel."

"She's very cute." Lexi had never considered getting a pet. She hadn't felt it would be fair to the animal because she was so busy with other things in her life.

"You should get one," Amelia said. "Dogs are the best."

"We're still not getting one, Berry," Blake said, running his hand over her hair as he walked by.

"But if Uncle Lee moves out, we're going to be so lonely."

"There are enough of us here. I don't think you'll be lonely," Blake assured her.

Amelia crossed her arms. "Maybe he should leave Elsa here. *She'd* be lonely without me and Layla."

"I'm sure she'll be fine."

Lexi was intrigued by the interactions within the family. What would it have been like as a little girl to grow up with aunts and uncles around?

Her dad had always said that his family and her mom's were the wrong sort of people. What Lexi had only recently discovered, thanks to her mom, was that her dad had distanced himself from his impoverished family when he'd started to earn more money. And when her mom's wealthy family had made it clear they didn't think he was worthy of their daughter, he'd forced her mom to cut them off, too.

Turns out, they'd been right.

In the one conversation she'd had with her dad following his arrest, he'd been adamant that he'd done what he had in order to make sure that their family always had money. And once she'd heard from her mom about her dad's growing-up years, she understood a bit more—even though she still didn't accept it—why he'd done what he had.

Unfortunately, he'd also said he'd stolen money from those people in order to fund her skating career. It left Lexi feeling guilty and angry. She didn't want to bear any responsibility for what he'd done, but it was hard not to. She had definitely benefitted from the wealth he'd accumulated through nefarious means.

"Let's pray," Blake said once everyone had gathered in the kitchen.

Wilder came to stand next to her, offering her a quick smile.

Lexi bowed her head, knowing that was expected when someone prayed. She wasn't a stranger to faith and prayer. Her mom had a strong faith, and she'd insisted that Lexi go to church with her. At one point, when Lexi had been seven years old, her mom had led her to the Lord, however, she'd never been as devoted to the church as her mom was.

Her dad had supported her mom's faith. Even insisting they go to church each Sunday as a family. They'd attended a large church in a nearby town, and her mom had been involved with the ministries there.

Her dad hadn't gone there because of his desire to be a good Christian, however. He had thought being a church-goer would make it easier for people to trust him. It had been a smokescreen persona to hide his true personality and his actions. In the end, he'd swindled people at the church too.

Since her dad's arrest, Lexi hadn't set foot in a church. Part of that decision had been the shame she'd felt over what her dad had done. But a bigger part had been her own struggle with her faith when confronted by the realization that she couldn't take anyone—even Christians—at face value.

When she'd accepted Alexander's offer to work at the rink, she hadn't thought she'd end up surrounded by people who were Christians, involved in their church the way her family had been. But here she was.

Once the prayer was over, the kids were quickly served. Then Wilder handed Lexi a plate and motioned for her to go ahead of him.

Glancing at him, she said, "Can you tell me what the different dishes are?"

"Sure." He came to her side and pointed out each dish, giving a brief description of it.

In the end, she took some rice, curry, and butter chicken. Then, at Wilder's insistence, she added a piece of naan bread to her plate.

"We're sitting in the dining room," Charli said, pointing at the doorway the girls had gone through once they'd filled their plates. "Do you want anything special to drink?"

"Water is just fine."

"Perfect."

Rori had her plate filled by then and smiled at Lexi as she tipped her head in the direction Charli had indicated. "We can go sit down, if you'd like."

She would have been most comfortable with Wilder, but Rori seemed nice enough, so Lexi followed her into the dining room.

"You can sit by me," Layla said when she spotted her.

The room was large with big windows. It was probably a sunny space during the day. But that wasn't the case right then, since the sun had already disappeared.

"We don't have assigned seating," Rori said as they approached the large rectangular table surrounded by chairs. "So, you can sit wherever you want."

Lexi appreciated Rori telling her that because she wouldn't have wanted to sit in someone's seat. Since Layla had requested to sit beside her, Lexi went to the chair next to the girl.

When Wilder appeared a few minutes later, he headed directly to where Lexi was and sat down beside her. It wasn't long before the table was full, and people were eating.

"How are you finding the food?" Wilder asked. "I know spicy isn't for everyone."

"I really like the butter chicken," Lexi said. "The curry is probably right at the top end of what I enjoy spice-wise, but the naan is delicious."

"I'm glad you're enjoying it."

Lexi still wasn't sure it was her favorite type of food, but it was something she wouldn't mind eating again. Part of the reason she enjoyed it so much was because she hadn't had to cook it.

She continued to struggle with making meals for herself, and a lot of days, the meal she ate at the resort was the only one she had. She had the money for groceries or even take out, but she just couldn't be bothered. It was easier to just eat at the resort, then have fruit, yoghurt, raw veggies, and protein bars the rest of the time.

When she'd been training, her meals had all been fairly basic. They'd been flavorful, but they hadn't had a lot of unique ingredients in them. Whoever her dad had hired to cook her meals had done a good job operating within the limited parameters they'd been given.

"So, I suppose we need to discuss the Christmas skating program," Kayleigh said after they'd been eating for a few minutes. "We should do that now, so no one has to stay late. Also, we don't want to keep Charli and Blake from being able to do their nighttime routine with the girls."

"I appreciate that," Charli said as she spooned some pureed food into the baby's mouth.

"If it's okay with Alexandra, I'll give you a brief overview of what we need."

When Wilder glanced at her, Lexi nodded, more than happy to let Wilder take the lead, since she still wasn't entirely sure what they were doing.

"I called around yesterday and determined that we can rent bleachers that would actually fit the area around the ice at the rink. That would save us from having to set up a rink outdoors. Plus, it means we won't be at the mercy of the weather for this event."

"That's good," Kayleigh said. "I'm sure Alexander would rather see the program performed in the rink that he spent so much money on."

"So with that settled, what we need next is skaters."

"How good do the skaters have to be?" Charli asked. "Are you going to want auditions?"

"I don't know about official auditions," Lexi said. "But we'll need to make sure that the kids—and adults—who want to participate can at least stay up on the skates to move about the ice."

"Would you want them to know jumps and spins?"

Lexi shook her head. "It would be too much with that many skaters on the ice. If we want to have some skaters do spins and jumps, we'll choreograph it so that it's just a small group of two or three doing that part."

"Would kids with a skill level similar to Layla and Amelia be okay?"

Lexi nodded. "Even a little less skilled would be alright."

"How about costumes?" Charli asked.

"I think we'd just have them go with a Christmas color shirt and maybe white pants," Lexi said. "So red or green or even gold would work. I don't want it too complicated because we don't have the time for that. And I also want the kids comfortable as they skate."

"We might not have many kids from the church as they're also practicing for the children's program there," Charli told them.

Kayleigh sighed. "I wish I understood why Alexander was so determined to have this. It's such short notice."

"Did he say he wanted a program with a bunch of kids and such?" Hudson asked as he rubbed his hand on his wife's back.

"Not specifically," Kayleigh said. "But what else could he mean?"

Hudson glanced at Lexi. "Maybe he just wants to see you skate."

Lexi frowned. "Just a solo program?"

Her stomach twisted at the thought of performing by herself. It was like a horrible reminder of what she'd lost. She'd rather deal with the hassle of a program with a bunch of kids than skate by herself.

"Maybe you could still use Amelia and Layla," Charli suggested.

Hudson leaned back in his chair, though he kept his hand on Kayleigh's shoulder. "I'm not sure why Alexander is so set on this ice skating rink. I think he's done it for you, to be honest."

Lexi frowned. "Me? Why?"

"He hadn't mentioned anything about building a rink here until after everything happened with your dad."

Lexi managed to keep from wincing at his words. "I never really knew him, though. So why would he care?"

"You are his goddaughter," Hudson said with a shrug. "And from what he said when I questioned him about the rink and hiring you, he said that he thought the rink would add value to the resort. When he told me he'd hired you, he mentioned that your mom had been worried about you and what your future would look like. She said you'd been struggling to find a way to support yourself."

Lexi felt like she was being stripped bare emotionally. How pathetic did she appear that she'd needed her mom to try to find a job for her? And on top of that, he'd spent a bunch of money on something to create a job just for her.

She was so confused and had no idea what to say to these people.

Glancing at her husband, Kayleigh then gave Lexi a sympathetic smile. "We're not saying you don't deserve the job or that Alexander shouldn't have built the rink. Alexander has helped several of us over the years. Wilder and I, especially. We've worked hard to make sure he doesn't regret the opportunities and money he's invested in us."

"I can tell you that as far as Alexander is concerned, you don't owe him anything more than your best effort in the job," Hudson said. "That's all he wants from any of us, even those he's taken a special interest in."

While this dinner may have gotten her out of the stress of planning the program, it had left her with a tangle of emotions that made her feel vulnerable in front of virtual strangers.

"I'll clarify with Alexander exactly what he wants," Kayleigh said. "Because I don't want to waste your time and energy, Alexandra, if he'd settle for a performance by just you. If you're willing to do that, of course."

Lexi really didn't know if she could handle working on a program that was to be a solo piece. Even if Layla and Amelia were there, she would still feel like she was skating alone.

"Perhaps we should have clarified that with him last week," Wilder said. "So we didn't waste Alexandra's time."

Lexi looked over at him to find that he was frowning at his sister. She wasn't surprised, as it had wasted his time as well.

"You're right," Kayleigh said. "I just didn't think about how much work it would require. I apologize for that, Alexandra."

Lexi's eyes widened. "You don't need to apologize."

"Of course I do. If I'd followed up with Alexander right away, it's possible we could have avoided all of this."

"What's the worst he'll do if he wants a full-blown performance, and we don't give him that?" Hudson said. "He's not going to fire all of us."

Lexi wasn't so sure he wouldn't fire her.

"Well, we know for sure he's not going to fire you," Kayleigh said with a laugh. "I don't think any of the rest of us are that safe."

"Are you kidding?" Hudson chuckled. "I think if he had to choose between you or me, he'd fire me."

"Hopefully he won't fire anyone," Wilder said. "If he still wants the bigger program, maybe clue him in on the excessive amount of work and money it will cost to bring it about."

"We'll get this sorted out," Hudson assured them. "And no one will lose their job in the process. I'll make sure of that."

As the conversation moved away from the program, Lexi pushed the food on her plate around, taking a small bite every so often. Her appetite had fled as she'd been harshly reminded of just what her life had been reduced to.

"You okay?" Wilder asked as he leaned close to her.

She gave him a smile, pulling up the one she used even when she wasn't feeling it inside. "I'm fine."

His gaze narrowed briefly. "None of this is a big deal. We'll roll with the punches and get it figured out."

Never in her life had Lexi been comfortable *rolling with the punches.* She much preferred everything to be planned out and organized well in advance. It wasn't like she'd never experienced things going wrong, but planning ahead often helped keep those instances to a minimum.

She was also very confused. Not just because of the program. She didn't understand why she had the job when there was no valid reason for the position to actually exist. Also, anyone that had been skating for more than a couple of years could have filled her role. She was overqualified for the job, which left her floundering.

Of course, she'd been floundering since the day of her dad's arrest, so this was the same book, just a new chapter of *Alexandra is Lost.*

Was this going to be the totality of her life in the years to come? Killing time at a rink that was hardly used, while trying to put together skating programs for kids who'd only been taking lessons for a short time and had no aspirations to become elite skaters?

Had she seriously reached the end of her career already?

It hurt to imagine that everything she'd worked for and everything she'd dreamed of was gone. Swept away by her father's greed.

Swallowing hard against the emotion that welled up inside her, Lexi scooped up another bite of food, though she struggled to put it in her mouth. Finally, they finished eating and moved on to dessert and coffee.

After dessert, when Charli tried to send the girls off to do their homework and received an argument in response from Layla, the dinner quickly drew to an end. Lexi was more than happy with that turn of events because she wanted to get back to the solitude and safety of her apartment.

There was nothing waiting for her there, but she needed to be alone with her thoughts. She needed to not have to school her expressions and reactions because of the presence of others.

"Sorry this evening kind of turned into a bust," Wilder said as they left the house after saying goodbye to everyone. "That wasn't how I thought it would end."

"I think we're all a bit confused about how to proceed."

"True, which is why we need to get clarification sooner rather than later. It might not matter to Kayleigh and Hudson, but clearly, it's important for you to know."

Lexi appreciated that Wilder understood that. She didn't like it when things were in flux, especially when it seemed there was no clear direction for moving forward.

She had experience with things being in flux. Every time she and Mik were creating a new program, things were in flux as they and their choreographer tried to figure out what worked best for the music they'd chosen. Sometimes they'd think one thing would work, but after skating it that way for a bit, they'd realize it needed to change.

Lexi could handle that because they were moving toward the ultimate goal of a perfectly choreographed program. They had an end point in sight, even if the journey to get there involved some twists and turns, and at times, some backtracking.

This mess, however, had no end point in sight—if there even was one at all.

"I know you're probably stressed out by this, but try to not let it get to you. We'll get it figured out."

Lexi appreciated Wilder's confidence. However, she did not share it.

"Are you off work tomorrow?" Wilder asked as he turned at the corner of her street.

"Yes. Tuesday and Wednesday are my days off."

"Those are supposed to be my days off, too."

"*Supposed to be?* What does that mean?"

"I usually end up working seven days a week."

"Why would you do that?"

"The money I earn at the resort goes toward the cost of my traveling in the off-season. Plus, I really enjoy working with people on the slopes. It's not a hardship."

Lexi understood that. When she was training, it was a seven day a week thing, although she had a much lighter workout on Sundays since her dad had insisted they attend church in the morning, and also, their bodies had needed a break.

"If you're off tomorrow, do you want to do something?"

"Do something?"

"Yeah. If you're not busy with other stuff."

Lexi often struggled to fill her days off, and usually ended up just reading or sketching skating costumes in her sketchbook once the rink had opened, forcing her to leave the ice.

"I'm not busy," she said. "What do you have in mind?"

"Is there anything you enjoy doing outside of skating? Like going to museums or to the movies?"

Lexi hadn't been to a movie in ages, and museums hadn't been things she'd had the time to explore. Both sounded interesting.

"Or... if you're up for a little adventure, we could try a Segway tour in Coeur d'Alene."

"Segway tour?"

"Do you know what a Segway is?" he asked as he pulled to a stop in front of her building.

"Isn't it some sort of electrical bike?"

"Sort of. You stand on a wheeled base and hold on to handles to guide it," he explained. "I think it's fun."

Lexi hesitated. Was this something she might enjoy? She wasn't one for stepping out of her comfort zone very often, and she kind of felt like she'd done a lot of that already since her move to Serenity. Was she really prepared to do it some more?

"I... guess so?"

"I think you'd have fun. We'll go on a tour around Coeur d'Alene. It usually lasts a couple of hours."

"What time would we go?"

"I'll have to see what time the owner has available tomorrow. I'll text you as soon as I know."

At least she wouldn't be bored.

"I guess I'll see you tomorrow then," Lexi said as she pulled the handle to open the car door.

"Don't back out on me," Wilder told her with a wink.

"I won't." Although the thought had crossed her mind. "Goodnight."

After closing the door, she made her way up the sidewalk to the front door. She used the code to open it, then glanced over her shoulder to see that Wilder's car continued to idle at the curb. He didn't pull away until she was safely inside the building.

It was a small gesture that her mom would have appreciated. The man might not be her type overall, but he still had good manners that made her feel valued.

It would be interesting to see what the next day held. If she could put aside the stress of the Christmas program for a few hours, perhaps she could actually enjoy herself.

# CHAPTER TEN

Wilder left the quiet house and jogged over to his car. Everyone was at work or school or, in Shiloh's case, hanging out with Grandma and Grandpa.

He couldn't wait until there was enough snow on the slopes for him to start work. Being alone in the big house wasn't his idea of a fun time, especially when he'd finished all his work.

He'd used part of his morning to finish up the edit on his Iceland collaboration video, getting it ready to be uploaded once he had the approval from the Icelandic company he'd worked with. He'd also taken the time to reply to emails and check in with the handful of marketing clients he had.

Now, after eating a quick early lunch, he was on his way to pick up Alexandra. When he'd called his buddy who owned the Segway tour company, Marty had been more than happy to give the two of them their own personal tour that afternoon at two.

Wilder was actually a little surprised that Alexandra hadn't backed out. However, he wouldn't be one hundred percent certain of her going until she was seated in his car next to him.

When he pulled up in front of her building, he sent Alexandra a text to let her know he was there, then he got out of the car to wait for her. She didn't reply, and it was several long minutes before she appeared, and when she stepped out of the door, she had a tall blond man with her.

After she gestured to Wilder, she turned away from the man and quickly headed in Wilder's direction.

Though her was tempted to ask who the man was, he bit his tongue. This wasn't a date. They were just two friends hanging out together. He cared that she was new in the area and likely hadn't made a lot of friends yet.

Plus, she'd seemed rather stressed the night before. Whenever he was stressed, doing something fun helped to put him back in a better frame of mind.

"Good afternoon," he said, smiling as she drew close.

"Hi." Her return smile was fleeting, but he thought it was genuine.

He opened the door for her, then waited for her to settle into the passenger seat before closing it again. After rounding the front of the car, he slid behind the wheel and started the engine.

"How was your morning?" he asked as he pulled away from the curb. "Anything exciting?"

"Not really. I was up at the rink early to skate, then worked out for a while."

"You skate even on your days off?"

"Of course. For the most part, I try to skate every day, usually early in the morning before anyone else is at the rink."

Wilder wanted to ask her why she did that if she wasn't going to skate professionally anymore, but he wasn't sure the question would be well-received. And possibly, it wasn't any of his business.

"That's some good devotion you've got going on there."

"It's more like a way of life that's engrained in me now. I can't remember a time when I haven't skated every single day. My skating sessions aren't as long as they once were, but I'm still trying to keep up my skills."

"I know it can be hard to get back on track after a time away," Wilder said. "My first time back on skis in the season is always fun as I try to get the feel for it again."

"Is it like riding a bike?" Alexandra asked.

"It does come back rather quickly, so I guess it must be."

They fell silent for a couple of minutes as Wilder drove through town to the road leading to Coeur d'Alene, with only music from a Christian radio station playing softly in the background.

"So you said it's about an hour's drive?"

"Yep. Did you want to grab a coffee or anything for the trip?"

"No. I brought my water, so I'm good."

"Still can't believe you don't drink coffee."

"If I get sufficient sleep, there's no need for the pick-me-up coffee might offer."

"I admire your discipline. If you're going to treat yourself or splurge on a food, what would it be?"

"I'd probably eat more pasta," she said.

"I suppose you're not talking about the boxed mac and cheese."

"Uh... no. Freshly made pasta is my favorite. I really like it with a bolognaise sauce."

"I'm a pasta fan too, but usually when I make the noodles, they're out of a box. I don't have the time—or the desire—to learn how to make my own pasta."

"I've never tried," Alexandra admitted. "We had a chef that cooked for us."

"Maybe you could learn. I'm pretty sure they sell affordable pasta making machines online, so that must mean it's not only chefs who make fresh pasta."

"I've never thought about learning how to do it myself."

"Honestly? I can't believe it would be more difficult than learning to do a flawless Triple Axel." Wilder glanced over with a grin. "I know I'd rather learn to make pasta than how to do that jump."

Alexandra gave a little huff of laughter. "Yeah. It took me a *long* time to get that jump to the point where I could land it consistently."

"Your hard work has definitely paid off. Which is why I think you'd be a primo pasta maker in no time."

"Does anyone in your family make it?"

"My brother Zane does. He's a chef and had already perfected it while he was still in high school. We were all appreciative recipients of his attempts along the way."

"What about Kayleigh? You said she likes to cook."

"She does, but as far as I know, it's mainly fancy French stuff. It's possible she's branched out though. You could always ask her if she does."

Alexandra hummed noncommittally, which Wilder took to mean she probably wouldn't say a thing to her about it. If he knew anything about Kayleigh—and as her brother, he certainly did—he was confident that she'd love to talk about food with Alexandra. And if she didn't know how to make pasta, she might be willing to learn along with her.

"So tell me more about your travels," Alexandra said as they left Serenity behind.

Wilder always enjoyed sharing about his trips and the places he visited. And though parts of his travels had taken a more serious turn in the past couple of years, he didn't think it was the time to share what he'd learned during his trip to Thailand and how that had led him to the orphanages he now spent part of his summer helping.

Maybe if he got to know her a bit better and felt like she would be receptive to hearing about it, he'd share more.

By the time they neared the place where they'd start the tour, he'd exhausted a lot of the more interesting stories he had about places he'd visited.

"Is this it?" Alexandra asked, skepticism in her voice. "It looks..."

"This isn't where we spend the whole time," Wilder said as he found a place to park. "We check in here, then Marty will give us a rundown on how to operate the Segway and have us practice a bit before we set off."

It wasn't the snazziest of locations, but since they weren't staying there, it really didn't matter. He was just lucky that Marty, who owned the place and gave the tours, was willing to make an exception for them, even though the tours were technically finished for the season. He probably wouldn't have considered Wilder's request if the weather hadn't been so nice.

It was a sunny day, and unseasonably warm, with temps nearing sixty degrees. Any hint of the snow they'd had several days ago was gone. It was nice for what they had planned that day. Not so nice for his hope that the slopes would open soon.

Once the car was parked, he turned to smile at her. "Let's go!"

She stared at him for a long moment, then nodded. "Let's go."

Her response wasn't quite as enthusiastic as his had been, but he thought she'd enjoy the experience once the tour was underway.

Marty strode over to meet them, his tall lanky frame clad in blue jeans, a long sleeve flannel shirt, and a vest. He pushed his sunglasses to the top of his head as he reached them and offered Wilder a wide, friendly smile.

"Good to see you again, Wild-man."

Wilder gave him a hug, with a firm slap on his back, before stepping back to introduce Alexandra. She smiled her professional smile at him as they shook hands.

Marty might look a little rough around the edges—because he was—but he had a heart as big as his home state of Texas. He and Wilder had met when Wilder had come with some friends to take the tour a few years ago.

Wilder had struck up a conversation with him, and they'd ended up keeping in touch over the years. Now he considered the man a good friend, and he tried to see him a few times over the winter season. Marty switched over to cross-country ski tours once winter arrived, and Wilder had gone on those a few times, too.

"So, have you ever ridden one of these?" Marty asked as he gestured to where three Segways sat next to a small building that looked like it needed some fresh paint.

"No. I've never had the opportunity."

"Well, you're gonna have one today," Marty said with a grin. "Let's get you suited up, and then we'll teach you how to ride a Segway. Don't worry. It's really quite simple. We have kids as young as twelve use them for the tours."

Alexandra was silent as Marty led them into the building and handed them headsets, helmets, and a reflective vest.

"The headsets are so I can speak to you as we ride, and the helmet and vest are for safety."

Wilder thought Alexandra might complain about how unfashionable both were, but she didn't. She just took the items and put them on.

Once they were all dressed for the tour, Marty walked Alexandra through the process of operating the Segway. She seemed hesitant at first, but soon, she was moving tentatively around the large space Marty had set up for people to practice.

"Doing good," Wilder said as she rolled past him.

She flashed him a quick smile, then focused on maneuvering the machine around some pylons Marty had set up. Though she moved slowly and cautiously, she was doing pretty good for her first time on a Segway.

Over the next ten minutes, she continued to ride it around, gradually gaining more confidence.

"Think you're ready to hit the road?" Marty asked.

"Yep."

"Perfect!"

The three of them wheeled out of the lot and onto the sidewalk that ran along the chain-link fence Marty had set up around the property. Wilder let Alexandra ride directly behind Marty, with him bringing up the rear just in case she needed something. He'd also see if she got into any trouble.

Marty kept them at a steady pace as they headed for the first location of the tour. Wilder had already heard the spiel a few times, but he still paid attention to what Marty had to say. Since it wasn't an official tour, Marty didn't stick to his usual script.

About forty-five minutes into the tour, Marty had them pull over in a park for a break. Alexandra headed off to use the bathroom, leaving the two men to chat.

"New girlfriend?" Marty asked as he sat down on the bench beside Wilder, stretching his long legs out in front of him.

"No. More like a new friend who's a girl."

"Really nothing more?" Marty didn't sound convinced.

"I only met her a couple of weeks ago," Wilder told him. "She's not from around here, so I thought I'd bring her on this tour so she could learn more about the area."

"How did you meet?"

"We're both working at the resort. She's a figure skater and is working at the new rink that's been built there. Of course, I'm still working the slopes."

"Not yet, though, huh?"

Wilder sighed. "Not yet. Hoping for a good dump to get the slopes covered."

"I can't wait either. Too much downtime between shutting down this side of the business and getting on with the ski tours makes me antsy."

"I hear ya. I came home a bit earlier than usual, so now I'm just trying to fill my time."

"Hence, why you're on a Segway tour with a beautiful woman?"

"Something like that."

"Is there a reason she isn't a girlfriend?"

Wilder pondered the question for a moment. "I think we're just too different."

Since deciding he was going to spend half the year traveling, Wilder hadn't been sure how to fit a relationship into his life, so he hadn't even tried. Over the years, he'd wondered what his life might look like in the future, but he hadn't envisioned anything that would make him eager to settle down.

Alexandra was uptight and so emotionless at times that Wilder never knew what she was thinking or feeling. He couldn't imagine a more stressful relationship than one where he'd have to be constantly trying to guess what the woman was feeling.

He had no idea what had made Alexandra that way, but he wasn't about to take on the job of trying to figure her out. Friendship he could do. He had friends with all kinds of personalities. Some types made friendships a bit more difficult than others, but he still made an effort to keep in touch with each of them.

"Sometimes opposites attract," Marty mused as he glanced in the direction Alexandra had taken.

"True, but there are a lot of things going on in her life. I'm sure she's no more interested in me than I am in her."

Marty seemed to accept that and let the subject drop. As they waited for Alexandra to return, Wilder told him how he'd spent his summer, updating him about the orphanages. Marty had become a financial supporter of one of them, so he was interested in what was going on with the ministry.

"Here she comes," Marty said as he pulled his legs in and got to his feet.

Wilder stood up as well and turned to see Alexandra striding toward them. Her cheeks were pink from the slight chill in the air, and her expression appeared to be more relaxed than Wilder had ever seen it.

"Ready to get back on the wheels?" Marty asked as she joined them.

"Yep. I'm really enjoying it." She turned to Wilder with a smile that reached her eyes, making them warm and sparkling like the waters of the South Pacific Ocean. "Thank you so much for planning this. It's not something I would have ever thought to do."

"You're welcome," Wilder said, trying not to think about how beautiful she looked when she smiled like that. "I'm glad you're having fun."

After they had their gear back on, they set off for more of the tour. Wilder once again followed behind Alexandra, watching as her hair flowed out in gentle waves behind her as she guided her Segway with total confidence along the sidewalk.

He was relieved that Alexandra was enjoying the afternoon. He hadn't been sure she would, but he'd hoped she'd at least give it a shot. Which she had. And then some.

Right around the two-hour mark, they made their way back to the lot. Once there, they got off their Segways and returned their equipment to Marty.

"Thank you so much," Alexandra said as she held out her hand to Marty. "This was a wonderful experience."

"You're very welcome." Marty gave her hand a shake and smiled. "Maybe you can come back again once the snow has melted in the spring."

Alexandra glanced at Wilder. "I think I might."

Wilder wasn't thrilled at the idea of her coming back on her own, but he also wasn't sure he'd have the time to come with her again in the spring before he left.

"See ya around," Marty said as he gave Wilder a hug.

"Let me know when you want to ski, and I'll set you up."

"Sounds good."

After saying goodbye, they made their way to the car. Once inside, Wilder said, "Hope it wasn't too cold for you."

Alexandra gave a huff of laughter. "I've lived a big portion of my life on the ice. The cold doesn't bother me."

"You sound like Elsa."

"The dog?"

Wilder turned to stare at her. "You've never seen *Frozen?*"

She shook her head. "I didn't watch a lot of television or movies."

"I might have to set up a playdate for you with Layla and Amelia to watch it."

"Is it a good movie?"

"It's an animated princess movie that was very popular. I think you might like it."

He expected her to shoot down the idea, but she just shrugged and said, "Maybe."

"Do you want to grab a bite to eat before we head back to Serenity? I know a great little place that has good soups and sandwiches."

"Sure. I kind of feel like I worked up an appetite, though I'm not sure how, since all I did was stand up and hold handlebars."

"It's all the fresh air."

Wilder guided the car out of the parking spot and drove to the small restaurant. It was a place he'd visited plenty of times over the years, and they'd never let him down.

There was no problem finding a spot to park, since it was early for the dinner hour.

"This is a restaurant?" Alexandra asked, skepticism high in her voice once again.

She was going to think he only took her to places that were a bit on the rundown side. If she did, he hoped she learned not to judge places by their appearance.

"Yep. This is it."

When they reached the entrance to the building, Wilder pulled the door open, then held it for Alexandra. She glanced up at him as she walked through the door, then turned her attention to the interior of the restaurant.

Its exterior had a bit of a rundown appearance. With it being so close to winter, all the flowers that were usually in the planters at the front were gone. Inside, however, it was cozy and inviting. At least it was to Wilder.

The sign just inside the door said to seat themselves, so Wilder let Alexandra decide where she wanted to sit.

They'd barely sat down at the table when a waitress approached them with menus and a smile. She told them about the specials for the day, then left to get their drinks.

"What do you recommend?" Alexandra asked as she looked over the large laminated one-page menu.

"That's a trick question. I really like their cream of tomato soup, especially when combined with their grilled cheese. But I also love their beef vegetable barley with a roast beef sandwich."

She nodded, then returned to perusing the menu.

When the waitress came back with their drinks, she asked if they were ready to order.

"Do you need a few more minutes?" he asked Alexandra.

"I think I'm ready," she said, then looked up at the waitress. "I'll have the cream of tomato soup and half a grilled cheese sandwich."

"Good choice. That's one of my favorites," the waitress said with a smile, then turned to Wilder. "And what can I get for you?"

"I'll have the beef barley soup and the roast beef sandwich. The whole thing."

The waitress chuckled. "Sure thing."

After she left them, Wilder relaxed back in his seat, searching for a topic of conversation. There was lots he wanted to talk to her about, but he felt like her life was a bit of a minefield. Since they didn't know each other very well yet, he didn't want to make her uncomfortable by asking questions that she didn't want to answer.

"How do you know Marty?" Alexandra asked.

Wilder would have liked to learn more about her, but as long as there was *some* conversation, he'd take it. As they waited for their food, he told her about how he and Marty had met and how their friendship had grown.

"Do you have a lot of friends?"

"I suppose I do," he said. "I consider anyone I've had positive interactions with a friend."

"So, I'm a friend?" Alexandra asked, her expression unreadable.

"We've spent time together, and I've enjoyed getting to know you. So yes, I consider you a friend."

He thought she might smile at that, but instead, her gaze momentarily dropped to her glass of water. "But this isn't a date, right?"

# CHAPTER ELEVEN

Lexi looked up in time to see Wilder's eyes widen. Why had she asked that?

He stared at her, not answering her right away, making Lexi wonder what was going through his mind. She didn't think he'd considered their time together a date, so she should have just left well enough alone.

Strangely enough, the thought of being on a date with Wilder wasn't as unappealing as she'd thought it would be. Did that mean she was over Mik?

Because of how their relationship had evolved, she'd never had another boyfriend. She'd never had the experience of dating or falling in love with anyone but Mik. Her heartbreak over what happened with Mik had been a constant in her life over the past year and a half.

And yet, when she was with Wilder, the hurt she'd carried for so long seemed to dim.

It was true that these days, when she thought of Mik, she found herself missing his partnership on the ice more than his romantic partnership in her life.

Unfortunately, Wilder wasn't a man she could ever consider dating because he was just so different from her. She had a hard time understanding the way he lived his life. With no real direction or focus on the future. She was being forced to live that way right then, and she absolutely hated it.

One of the things she'd loved about her relationship with Mik was that they shared a passion and a drive for skating. And she had no doubt that if they'd been able to stay together, they would have achieved everything they'd planned for their future.

"No. Usually when I ask a girl out, I make it clear that it's a date."

"Okay. Good. I just didn't want there to be a misunderstanding."

"This is just friends hanging out together. I wanted to show you a bit about the area since you're new here."

"I appreciate that. It was a lot of fun." Lexi searched for a way to continue their conversation. "What's been the favorite place you've visited?"

Wilder's expression turned contemplative. "It's hard to pick just one because I've enjoyed several locations for different reasons."

"How about places you don't want to visit again?"

A smile tipped the corners of his mouth. "Honestly, I'm not trying to avoid answering your questions, but that one is also hard to answer."

"Why?"

"I've had plenty of negative experiences over the years, but none bad enough to keep me from going back to a country where I've also had positive experiences."

"Dare I ask if there are countries you haven't visited and never will?"

"That one I can answer a bit easier. There are countries I haven't been to and, as it currently stands, some I never will. Those are places where my personal safety is a concern. My parents worry enough about me as it is. I don't feel so drawn to visit those countries that I'll ignore their concerns."

"Do you already know where you're going when you leave here in the spring?

Right then, the waitress returned with their meals, and after setting them down, she left them again. Lexi opened her mouth to ask her question again, but then Wilder bowed his head for a moment.

She snapped her mouth shut, waiting until Wilder looked up again before picking up her spoon.

"To answer your question," Wilder said after he'd taken a couple of spoonfuls of his soup. "I don't have a definite idea. Something usually comes together in the weeks before I plan to leave."

And there was the proof of how differently they lived their lives. She needed a plan. Uncertainty stressed her out.

"Oh, this soup really is good," Lexi said, deciding to change the subject.

"Make sure you dip your sandwich in the soup. It's the best way to eat it."

Lexi frowned. "Dip my sandwich in the soup?"

"Yep. Trust me. It's divine."

She really wasn't sure it would be, but Wilder's excitement about it made her want to try. Picking up the thick triangle of sandwich, she carefully plunged one corner of it into the bowl of soup.

After she took a bite of it, she had to admit Wilder was right. "It really does taste good."

Wilder grinned at her. "Told you."

Lexi's stomach flipped a little, taking her by surprise. "Guess it's important that you have at least one talent."

That made Wilder laugh, harder than Lexi really thought the comment was worth, but she enjoyed the sound of his laughter. "Never thought knowing that dipping a grilled cheese sandwich into tomato soup was a talent, but I'll take it."

As she was introduced to all these yummy foods by Wilder, Lexi wondered what else she'd been missing out on by eating strictly by numbers. She'd have to be careful, or she'd end up gaining weight. Eating high calorie food when she wasn't training as strenuously probably wasn't a good thing.

But that was a problem for tomorrow. Right then, she was going to enjoy her soup and sandwich. She almost wished she'd gotten a whole sandwich instead of just a half.

"Do they do takeout here?"

"Pretty sure they do," Wilder said as he lifted his sandwich. "Wanting to take something home?"

Lexi hadn't planned to, but now that she'd tasted the food—especially the soup—she thought it was an excellent idea. And it would help solve at least one meal debate in the near future.

"I think I'd like to take some soup home."

"I don't blame you. I might do that as well."

When their waitress returned to check on them, Wilder asked her about the availability of takeout.

"We definitely do takeout," she said. "Do you want me to bring a takeout menu for you to look over?"

"That would be great," Wilder told her with a smile.

She came back a couple of minutes later with two smaller folded paper menus. "You can order off the main menu, but we also sell in bulk if you wanted larger portions to take home to share or to freeze. You can take these menus with you too, in case you want to order again. That way you can call ahead."

Wilder took the menus, then handed one to Lexi. "Thank you."

"Just wave me down if you want to order something to go."

As they continued to eat, they discussed the items on the takeout menu. Lexi quickly decided to get two different soups so she could freeze them for future use.

Near the end of their meal, Lexi noticed that the place was filling up. There were all kinds of people coming in. Old, young, families, couples. It didn't surprise her now that she'd had a taste of the food.

In between greeting newcomers, the waitress stopped at their table to take their orders for takeout.

"Is this all on one bill?" she asked.

"Yes—"

"No—"

Lexi glared at Wilder. "I can pay for my own food."

"I know that, but I don't mind doing it."

It seemed far too much like a date if she let him pay, so she looked up at the waitress and said, "Separate, please. And add a tub of cream of tomato soup and one of the minestrone to my bill. Thank you."

Lexi thought Wilder might be mad at her for overriding him, but he just placed his own order for takeout. Once the waitress left, he said, "I'm sorry for assuming."

"It's fine. I just don't want you to feel obligated to pay for me when we hang out. You said this wasn't a date," she reminded him.

"I did. And it's not."

"This isn't going to be an issue, is it?" Lexi wanted to be sure that things wouldn't become awkward between them.

"Of course not." Wilder smiled. "I just thought that since I suggested going for dinner, I should pay."

"So if I invited you, you'd expect me to pay?"

"Probably not."

Lexi gave him a quick smile. "So let's just make a deal that we'll pay our own ways if we hang out."

"If you're sure."

"I am. There's no reason you should pay for me."

Wilder nodded. "I get it."

"Thank you."

Lexi appreciated the fact that he wanted to treat her, but she also appreciated that he backed off when she asked him to. Often, she and Mik had butted heads when she objected to something that he'd decided for them both without talking to her. And her dad could be the same way with her and her mom.

When the waitress returned with their takeout orders and their bills, they quickly took care of them, then left the restaurant.

On the trip back to Serenity, Wilder once again did most of the talking. This time, he shared about his life growing up there, how he ended up working at the resort, and he also touched on his faith.

"Do you attend church?" he asked, glancing over at her.

"I used to. My dad made us go to church every Sunday. Well, I guess he didn't *make* us go because my mom was a Christian and wanted us to go as a family. I figured out later that my dad wanted us to go because he thought his church attendance would balance out the bad that he was doing behind the scenes."

Lexi knew that her voice probably betrayed her feelings about her father, but she couldn't seem to contain it.

"Not everyone who goes to church does so with a heart to worship God. But you shouldn't let the actions of your dad dictate your own feelings regarding Christians and the church. There might be people who are hypocrites when it comes to God and their faith, but we can't control them. We can only control our own hearts and actions."

"Why do you choose to be a Christian?" Lexi asked.

Her mom's faith had been important to her, and Lexi had never asked her *why* she'd become a Christian. It was just a part of their life. She thought she'd understood why people went to church. Why they claimed to be Christians. But that understanding had flown out the window when her dad's actions had been revealed.

Once that had happened, she'd begun to wonder about people's motives and who she could actually trust in the church or who claimed to be Christians. Even though her mom's faith had remained steady—and she'd married another man who claimed to be a Christian—Lexi's faith in God had faltered.

"I've been a Christian for as long as I can remember," Wilder said. "Being raised in a Christian family, I learned what being a Christian meant at a very young age. But as an adult, I've chosen to continue to embrace the faith of my parents and make it my own, believing it to be true."

"Is that the case for everyone in your family?"

Wilder didn't answer right away, seeming to give her question some thought. "To be honest, I'm not sure about two or three of them. It's been awhile since I've had an in-depth conversation with them about where they are in their walk with God."

Though they'd attended church regularly, Lexi hadn't really socialized with anyone from the congregation. However, her mom had. Since she hadn't worked, she'd built a small community of church friends. Sadly, they had turned on her once her husband's misdeeds became known.

Being around a whole family who were Christians was something new to her. They weren't preachy about their faith, but she'd gotten several glimpses of it as she spent time with Kayleigh, Hudson, and especially Wilder.

"If you want to go to church, you'd be more than welcome at ours. It's the church we've attended our whole lives, and Will's dad is the pastor there."

"Janessa's husband?" She was still putting names and faces together.

"Yep. He's been the pastor there for a long time."

"I can't go because I work on Sundays." It was a valid reason, which Lexi was glad for because she wasn't altogether sure that she wanted to go, anyway.

"Yeah. I do too. Thankfully, I managed to adjust my Sundays so that I go to work at one. If someone wants to book a one-on-one session with me, they know not to book anything before that time on Sundays. You could probably work out something similar if you wanted."

"I'll have to see," Lexi said, uncertain that she wanted to ask for that just yet.

"If you do decide you want to come to church, let me know, and I'll get you the information."

"Okay." That might not be a conversation that ever happened, but anything was possible, she supposed. Like her dad being a convicted felon, and her losing her whole career.

"Are you going to be here for Christmas?" Wilder asked. "Or will you be with your mom?"

"I'm not sure," Lexi said. "We never really made a big deal out of Christmas, though we always celebrated. It fell in the middle of the competition season, so I couldn't take too much time off. I'm sure my mom will want me with her, but I don't know if that's what I'll do."

"Well, if you're hanging around here, you'd be welcome to join us for our Christmas celebrations."

"Isn't Christmas usually for family?"

"Sure, it's mainly family, but we've always included people who might not have anywhere else to go. Or if they're a close friend to someone in the family."

Lexi could only imagine how chaotic a celebration like Christmas would be with so many people present. Her Christmases with her folks had been very low key, and it had been the one day of the year that she hadn't skated at all. They'd opened presents they'd bought for each other and had a dinner that was tasty but nothing too elaborate, since she was in competition mode and training, so she'd needed to watch her diet.

Her mom had tried to create traditions for them at Christmas, but the only one that had stuck had been the two of them attending a Nutcracker ballet performance at some point during December.

Thankfully, she had a bit of time to see how things went before committing to anything.

"Well, here we are," Wilder announced as he pulled to a stop in front of her building.

"Thank you again for a fun afternoon," Lexi said. "It was a nice break."

Wilder smiled at her. "I'm glad you enjoyed it. We'll have to do it again sometime."

"Sounds good." Lexi pushed open the door. "Have a good evening."

As she stepped into the foyer of her building, she glanced out the window in time to see Wilder's car pull away. Smiling, she made her way to the elevator and pushed the button.

As the elevator doors slid open, the man she'd met earlier stepped out. Seeing her, he smiled.

"Alexandra, we meet again."

"Hello, Colin."

He was the first neighbor in the apartment building she'd met, mainly because he'd taken the initiative and introduced himself.

"You've been out for several hours," he said, which made her feel a little put off. "I hope you were having fun."

"I was." She didn't volunteer anything more because it felt like he was fishing, and she wasn't going to give him any information. "And now I need to get a few more things done before bed. Morning comes early."

"That it does," he agreed with a nod. Walking backward, he smiled again and said, "See you around."

She nodded, then stepped into the elevator. Not wanting him to change his mind and join her, Lexi jabbed the button to close the doors, then hit the button for her floor.

Once the door had closed completely, Lexi exhaled in relief. The guy had been super friendly when he'd introduced himself earlier. And he was even friendlier this time around. That didn't make her feel very comfortable.

She hoped he didn't become a problem. That would be the last thing she needed in her life. Plus, she didn't want to have to move. Something told her that apartments of the quality in that building weren't plentiful in Serenity.

Back in her apartment, Lexi put her soups into the freezer, then went to the bedroom and changed into her favorite pajamas. Now that she was on her own, she relaxed, allowing the smile she'd been feeling all day to come out fully.

It had been a *great* day. She couldn't remember the last time she'd enjoyed something that wasn't related to skating. The time spent with Wilder had been a reminder that there was more to life than training and ice skating.

And with the distraction of the day, she had also not dwelled on whatever was happening with the Christmas program. It had been a nice break from that.

Unfortunately, it couldn't be ignored forever. Sooner or later, it had to be dealt with. She could only hope that Kayleigh or Hudson had spoken with Alexander that day and gotten some answers for her.

After the relaxing day she'd just had, she didn't feel as over-whelmed by whatever was to come. Somehow, she knew that Wilder wouldn't abandon her to deal with it on her own. And she didn't think Kayleigh and Hudson would either.

It felt weird to trust someone who wasn't her parents, a coach, or Mik. Hopefully, they didn't end up betraying that trust the way everyone but her mother had.

# CHAPTER TWELVE

Wilder had hoped to run by the resort—the rink, to be precise— the next day, but when his dad asked if he could help him paint at the house, he'd had no good reason to say no. Without significant snow on the ground, he was still killing time, waiting for his job to start.

There was snow on the higher slopes, but they needed a good dump all around to be able to open. He'd known when he decided to come home earlier than usual that he'd have downtime before getting to work, so he wasn't that upset about it.

His desire to go out to the resort that day had more to do with checking to make sure Alexandra was doing okay. Even though he knew that there couldn't be anything romantic between them, he enjoyed hanging out with her.

The frosty exterior he'd been faced with when they first met was slowly melting. That woman probably wouldn't have agreed to go on the Segway tour with him. It made him hopeful that Alexandra would continue to open up and do things she hadn't experienced before.

More and more lately, she'd become *Lexi* in his mind. *Alexandra* just seemed so formal, and the more he got to know her, the less formal their friendship became. He had no idea what she'd say if he started calling her Lexi.

Maybe he'd give it a try. He was known to live dangerously at times.

"What's making you smile, son?" his dad asked from where he was adding more paint to the tray for the roller.

"Have you heard about Alexandra?" Wilder asked as he slowly rolled the sage green color his mother had chosen for one of the guest bedrooms on the large wall.

"Is she the ice skater that Kayleigh hired?"

"Yep. Did Kayleigh tell you anything about her?"

His dad pounded the lid back onto the can. "Not much. Just that she wasn't sure why Alexander had built the rink or hired someone like her to work there."

"Someone like her?" Wilder returned the roller to the tray for more paint, wondering what Kayleigh had shared about Alexandra with their parents. It didn't sound like it was positive.

"She just said that Alexandra is definitely overqualified for the job, given her experience as an Olympic gold medalist."

"I get the feeling that she's been blackballed in the skating community because of what her dad did. Her coaches and her partner all dropped her when he was arrested, and it was revealed what he'd been doing."

"That's a shame," his dad said as he picked up the roller he'd been using and continued his work on the opposite wall. "Unless she played a role in what he did, she shouldn't have to pay the price."

"I'm sure it's been difficult for people to separate her from her father. It's probably why she's ended up here. Sort of like a place to hide."

"So you brought her up after I asked you what was making you smile," his dad reminded him. "Is she making you smile?"

"Not in the way you think." Wilder carefully maneuvered the roller toward the upper part of the wall, mindful of not getting paint on the ceiling. "I was just wondering what she'd say if we started to call her Lexi instead of Alexandra."

"You don't think she'd react well? Nicknames can be a sign of a person's affection and desire for a closer friendship."

"Two things that would probably scare her off," Wilder said. "She's a bit standoffish and aloof, so I'm not sure she'd accept a nickname."

His dad grinned at him. "Only one way to find out."

Wilder laughed. "Well, you might have to use Mom's blow dryer to thaw me out if Alexandra doesn't like the nickname. She's got a look that I'm convinced can freeze a person in their tracks."

"If you try it out, be sure to let me know what happens."

"Will do."

"You two need to quit chitchatting," his mom said as she walked into the room. "You're never going to finish."

"Yes, ma'am," his dad said, snapping a salute at his wife.

"All you're missing is a whip," Wilder told his mom. "Where's the threat?"

"I've got plenty of threats for your dad," she said with a wink. "I'll figure something out for you."

Wilder grinned as he went back to work. Though he might have liked to go to the resort, he also enjoyed hanging out with his parents.

He appreciated that, aside from encouraging him to go to college, they let him live his life. And they'd become more involved in it when they'd joined him at the orphanages that he'd visited.

"Are you staying for supper, sweetie?" his mom asked. "I'm making spaghetti."

"I guess I'll risk it."

"Ha. Very funny," she said. "It's not that bad."

"I think it's one of your better dishes these days."

"It is," she agreed. "Even your dad likes it."

"As long as I don't have to make it after painting all day, I'll eat pretty much anything."

"Well, I'll leave you two to it, so you're done in time for supper."

They continued to work steadily, getting all the walls painted. They had to work around the furniture since it had all been pushed into the middle of the room, but they managed to get it done.

Once the walls were all painted, they cleaned up the brushes and rollers they'd used. The trim for the windows and the door was in the garage, where his dad had already painted them white. They'd install them and move the furniture back after supper, when, hopefully, the walls would be dry enough.

Over spaghetti, garlic bread, and salad, they talked about the orphanages. His parents had stayed in touch with the people running them, so they had constant updates on the kids and the ministry.

"I would like to do a fundraiser for them," his mom said. "They each have a stateside organization set up, so donations could go directly to them."

"I'm sure we could come up with something." Wilder knew his siblings would jump at the chance to help. "Too bad we couldn't combine the skate thing Alexander wants with a fundraiser."

"What skate thing?" his dad asked.

Wilder explained to them what had been going on with Alexandra and the skating program. "It's all up in limbo at the moment. We're hoping that Kayleigh or Hudson can get some clarification on what exactly Alexander wants."

"Alexander and Alexandra," his mom muttered. "How confusing."

"Yeah. I'm assuming that Alexandra was named after Alexander. He's her godfather."

"I guess that's probably why he's helping her out."

Wilder nodded. "That's what we're all assuming."

"Well, maybe we should talk to Kayleigh and see if we could combine the program with a fundraiser." His mom smiled. "Who knows? Maybe Alexander would cough up a sizable donation. That would be wonderful for the orphanages."

"It would be," Wilder agreed. "I plan to go up to the resort tomorrow, so I'll see if Kayleigh has time to talk. Having a specific goal might help to give the program some direction."

"Do you think we can pull something together in less than two months, though?" His mom didn't sound convinced.

His dad leaned over to kiss the side of her head. "Honey, you know that when our family sets their mind to something, we can make it work."

"Just let me run this by Kayleigh, and possibly Hudson, first," Wilder said.

His mom nodded. "Try to get her to see how beneficial this could be all around."

"I will." Though he and Kayleigh were quite different in their approach to things, he knew she would at least listen to what he had to say.

By the time he got back to the house, it was almost nine. He was tempted to call or text Alexandra, but he knew that she got up early to train. He didn't want to take the chance of keeping her up later than usual.

Besides, he really didn't have a reason to call her.

Late the next morning, Wilder drove out to the resort. He'd called Kayleigh, and she'd said that she and Hudson could meet with him for lunch. Since he knew they were both busy, he was glad they were willing to squeeze in some time with him.

He parked outside the entrance to The Steakhouse, then headed for the doors, hands in his pockets to ward off the chill of the day. Dark clouds hung heavy in the sky, and the forecast was for snow. Wilder hoped that, for once, they weren't wrong.

Inside the restaurant, the hostess greeted him by name with a smile. "On your own, or are you meeting Kayleigh?"

"I'm meeting Kayleigh and Hudson. Are they here?"

"Not yet, but I'll show you to their usual table."

Wilder followed her through the restaurant to the table he'd sat at before with his sister. He settled into the booth, then pulled out his phone.

He'd given himself enough time to stop by the rink to say hi to Alexandra, but she hadn't been there. So now he was early for his lunch with Kayleigh and Hudson.

As he waited for them to show up, he checked the stats of his latest video, then went through his social media, responding to comments and answering DMs he'd received.

He contemplated texting Alexandra but decided to just stop by the rink again after lunch to talk with her. Hopefully, it wouldn't be too busy.

"Hello, brother dear," Kayleigh said as she slid into the booth across from him. Hudson followed, unbuttoning his suit as he settled next to her.

"How's it going?" Hudson asked.

"Good. My shoulders are a little sore from helping Dad paint the guestroom yesterday."

"Better you than me," Kayleigh said.

"Mom made me supper as a way of saying thank you."

Kayleigh laughed. "Then *definitely* better you than me."

"Hey. It wasn't *that* bad. She didn't mess up the spaghetti at all."

Their waitress appeared with a tray holding three glasses of water and set them on the table in front of them. "Do you need menus?"

"We don't," Hudson said. "How about you, Wilder?"

"No, I don't either."

The waitress smiled. "Alright then. What can I get for you?"

They quickly placed their orders, then once they were left alone again, Wilder laid out what he and his folks had talked about the night before. Since he had just the lunch hour to present the idea to Kayleigh and Hudson, he didn't want to waste any time.

The waitress returned with their food mid-conversation, so they took the time to pray for their meal before diving back into the discussion.

"I could see Alexander getting on board with this," Hudson said. "He's pretty generous when it comes to good causes."

"Maybe instead of making it strictly a performance for Alexandra, we could have it be a skate with Santa and Mrs. Claus sort of thing," Kayleigh said. "Then we could also have some elves available to skate with kids."

"And we could have the café there sell hot chocolate, apple cider, and coffee. Maybe have some decorated Christmas cookies, too."

Kayleigh smiled. "I think this will work so much better. We just need to see if Alexandra will be on board with it."

"I think she will be," Wilder said. "But I don't think we should hype it up using her fame, if you know what I mean. Wearing a costume would help her keep a lower profile, which is what I think she would want."

"Will you talk to her?" Kayleigh asked. "The two of you have seemed to hit it off."

"We get along," Wilder agreed.

"Once you've had a chance to talk to her, let me know what we can do to help. We'll need to get posters designed and printed, and maybe start spreading the news on social media."

"Sounds good." He paused then said, "Something else that might sound good is if you bail on the 80s night idea. I just don't think it's going to fly."

Kayleigh sighed. "Yeah. Let's put that idea on the back burner for now."

"Put it into the garbage as far as I'm concerned," Wilder said.

Hudson chuckled. "I'm with Wilder."

Kayleigh waved her hand dismissively at them. "We'll talk about it in the new year."

Wilder could live with that, and he had a pretty good idea that Alexandra would, too.

They finished up their meals, then Wilder left out the front door, planning to go back to the rink, while Kayleigh and Hudson returned to the hotel part of the resort where their offices were located.

He noticed a shiny Audi parked in the lot by the rink that hadn't been there earlier and wondered if it belonged to Alexandra. Getting out, he headed for the entrance to the rink. There weren't many cars in the parking lot, but that didn't mean anything, since guests often used the golf carts with drivers that the resort offered to get them from place to place.

As he stepped into the rink, Wilder's gaze swept the space, looking for Alexandra. He spotted her on the ice, so headed in that direction.

She had a couple of kids on the ice with her, so Wilder just stood next to the boards without calling out to her. A woman he assumed to be the mother of the children stood a little further down the boards, her gaze on the trio.

Alexandra wore her usual fitted black workout jacket and leggings. Her hair was pulled back in a ponytail, and she had a pink band on her head that covered the tops of her ears.

"Look at us, Momma!" one of the kids called out.

"I see you, sweetie. You're doing great!"

The kids each had a skating aid that they were holding on to as they made their way around the rink with Alexandra. She was showing them how to glide, which the older one was picking up much quicker than the younger one.

"Are you a guest here?"

Wilder turned to see the woman had moved closer to him. "No. I'm not."

"Do you really think it's appropriate for you to be hanging around watching children like this?"

There were so many things that Wilder wanted to say to her. Stuff like *My sister is married to the son of the man who owns this whole place, so I can go where I want.* Or *I'm actually watching the woman, not the children.*

Instead, he just said, "I'm here to speak with Alexandra. And while I'm not a guest, I am an employee."

"I'm afraid you're making me uncomfortable. Can I have your supervisor's name?"

He debated whose name he should give. Technically, Trev was his supervisor, but Kayleigh could probably get the woman to back down better than Trev could.

"Sure. I can even give you her phone number."

While the woman fished her phone out of her pocket, Wilder sent off a quick text to Kayleigh to give her a head's up on the incoming call.

"What's her name and number?"

"Her name is Kayleigh St. James," he said, then gave her Kayleigh's number. "And my name is Wilder."

Her brows lifted when he volunteered his name, but she didn't say anything as she focused on her phone.

Hopefully, Kayleigh wouldn't kill him for causing a problem with a guest. He understood why the woman might be concerned, but he had absolutely no interest in her children. All his attention was on the woman skating with them.

While the woman made her call, Wilder wandered over to the café and ordered himself a coffee. The guy working there knew him, so punched in his employee discount, even though, technically, he wasn't an active employee yet.

Rather than return to the boards with his coffee, Wilder headed for one of the tables that had a great view of the forest around the resort and the mountains in the distance. Soon, he'd be on one of the closer ones.

From his seat, he could see Alexandra but only the tops of the kids' heads. He wasn't surprised when his phone rang after he'd been there for a couple of minutes.

"Hey, sis," he said when he saw Kayleigh's number on the screen.

"Don't *hey, sis* me. I can't leave you alone for five minutes..." she said with a sigh. "What were you doing?"

"I came to the rink to see if Alexandra was busy, and all I did was stand at the boards while she worked with a couple of kids. I guess their mom thought I was creeping on them or something."

Kayleigh sighed again. "Sometimes..."

"She's not hunting me down, so you must have said something to reassure her."

"Yep. I told her that you were there at my request to speak with Alexandra." She paused, then added, "And I told her that I thought you had a bit of a crush on Alexandra."

"Kayleigh! What?"

"Hey. It's all the truth!"

"You think I have..." He glanced at the rink, then lowered his voice. "You think I have a crush on Alexandra?"

"Well, you seem to be spending a lot of time with her."

That was true, but it hadn't been prompted by him having a *crush* on her. "I don't have a crush on her."

Kayleigh hummed in response. "Regardless. The woman seemed happy enough with that explanation, so be glad I got her off your back."

"Thank you," he said, meaning it, though he was still annoyed with her.

"Anyway, I've got to get back to work. Try to stay out of trouble."

Before Wilder could give her a snappy comeback, she hung up on him. Wilder set his phone on the table and picked up his coffee to take a sip. He hoped that this wasn't going to be the start of rumors among his siblings, but he figured that was too high of an expectation of them. His sisters, especially.

Finally, the kids came off the ice, turned in their skates, then left with their mom. Wilder got up as Alexandra also skated to the break in the boards and bent to slip the guards on her skates.

"Hey," he said as she straightened.

She gave him a brief smile. "What brings you by?"

"I wanted to run something by you. A possible option to the Christmas program."

"Sure. Just let me return these to the skate rental," Alexandra said, patting the skating aids.

"I can do that for you," Wilder said. "Why don't you go sit down? Do you want a coffee or something?"

"I'd like a cup of tea, please. If you tell Luke it's for me, he'll know what I want."

Puzzling over why he wished that *he* knew what she wanted to drink, Wilder went to the skate rental place and returned the skating aids. When he stepped up to the counter at the café, Luke said, "Back for a refill?"

"Sure, why not? But also, Alexandra wants tea."

"I'll get those for you right away." Luke moved to where the coffee machine sat and quickly filled a cup with coffee, then another one with hot water and a tea bag. When he returned with the two cups, he said, "Want a cookie or a cinnamon bun? They were made fresh today."

Wilder considered it for a moment, then nodded. "I'll take two cookies, please."

He doubted that Alexandra would eat one, but he didn't mind eating both if that ended up being the case. "Thanks."

Cups and cookies in hand, Wilder headed back to where Alexandra waited at the table he'd been seated at earlier. She had her legs stretched out, her skates balancing on the back of the blade.

"Here you go," Wilder said as he set her cup of tea down in front of her, then sat down across from her. "Did you want a cookie? Luke said they were freshly made."

Alexandra stared at the cookie he held out to her, then slowly, she reached out and took it. That surprised Wilder, but he kept his thoughts to himself. If she wanted to enjoy the treat, who was he to draw attention to it?

"How did the lesson go?" Wilder asked after he'd taken a sip of his coffee.

"It went well, though it was a bit weird at the end."

"Why's that?"

"As they were leaving, the woman said to me that he looked like a nice guy and that I should give him a chance. I have no idea what that means."

Wilder fought the urge to facepalm himself. "Oh, well, I can probably shed some light on that."

"You can?" Alexandra asked, her eyes wide.

"Yep. When I got here earlier, I was standing at the rink watching your lesson. I guess the mom got a little concerned that a guy was standing there watching her girls. She demanded to speak to my manager."

"Oh dear."

"It was fine. I gave her Kayleigh's number, so she was able to talk her down," Wilder said. "However, she wanted to make sure she didn't try to bring it up again in the future, so Kayleigh made it seem like I was hanging around the rink because I have a crush on you."

Alexandra choked on the sip of tea she'd just taken, covering her mouth in time to keep it from spraying everywhere. "What?"

"Kayleigh made it seem like I had a crush on you so the woman would understand I wasn't there to watch her young daughters."

"So... it's not for real?"

"Only in Kayleigh's imagination."

No emotion crossed Alexandra's face, so Wilder had no way of knowing if she was relieved or disappointed. However, given their conversations of late, he was going to go with relieved. Which, in turn, made him feel rather disappointed.

"I'm glad she's protective of her children," Alexandra said. "But there's no need to go after every single guy she thinks is watching them."

"Hopefully, Kayleigh put her mind at ease, and she'll leave me alone." He thought back to the incident he'd had where he'd been accused of sexually harassing a woman. Was there something about him that made people think he was a good candidate to accuse of stuff like that?

"Anyway, I did have a valid reason for stopping by," Wilder said. "And it had nothing to do with a crush."

Or at least he didn't think it did.

# CHAPTER THIRTEEN

Lexi wrapped her hands around her cup of tea, appreciating the warmth that seeped into her fingers after her session on the ice. She'd spotted Wilder when he'd walked in and had been conscious of his gaze on her as she'd worked with the children. But then he'd left to go sit at the table, and she'd been disappointed.

Why? She had no idea.

But she had to admit that she'd enjoyed sitting there with Wilder. It had been relaxing until he'd said that Kayleigh had told that woman that he had a crush on her.

Lexi didn't know how to respond to that. Did she *want* him to have a crush on her?

It was weird to acknowledge that part of her actually did. At least it would explain why he was spending time with her.

"So, why did you come by?"

"I was planning to come see you regardless," he said. "But I had lunch with Kayleigh and Hudson first."

"I saw you there."

Wilder's brown eyes widened. "You did?"

"Yes. I usually go for lunch at one of the restaurants before I start work."

"Why didn't you say hi?"

"I didn't want to interrupt."

She still wasn't sure about where she stood with them, especially Kayleigh and Hudson. They were her bosses, and Wilder was... well, he was her co-worker. But the three of them were bonded by blood and marriage. Which was more than any connection she had with them.

"You could have," he said. "We were actually talking about the Christmas program."

"What did you discuss?"

"Well, backing up a bit, I need to tell you about what prompted the change in the ideas we had for it."

"Okay?"

"A couple of years ago, while I was traveling, I came across a situation where a child was... being hurt. I rescued the child, and, in the process, I became involved with a couple of orphanages. They are supervised by missionaries from the States, and they do good work in countries where poor and orphaned children are especially vulnerable."

As he spoke, Lexi could hear the passion and care in his voice. Though he'd sounded excited when he'd spoken of his travels before, this was different.

"I've continued to keep in contact with the orphanages and usually spend time there during my summer travels. Mom and Dad were also with me this summer, offering their medical services at the orphanages. Anyway, they are always in need of money to keep the orphanages operating. They've hired people to staff the orphanages, and they need to be able to buy clothing and food for the children. And, of course, there are all the other expenses that come with operating and protecting a compound filled with vulnerable people."

Lexi had never thought much about what life was like in countries that had a large poor population. Even though she'd skated in some of those countries, she hadn't ever ventured beyond the rink or where they were staying.

There had been no exploring or viewing the sights. Other skaters might have taken the time to see the sites in the countries where their competitions were held, but Lexi never had.

"We thought that maybe we could shift the focus of the program. Make it into an event of skating with Mr. and Mrs. Claus.

Parents could pay for their kids to skate, and we could have stuff like hot chocolate and mini donuts for sale. Maybe even have some auctions. All of it to raise money for the orphanages."

"It definitely sounds better than having to come up with a program that would require a bunch of skaters."

"We thought so," Wilder said, his excitement showing in his eyes. "And maybe the girls, and a couple of other people they know who skate, could be dressed as elves."

"I assume I'm to be Mrs. Clause," Lexi said.

"Yep."

"And Mr. Claus?"

Wilder shrugged, though there was a gleam of humor in his eyes. "Do you know any guy who might want to fill the role?"

"Just one."

"Who?"

"You."

Wilder grinned. "You want me to be Mr. Clause to your Mrs. Clause?"

Lexi felt a flutter in her stomach. Apparently, that was what she wanted. But she wasn't going to let him know that.

"Well, you're the only guy I know around here who skates," she said. "And you're not too bad at it."

Laughing, Wilder said, "I'm pretty good at staying up on my skates. And if necessary, I could probably even do a jump or two."

Did she want to skate with a partner again? Even one who was technically not a figure skater?

"Are you going to be a fit or a fat Santa?" she asked.

"I don't know. Would you be a fit or chubby Mrs. Claus?"

"Depends on whether I need to do jumps and spins. I'm not sure I'd be able to do that with too much extra padding on me."

"So you wouldn't be opposed to this?" Wilder asked as he leaned back in his chair.

"No. I think it's a good idea." She hadn't been a part of any fundraisers, but it was probably never too late to start participating and supporting something outside of herself.

And the bonus would be that she would be in costume, so hopefully no one would recognize her. "I don't mean to sound... arrogant or anything, but I'd prefer if my name wasn't attached to this. I just want to be Mrs. Claus, not Alexandra Corbyn."

"I get that," Wilder said with a nod. "How do you feel about Lexa? Or Lexi?"

Lexi lifted her brows at him. "You don't like Alexandra?"

"It's not that at all." He smiled. "Alexandra just feels really formal. Have you never had a nickname?"

"My mom calls me Lexi. My dad hated that name, so he always insisted that everyone call me Alexandra."

"I won't call you something you don't like," Wilder said. "It's just that I'm kind of a less formal guy."

"Do you have a nickname?"

"Not really. Sometimes people will call me Wild."

"That seems appropriate."

Wilder laughed. "I do have my moments."

Only her mom had ever called her Lexi. In her mind, the shortening of her name denoted a closeness that she'd never felt with anyone outside of her small circle. But even then, Mik, her coaches, and her dad had always called her Alexandra.

Did she want Wilder to use her nickname? Was he important enough to her?

Having Wilder use a nickname for her felt like a step in a direction she wasn't sure they should go. Her future was uncertain. He was going to be leaving. She didn't want to even entertain thoughts of anything but friendship between them.

Wilder was just so different from the men she'd known. His easy-going, laid-back attitude was totally foreign to her, which made her curious. And without even realizing it, she'd begun to look forward to seeing him, and when they didn't get a chance to talk, she missed him.

"You can call me Lexi," she told him, deciding that he'd been a good friend to her and treated her well, unlike some in her life.

Wilder's smile took over his face, and his brown eyes sparkled. "Perfect! Lexi fits you, I think."

She had no idea what to say to that. "So, what do we need to do for this fundraiser?"

"I'm glad you're on board with this. I really think it will be a good time, and I'm hoping that Alexander will cough up some money to help out."

"That would be great of him." Lexi would help as much as she could, too, but she'd been living on a pretty strict budget since her dad's arrest.

Thankfully, her financial advisor had helped her set up a livable budget using the money she'd saved from collaborations and endorsements she'd done over the years. Saving the money had been about the only good financial advice her dad had given her.

"Maybe you could think it over and see what other ideas you can come up with for the event. Then we'll have another meeting with Kayleigh and Hudson to pool our ideas."

"I guess we can't delay too much if we need to get things like costumes."

"This is going to be fun," Wilder declared, and Lexi had no reason to doubt him. His confidence and excitement were catching.

She felt a lot more at ease with this kind of setup than she had with the previous idea. The focus wouldn't be on her as a skater. She'd just be one person in a group putting on a show.

At one time, she'd loved the spotlight. Skating out on the ice with Mik had always given her such a rush. And completing a program with no mistakes was a high that nothing else in her life had matched.

This event wouldn't give her that rush or the high, but as she thought about it, she realized that it would give her direction. At least until Christmas. She'd have something to focus on. A goal. That was something that had been sorely missing in her life, which was why she'd felt so adrift since everyone had abandoned her.

To Wilder, this might be a fundraiser for something he was passionate about, but for Lexi, it felt like a lifeline.

They talked a bit more about when they could schedule a meeting, with Wilder deciding to see if Kayleigh and Hudson would be available for one during the day. Lexi's schedule at the rink wasn't usually too busy. In fact, that day was her busiest yet, with four different groups booked in.

The next one was coming soon, so she needed to finish up with Wilder before they arrived.

"Are you sure you're okay with this?" Wilder asked as they got to their feet. "I don't want you going along with it just because you feel like you don't have another choice."

"I'm definitely okay with it. This idea is far more appealing to me than the initial one we had."

"And I like it because we can share the burden and not have so much of it land on you. It will be more of a group effort."

"I appreciate that." She really did.

"Oh, and one other bit of good news for you," Wilder said. "80s night is cancelled."

Lexi's eyes widened. "Really? Seriously?" She frowned at him. "You're not joking, are you?"

She wouldn't put some teasing past him, but she didn't think he would lie.

"Nope." He lifted his hand. "Absolutely one hundred percent true."

"Oh, that's great news."

"I thought you might feel that way."

"You were just the bringer of all the good news today."

His grin took over his entire face, and Lexi's heart skipped a beat. The joy with which he lived his life was so appealing to her. Why did that way of life have to take him far from Serenity?

The door to the rink opened, and a group of six filed in, four of them children.

"Time to get back to work."

Wilder glanced over at her. "Good luck."

She rolled her eyes at him. "Thanks."

"I'll talk to you later."

Lexi would have liked to watch him leave, but the group immediately demanded her attention. After getting them sorted with skates and skating aids for the younger two, she took to the ice once again.

These moments were a far cry from any other time she'd spent on the ice, but they were also fairly low-key stress times. So, for the time being, she'd embrace this new part of her life until she had a better idea of how to proceed.

When Layla and Amelia showed up for their skating lesson the next day, they came without their parents. Instead, Wilder, Janessa, and her husband accompanied them with Shiloh in tow.

"We decided to give Charli and Blake a break," Janessa said as the men helped the girls tie their skates. "It's been a rough week for Charli especially, so hopefully this will help her regroup."

"I'm sure she appreciates you doing this for her."

"She'd better," Janessa said with a frown that then relaxed into a grin as she laughed. "I know she will. Blake planned to take her out for breakfast, and then I think he said they were going shopping."

That didn't sound like a break to Lexi, but what did she know? Her idea of a break was going for a mani-pedi or a massage.

Once the girls had their skates on, they came over to where Lexi stood. All three of them removed their guards, then pushed away from the boards.

"Did you get a chance to practice this week?" Lexi asked as she led them through some stretches on the ice, limbering up their muscles.

"Yes. Uncle Wilder took us," Layla said. "I was able to land my single toe three times in a row."

"That's great. You'll have to show me." She turned to Amelia. "How about you? How did your skating go this week?"

"I got more rotations on my spin."

"Good job! Keep up the hard work."

As she had them show her what they'd been working on, Amelia's natural ability to move on the ice once again impressed her. She had a gracefulness that went beyond her years.

Lexi didn't know if Amelia was Olympic quality, but with some hard work, she would definitely be a solid competitive skater.

She enjoyed that day's skating lesson the most of all she'd had so far. The girls paid attention and tried their best to do as she asked. Overall, it was more relaxing than her skating lessons as a young girl had ever been.

Occasionally, as the girls practiced, Lexi would glance over to where Wilder stood at the boards with Will and Janessa. She liked that he came with the girls and that he showed such an interest in what they were doing. What she was doing.

Will and Janessa could have brought the kids on their own. But for whatever reason, Wilder had tagged along, and Lexi was happier about that than she probably should have been.

Unfortunately, she didn't have much time to chat with them after the lesson was over because her day was busy. The afternoon was booked with individual groups, and then she had to stay until the rink closed.

"Hey, you want to grab coffee or something after you're done here?" Wilder asked once the girls' lesson was over and they'd left with Will and Janessa.

"I'm not finished until eight."

"That's okay. If you don't mind a bit of a late evening, I don't either."

"Why?"

"I don't know." Wilder shrugged. "I just thought you might like to get out for a bit. Do you like ice cream? We have a great ice cream parlor in town. Or if you prefer an actual dessert like cheesecake, there's another small place that serves the best brownie cheesecake around."

All of that sounded like a plan to put several pounds on her frame, but Lexi found herself reluctant to turn him down. The truth was, she enjoyed her time with him, and it hadn't helped her state of mind to spend so much time alone.

"Okay."

Wilder grinned. "Great. Do you want me to pick you up from your place?"

The smile he gave her whenever she agreed to do something with him made her feel like she'd just given him a great gift. It didn't make a lot of sense, but she couldn't deny how it made her feel.

"You don't want me to just meet you somewhere?"

"You could, but I don't mind picking you up," he said. "Then you can just relax after being on your feet all day."

That did sound very appealing. "I usually get home around eight-thirty."

"I'll be there."

With that plan made, they said goodbye, and Wilder headed for the exit of the rink. Lexi sighed as he disappeared out the door, and she stood there for a moment, trying to tell herself to *not* get excited about their evening plans. They were new friends hanging out and getting to know each other. And that was that.

But perhaps Wilder hadn't gotten that memo?

She was beginning to think she hadn't gotten it either. Or if she had, she'd read it and tossed it into the garbage.

Her mom was still trying to get her to join them in France, but for some reason, Lexi just wasn't convinced it was the best move for her. She'd been in survival mode for a year and a half, just wanting to escape the spotlight and judgment that had fallen on her because of her dad.

If she'd been a nobody, her dad's crimes wouldn't have drawn the attention to her the way they had because of her career. She could have just continued to live her life without people gossiping about her all over the internet.

France might have given her the anonymity she wanted, but she couldn't have done anything there. She'd have had no opportunity to work.

For all that some might have considered her a spoiled rich girl, she had a strong work ethic and didn't know what to do with herself when she didn't have something to keep her busy.

The months immediately following her dad's arrest had seen her and her mom moving from Maine to New York City, where they had an apartment which had been in her mom's name, so it hadn't been seized along with all their Maine properties.

They had gone into seclusion together, trying to find ways to fill their days that didn't involve going anywhere someone might recognize them. Somewhere along the way, her mom had reconnected with a man from her past, and they'd eventually gotten married.

When they'd moved to Leland's home in the south of France instead of staying at one of his US properties, Lexi had stayed behind in New York, hoping to find a way to move forward. Things had gotten worse for her when her dad's trial got underway, and the full extent of his crimes was brought to light.

Thankfully, because it was a federal trial, there were no cameras allowed in the courtroom. That didn't stop people from reporting all the details, however.

Her dad had asked her to come to the trial and show support, but that was a solid no on her part. She didn't support him or his actions at all. Though he'd stolen from the rich, he'd also stolen from the less fortunate, and none of it sat well with Lexi.

So now she was completely on her own.

Wilder's face came to mind, and for a moment, she didn't feel alone. His presence in her life had taken some of the sting out of being on her own in Serenity.

When her day ended at the rink, Lexi headed for home, for once feeling like she'd actually had a decent day. Though it looked very different from how she'd imagined her future, it hadn't been the worst thing ever.

She rushed home from the resort, hoping to be able to change before heading out. A shower would have been nice, but she didn't have the time. Moving quickly, she swapped out her skating clothes for a pair of fitted jeans and a loose sweatshirt.

If this had been a date, she might have spent a little more time on her appearance. But since they'd agreed there was no dating, she just smoothed her hair into a ponytail and made sure her makeup wasn't smeared.

By eight-thirty, she was ready for Wilder, reminding herself as she waited that there was nothing but friendship between them.

A guy and a girl could just be friends, right?

# CHAPTER FOURTEEN

"How did the rest of your day go?" Wilder asked as he drove to the small café they'd decided to go to instead of the ice cream parlor. The café was open late, which wasn't usual for places in Serenity that weren't bars.

"It went fine. The kids that came to the rink were kind of spoiled, though. But nothing I couldn't handle."

"Spoiled kids are my least favorite people to work with," Wilder said. "I can deal with them in passing, but trying to get them to understand that we do things a certain way for safety's sake and not just to be bossy can sometimes be stressful."

"Have you ever had someone get injured?"

"Pretty much every season we have at least one person who ends up with a broken bone. It's always a risk when you have people on the slopes for the first time."

"I'd be afraid that would be me."

Wilder glanced over at Lexi. "You've never skied?"

"Nope. I couldn't risk getting injured," she said. "I still don't have any real desire to try."

"I'm wounded," Wilder said, pressing his hand to his chest.

"I'm afraid I would be too," Lexi said, humor edging her words. "Haha."

"I rarely did anything that might result in an injury that would keep me off the ice."

"But what about injuries while you were skating?" Wilder asked. "Didn't you have any of those?"

"Oh sure, but I've never had anything like a broken leg or arm. Mainly I had sprains or torn muscles. I did fracture my wrist once during practice when I fell on a throw jump we were trying to learn."

"I've broken my leg once and my arm twice over the years of skiing."

"And that's why I'm going to stay off the slopes. I still need to be able to skate for my job, so I'm not going to risk getting hurt."

"Ah, that's too bad."

"Why?"

"I thought I might be able to convince you to come skiing with me."

"Sorry to disappoint."

When they reached the café, Wilder found a parking spot not too far from the door. A cold wind greeted them as they got out of the car and headed for the front door.

As they stepped inside the building, Wilder glanced around. He grinned when he spotted Lee and Rori seated at a table set against the exposed brick wall opposite the entrance.

Rori spotted him and waved, making Lee look in their direction. Lee motioned for him to come over, and by the time they got there, Lee had shifted to sit beside Rori instead of across from her.

"Join us," Rori said.

Wilder shook his head. "Oh, we don't want to interrupt your date."

Rori smiled at them. "It can be a double date."

"It's not a date." He and Lexi were a duet in their response.

Lee laughed. "Okay. Then we'll be on a date, and you can just be friends."

"Do you want to join them?" Wilder turned to ask Lexi, aware that he probably shouldn't be putting her on the spot.

"Sure," she replied with a shrug.

Wilder stepped to the side so Lexi could take the spot across from Rori. He hoped she really didn't mind spending some time with Lee and Rori. Of all his siblings, Lee was probably a good one for her to be around. And from what he'd seen, Rori was sweet and friendly.

Once they were seated, a young woman approached the table. "More guests, Dr. Lee?"

"Yep. This is my brother, Wilder, and his... co-worker, Alexandra."

At the revelation that Lexi wasn't his girlfriend, a gleam of interest appeared in the woman's eyes. "Welcome. What can I get you this evening?"

"We'll need a few minutes with the menu," Wilder told her. "But for now, I'd like a cup of decaf."

"Sure thing." She directed her attention to Lexi. "And for you?"

"Just water, please."

The waitress nodded, then headed in the direction of the bakery cases.

"How do you know her?" Wilder asked Lee.

"She's the sister of Alys, our vet tech at the clinic."

Wilder lowered his gaze to the single page menu. "It's ages since I was last here. What do you two recommend?"

"I love the warm brownie with ice cream," Rori said. "So yum."

"I go for the mocha cheescake," Lee said. "But you can't go wrong with anything here, really."

"I think I'll get the brownie," Wilder said, then looked at Lexi. "How about you, Lexi?"

"I think I'll have the strawberry shortcake," she said.

"Oh, that's good too," Rori told her.

With that settled, they placed their orders when the waitress returned with their drinks. It didn't take long for her to return with their desserts, then after refreshing Lee's coffee, she moved off toward another table.

"How is life at the resort?" Lee asked as he lifted his mug.

"It's good," Wilder said. "We've finally got a plan for the Christmas program, which is no longer a program."

"Oh really? Do tell."

As they ate, they shared what had transpired and what they hoped to pull off.

"If they do an auction, we might be able to donate something from the clinic. Like a grooming."

"You offer grooming?" Wilder asked.

"Not by an employee at the clinic," Rori said. "But we have a groomer who comes to the shelter to cut nails and such. I'm sure if we said we'd pay for her time, we could offer her services for the cause."

"You wouldn't offer a spay or neutering?"

Lee chuckled. "I supposed we could. I just thought a grooming might be better suited for a Christmas themed event."

"True. You could offer a coupon for a certain amount of money, which would cover the cost of that service or anything else the clinic offers."

"If this comes together like you hope, I'll talk to Carl and see what he's willing to do."

"We'll need some help contacting people to donate to the auction if this idea gets approved. It's unfortunate that it falls at a time that's busy for me or I'd happily go around talking to people."

"You should have a bake sale too," Rori said. "You have several great bakers in your family, and probably at the church, too."

"That's a great idea, Rori," Wilder said.

Rori's cheeks pinked as she smiled. "I'd like to help out wherever I can."

"Can you skate?" he asked. "We might need elves."

She shook her head. "Sorry. I can't help with that."

"And even though I can skate, I think I'm too big to be an elf."

Rori laughed as she leaned against Lee's arm. "I can't imagine you in tights and a Santa hat."

"Maybe you could take pictures," Lee said as he slipped his arm around Rori and pressed a kiss to her forehead. "Pictures of the kids with Santa."

"But Santa would be on the ice, and we wouldn't want to confuse the kids by having two Santas. I doubt that's the goal of the event."

Lexi had stayed quiet at first, eating bites of her strawberry short-cake, but gradually she joined in the conversation. Though Wilder might have wanted to just hang out with her, it had turned out better being with Lee and Rori because they'd had some good ideas for the Christmas event.

Now, if Alexander would just give them the green light to go ahead with everything.

Once they'd finished their desserts, Lee said, "We'd better get going. We've got church in the morning."

"Will you be joining us, Alexandra?" Rori asked.

"By the way, you can call me Lexi," Lexi said. "And I'm afraid I can't. I have to be at the rink before it opens at eleven."

"Oh, that's too bad," Rori said. "You could always watch the service online after the fact."

"They record it?" Lexi asked.

Lee nodded. "They stream it live, but it's also available for people who want to watch it at a different time. Get the info from Wilder, so you have it if you want it."

"I'll do that," she said as they got up from the table after taking care of the bill.

Wilder wasn't sure if she would actually ask him for the information, so he planned to offer it anyway. He had a sense that she was searching in her life. She'd lost a lot, but it didn't seem like she'd succumbed to despair. At least not yet. But maybe she would be able to find an anchor in her life if she turned it over to God.

"It's snowing," Lexi said as they stepped outside.

"Woo hoo! Maybe we'll get enough on the slopes for me to start working."

"It was nice spending time with you, Lexi," Lee said. "We'll see you around. Bro, catch you at home."

Rori said goodbye to them, then walked away hand-in-hand with Lee.

"Are you really excited about getting to work?" Lexi asked as they walked to his car.

"I am." Wilder pressed the fob to unlock the doors. "I'm not one who enjoys sitting around for days."

"Even if you're at a beach?"

"If I'm at a good beach, I'd be surfing."

"Do you snowboard as well or just ski?"

"I can snowboard, but skiing is my preference."

After they got in the car, he started it and cranked the heat. He turned on the wipers to clear the windshield of the melted snow, then backed out of his parking spot.

"I guess you get lots of snow around here."

"Yep. We do. And the occasional blizzard just makes it loads of fun."

Lexi let out a huff of laughter. "You are crazy."

"I've been told that plenty of times, and I embrace it. Give me enough snow and I'll be out there making snowmen and throwing snowballs with the kids."

"Your nieces and nephews must love you."

"I think they do. I certainly love them."

"Do you like kids in general, or just them?"

"I like all kids. That's why I'm working with the orphanages."

"Do you plan to have some of your own some day?"

Wilder wasn't sure what to make of her question. It wasn't a question he got a lot, though now that his siblings were married and having children, he was getting it more. Well, he was getting the marriage question the most, but the children question was in there too.

"Honestly, I don't have a plan when it comes to kids. Just like I don't have a plan when it comes to marriage."

"What does that mean? Don't people usually plan if they're going to get married and have kids?"

"I suppose some do," Wilder agreed. "But I'm choosing to believe that if God wants me to marry and have kids, He'll bring the right woman to cross my path at the right time."

"And if that never happens?"

"Then I'll be content with loving on my nieces and nephews and any other children God brings into my life. Marriage should never be the be all and end all of a person's life."

"What do you mean?"

"As a Christian, I believe that the be all and end all of my life should be honoring God. If it's not His will that I marry, yet I pursue that, I might struggle with joy and contentment in my life."

"I was going to get married. Mikhail and I were engaged."

"Did you plan to have kids?"

"Only once we retired from competition," she said. "Then we figured I could safely get pregnant since I could still help Mik coach. We used to talk about how we'd raise the next generation of Olympic skaters."

Her voice was completely emotionless as she spoke, which Wilder had come to realize meant she was keeping her emotions locked down.

"You can still raise the next generation of Olympic skaters. I doubt you're going to give up skating or coaching."

"Maybe not, but I won't be competing anymore."

"Are you sure?"

Lexi didn't reply right away, making Wilder think that deep down, she really did want to continue to compete. Which made complete sense. Competing had been her whole life. And she hadn't left the sport on her terms. Other people's decisions had ended her career.

"I can't go back. The scandal would follow me everywhere. And if I can't compete at the top of my game, I don't want to compete at all."

Wilder didn't subscribe to that theory himself. He was motivated to give everything his best shot in the moment, even though it might not be the best he'd ever been. As he aged, he felt the effects of the skiing season on his body more and more, but he still believed he had something to offer.

And he believed that Lexi still had lots to offer as well. "Could you do singles skating?"

"Probably," she said. "But not well enough to win gold, I don't think. So many of the female skaters competing now are young and strong, performing amazing jumps. I'm old compared to them."

Their discussion came to an abrupt end as he pulled to a stop in front of her building. "Listen, I'm going to send you a text with a link to our church's website in case you're interested in watching the livestream."

"Okay. Thank you." She opened the door, which flooded the interior with light. "I enjoyed tonight."

"Me, too. Have a good night and a good day tomorrow."

"I'll certainly try. Goodnight."

Wilder kept watch as she shut the door, then made her way to the entrance to the building. He waited until she was safely behind the locked door before he pulled away from the curb.

As he drove home, Wilder braced himself for curious siblings because he was quite certain that Lee wouldn't keep it to himself that he'd run into them. No one would believe him that it hadn't been a date.

Pushing that aside to deal with when his siblings confronted him, Wilder instead turned his thoughts to Lexi and church. He wondered if she would have wanted to attend with them if her schedule had allowed.

If she really did want to go to church, Wilder was sure Kayleigh and Hudson would approve changing up her schedule a bit. He didn't want to pressure her, but he got the feeling that despite attending church previously, she'd never had a close personal relationship with the Lord.

Maybe he'd broach the subject again to see if she'd be willing to talk about her faith. It had seemed that her father had gone to church as a way to maintain an image and cultivate relationships that he could then abuse.

Wilder didn't blame her for having a rather jaded view of church, if that was the experience she'd had. However, it made him long to introduce her to something that might help to offset her previous experiences.

Even if she watched the stream, it was better than nothing. When he was traveling, he often tuned into the livestream or watched it later if the time difference didn't work out favorably. It was a nice way to stay connected to his church family, and to be spiritually fed from a pastor he trusted and respected.

When Wilder got to the house, he pulled to the curb to park. Before he had a chance to get out, lights appeared in his rear-view mirror, and he figured it was Lee. He got out and waited for his brother to join him.

"Thanks for letting us crash your date," he said.

"No problem. I think it was good for Rori. She's trying to make new friends, so it was good that she could be around Lexi, especially if Lexi's going to be hanging out with us."

"I don't know if she will be or not. For now, we're all kind of forced to spend time together as we sort out this Christmas program," Wilder said as they approached the front door. "I don't know if she'll still want to be around us afterward."

Lee opened the door and stepped into the foyer. "So it really wasn't a date?"

"Nope. Dating isn't something that would work for us, but a friendship is always doable."

They headed for the kitchen, where they found Janessa and Will.

"Where have you two been?" Janessa asked.

"Rori and I were at the café, then Wilder and Lexi showed up."

Janessa arched a brow at Wilder. "Date?"

"Nope. We planned to discuss the Christmas program, but then saw Rori and Lee there and decided to join them."

"Really?" Janessa didn't look convinced. "Not a date?"

"Both of them said it wasn't a date," Lee said as he settled on a stool at the counter. "So I guess it wasn't."

"Neither of us is in a place to date," Wilder said. "I'll be leaving again in the spring, and who knows where she'll end up."

"You don't think she's here long term?" Janessa asked.

Wilder shrugged. "I have no clue. And I don't think she does either. She seems quite... unmoored, for lack of a better word. From the few conversations we've had about her career, I think she doesn't know what to do with her future."

"I imagine losing everything the way she did must be very hard to deal with," Janessa said. "I mean, she's lost her dad, and because of him, she's also lost her career."

"Learning her father wasn't who she thought he was has probably also caused her some trust issues."

Janessa and Lee exchanged a glance that Wilder didn't understand, but before he could ask about it, Will said, "Maybe she'll find a future in Serenity. For whatever reason, she's ended up at the resort. Perhaps God has a purpose for her here."

Wilder had a hard time envisioning what that future might be. If she wanted to coach, the resort probably wasn't the best place for her. And if she returned to competing, it was unlikely that Serenity would be a good base for her training.

"I hope she finds what she needs," Janessa said. "She seems to be a very uptight and... controlled person."

"Of course she's controlled," Wilder said, feeling the need to defend Lexi. "When she competes, she has to be able to keep her emotions under control no matter how her skate goes. And she has to leave anything she might be struggling with behind when she steps on the ice so she's not distracted."

"That does make sense. I've just never met anyone like her before."

"Rori isn't super open with everyone," Lee said. "But you're not saying that about her."

"Rori can be reserved, but I've always had the sense that she was willing to open up if someone expressed an interest in truly knowing her. I don't get the feeling that Lexi is that way."

"You have to understand, though," Wilder began. "Her trust has been betrayed by people who were supposed to have had her best interests at heart. Who were supposed to love and support her. She lost her dad. Her coaches dropped her. And her fiancé not only broke off their engagement, he dropped her as his partner. Her ability to trust is going to be very low for the time being."

"She seems to trust you," Janessa said. "At least enough to spend time with you."

Wilder didn't know how much Lexi trusted him, but he had a feeling that she was spending time with him because she didn't have any other options. Plus, they needed to work together for the program. He sincerely doubted that she viewed him as a confidante or anything beyond an acquaintance.

He'd know that they'd officially moved from being acquaintances and co-workers to friends when she initiated contact with him without it being work related. Wilder didn't plan to hold his breath waiting for that to happen.

If they could get through this Christmas program without her cutting him with her skate blade, he'd count it as a win. And if they managed to forge a solid friendship in the process, that would just be a cool bonus.

# CHAPTER FIFTEEN

Lexi listened as Kayleigh outlined what she had proposed to Alexander for the Christmas fundraising event. She wasn't sure if she was surprised or not that he'd agreed without requesting any changes.

Granted, she didn't know the man well—or at all, really—but Kayleigh and Hudson seemed to have a good relationship with him, so perhaps he was deferring to their judgement.

"There are lots of moving parts for this, but only some of it will fall on your shoulders," Kayleigh said. "Basically anything that involves the ice will be what you need to plan."

Lexi nodded. "The costumes and decorating, too?"

"We can discuss the costumes and where to get them. The decorating will be done by whoever we get to decorate the resort. I think you should have just a short program for the skating with the Santa thing. You, Wilder, and whoever you choose as elves."

"I think I can do that."

"Oh, and if you want, you can set up a playlist of Christmas songs that would be fun for people to skate to."

That shouldn't be too hard. "How long will the fundraiser last?"

"I think we're going to run it for a few hours. Probably from one until six. That way, we will hopefully not get a huge rush of people trying to get here for just a couple of hours."

"And what else will the time entail?" Lots of ideas had been tossed around, so she was curious about what they'd ended up with.

"We'll have an auction to raise money for the orphanages. We're also going to have a bake sale."

"A bake sale?" Rori had mentioned that, but Lexi hadn't asked her for further details.

Kayleigh gave her a curious look, then said, "People will bake things and donate them to us to sell. We have some really great home bakers in the church who will be happy to help."

"I've never heard of that before."

"We have a few of them each year, helping to raise money for various things. The school has done them to raise money for student trips. The church has one or two a year to raise financial support for missionaries. It's something that people like, so I think it will go over well, especially if the baked goods are Christmas themed."

Lexi felt like she had fallen into one of those Christmas romance movies her mom loved to watch.

"We'll also sell hot beverages and mini donuts," Kayleigh added. "And we're still trying to figure out the logistics, but Rori is willing to take pictures of the kids with Santa."

"It's grown to more than I thought it would be," Lexi said. "For a bit there, I was worried about how it was going to work out."

"You and me both," Kayleigh told her with a grimace. "But sometimes all you need is a starting point. We had that—even though it wasn't a great one—and I think we'll end up with something that's amazing. Perhaps it will become a tradition for future years."

For a moment, the idea of it was appealing to Lexi. Then she remembered that she might not be there next year. She had no idea what the future held for her, and it was entirely possible she wouldn't be around in a year.

The door to the rink swung open, and Wilder walked in, grinning as he headed in their direction.

"What have I missed?" he asked as he unzipped his jacket and shrugged out of it, then hung it on the back of the chair and sat down.

"I'm just giving Lexi an update on the fundraiser since Alexander gave his approval," Kayleigh said.

Seeing the two of them together, Lexi could see the similarities in the siblings, though she'd missed them back when she'd first met the pair. However, while their smiles were similar, Wilder's came quickly. Kayleigh was more reserved. Of all Wilder's siblings that she'd met so far, Lexi found that she related the best to Kayleigh.

"So what do you need me to do?" he asked, leaning forward to look at Kayleigh's tablet.

As Kayleigh filled him in, Lexi stayed quiet and sipped on the tea she'd made herself at home and poured into an insulated mug. Like her, Kayleigh came into work early, so they'd decided to meet at seven before the day got underway.

After steady snowfall through the weekend, it seemed that perhaps Wilder would be starting work soon. Lexi wondered if that meant she'd see more or less of him.

They had the same days off, but that didn't mean Wilder would want to see her on those days. Lexi hoped that wouldn't be the case. Even though she knew there was no way there could be anything between them, she was reluctant to give up time with someone she'd come to view as a friend.

"So, are you going to design a program for us?" Wilder asked, his gaze meeting Lexi's. "You just have to make it really simple. Like make Santa a hockey fan so I can use a stick on the ice."

"You want Santa to be a hockey fan?" Lexi asked.

"Of course. Don't you think Santa is a fan of all winter sports?"

She stared at him for a long moment, her pulse fluttering. When he returned her gaze, his brown eyes sparkled with laughter.

"I honestly haven't spent even a second of my life thinking about what sports Santa might be a fan of."

Kayleigh laughed. "I have to say I'm with you there, Alexandra."

Hearing Kayleigh call her by her full name felt weird after Wilder had started to call her Lexi. She found that she wanted Kayleigh and the other Halversons to call her Lexi. The desire to lessen the formality of her relationship with them surprised her. But it also filled her with a warmth that made her certain it was the right decision.

"Well, I've given it some thought over the past few days," Wilder said, relaxing back in his chair as he crossed his arms over his chest. "And I think it's only right that Santa be a fan of hockey and other cold weather sports. Like figure skating. I'm pretty sure he's a fan of yours."

Lexi couldn't keep the smile from her face at his words. "Well, if he wants an autograph, let me know."

"He's very excited to be skating with Mrs. Claus," Wilder said with a wink.

"Well, I, for one, am very excited to see how all this works out with Santa," Kayleigh said as she picked up her tablet. "I think it's going to be a lot of fun."

"I do too," Wilder told her. "This is going to be an amazing fundraiser for a great cause."

"Now that we've got a direction to move in, I agree." Kayleigh got to her feet. "I'm going to head back to work, but feel free to contact me if you have any concerns, Lexi."

"What about if I have concerns?" Wilder asked.

Kayleigh rolled her eyes as she bent over to kiss the top of his head. "I've never had to tell you to contact me with your concerns, little brother. You seem to know to do that without any guidance from me. I'll see you guys later."

Once it was just her and Wilder, Lexi said, "I have never been involved with something like this. I really hope it works out."

"I'm sure it will." Wilder's expression turned serious. "Are you worried that you might make a mistake somewhere with this?"

She shrugged, her gaze dropping to the insulated mug she gripped between her hands. "I don't want to do something that might negatively affect the fundraiser."

"You won't." His words were immediate and held a confidence she didn't share. "The whole point of this is to have fun. There are no judges handing out scores. It'll just be people looking for a fun experience."

Lexi wasn't used to not being judged when performing. There hadn't been judges at the galas following competitions, but there had still been plenty of dissecting of their performances by the spectators and online. Even their practices had been judged by their coaches and by commentators, who were allowed to view the practice sessions at competitions.

"Seriously, don't let this stress you out. We're going to have fun, I promise you."

"I have a feeling that my idea of fun and yours are slightly different."

"Maybe, but I think you'll come around to my idea of fun for this."

"Okay." She wasn't going to argue with him about it. Time would tell. "Are you going to have time to practice once you start work?"

"Yep. If you want, we can practice around this time."

"What time do the slopes open each day?"

"Nine o'clock on weekdays. Eight-thirty on the weekend."

"We don't have to start practicing right away. I'll need some time to sort out what I think we should do."

"Just don't forget to work in a hockey stick for Santa."

Lexi gave an exasperated shake of her head. She was going to have to work it into whatever she planned, because he wasn't going to let it go.

"I'll make sure you have a hockey stick."

Wilder beamed at her. "Perfect!"

His smile warmed her, making her feel things she hadn't felt in a long time.

"Well, I need to go talk to Trev. He asked me to come in today to make up the schedule, since it looks like the ski instructors will be back at work soon."

Lexi got to her feet when he did and followed him to the door. He pulled on his jacket, then zipped it up.

"It's definitely gotten colder over the past couple of days, so dress warm if you go out."

She didn't bother to remind him that she was used to the cold. His concern made her feel like he cared, even though he probably said the same thing to everyone. She'd come to see that he was just an overall caring person, like all the members of his family that she'd met so far.

Lifting his hand, he said, "See you later."

She nodded, then wrapped her arms around herself as she watched through the glass doors as he jogged to his car. It was only once he'd driven away that she moved away from the door.

After returning to her small office, she pulled out her phone and went to the site for the scores for the weekend competition. She hadn't been able to break the habit of looking, but she at least she'd managed to resist following along when the competition was live.

Mikhail and his partner had finished sixth in the short, but then had withdrawn from the competition. She wished she knew what had happened, but she knew better than to go to any forums to see what people were saying.

Some of the posts on the forums were fine, with people sharing their thoughts in kind ways on programs and costumes. Others were cesspools of negativity, where skaters' looks and performances were torn apart and made fun of.

She'd made the mistake of going to the forums after her dad was arrested and she'd been dropped. There had been no positive posts about her. Every single one had ripped her to shreds. Her looks. Her skating ability. Her costumes.

It had been horrible, and she hadn't gone back since.

She wondered if Mik or his partner had posted on their social media about it. After a brief hesitation, she went onto her new social media accounts and checked their pages. There was nothing there about the reason for the withdrawal.

In fact, on Mik's, the last post had been months ago, which was different from when they'd been together. Back then, he'd posted a lot of little videos and photos from their practices and performances.

Her coaches had social media, though they hadn't posted as frequently as Mik had. She went to theirs, but found nothing there either.

Lexi started running scenarios in her mind, but then stopped herself. It was no longer her concern what had happened. Still, she was curious if their short program might indicate what the problem was. Sometimes the commentators had information that had been passed on to them.

In the end, she couldn't resist.

She switched to her laptop, which was sitting on her desk, and opened YouTube to the skating channel. After scrolling past all the individual videos of the programs, she found their short program.

When she'd last watched them, she had felt anger and regret, and maybe some jealousy. This time, though, as the program began, she compared it to the last one she'd watched, critiquing it just like her coaches would do if they'd had a less than stellar skate.

Lexi winced as she watched Mik throw Amberlyn into the air, but not high enough for her to get the rotations needed before he caught her. She came down too soon and at an awkward angle, sending them both crashing to the ice. From the length of time it took them to get back up, especially Amberlyn, she knew the fall had to have hurt.

When the program ended, there was no hiding their exhaustion and pain as they skated to center ice for their bows and then off the ice to the kiss and cry area.

At one time, she would have kind of felt like Mik deserved what he was enduring, but right then, she just felt badly for both of them.

Sitting back in her chair, she stared at the image frozen on the screen. She didn't know what was going on with her coaches, because there was no way they would have let them on the ice at an elite competition with the possibility of making an error like that.

Leaning forward, Lexi reached out to close the laptop, then settled back in her chair. She crossed her legs and gazed blankly out the open door toward the rink.

Why wasn't she feeling the intense emotions she usually felt when viewing her ex-partner/ex-fiancé skate? Oh, she still had plenty of feelings about him and how the whole situation had unfolded. But they weren't as overwhelmingly negative as they had been in the past.

She still wished she was competing with Mik, though she wasn't sure she'd want him back as a fiancé. He'd clearly shown that his love for her wasn't strong enough to stick by her side in a time of crisis.

But as a skating partner? They'd truly been the perfect match.

Lexi thought of all the beautiful costumes she'd worn, now sealed and packed away in a trunk that sat at the foot of her bed. Soon she'd have another costume, but it was one she'd never have imagined wearing.

Mrs. Claus.

It was probably the least pressure she'd ever faced for a program. But at the same time, she felt an intense need for whatever she and Wilder came up with to be the best. She wanted people to enjoy it and for Wilder to be happy with it.

With that in mind, she sat forward and grabbed her phone. Opening her music app, she searched for some Christmas music.

She decided rather quickly that, of course, they'd skate to *Here Comes Santa Claus.*

Putting the song on repeat, Lexi leaned back in her chair and closed her eyes. Once the rhythm of the song had gotten into her mind, she began to see ways that she and Wilder could move to it.

By the time she'd listened to the song for the tenth time, she had an idea in her mind. Picking up the phone, she went to the bench where she'd left her skates earlier and sat down to put them on. After they were laced, she hooked her phone up to the Bluetooth speaker system in the rink.

As the song played, she tried out on the ice what she'd envisioned in her head. Skating Wilder's part, and then her own. As the song finished for the second time, Lexi smiled. This could really work. And Wilder would be happy because she found a way to incorporate the hockey stick.

She wasn't sure when they'd be able to practice, but hopefully it would be soon. There would still be changes to the program that would come about as a result of them actually practicing it together, but that was to be expected. It was possible the final product wouldn't look much like what she had in mind right then.

But without the complicated jumps and spins that competitive programs had, they should be able to perform what she'd mapped out without too much trouble.

It was a quiet day at the rink, with only a few people wanting to skate. None needed Lexi's attention, so she sat in the small booth where the sound system was located. Sometimes people had requests for music, which she played for them. That was the case that day, with some Taylor Swift fans wanting her to play the singer's latest album all the way through.

As she sat in the booth, she tapped out a message to Wilder.

*I think I've figured out a program for us. Could you come by early tomorrow to try it out?*

Tuesday was her day off, but she had no problem coming in before the rink opened to practice. This program and the fundraiser would be something she could focus a lot on over the next few weeks. She was grateful for that, because while it wouldn't help her figure out her future, it gave her something to work towards in the present.

When her phone's text alert sounded, Lexi looked down at the screen.

**Wilder:** *Yep! I can do that. Have you figured out the costumes yet?*

*No. I thought maybe I could find something on Amazon. Or do you have another idea?*

**Wilder:** *I have no ideas for that. Amazon is probably a good place to start.*

*What size should I get you if I order something? We can always return it if it doesn't work. I'd like to place an order soon, though. So we can practice with the costumes on.*

**Wilder:** *I think an extra large if we're thinking of adding some padding.*

*Okay. I'll see what they have.*

Once their conversation was over, she retrieved her laptop from the office and logged onto Amazon to see what she could find there. After searching for a bit, she found a Santa suit that looked like it would work. It didn't look cheap, and it had a nice blue toned red instead of an orange red that others had. So into the cart it went.

Finding an outfit for Mrs. Claus was a little more difficult. Too many of the outfits were for a sexy Mrs. Claus, which she knew wouldn't be appropriate for this particular program.

Finally, she found one with a full skirt that ended around mid-shin. It was the same rich red color as the costume for Wilder. The hem of the skirt had a fluffy white fringe on it, and that same fringe went around the hooded cloak that came with it. She thought it would be comfortable to skate in.

After she had them both in the cart, she completed the order, which should arrive in two days. Hopefully Wilder was okay with what she'd chosen. At least they had a little time to get the costumes sorted out if he wasn't.

For the first time in a very long time, she felt a frisson of excitement that was related to skating. Now that they'd gotten the program sorted out, she was looking forward to it. And not just to the program itself, but she was anxious to have a purpose in the practicing she did each day.

And though she might have questioned the whole idea of a Christmas program at the start, she was definitely on board now.

She might not be competing, but she was putting to use the only skills she had. It was a good feeling, and it made her happy.

# CHAPTER SIXTEEN

Wilder was up early the next morning and dressed in a pair of joggers instead of his normal jeans, thinking they might be better for the practice with Lexi. He'd gone to his parents' place the night before to find a hockey stick since they didn't have one at Charli and Janessa's.

When he walked into the kitchen, he was greeted by a room full of activity as people got ready to leave for school and work. Wilder made himself some instant oatmeal, then stood next to the counter eating it, while Layla and Amelia sat hunched over bowls of cereal.

"Okay, I'm off," Blake said as he picked up Shiloh's car seat.

Charli gave him a kiss, then bent to press a kiss to Shiloh's forehead. Blake would be dropping the baby off with his and Charli's parents before he went to work, while Charli took Layla to the middle school, then went with Amelia to the elementary school.

After he finished his oatmeal, Wilder rinsed the bowl and put it into the dishwasher. He filled a travel mug with coffee, then said goodbye to the people still there and headed for the rink.

Wilder was excited to see what Lexi had come up with. He hadn't been sure how she'd approach a program that had no real significance to it. This one wouldn't have any of the intricacies or difficulty of a competitive program. Or at least he hoped it wouldn't. There was no way he'd trust himself to throw—let alone catch—Lexi.

There was only one car in the parking lot at the rink. It was the Audi he'd seen before, which seemed to confirm that it was Lexi's car.

Grabbing the hockey stick from the back seat, he locked the car, then headed for the rink. Christmas music was playing as he walked inside, making him smile. The music of the season was just one of many things he liked about Christmas.

He spotted Lexi on the ice already, and as he neared the boards, he stopped to watch as she glided on her skates, then popped up into a jump that looked absolutely flawless. Wilder couldn't help but admire how she took something that was so challenging for the average person and performed it effortlessly.

Except he knew that even though the jump looked flawless and effortless, a lot of work had gone into making it appear that way.

"Good morning," he said, making his voice loud enough to be heard over the music as he leaned against the boards.

Lexi turned toward him with a smile, then skated to where he stood. "Good morning."

It seemed she had a uniform for when she was on the ice. The dark blue workout pants and jacket skimmed her figure, allowing him to see the lines and positions she'd focused on with Amelia and Layla. He could see the elegance that resulted from her paying attention to those things, though he had a feeling it came naturally to Lexi.

For the first time, it seemed her expression was open and re-laxed. There was even a spark of excitement in her eyes.

"Ready for the program?" she asked.

"Ready as I'll ever be. I just hope you're going to take it easy on me."

"It's not super complex," she said. "And if we need to change stuff, we can do that. Nothing is set in stone with this. We don't have to worry about maximum point value for anything."

"I'm glad to hear that."

"Well, get your skates on and let's get going."

Wilder grinned as he went to the bench to swap his boots for his skates.

"I got us costumes," Lexi said as she rested her arms on the top of the boards. "They should be here tomorrow."

"You didn't have any trouble finding good ones?"

"I don't think so, but we'll only know for sure once we get them and try them on."

With his skate laces tightened comfortably, Wilder made his way to the entrance to the rink, then removed his guards before stepping out onto the ice, hockey stick in hand.

Lexi skated backwards away from him, hands on her hips. "I see you brought your prop."

"I certainly did." Wilder put the blade of the stick on the ice, then pretended to skate with a puck, dashing around Lexi and taking off down the rink. When he circled back to where Lexi stood watching him, he said, "I couldn't trust you to bring one for me."

"Rightfully so," she said with a grin. "Ready to get to work?"

Wilder nodded, leaning on the stick. "What do you want me to do?"

"I'm going to walk you through the whole thing, then we can figure out if it works for you."

Wilder moved off to the side, watching her as she turned on the music, then began to skate. He'd watched some of her competition programs on YouTube, but this was different.

This program was lively and fun. And he could see on her face that she was enjoying herself. Smiling, she went through different steps, but nothing too difficult. Wilder thought he could do it.

When the music ended, she skated to a stop in front of him. "So, what do you think?"

"Amazing! That was great."

"Now your turn," she said. "And I'll add in my parts as we go along."

Without turning the song back on, she had him mirror her steps. It was slow going, but thankfully, she was very patient with him and didn't get upset with him when he made mistakes.

His natural inclination was to joke around, but it only took one look from Lexi to get him back in line. She was definitely all business, even though the program itself was fun.

He hadn't put much thought into how difficult figure skating could be, even on the simplest level, like their Santa program. Hockey was more about speed and adaptability—both of which he was pretty good at—but not a whole lot of finesse. Lexi was alllllll about finesse, however. Even for the simple steps.

The first part of the program, he skated alone with the hockey stick, moving down the ice like someone had passed Santa the puck. Then Lexi joined him, taking the stick from him and leaving it against the boards as she circled around him, though the actual plan was for one of the elves to take it from him.

At her instruction, he reached out and took her hand. She wore thin gloves, but they didn't interfere with her grip.

At her direction, he lifted their joined hands above her head so that she could spin in circles. Then they moved into the waltz position, with his hand resting lightly on her waist and hers on his shoulder. They kept several inches of space between them as they skated around the ice, which was good because he didn't want to get his skates tangled up with hers.

The song wasn't really a waltz song, but they kept to the rhythm of it as Lexi skated backwards, letting Wilder guide her around the ice. They did some more twirls and simple spins, then she had him go down on one knee while she sat on the other, both of them lifting opposite arms in the air.

It was the perfect ending pose for Santa, who was known for having people sit on his knee. So it was only natural that he'd have his wife do that.

It was nice to have Lexi close, but he tried not to focus on that. It was just part of the program. It was all an act.

When Wilder heard clapping, he looked over and saw Kayleigh and Hudson standing at the boards. Helping Lexi onto her feet, Wilder got up and gave his sister and her husband a bow.

"That looked like a lot of fun," Kayleigh said as Wilder and Lexi skated to the boards.

"I'm impressed that you managed to get a skier to do so well on skates, Alexandra," Hudson said.

"Hey, I'm multi-talented," Wilder said. "I can ski. I can skate. I can do a lot of things."

"Are you going to skate the program just once on the day?" Kayleigh asked.

"I wasn't sure about that." Lexi rested her arms on top of the boards. "Maybe we could skate it once every hour? Like at the top of the hour?"

"That could work," Kayleigh agreed. "I think it would be a shame for you to only perform the program once after all the work you guys are putting into it."

"I was thinking we could skate and then have the kids join Wilder on the ice. Somewhere in there, we'll need to figure out how to do pictures with Santa."

Kayleigh nodded. "Are you going to utilize Layla and Amelia?"

"Yep. I have a few little steps and spins for them to do during our program."

"We need to get their costumes," Kayleigh said.

"I've ordered mine and Wilder's." Lexi picked up her phone and tapped the screen a few times, then held it out to Kayleigh. "These are the ones I got."

Kayleigh looked down at the phone, then smiled. "Those look great. I thought you might not be able to find a pretty but non-sexy Mrs. Claus."

Wilder held out his hand for the phone so he could see what they were going to wear.

"There were a lot of those, but I found that one, and I actually liked it."

"We need to send those pictures to Charli so she can find elf costumes that match."

"Remember to turn in your receipts for this," Hudson said. "Since Alexander initiated this idea and has approved the direction we've taken, the resort will cover all costs."

"That's great," Wilder said, though he would have covered the costs of their costumes himself.

"Well, we need to get back to work, but I just wanted to check in and see how things were going," Kayleigh said. "Wilder let me know you'd be rehearsing this morning, so I thought we'd come by."

"You're doing a great job," Hudson said as he held out his fist.

Wilder bumped it with a grin. "Sure you don't want to be an elf?"

"Oh, I'm quite certain I don't want that."

Laughing, the couple headed for the door.

Once they were gone, Lexi turned to him and said, "So, what do you think?"

"We definitely need more practice, but I think it's going to turn out really well. I like it."

Lexi smiled at his words. "Thanks for going along with this."

"You say that like it's a hardship for me," Wilder said. "It really, really isn't. I'm up for any adventure, and this feels a bit like an adventure."

"I'm still getting used to that mindset. I haven't met anyone quite like you before."

"I am one of a kind," Wilder said with a laugh. "God broke the mold after He made me."

"Aren't we all one of a kind?"

"I suppose. My mom always said she was glad God only gave her one of me."

"Did you give her a run for her money?"

"I think I'm responsible for every gray hair on her head." Wilder pushed back away from the boards, then stroked forward again. "I did all kinds of things when I was younger that scared my mom."

"Like what?"

"I jumped off the first-floor roof onto the trampoline when I was ten. I built a five-foot bike ramp. Broke my collarbone on that one. I think I've climbed every tree on our property. When my dad got us a dirt bike, I was the one who was banned from driving it because I always went too fast."

"Your poor mom."

"Are you telling me that your mom didn't have any thoughts about you being flung into the air for jumps and twists? Or hanging upside down for a lift?"

"She didn't have a problem once we had them perfected," Lexi said. "But when we were learning a new high-flying skill, she was nowhere to be found."

"I think my mom would have been the same."

The door to the rink opened, and the guy that worked in the skate rental walked in.

"Hey, Alexandra," George said with a lift of his hand. "Wilder."

The middle-aged man handled several parts of the rink. From taking care of the ice, to sharpening skates, to renting them out, he was a bit of a jack of all trades.

"How's the ice?" he asked as he joined them at the boards.

"I have no complaints," Wilder said with a grin. "But then, I'm not the pro."

"I think it's still fine," Lexi said. "These are the slow days of the week, so it'll probably be okay until Thursday."

George looked out over the ice, then nodded. "I'll keep an eye on it."

He headed back to the rental area, flipping on the lights of the room behind the pass-through. His arrival meant it wasn't long until the rink opened, so they needed to wrap up their practice.

"I guess our practice time is over," Wilder said. "I need to get going anyway. I promised my dad I was going to help him out with some stuff around their house. Today and tomorrow are probably the last days for a little while that I can help him."

"Do you want to practice again tomorrow?"

Wilder nodded. "I'll be here. Same time."

"I'll be here too. And then maybe on Saturday, I'll do a little work with the girls on their part in the program."

"Unfortunately, I won't be able to come for their practices anymore," Wilder said with a frown. "If we're all going to practice together, I might have to see if Charli would be willing to get the girls up early on Saturday so we can do it before I have to go to work."

"I have to say it's taken a little to get used to working weekends and having my days off during the week."

"Did you take weekends off when you trained?" Wilder asked as he slipped his guards on, then walked across the carpet to the bench to take his skates off.

Lexi sat down next to him and bent over to untie her skates. "Nope. We trained pretty much every day, though Sundays were less intense, just to give our bodies a bit of a break. It probably wasn't what would be recommended, but it worked for us."

"So all you had to juggle was your training?"

"Yes. Here, I'm also coaching, along with working, and now I have the fundraiser program. There's a lot of different things on my plate."

"If you need to offload anything, just let me know. We'll work around what you need."

"I'll be fine. I've never had a problem with a busy schedule."

"I'll chat with you later," Wilder said once he'd gathered up his things. "I'm going to head over to the slopes now and take a test run to see how things are before going to my folks' place."

"Try not to get hurt," Lexi said as she walked with him to the door.

Wilder flashed her a grin. "That's always the goal, but some-times things happen."

"Well, try not to let it."

"For you, I'll try harder than normal."

Wrapping her arms across her waist, Lexi smiled at him. Though it was small, it reached her eyes, and Wilder knew it was genuine, as most smiles she gave him these days seemed to be. Things between them had progressed enough that Lexi appeared willing to let down some of her walls, and Wilder couldn't be hap-pier.

It also warmed him that she was concerned for his safety. Each time they were together, his emotional reaction to her got more and more tangled. He found himself wondering if she felt anything like he did.

And if she did, was there a way to bring their lives into align-ment?

CHAPTER SEVENTEEN

Lexi wasn't sure why she was so focused on Wilder's safety when she was aware that her own sport also had the potential for injury. But the very idea of something happening to him didn't sit well with her.

She tried to tell herself it was just because it would mess up their plans for the Christmas program if he ended up with a broken arm or leg. However, deep down, she knew it was more than that.

After he'd left, she returned to the ice to do a bit more skating before Talya showed up for her shift on the ice with the guests. These quiet moments in the rink were her favorite—second to when Wilder was there with her. Somewhere during these past few weeks, she'd found her joy in skating once again.

Joy, and something more. There was a lightheartedness present in what she was doing now that hadn't been there when she'd been so intently focused on perfection and gaining medals and recognition. Still, she wasn't going to slack on keeping up with her training, even if her approach to it was a little different than it used to be.

As she usually did, Lexi worked her way through her jumps and her more difficult spins. There was no reason to, since she wasn't utilizing those skills right then, but it would feel like a failure if she stopped being able to do the things she'd worked so hard to achieve.

Hours and hours and hours of her life had gone into perfecting those skills. She couldn't let it all slip away like her career and engagement had. She wasn't responsible for losing those two things. But if she lost her skills, it would be her own fault.

When Talya arrived, Lexi skated off the ice, then spent a few minutes talking to her before she went to the office. She put her skates in her bag, then said goodbye to Talya and left the rink.

She didn't need to take her skates home every day, but there was no way she would ever leave them where they could be stolen. The boots had been broken in just perfectly, and it would hurt and be incredibly frustrating to lose them and have to start over with a new pair. These ones still had some wear left, so she took special care of them.

Once home, she made herself a cup of tea, then sat down at her laptop to check her email and social media. She'd protected that address closely, so unlike her social media, she hadn't had to abandon it. It was rare that she had email of any importance in her inbox these days, but she checked it once a day, just in case.

When her inbox loaded, she stared at the message buried between junk emails.

**Help!**

The email address showed it was from Mik, which made Lexi wonder if he'd been hacked. There was no other reason he would be contacting her.

Curiosity got the better of her, however, and she clicked on the subject line to open the email.

*Lexi ~ I know I'm probably the last person you want to hear from, but I'm desperate, and you're the only one who can help me. I want to ask you to please consider partnering with me again for the Olympics. If you've watched any of the footage from recent competitions, I'm sure you've seen that I'm struggling. My current partnership just isn't working, and I know there's only one person available who can perform at a level to match mine, and that's you.*

Lexi laughed as she read his words. He'd dropped her like a burning coal and now he wanted her to save him? He had to be out of his ever loving mind.

*Lev and Irina agree that if I want a chance at a medal at the Olympics, it's going to have to be with you. Even though we've not skated together for the past year and a half, I believe we'll still rank better than I have recently.*

*I don't have your number, or I would have called, since I'd rather talk to you about this over the phone. Please, give me another chance. I promise I'll make it up to you.*

Make it up to her? There was nothing he could do to make up for the hurt he'd inflicted on her.

And yet... she found herself contemplating calling him. Which was absolutely ludicrous. She owed him nothing.

And yet... there was a part of her that wanted to compete again. To prove to the world that she was still great at her sport. That they had tried to shoot her down, but she was strong enough to rise again.

But did she want to do that with Mikhail?

Curiosity got the better of her, so she picked up her phone and after figuring out how to hide her number, she tapped *67 and then the number Mikhail had included in his email. She doubted he'd answer an unknown number, but he might take a chance since he was hoping to hear from her and obviously knew she'd changed her number.

It rang three times before he picked it up.

"Hello?"

The familiar sound of his voice took away her breath for a moment. She was thrown back in time, leaving her torn between starting the conversation and ending the call.

"It's Alexandra," she finally said, forcing the words out through tight vocal cords.

"Hey! I'm so glad you called. I assume you got my email?"

"Yes. I did," she said, relaxing just a bit. "It was a surprise."

Mik sighed. "I know, but I really need you."

In the months immediately after being dropped by everyone, those words would have been a lifeline that she would have grabbed onto with both hands. Now, however...

"What about Amberlyn?" she asked.

"We've dissolved the partnership."

"Already? You aren't even going to try for the Olympics with her?"

"No. It's been a disaster from day one. We just don't mesh, and it shows on the ice."

That was very true. Lexi had seen that herself. She also had a feeling that the way Mik, Lev, and Irina operated was too much for the girl. Because they'd all been together so long, Lexi had never had a problem with the coaches' straightforward, often forceful, way of training.

"You need to come back," Mik said. "We could take gold again, I'm sure of it. I'm prepared to do the work, and I know you are too."

Lexi sighed. "You think they're just going to let us waltz in and take a place on the Olympic team?"

"If they think we're going to bring home a medal, they certainly will."

She didn't share his confidence. "Why are you so determined to do this? I'm sure you could find another partner."

"I need this medal. I can't have everything fizzle out because I don't have the right partner. Who is going to want me to coach their kid if I have such dismal results on the ice?"

Of course. It made sense that he was looking to the future. His future. He hadn't cared at all about helping her achieve her future when he'd dumped her. Why should she help him?

Except, maybe it would help her too. She could come out of it with prospects for coaching, too. Leaving competitive skating on a high note rather than the devastatingly low note previously might be a big help for her future.

They could have selfish personal goals while working toward a joint one. Maybe?

When they'd been together before, their personal goals were identical in the same way their professional ones were. It had made things easier.

"I have commitments," she said. "I can't just up and leave where I am."

In that moment, Lexi acknowledged to herself how important it was to her to carry through with the commitments she'd made there in Serenity. There was no way she wanted to disappoint Wilder or any of the others. They were relying on her, and she wasn't going to let them down.

Not even for an Olympic medal.

That realization shook her up a bit. When had the connections she'd made in Serenity risen so high in her priorities?

"Are you near a rink?" he asked. "We'll come to you."

"Do Lev and Irina know you're talking to me about this?"

"Yes. We had a conversation about it, and we decided we had to at least try to convince you to partner again."

"And if I say no?"

"You won't."

She hated that he knew her well enough to be able to say that. "I have a job that we'll have to work around. Plus, I'm involved with a Christmas skating program that I can't abandon. I won't have the same number of hours available to train."

"We'll make it work," he said. "It might take a bit to get you back up to speed, but I think we'll be successful."

"I don't need to get back up to speed. I'm still capable of doing all my jumps and spins. We'll just need to spend some time on the pairs' elements." She paused, then said, "One more thing. I'm not willing to do the program we were working on. We'll have to do an old one."

"An old program for the Olympics?" he demanded.

"I don't have the time to learn a new one, and I have no desire to skate to the one we had planned," she said, keeping her tone firm. "Also, I'll want a new costume for whatever program we choose."

"Why?"

She wasn't sure how to explain it to him when she wasn't entirely sure she understood it herself. All she knew was that she wouldn't want to stand in front of Wilder in any of her previous costumes.

"Because."

"That's not an answer, Alexandra."

"I don't have to give you a reason. It's what I want."

"Fine."

"And before we make this official, I want us to skate together to see how much work we might need to perfect the program. If it's too much, I won't be able to do it."

"You've never backed away from a challenge before," Mik said.

"This isn't about me backing away from a challenge. It's about finding balance with the life I have now." She took a deep breath. "You dropped me, Mikhail. I had to find a new direction in life. It's not fair to expect me to drop it all for you now."

"This will benefit you too," he said defensively.

"Perhaps, but I'm also not willing to trash my life here for people who had no use for me when I was going through a really rough time."

"You have to let that go."

Did she?

He'd never apologized for what had happened. For what he'd done to her. Could she work with him without that?

She would only know once she was around him and the coaches again.

"Fine. But if I don't feel comfortable with you, I won't hesitate to shut it down."

Though she wanted to tell him that he had more to lose than she did, at the heart of it, she wasn't sure that was true. She wanted him to be professional, and she hoped that the threat of her pulling out would keep him in line. If he wanted it badly enough, he should be willing to agree with any of her demands.

After the call ended, Lexi stared blankly at her phone, fighting her first instinct, which, for some strange reason, was to call Wilder to see what he thought of Mik's request.

She wouldn't call her mom, because she already knew what she'd say. Even though her mom had known Mik since he was a boy, she'd never been his biggest fan. And after what happened between Lexi and Mik, she'd viewed him as their enemy. She wouldn't want Lexi to even consider it.

Wilder, however... her mom would probably love him. She'd enjoy his personality, but it would be the way he embraced his faith that would make her happiest. Mik had never taken a real interest in church or Christianity. He'd tolerated it in Lexi's life, probably because it hadn't taken up that much of her time.

But Wilder? Lexi knew that he would help her embrace her faith more fully. She also thought he'd be able to give her some good advice. From the conversations they'd had, she knew that, while he might be laid back in his life, it didn't mean he didn't know how to consider things seriously.

What would he advise her about this situation? Would he encourage her to go for it? Or would he caution her about joining up with Mik and her old coaches again?

Maybe the bigger question was how she could trust a man she'd only known for weeks, more than one she'd known for years. Somehow, she knew that Wilder would never treat her the way Mik had. He'd already gone to bat for her, and in his own way, he'd been protective of her.

At one time in her life, she would have said she didn't need that. But having experienced abandonment by the man who claimed to love her, she knew that she'd much rather have a man who was interested in shielding her from hurt, than one who willingly inflicted it on her.

Still, this had to be a decision she made on her own, since it was her life. Her career. Her future.

# CHAPTER EIGHTEEN

Lexi skated around the ice, stretching one way, then the other to get her body prepared for the skating that was to come.

Mik had texted her the previous night to let her know they'd arrived and were at their hotel. Perhaps she should have gone over to meet with them, but she was really determined to keep their interactions strictly at the rink and on the ice. No personal interactions, only professional ones.

Nerves fluttered in her stomach, but Lexi was confident she could keep them from showing. She'd learned how to do that early on in her competition career. In the past, she hadn't tried to hide what she was feeling from Mik and her coaches, but everything had changed.

She had to hide what she was feeling because she wasn't going to let these people hurt her again. They were together for one reason, and one reason only.

Ever since her conversation with Mik, she'd been praying that this skate would give her clarity about moving forward with him and the coaches. She'd never really sought God's guidance for her career, but this time around, she knew it was important that she at least try.

She was at a crossroads unlike any she'd ever been at before. More than anything, she needed to be able to walk away if this wasn't what God wanted for her. If it didn't go well that day, it was imperative that she not compromise.

At the sound of the rink's door opening, her stomach clenched. She turned on the ice to see Wilder walk in. Though she'd told him what time she and Mik were practicing, she hadn't thought he'd show up. Seeing him there bolstered her confidence, and suddenly she was glad he was going to be nearby for this.

"Do you mind that I'm here?" Wilder asked as he came to stand at the boards.

Lexi skated closer. "No. I don't mind."

"Will they?"

"I don't really care if they do," she said. "As long as you don't interrupt, they can't object. You're the resort manager's brother, so I think you have the right to be here if you want."

"I won't interfere," Wilder said. "I promise."

Since he didn't have his duffle bag this time, she knew he wasn't there to skate. He had on a pair of jeans, and when he removed his jacket, she saw he was wearing a sweatshirt featuring the resort logo.

"Are you nervous?" he asked.

"A little bit, but nerves don't do me any good when I need to perform, so I'm trying to keep calm."

"I think you're going to do great. I've watched you practice, and I'm not sure I've ever seen you fall."

"Oh, I've fallen." She propped her arms up on the boards. "I'll probably fall today as we try to get back into the swing of things. Pretty sure the first few throw jumps are going to end up with me on the ice."

Before Wilder could reply, the door to the rink opened again. They both turned to see Mik walk in with Irina.

Lexi waited for some sort of rush of emotions to overcome her as she saw her ex-partner—her ex-fiancé—again. However, there was nothing. No anger. No joy. Nothing.

"I'll go sit over there," Wilder said, pointing to a table on the far side of the rink.

She gave him a smile, then turned her attention to Mik and Irina as they neared the ice. Mik was as tall, dark, and handsome as he'd ever been. He was dressed in a pair of workout pants and a jacket.

Meanwhile, Irina wore her signature fur coat—totally uncaring of the fact it might offend some people.

"Hello, Alexandra," Irina said, her Russian accent heavy in the words.

"Irina. How are you?"

"I'm fine. And you?"

"I'm also fine."

The words were stilted, but that was to be expected. She looked at Mik and gave him a nod. "Mikhail."

"Alexandra."

"If you want to put your skates on, you can do it there," Lexi said as she pointed to the bench. "I'm ready whenever you are."

Irina nodded at Mik, who then went to sit on the bench. Turning her attention back to Lexi, she said, "Show me your jumps."

And just like that, they were back to coach and skater.

Lexi pushed away from the boards and circled the ice. She started with her easiest and favorite triple jump, then worked her way up to the Axel. She kept her feet under her for each landing, and she felt a sense of triumph that she'd proven that she still had her individual jumps.

Of course, it wouldn't have been Irina if she hadn't had a critique for each jump. Nothing was ever enough for the woman, but that was how she'd always been. She pushed and pushed for whatever elusive level of perfection she had in her mind.

"Who's that?" she said when Lexi skated to a stop in front of where she stood on the ice right by the entrance, trying to catch her breath. "Boyfriend?"

Knowing she was gesturing to Wilder without looking in that direction, Lexi said, "Not my boyfriend. He's the brother of the manager, and he knows the owner of the resort. He's just here to observe."

Irina's frown deepened. "Why?"

"Curiosity? The owner had this rink built recently and probably wants to know how it's being used."

Mik came over to where they stood, then removed his skate guards and stepped out onto the ice with them.

"Warm up," Irina said to Mik, shooing him away with a flick of her hand.

Lexi didn't bother to watch him head off across the ice. She was nervous about the partner elements. While she'd definitely kept up with her jumps, there had been no way to practice the throws and lifts. That could only be done with a partner, and she hadn't had one.

"Spin," Irina demanded, then told her which ones she wanted to see.

By the time Lexi was done, Mik was back, waiting at the boards. Lexi glanced at him, but then focused on Irina. It was time. After a year and a half, she was about to take the hand of the man who'd abandoned her at the most vulnerable point in her life.

She glanced over to where Wilder sat. When their gazes met, he gave her a quick smile and a nod, offering her the encouragement she needed.

"I'm going to call Lev so he can watch," Irina said, pulling her phone from the pocket of her coat. "Skate together, then do a throw triple toe."

Lexi took a deep breath, then grasped the hand Mik held out to her. Familiarity washed over her as they skated across the ice, preparing for their first throw jump.

With a countdown, Mik got them into position, skating backwards with his hands on her hips. Her hands rested on his, then he picked her up and flung her into the air.

Unfortunately, Lexi felt the lean in the air and knew she was going to have to fight to stay on her feet. It wasn't the first time she'd had to fight for a landing, but this one felt more important than any of those.

She had to show Irina and Mik that she hadn't let herself go since she'd last skated with Mik.

Tightening her core, Lexi tried to keep from two-footing the landing and ended up having to put her hand down. Right on cue, she heard a shout from Irina to do it again.

Without argument, they circled around to try once more. They didn't have to communicate much, as the many, many times they'd performed that jump came back to them.

This time, they had a more balanced launch, and she was able to hold on to the landing, even though she had to sink low into her knee. She managed to keep her free leg straight as she followed through on the landing. It was by no means perfect, but it was closer.

Not close enough for Irina, however.

After they'd run through all the throw jumps and pairs' lifts, Irina declared it was time to do a program run-through. They had a bit of a debate on which one to try. Mik was still pushing to do the one they had been working on for the Olympics, but Irina cut that suggestion down without any sort of discussion.

Lexi was most willing to do their Romeo and Juliet program because it seemed somewhat appropriate. A doomed love story. That's what hers and Mik's had been.

She was tired, but not as exhausted as she would have been if she hadn't continued to work out and train, practicing all her jumps and spins. But no matter how tired she was, she would complete this program.

"Okay," Irina declared. "Romeo and Juliet. Go."

Lexi cued up the music on her phone which was connected to the BlueTooth sound system in the rink, then waved for Wilder to come over.

"What's up?" he asked, giving her a warm smile.

She handed him her phone. "Can you start the music for us?"

When he nodded, she showed him what button to tap on her command. She could have given it to Irina, but Lexi didn't trust her with her phone.

"You're going to do great," he said, giving her a smile that bolstered her confidence.

As Lexi skated to join Mik for their starting position, she took several deep breaths. She could do this. She believed in herself. Wilder believed in her. It was amazing how much energy that thought gave her.

Rather than gaze into Mik's eyes at their starting position, Lexi looked at his left ear and waited for the music to start. Like she'd told Wilder, the moves came back as soon as the music began.

This had been one of their highest scored programs, and it had been one she'd enjoyed skating.

The surprising thing that revealed itself as they skated was that Mik struggled more than Lexi. When they reached their ending pose, each stretched out on ice, Irina began shouting her critiques, which, thankfully, were mainly directed at Mik.

Even Lev could be heard yelling through the phone, as he'd watched their program courtesy of Irina's phone.

"I'm not used to skating with Lexi anymore," Mik told Irina angrily. "Her jump speeds are different from Amberlyn's. Her height and weight are different from Amberlyn's."

"Shouldn't have mattered," Irina retorted. "Even if your jumps weren't the same speed, you should have stayed on your feet. Do the jump five times."

Previously, Mik would have just set off to do it, but this time, he was grumbling as he went.

Lexi wasn't immune from criticism, however. Irina had some thoughts for her as well, and soon she was out there working on two of the jumps that she'd been wobbly on.

Finally, they came back to Irina, and she looked back and forth between them, her gray gaze hard. "Thoughts."

Lexi thought Mik was going to jump right in, but he didn't. She glanced at him, then said, "I'm fine with moving forward, but only if we can do our training here. I'm not leaving Serenity."

"Where can we live?" Irina asked.

"There are rentals in the area. I'm sure I can get someone to help find you places to live."

"Is this where we'll train?" Mik asked, waving a hand at the rink.

"We can only practice here when it's closed, like now. The rink opens at one on weekdays and eleven on the weekends. There's a rink in town that's used for hockey practice and games, but that usually only happens in the evenings since those involved go to work or school during the day."

"We can use that one all day?"

"During the week." Lexi was glad she'd made the call to the rink to ask about that. "But I'll still need for us to practice early in the day because I have to be at work by one."

"You're going to keep working while we train?" Mik asked.

"I told you I would," Lexi said. "I need the money, especially since we'll have to pay if we use the rink in town."

"Can we perfect this in time for Nationals?" Irina asked. "Are you prepared to work for it?"

"Nationals?" Lexi asked.

"Yes. We need to go to Nationals." Irina frowned. "We must prove that you are worthy of a spot on the Olympic team."

That was about a month before the Olympics. Would they have time to polish everything to a high enough level to make the podium? Especially since she didn't have unlimited hours in a day to train.

"I have a life here, and I can't practice as many hours as I used to." Lexi knew it probably sounded harsh, but they had hurt her, and she wasn't going to give them the opportunity to do it again. "And I won't have time to hang out with you either."

"That's fine," Irina agreed quickly, making Lexi think that she wasn't any more anxious to spend time with Lexi than Lexi was with her.

"Mik?" She turned to look at him.

He was frowning at her, but he gave a sharp nod.

"We'll fly back to Maine tomorrow," Irina said. "And we'll return next week to start training."

Lexi hoped she hadn't bitten off more than she could chew. But she was determined to make it work. She just hoped that Mik was coming into it with a similar mindset because they were going to have to work hard. They were not at their peak as a pairs team anymore.

Wilder had left earlier, setting her phone on the top of the boards, then gesturing toward the door. She wondered what he'd thought of the program, but she'd have to ask him later.

They continued to practice until it was time for the rink to open, then Mik and Irina left. She wouldn't have to practice with them for a few more days, but then it was going to be all out.

It was time to get back on track with her eating too, making sure to fuel her body with the nutrients it needed to perform at its highest level. She was going to need some help with that, and she hoped that if Wilder didn't know someone who could help her, maybe Kayleigh would.

She was tempted to take off her skates, but she was sure her feet would protest if she tried to put them back on. There was no one who had booked one-on-one time with her for the afternoon, but that could change at any time.

As she sat on the bench, Lexi finally allowed herself to think about the one person she hadn't told about what was happening with Mik. Now that the reconnection was a reality, she had to tell her mom.

Could it wait, though?

Maybe she'd tell her during their call the next day. If she called right then, they might get into a fight, and she couldn't deal with that when she was supposed to be working.

"Want some tea?"

She looked up to see Luke from the café coming toward her with a steaming cup. "Thank you."

"Looks like you were really put through the works."

Lexi nodded. "It's going to get worse."

The guy shook his head. "Don't think I could do it."

Lexi took a sip of her tea and let out a sigh of appreciation. "Do you know if there's any way to get some food brought down here? I'm starving, but I don't have the time to go up to the restaurants."

"Let me take care of that," Luke said. "What do you want?"

She thought about it for a moment, then said, "The steak salad, please."

"Anything else?"

"Nope. That'll be good. Thank you."

Lexi shifted over to one of the tables near her office, then propped her skates up on the chair across from her. Was she going to be able to endure the intense training that was to come? When push came to shove, it didn't matter. She'd committed to it, so she had no choice.

She'd do it, though. One day at a time, she'd do it.

She had to. She had to prove that she could still rise to the top and skate with the best of them. That even though they'd abandoned and ostracized her, she still had much to offer the skating world. Starting with one or two more competitions.

And hopefully, she'd walk away from the Olympics with a podium finish.

Maybe even a gold medal. Which, if she got one, she'd bring back to Serenity and pack away with her other medals.

# CHAPTER NINETEEN

Wilder held open the door of the rink for Amelia and Layla, then followed them inside. Even though the rink was never the warmest place because of the ice, that day it was definitely warmer inside than outside.

The girls ran ahead of him to where Lexi stood in her skates on the ice. It was seven-thirty, which was an hour and a half earlier than the girls usually came for their lesson, but since he had to be on the slopes at nine, this was the only time they could all practice together.

"Good morning, girls," Lexi said. "How are you today?"

As they chatted for a bit, Wilder watched Lexi, still trying to process what he'd seen her and Mik do the day before. He'd seen pairs skating before, had even seen videos of her and Mik skating together, but it was a different experience when it was live and it was someone he knew and cared about being thrown into the air.

He'd never questioned her skill and talent, but he'd only had half the story. When Mik had flung her into the air, her blades had cleared the top of the boards, and still, she'd managed to land on her feet.

"Let's get your skates on," Lexi said. "Then we can do a little warmup before I show you your parts for the Christmas program."

Wilder went with them to the bench and helped them lace up their skates. Then, while they were on the ice with Lexi, he put on his own. He joined them, skating around the perimeter of the rink as Lexi worked with the girls.

He wanted to know in detail how the rest of the practice had gone with Mik, but when he'd texted her the night before to ask, she'd just said it had gone fine.

Given what he'd seen the previous day, she needed to compete. Her talent and skill were very evident. And even after not competing for a year and a half, she *still* skated better than Mik. He'd known she loved to skate. But seeing her with Mik, skating one of their programs, it was clear she belonged on the ice.

Would dipping her toe into the competition waters again draw her away from Serenity?

After Wilder circled the rink a second time, he stopped against the boards near where Lexi was working with the girls. It seemed that perhaps they were going to be the only elves on the ice for the program, which made sense since Lexi needed it to be less complicated considering everything else going on.

"Why don't you two stand here while your uncle and I show you our part of the program, then we'll try it all together."

Amelia and Layla skated to the edge of the ice where Lexi indicated. Lexi waited for Wilder to get into position with his hockey stick, then she started the music. After setting her phone on the boards, she waited for him to complete his moves before joining him.

The girls were clapping and cheering from the sidelines, and when Lexi and Wilder finished, they exclaimed how much they loved the program.

For the next forty-five minutes, they rehearsed with the girls. Since it wasn't a very complicated program, they picked it up quickly and had a lot of fun with it.

As eight-forty-five neared, Wilder said, "Are you okay with the girls until Blake comes to pick them up? He should be here around nine."

Lexi smiled as she nodded. "We'll be fine."

Wilder put his skates in his bag. "Would you mind if I came back after I'm done for the day?"

"I wouldn't mind."

"I could bring you supper."

"That would be nice."

"Text me what you want, and I'll pick it up."

"Okay."

Wilder was glad she'd agreed. He hadn't been sure how she'd be now that her old life was back in play.

After threatening the girls to be on their best behavior, Wilder said goodbye to the trio, then left for the ski shop. He wished he could stick around, but he was needed for what was likely to be a very busy day on the slopes.

It was just after six when he got back to the rink with food for him and Lexi. He was glad that he was able to get food at the restaurants at a very reduced price because otherwise he wouldn't be able to afford it.

When he walked into the building, he noticed there were more people there than he'd ever seen in the rink. There were a few on the ice, but most of them were seated at the tables around the ice.

A fire was glowing in the large stone fireplace set in the far corner of the space. It took some of the chill out of the air the closer someone sat to it, but it wasn't strong enough to make the area nice and cozy.

He glanced around for Lexi and spotted her on the ice. Before heading in that direction, he took the bag of food to her office and dropped it off.

It didn't look like she was working with anyone, so Wilder approached the boards. The sound system was playing some upbeat pop music, and the people on the ice appeared to be couples. All teens or older.

"Hey there," Lexi said as she skated to a stop in front of him, a smile on her face and her eyes sparkling.

"Hey." Wilder smiled at her, glad that she seemed happy to see him. "Looks busy here tonight."

"Yep. But not a lot of people are wanting to skate. I guess they just like the atmosphere here. I wouldn't think this would be the favored destination since it's colder here than in most buildings at the resort."

"Can you take a break?" he asked. "I put the food in the office."

"Yep. I'll just let George know."

She skated to the entrance to the ice, then grabbed her guards. After she had them on, she walked to the skate rental area and spoke to the man working there. Wilder waited for her, then they went to her office.

"This looks so good," Lexi said as she opened the lid of the container that held her steak salad. "I'm starving."

"Do you follow a special diet when you're training?"

"I did last time," she said. "But I had someone who prepared all my food for me, so I didn't have to think about it. I'm not sure what to do this time around."

"What was the prepared food?"

"My dad hired a nutritionist to work with a chef, and she gave the chef all the details on what each meal should contain. I don't have that this time around."

"It's too bad my brother's not here. He's a chef."

"I was wondering if there was someone in the area that did meal prep."

Wilder hadn't heard of anyone specifically, but he could probably check around. "Let me ask Charli and Janessa if they're aware of anyone."

"I'd need someone who will cook to my specifications."

"It's possible there's someone who could do that for you," Wilder said. "We just have to find them. I know Denise loves to cook, and she probably would do meal prep for you. The only downside is that her specialty is comfort food. It is all yummy, but probably contains more calories than you'd want."

"I might have attempted it myself, but I just don't have the time."

"How did it go yesterday?" Wilder asked after he said a quick prayer for his food.

"It went about as well as I expected it to. We're rusty, but I don't think it's anything a little practice won't clear up."

"It looked really good to me, but I realize coaches and judges look at things differently than I do."

"Irina seemed satisfied with what we were able to do, given we haven't skated together in over a year and a half."

"She yelled a lot."

Lexi smiled. "That's just how she is. She and her husband have been my coaches since I was five years old, so I'm very used to how she communicates."

"It was a little surprising to me, but then I'm not used to being around people yelling like that."

"I imagine that's true for a lot of people."

"So you've decided to go ahead with it?"

Lexi nodded. "Do you know if there is a place in town that they could rent for the next few months?"

"I don't, but I could ask a couple of people who might be able to help." He knew that Jackson's parents owned rentals, but he didn't know if any were available and would work for this situation.

"How was it training with them again?" Wilder asked as they continued to eat.

Lexi shrugged. "It was fine. We didn't discuss the past. Just focused on the present and the future."

"Do you see this turning into a long-term thing?"

She stared down at her salad, stabbing at a piece of lettuce. "I don't know."

For some reason, Wilder didn't like the uncertainty. He wanted her to say that she was only training for the Olympics, and that she wasn't going to go back to training and competing full time. But he knew that was completely selfish of him.

He shouldn't be selfish about something like that. Not wanting her to leave Serenity to go back to training wasn't fair when he was going to be leaving in April.

He had no idea why he felt that way, except that he really enjoyed being around her. Even more so now that she'd begun to warm up to him. Her smiles were more genuine these days, and they came more easily, which was also something new. And something he really liked.

"I told my mom this morning that I'm going to be skating with Mik again."

Wilder looked up from his burger to see Lexi frowning at her salad. "How did she take that?"

"About as well as I expected."

"Not happy, huh?"

"Not at all," Lexi said with a sigh, her shoulders slumping. "She really doesn't like Mik and the coaches."

"From what you've said, perhaps she has good reason to feel that way."

"I know. I don't really like them myself, but this is a chance to write another more positive chapter to the story of my competitive skating career."

Wilder could understand that. He just hoped that it didn't affect her mentally. Working with people one didn't like could be a strain.

"Do you need to connect emotionally to skate together?"

"For sure it's better if you can connect that way, but there have been times we've skated while being annoyed with each other. We're not perfect, but the show has to go on, regardless of where we might be in our relationship as pairs skaters."

Wilder wanted to ask if she thought she'd get back together personally with Mik instead of just professionally, but he also wasn't sure he wanted to know the answer.

"Do you think your mom will come around?"

"Well, that depends on your definition of coming around. She won't ever have anything to do with Mik or the Ivanovs, but she and I will be fine."

"Will she come to visit?"

"She might. And though I'd love to see her, I'm not sure I want her to come while Mik and Irina are here."

"Does she go to your competitions?"

Lexi shook her head. "She can't handle being there in person, though she does watch from home."

"Did your dad go?"

A fleeting emotion crossed her face. "Yes. He was always there."

Wilder realized that she'd be competing for the first time without him. That would probably be a difficult thing for her.

"Is it hard to get tickets to the competitions?"

Lexi gave a huff of laughter. "I have no idea. I've never had to buy one. My dad always bought his own tickets. Or had his assistant get them for him."

The phone on Lexi's desk rang, and she stared at it for a moment before picking up the receiver. "Hello?"

After listening to whoever was on the other end, she said, "I'll be right there."

Hanging up, she gazed down at the remainder of her salad with a rueful look. "Guess this will have to wait."

"Make sure you eat it later," Wilder said. "You're going to need to keep your strength up."

She gave him a quick smile. "I will. Thank you for getting it for me."

"Anytime." He closed the lid on his own food and got to his feet. "I'll see you later."

She hesitated for a moment, then nodded and left the office, heading in the direction of the skate rental. Wilder put his jacket back on, then picked up his takeout container and walked out of the office. He paused to observe everyone there before he went to the exit and left the rink.

What was he doing?

For the first time, Wilder had to admit that the time he spent with Lexi was more than just a guy hanging out with a friend who happened to be a girl. Lexi had started out as a mystery that he'd been interested in unraveling. And he'd thought she needed a friend.

Now, though, he'd gotten a glimpse behind the walls she'd erected, and he'd discovered a woman with passion, humor, and a strength that had allowed her to walk through the fire of her father's making. She'd come out on the other side singed, but not burned beyond recognition.

She had a physical and inner strength that he could only admire.

But his life wasn't really suited for a person like her. He'd always thought that any woman he got serious about would be someone who could embrace the nomadic lifestyle with him. She'd have to have a job she could do from anywhere.

That was definitely not the case with Lexi. She was firmly stuck to the ice. Even if she didn't choose to continue to compete, she would want to coach, which she also couldn't do remotely.

Wilder had never bothered to try to cultivate something with women who wouldn't fit into the life he'd chosen for himself, and regardless of his developing feelings, he wasn't sure that now was the time to change that practice.

His thoughts went to Miriam, who worked with her parents in the orphanage. Her commitment to the kids at the orphanage had been something Wilder admired, but it had also been what kept him from pursuing a closer friendship with her. Her life was firmly rooted in the orphanage in Thailand.

And for all that he enjoyed traveling around that part of the world, he wasn't sure that he wanted to live there permanently.

But he had to be honest that his interest in Miriam hadn't come close to what his interest in Lexi had become, which was probably why he hadn't even considered settling down in Thailand.

Of the two women, if he was going to settle down with one, it should be with Miriam because their lives meshed better on other levels. Miriam's life was definitely more altruistic than Lexi's. And Miriam had a stronger faith.

And yet... there was no denying that Lexi had captured his emotions in a way Miriam hadn't, despite the time they'd spent together.

Wilder headed home, pondering the fact that he hadn't guarded his feelings as well as he should have, and where it had left him.

Maybe it was a good thing that Lexi was going to be busy in the upcoming weeks. He'd be spending time with her because of the Christmas program, but beyond that, her time would be limited by her training and her work at the rink.

When he got home, the house was quiet, unlike how it had been the night before for the pizza supper they'd had. He'd wished that he could invite Lexi. But now, realizing the extent of his feelings, it was probably good that he hadn't been able to.

"Hey there, brother," Janessa said as he walked into the kitchen. "How's it going?"

"Good." He went to the cupboard and grabbed a plate. After dumping the fries onto it and adding the patty from his burger, he put the plate into the microwave.

"That your dinner?" Will asked. He sat at the counter with a mug and a plate of cookies in front of him. They looked like the gingerbread cookies Will's mom always made for him.

"Yep. I ate part of it at the resort but brought the rest home."

"How was work?" Will asked as he picked up a cookie and dunked it into his coffee. "Busy on the slopes?"

"You know it. The first Saturday after opening is always crazy."

"I suppose the nice weather helped."

"How was practice with Alexandra?" Janessa asked. "The girls were excited about their part in the program."

"I think it went well. We'll be ready."

"I'm glad it all came together after the mess it was originally."

"Me too. Even if I have been cast as Santa."

"You'll make a great Santa," Janessa said. "You like kids. Alexandra as Mrs. Claus is a bit more of a stretch, but I think she'll do okay."

"It'll be interesting, that's for sure."

Janessa didn't say anything about the two of them making a cute couple, which made Wilder think that she also could see that it wouldn't work for them. Usually his siblings were all over matchmaking the ones of them that were still single, especially now that so many of them had significant others.

"What do you think of her chances at the Olympics?" Will asked.

"If they can get enough training in, I would imagine they're pretty good. Lexi said they're using an old program, so at least they're not having to learn a new one."

"Will they get marked down for that?" Janessa asked.

"No clue, but I suppose they're better off skating a flawless old program than stumbling through a new one."

"Are you going to the Olympics to watch her?"

Wilder gave his sister an incredulous look. "No. I'm not going to spend a ton of money to go see something I can watch on my television from the comfort of my couch."

Plus, being at the competition wouldn't help keep his emotions in check.

"I would have thought you'd go to support Lexi," Janessa said, using the shortened version of Lexi's name for the first time.

"Her own mother doesn't even go to her competitions."

Janessa's brows lifted. "Really?"

"Yep. She said that she finds it too stressful to be there in person."

"I can understand that," Will said. "I think my mom would have a hard time watching any of us kids compete in something like that."

Wilder wished he could go to the Olympics to watch Lexi skate. It would be an experience for sure, on top of being there as a support for Lexi. But she probably wouldn't even be able to find him in the crowd, especially when she was focused on what she was there to do. Plus, she'd be staying in the Athlete's Village, so he wouldn't see her outside of the competition either.

His going to the Olympics to support her felt like it would be making a statement he knew he shouldn't. He would support her from afar and hope that he could keep his feelings from growing even stronger.

"We'll need to plan a party around her competitions. All get together and watch on the big screen."

"She said she was also going to Nationals in January."

"Yay! Two viewing parties."

"More like four," Wilder said.

"Why?"

"Two for the short programs. Two for the free programs."

"Oh right. Forgot about that."

Wilder wondered what Lexi would think if he told her his family were planning to have viewing parties for her competitions. He hoped that she'd be pleased that they were excited for her and cheering her on.

They had to get through the Christmas program first though, and Wilder was going to do his best to be a partner she was proud of, even if he wasn't Mikhail.

# CHAPTER TWENTY

Lexi was exhausted when she got back to her apartment on Sunday evening. With the opening of the ski slopes, a lot more people than usual had been at the resort, and a good chunk of them had ended up at the rink.

A lot had apparently come to check out the rink, ending up at tables with coffee, hot chocolate, and pastries in hand. Not everyone had an interest in skating. But among those who were, there had been several who were getting on the ice for the first time, needing her help to learn the basics of skating.

She'd helped those who had requested it and remained thankful that no one had seemed to recognize her. It hadn't been a difficult day, but she'd once again been up early to work out and spend some time on the ice, even though Mik and Irina weren't back in Serenity yet.

Add into that the ongoing disagreement she had with her mom, and she was ready for some downtime.

Lexi went into her kitchen and opened the fridge. Her empty fridge.

Her biggest challenge at the moment was figuring out how to feed herself. Not just that night, but in the coming months. Her schedule was going to be much busier than it had been the last time she'd trained. Making herself meals was just not going to happen.

With a sigh, she closed the fridge door, then went to the pantry where she had a box of protein bars. Not the best, but it would have to do.

Taking the protein bar and a glass of water into her bedroom, she set them on her nightstand, then decided to take a shower before eating.

As she stood beneath the hot spray, letting it beat down on her tired body, Lexi's thoughts went to her mom. They'd had two conversations since she'd broken the news to her about returning to competing with Mik.

Her mom had made it clear she wouldn't have had any issues with Lexi re-entering the world of competitive skating if she'd been paired with someone else. Or if she'd chosen to do it as a solo skater. But she didn't want Lexi to be with Mik.

Lexi understood that, but her mom needed to understand that she was going into this with her eyes wide open. Mik, Lev, and Irina were getting her professional commitment, but nothing on a personal level. They were now on the outside of the wall she'd built to protect herself.

The odd thing was that there were people within that wall who she never would have imagined ending up there. Wilder, for example. That man had managed to sneak through a crack she hadn't even known was there until she'd suddenly realized that his presence in her life was a good thing.

And right then, she was a bit disappointed that she hadn't seen or heard from him that day. Although she knew that he'd likely had as busy a day on the slopes as she'd had at the rink. Plus, he'd probably gone to church.

Thoughts of church stayed in her mind as she finished her shower and dried off, then pulled on her comfiest pajamas. Now that it was winter, she loved to wear cozy, fleecy things when she was at home.

Going through the apartment, she shut off all the lights and made sure the door was locked and the alarm was armed. Back in her room, she crawled beneath the covers of her bed, then reached for her laptop, where she'd left it on the other side of the bed.

After opening it, she clicked on a browser and typed in *meal prep Serenity Point,* and as she looked through the search results, she ate her protein bar and drank her water. She'd have to get back out of bed to brush her teeth, but that was fine.

There was one result that looked promising. She clicked through to the website, then read the information provided.

It was the best option so far, so she located the contact information for the woman and typed out a quick email, letting her know she was a professional athlete who needed meals prepped according to nutritional values.

She hated to think how much the service was going to cost her, but it was a necessity. At least she wasn't paying for coaching. If Lev and Irina wanted her back that badly, she wasn't going to be the one to pay them. She wasn't earning any money from her skating the way Mik was. Plus, they didn't have to pay rink rental at the resort because of her.

Mik had texted earlier to let her know they'd be arriving the next day and would be staying at the cheapest hotel in town until they could find rentals.

They were obviously pinning a lot on this reunion. Lexi, however, didn't feel like she had as much on the line. Still, she was going to do her absolute best. She had nothing professionally now, so anything positive that came from this would be a step up.

She just hoped that her mom would come around and support her and Mik, but she knew it might not happen.

As she stared at the laptop screen, Lexi wondered if she'd see Wilder and other members of his family if she watched the livestream from their church. She put the name Wilder had given her into the search bar, then opened the site. It didn't take long to find the livestream from that morning.

Relaxing back into her pile of pillows, Lexi began to watch it. Announcements scrolled through first, so she moved the video past those. When the stream went live, it was a wide-angle shot that showed a fairly full sanctuary.

She leaned forward to see if she could spot anyone she knew.

A tall Black man drew her attention, and when she spotted Charli standing next to him, she realized that he must be Jay. She hadn't met him yet, but she knew he was Janessa's biological brother.

Soon, Wilder stepped into view, reaching out to hug Jay and the Black woman standing next to him. Other people she didn't know greeted Wilder with hugs or handshakes.

When the music began, the camera zoomed in on the group of musicians on the stage at the front. The screen no longer showed Wilder, but Lexi didn't end the livestream.

It might be a nice way to wind down before she went to sleep. With that thought in mind, she let it continue to play while she dashed into the bathroom to brush her teeth, before she went back to the bed.

The songs were familiar, and she found herself singing along. She had always enjoyed the music at their church in Maine. As far as she was concerned, it had been the best part of the service.

When it was time for the sermon, Lexi almost clicked to close the livestream. But she wanted to know what it was that drew Wilder there of his own free will. She'd attended church because her parents had told her she had to, but she didn't think that was the case for Wilder. And she wanted to know why.

The music had been good, but it was something he could have heard on any Christian music radio station. So it had to be the sermons.

The pastor had a surprise for her, however. "Before I bring the message this morning, I'd like to ask Wilder Halverson to come up and share a bit about what he was doing last summer."

Lexi made the livestream full screen, then leaned closer as Wilder walked up onto the stage. The two men shook hands, then the pastor left Wilder alone on the stage. She'd only ever seen him in jeans and T-shirts, but that morning, he had on a pair of black pleated slacks and a light blue, long-sleeved button-up shirt.

"Good morning," Wilder said, The warm smile he gave the congregation made her skip a beat even though it wasn't directed at her. He gripped the edges of the podium as he gazed out at the congregation, apparently not needing any notes. "Most of you know me, but if you don't, you probably know at least one of my family members. I fall in the lower half of the order of us children, and I still hold the title for giving Mom the most gray hair.

"For reasons my parents have never understood, each spring, I choose to head off for places around the world before returning in time for winter to work at the resort as a ski instructor. Throughout my travels, I've visited a lot of beautiful places."

Wilder shifted behind the pulpit. "It might seem to be a frivolous way to live life, but staying in hostels has given me the opportunity to connect with people I might not have, otherwise. I've been able to share about God's love with many of them.

There was a shift in his expression. "But a couple of years ago, as I visited one of those beautiful places, I stumbled across something ugly." Wilder looked down at the podium, clearing his throat before lifting his head. "In the process of rescuing a child who was being hurt, I came in contact with an orphanage there. The people operating that one, in turn, introduced me to another orphanage in another country. It opened my eyes to a whole new world. One where good people work hard to rescue the most innocent among us, who are preyed on by the most evil."

Lexi frowned as she listened to Wilder speak. This was a side of him she hadn't seen before. So far, she'd known him as a lighthearted man who liked to travel and ski. Oh, she'd seen moments of seriousness, but most of them had been related to her life.

But this... His passion and emotion bled into his words in such a compelling way.

"At those orphanages, I witnessed the resilience of the children. Given a safe place to live with food and a roof over their heads, they blossomed. It was my privilege to be able to spend some time helping at these orphanages and to see how God is using His people to care for these children.

"Being there also showed me the needs that they have. It's not cheap to run a large home for many children and to pay for people to help them and still be able to buy food and clothing. So many things are needed to raise kids, even very simply.

Smiling at the pastor in the front row, Wilder said, "Today, Pastor Kennedy has given me the opportunity to share this need with you. I've put together some pamphlets with more information on the orphanages and how you can help them. They're at the table in the foyer, so please pick one up and pray about how you can support this very valuable mission.

"Also, in a few weeks, we'll be having a fundraiser for the orphanages out at the resort. Stay tuned for more details on that. As we move into a time of year that's characterized by generosity, I hope that you can spare a few dollars to help those who have next to nothing. No donation is too small. And whether or not you can donate, I ask that you pray for the orphanages, especially for their safety, as not everyone where they're located supports what they do. Thank you."

Wilder waited for the pastor to come back up on the stage. This time, the pair exchanged a hug, then Wilder walked down the steps and disappeared out of the view of the camera.

Lexi sat back, mulling over what Wilder had shared. She knew about the orphanages, but for some reason, it hadn't resonated with her just how important the cause was to him.

Now she really wanted to spend more time with him, to learn more about the things he was truly passionate about. And it made her realize that she was very one dimensional with her passion for skating. It would always be something she was passionate about, but maybe it was time to expand her passions to more meaningful things.

"Thank you for sharing, Wilder," the older man said. "I join him in urging you to pray for these orphanages and the people who work there, and, if you are able, to send some money their way. In fact, let's take a moment to pray for them right now."

Lexi bowed her head, then remembered that the service wasn't live. Still, she remained that way, listening as the pastor prayed for the orphanages and their needs.

When the prayer was over, she shifted onto her side, moving the laptop onto the bed beside her so she could still see it.

"In everything, give thanks," the pastor said as he gazed out at the congregation. "For this is the will of God in Christ Jesus concerning you. That is Thessalonians 5:18, and today, I want to talk about our thankfulness as Christians. I figured it was a good time for that, as we'll be celebrating Thanksgiving in a few days."

Thanksgiving? Already?

Her dad had been even less interested in Thanksgiving than he'd been in Christmas. And because their Russian heritage hadn't included celebrating Thanksgiving, her coaches hadn't seen a reason not to go to the rink for at least a few hours on that day.

She'd be at the rink this year too.

As she listened to the sermon, Lexi felt convicted over how unthankful she'd been in her life. Because even in the midst of a horrible couple of years, she'd had a few reasons to be thankful.

Thanks to the money she'd saved from collaborations and endorsements, she hadn't been left financially destitute. And while one parent had ended up behind bars, she'd still had her mom. During the worst time of their lives, the two of them had been a support for each other.

Even now, she had things to be thankful for. A nice rink to work at. The opportunity to coach. And people who were offering her friendships like she'd never experienced before.

And, of course, she was thankful for the opportunity to compete one more time.

When the pastor finished his sermon, the congregation sang another song before they were dismissed. Lexi watched to see if Wilder would reappear, but then the stream went to a static image and began to scroll announcements again.

Lexi reached out and closed the lid of the laptop, plunging the room into darkness. Rather than focusing on the downsides of her life right then, she took a moment to talk to God, thanking Him in a way she never had for the good in her life.

She resolved to be more thankful—more faithful—even as the weeks ahead promised to be difficult at times. As she fell asleep, she did so with a lighter heart than she'd had in... ever?

The next morning, Lexi was at the rink at her usual time, long before anyone else would be there. After she flicked on the lights, she stood staring out at the rink.

The ice sparkled, reminding her of George, and the way he took care of the ice, sharpened skates, and helped the people who wanted to rent skates. He always had a smile and a greeting for her. Knowing that she could have ended up with a much different type of co-worker, Lexi was thankful for him.

She was also thankful for Luke, who'd learned her favorite drink and made it whenever he saw her headed his way. And though she didn't see Talya much, she was thankful for her as a co-worker so she could have two days a week off. She'd also been nice to Lexi whenever they had spoken.

Smiling, she headed for her office, where she took off her boots and outerwear, shoving her mitts into the pocket of her jacket before hanging it up. It had been below freezing that morning and had reached a cold even she found uncomfortable.

Once she was just in her skating workout clothes, along with the thin gloves she wore to ward off the cold while she trained, Lexi grabbed her skates and sat down to tug them on. After tying the laces, she picked up her phone and left the office.

Since she'd already worked out that morning, Lexi only needed to stretch a little before she got on the ice, even though she'd been out in the cold. After taking a couple of smooth strokes, she alternated lifting one leg, then the other up behind her, holding onto her ankle to stretch out her quadriceps.

She'd completed a couple of laps and had done some spins, when, as she came out of one, she noticed Wilder standing at the boards. Glancing at her watch, she saw it was nearly eight. That meant that he had a bit of time before he started work at the ski shop.

Smiling, she stroked over to where he stood. "Good morning."

"Good morning," he replied, giving her a warm smile in return. "How's the ice?"

"It's good. Just doing some spins and footwork. I don't want to strain my legs too much in case Irina has a big day planned for us tomorrow. I'd rather not go into our first training session with legs that might be tired."

"Are you nervous?"

"Not really. I just want to get going. We don't have a lot of time to prepare, so I want us to just get to work."

"Will it bother you if I stop by here in the morning to see how it's going?"

"Won't bother *me*," she said with a laugh.

"Might bother them?"

"Might."

"So should I stay away?"

"Nope. Feel free to come by. I've already told them you're friends with the owner, so they can't really complain."

Wilder chuckled at that. "Friends might be stretching it. More like an acquaintance. Kayleigh and Hudson are closer to him. I'm closer to his kids since they always want me to be on the slopes with them when they come."

"Guess you'll be seeing them in a few weeks then, since Alexander appears to be planning to spend Christmas here."

"Yeah, he is, but he'll have to come in early for the fundraiser, since we're not going to schedule it that close to Christmas. It's a busy time for people, so we'll get a better turn-out if we have it early in the month."

"I saw you telling people about it at church yesterday."

Wilder's brows lifted. "You watched the livestream?"

"Not when it was live," she said. "I watched it last night when I got home."

"The whole thing?" he asked.

"From start to finish."

He smiled, his brown eyes showing his happiness. "Nice. Did you enjoy it?"

"It was a good service. Probably the first one I've ever actually chosen to sit through of my own volition."

"What did you think of my presentation?"

Lexi stared at him, contemplating her response. "It was really good. You did a great job sharing about the orphanages and how people can help."

"I was thankful that Pastor Kennedy was willing to give me the time to talk about it all."

"How did the people there seem to react to what you shared?"

"I had several people tell me they planned to donate, and I had several more that asked how they could help with the fundraiser."

"How is all that coming along?"

"It seems to be coming along well. My mom and Denise— Misha's mom—have really stepped up to help out. With them taking charge, I think it will all work out just fine."

"Sorry if me deciding to train again has messed things up."

"It hasn't. Not at all. No one else is putting their life or job on hold for this, so you shouldn't have to, either."

Lexi appreciated that sentiment, but she still wanted to make sure that she was pulling her weight for the fundraiser. "Oh. Did the Santa Claus outfit work?"

Wilder grinned. "It sure did. How about yours?"

"Yep. Mine fit too. I need to wear it on the ice at some point to make sure I can move okay in it."

"Are you wearing a new outfit for your skating program?"

"Yes. Mik can keep his old costume, but I want a new one."

She'd sent an email off to her costume designer, along with a sketch she'd made, to see if she could do a new costume in a short period of time. So far, she hadn't heard back from her, which might mean she wasn't interested in working with Lexi. But she really hoped that the designer's lack of response was just because it had been the weekend.

If the woman wasn't willing or able to help her out, Lexi wasn't sure where she would go. There were other costumers that they'd worked with over the years, but the woman she'd contacted had been her favorite. Plus, she'd made the original costumes for this program, so she would still have the swatches from Mik's outfit to match hers.

The woman had file cabinets full of envelopes containing the swatches of each and every costume she'd made. So she'd have that for this particular set of costumes, which would be helpful for her if she agreed to work with Lexi.

"Are you diving right into things tomorrow?" he asked.

"I assume so. Irina hasn't given me a definite schedule, but I'm operating under that assumption."

She'd been surprised at how quickly Irina and Mik were returning, but she knew they were anxious to get things going. And they were right. The more time they had to practice before Nationals, the better.

"I talked to my friend's dad about whether they had any rentals available, and he said they have two one-bedroom apartments at one of the fourplexes they own."

"Really? That might be perfect for them."

"What are they doing for a car?" Wilder asked. "There's no public transportation out here from Serenity."

"Mik said that they'd be renting a vehicle at first, but his dad will be driving Mik's car out for them to use."

"That's good."

It would be good as long as she didn't have to see the man. He'd been one of the many willing to take his anger out on Lexi and her mom. No one seemed to want to believe they hadn't been aware of what her dad was doing.

Over the next few minutes, they talked about their weekends, which hadn't been terribly exciting since they'd both been working. As it neared time for Wilder to go to work, he said, "So you'll be training early in the morning each day?"

"That's the plan. Kayleigh said we could use this rink during the hours when it's not open to the public. Hopefully, it will be enough for Irina. If not, we'll look into using the rink in town whenever it's available."

Lexi had no doubt that they would both object to the setup. It was definitely a few steps down from the rink her dad had had built just for her and Mik. They hadn't had to work around anyone else's schedule, which had been perfect. That wouldn't be the case in Serenity.

It just showed how desperate Mik and the coaches must be. Even knowing the setup and that they'd have to train around her work schedule, they were still willing to tackle it.

Only time would tell if it was going to work or not.

# CHAPTER TWENTY-ONE

Wilder jogged down the stairs after taking a quick shower and changing into clothes that would be appropriate for their family's Thanksgiving dinner. His hair was still a little damp, but it would dry quick enough.

"Is Lexi joining us?" Charli asked.

Wilder frowned at the question. He'd invited Lexi, but she'd said she'd be working. "Nope. She's working."

"I offered her the time off," Kayleigh told him. "But she said she was fine to work."

"I still think it's ridiculous that everything at the resort is open on Thanksgiving," Charli muttered.

"It's because we have people coming specifically for the long weekend," Kayleigh explained in an exasperated voice. "They're not choosing to come to the resort expecting everything to be closed. It's the nature of the business."

Wilder had worked until three, though the slopes were open until four. Trev had had no problem letting him leave an hour early.

They were having their family dinner at four there at Charli's. Most of the family who were coming were already present, though noticeably missing were Zane, Cole and Skylar.

It was a typical Halverson gathering with lots of chaos as they all stepped in to help get the dinner on the table. The older kids were keeping the younger ones occupied while the adults pitched in.

"Okay, everyone," Charli said loudly. "Let's sit up."

There was a flurry of activity as parents rounded up the children and got them into their seats. Wilder waited until all of them were settled, then he sat down on an empty chair next to his dad.

Once they were all seated, his dad said a prayer for the meal, adding on a prayer for those who weren't there. Absent were Zane, Cole, and Skylar. Zane not being there wasn't unusual. Cole and Skylar not being there was.

When he'd asked Charli about Cole and Skylar's absence, she just said they'd decided to stay at college because of their jobs. Hopefully they'd be able to make it home for Christmas.

"Here you go, son," his dad said as he passed him the platter with turkey heaped on it.

Soon, his plate was filled with all the food that was common for their family Thanksgiving dinner. Turkey. Mashed potatoes. Sweet potato casserole. Fresh buns. Green bean casserole. Cranberry sauce. Two different types of salad. Corn bread stuffing.

Their Thanksgiving dinners had always been good, but since Misha's mom, Denise, had joined them, they were even better. There was never a shortage of food.

"I didn't eat breakfast or lunch because I wanted to eat lots for dinner, but I'm already full," his dad said after they'd been eating for a while. "It is all so good."

There were murmurs of agreement as people around the table cleaned off their plates. Wilder had managed to put away a plateful and then some. He had also skipped lunch, but since he was physically active, he didn't feel too guilty about taking seconds of several of the dishes.

They didn't eat dessert right away because everyone was full. Instead, they all helped to clean off the table and put away the food, then they went into the living room for their thankfulness time.

Wilder loved that part of the evening, and he wished that Lexi could be there so he could hear her share what she was thankful for.

"I'm thankful this year for how God brought our family together and helped us grow," Charli said as she smiled at Blake. "I'm thankful that He brought forgiveness and grace into my life so that Blake and I could be together. I'm so grateful for our love and for the three precious girls we get to call our daughters."

Wilder appreciated being able to hear from his siblings because it gave him a glimpse into their hearts.

When it was his turn, he said, "I'm grateful that God led me to the orphanage ministries, and I'm thankful for how people are joining me in supporting those organizations. Seeing the joy of the kids at those orphanages, when you know what the alternative would be for them without it, is so great. It's a real blessing."

His parents added their thankfulness for having been to the orphanages as well. Lee shared that he was thankful for his job, being back in Serenity, and Rori's love. Her response was similar. Their love for each other was clear, and Wilder was happy for his brother.

"I'm thankful for a lot of stuff," Janessa said. "It's been great having my two brothers living here and being part of my nieces' and nephews' lives. And in a few months, we'll be adding to the group, and we're very thankful for that."

For a moment, there was just stunned silence, then his mom said, "Are you... pregnant?"

Janessa and Will both beamed as they nodded. "I'm just two months along, but I couldn't keep it a secret any longer since every day I'm having worse and worse morning sickness."

His mom and dad got up to hug them, and everyone else joined in on the congratulations. The next generation was well underway, and Wilder couldn't have been happier about it.

Once they were done sharing, they had a time of prayer, then dessert appeared with coffee and tea.

The older kids took their dessert downstairs to watch a movie and play some video games. Ciara and Timmy had to stay upstairs with the adults, and they weren't overly impressed, but cookies ended up being the distraction that they needed.

When he'd finished his coffee and dessert, Wilder went into the kitchen to find Charli.

"Would it be okay if I took a plate of food to Lexi?" he asked her. "I'm pretty sure she's not going to have a Thanksgiving dinner since she's working late."

"Sure. We've got so much food, you could take her a couple of plates, and we'd still have lots left."

Over the next few minutes, Charli pulled out containers of food, and Wilder put some of each of the dishes onto two large paper plates. One held stuff that needed to be heated up, and the other held the salads. He doubted she'd eat everything that he was putting on the plates, but maybe she could divide it into two meals.

They covered the plates, then carefully packed it all into a bag, along with some dessert. Once it was all ready, Wilder said goodbye to the family members who didn't live at the house in case they left before he got back, then he carried the bag out to his car.

It was nearly seven by the time he pulled into the parking lot of the rink. There were a few cars there, but that might not accurately reflect the number of people inside. He knew that people often used the golf carts with drivers offered by the resort to get from the hotel to other places at the resort.

He got out, then picked up the bag from the back seat. It had started snowing earlier, and the flakes drifted down lazily, glinting in the lampposts that were situated around the parking lot.

Music, murmurs of conversation, and the scent of coffee greeted Wilder as he stepped into the building. He stamped his feet to get rid of the snow, glancing around to see how many people were there.

He saw that several tables were full, and there were quite a few people on the ice, including Lexi. Keeping an eye on her, Wilder made his way to her office. He set the bag with food in it on her desk, then took off his jacket.

Deciding he could do with another coffee, he went to the counter at the café, where he recognized the guy working there.

"Hi, Luke. How's it going?"

"Busy today."

"Did you miss out on Thanksgiving dinner?" Wilder asked after he gave him his order.

"Nope. My brother had to work today too, so my mom said we'll have it on Saturday."

"That's good."

"What're you doing here at this time of night?" Luke asked as he set the to-go cup of coffee on the counter and moved to the cash register.

"I figured Lexi wasn't going to get Thanksgiving dinner since her family isn't here. I brought some food for her from our dinner."

"That guy she's been skating with has been hanging around."

"Causing any problems?"

"Not really," Luke said. "Lexi just ignores him."

Wilder hoped that Mik wouldn't end up being a problem. The guy needed to find something else to do while Lexi was working. But as long as Lexi didn't care if he was there, they probably wouldn't do anything about him loitering.

"Well, if it becomes a problem, let Trev know. Lexi might not say anything."

"Will do."

With coffee cup in hand, Wilder walked to where there was an empty table and sat down. Lexi was interacting with the people on the ice, so he wasn't going to interrupt her.

As he sipped his drink, he glanced around the rink to see if he could spot Mik. There was no sign of him, so maybe he'd left already.

Wilder pulled out his phone and opened his email program. He hadn't had the chance to check it yet that day.

A text from Charli came in while he was sorting through the junk mail.

**Charli:** *Are you working tomorrow?*

*Yep. 9-4 Why?*

**Charli:** *We're going to chop down our Christmas tree and wondered if you wanted to come with us.*

*Sounds like fun, but no can do.* 😞

**Charli:** *That's too bad. I think the kids would have loved having you come along.*

*I'll help decorate it!*

**Charli:** *Sounds like a plan.*

As a kid, going to get the Christmas tree each year had been one of his favorite parts of the season. Becoming an adult with a weird schedule had required the sacrifice of some of the things he'd loved as a kid—chopping a Christmas tree being one of them.

But he got to earn a living doing stuff he loved, so it balanced out. And he'd still get to help the kids decorate the tree, which promised to be a lot of fun.

The sound of laughter increased, and Wilder looked up to see that quite a few of the people who'd been on the ice were now exiting it. He watched as they found places to sit down and take off their skates. That left only two people on the ice with Lexi.

The couple appeared to be in their own little world, not talking with Lexi as they circled the ice hand-in-hand.

Wilder decided to take a chance that Lexi would be available to chat and got up to approach the boards. When she spotted him, her brows lifted, and after a brief hesitation, she headed in his direction.

"Happy Thanksgiving," he said as she came to a stop on the other side of the boards.

She reached out to grab the top of the boards, giving him a brief smile as she said, "Same to you."

"Are you able to take a little break?" he asked.

"I should be able to. It's been pretty busy," she said. "This is the lowest number of people we've had on the ice since about two this afternoon."

"C'mon," he said, tipping his head toward the office. "I brought you some supper."

"You did?" Her smile grew. "That's nice of you."

Wilder walked along the boards toward the entrance as she skated on the ice. "Figured you might like some Thanksgiving dinner. We had a *ton* of food."

When they reached the entrance to the ice, she retrieved her guards. Together, they walked to the office, where Lexi dropped down into her seat.

"Oh, that feels good."

"Is there a microwave here?" Wilder asked as he lifted the plates out of the bag.

"Yeah. Behind the counter at the café." She gestured to the plates. "Didn't you have dinner already?"

"I sure did," he said as he lifted the plate with the food that needed to be reheated. "This is all for you."

She gave a huff of laughter. "I think not."

"You can always eat more of it tomorrow." Heading for the door, he said, "I'll be right back."

Luke smiled as he took the plate into the small kitchen behind the counter. When he returned a couple of minutes later, he carried the plate of warmed up food.

"Smells good," he said as he handed it over to Wilder, along with a fork and knife.

"Sorry I didn't bring some for you."

"No worries. My mom and grandma cook up a storm, so I'll be eating plenty on Saturday."

Taking the plate back to the office, Wilder spotted Lexi bent over with her head on her arms. He paused, not wanting to disturb her if she needed some rest.

Lexi straightened before Wilder could decide what to do. Walking to the desk, he said, "Do you want to take a nap?"

"I'm fine. Just glad to be off my feet."

Wilder set the plate down in front of her, along with the silverware, then uncovered the plate with the salad. "Do you want a water?"

She picked up her water bottle, then frowned. "You don't have to get that for me."

"I don't mind." He pointed at the plate. "Now eat."

It only took him a minute to return with a bottle of water for Lexi. She looked up as he set the water down on the desk.

"This is amazing."

Wilder grinned as he sat down across from her. "What, in particular, are you referring to?"

"All of it."

"My mom, Charli, Kayleigh, and Denise prepared most of it, I think."

"Seems like you have several people in your family who are great cooks," Lexi said. "I don't think I could ever produce something like this."

"I'm sure if you wanted to, you'd figure out how."

"I can only make a handful of extremely simple dishes, and none of them are healthy, which is why I'm glad I managed to line up someone to do meal prep for me."

"Did you? That's great."

In between bites, she told him how she'd found someone online, then had a conversation with her. She'd had all the nutritional information from her previous training, so she'd passed that onto the woman.

"Are you sure you're not burning the candle at both ends?" Wilder said. "You have a crazy schedule."

"It will take some getting used to, but it'll be fine."

Wilder knew it wasn't his place to interfere with her schedule, but she was going to burn out. There was no way she could continue at such a high physical performance without adequate rest.

"Did you have any sort of vitamin routine?"

"Yes. My doctor ran a bunch of tests to check my levels, then prescribed what I needed. He kept an eye on all that kind of stuff. I still take some vitamins, but I'm not sure if they're enough."

Maybe she should see Gareth or Misha to at least get an idea of where her levels were. "My brother and sister-in-law are doctors at the clinic in town. Would you like to see one of them?"

"Would they be able to fit me in?"

"Yep. I'm sure they could. I'll talk to Janessa tonight so she can sort it out on Monday."

"Thank you," she said. "I appreciate that." She gestured to her plate. "And I appreciate this."

"You're very welcome." He sat back in his chair, crossing his arms over his chest. "How have the rehearsals been going?"

"Pretty good." She lifted the lid off the dessert container. "Oh, I really shouldn't eat any of this."

"Just have one tonight. Thanksgiving dinner requires a dessert."

"Requires, huh?" she asked, one corner of her mouth lifting in a half smile.

"Definitely."

"Well, in that case." She picked up one of the decorated gingerbread cookies. "This will be my choice for tonight."

"Excellent choice. Will's mom makes them for him. For awhile, they were his breakup cookie."

"What's that?"

"When he and his girlfriend—the one prior to Janessa—broke up, his mom made him his favorite cookie to help him feel better."

"And this was the cookie?"

"Yep. And even though it wasn't Christmas, she made dozens and dozens of them. Will brought them to every gathering. He finally had to tell his mom that if she didn't stop, he was going to start hating them."

"They're delicious, so I can understand why they're Will's favorite."

"None of us would have been happy if his mom had stopped making them permanently."

Lexi relaxed back into her chair with a sigh. "That was very delicious. Now I can go home and just fall into bed."

Though she'd said she wasn't overwhelmed, Wilder thought she looked tired. He wanted to say something, but he held his tongue.

"I should probably get back out there to finish off my shift," she said as she got to her feet.

"I'll get everything put away," Wilder said when she reached for the plates.

"Okay." She gave him a smile. "Thanks."

He carefully repackaged everything, returning it to the bag. Though he hadn't been sure if he should bring Lexi food or not, seeing how much she'd enjoyed it, he was glad he had. If it meant she went to bed sooner and with a full stomach, that would be the best part.

Since it was almost nine, he decided to stick around. When he walked out of the office, he noticed that everyone had left the ice. The lights in the café area were dimmed, but he could still see Luke moving around in the kitchen.

Lexi was walking around the rink space, still wearing her skates, stopping to talk to a few people before making her way over to the skate rental place. George was taking in the last of the skate returns.

When Wilder joined them, the older man greeted him with a smile. "How's it going, Wilder?"

"Very good. Happy Thanksgiving."

"Same to you."

"Busy day today, huh?"

"Busiest day yet," George said. "Seems that Mr. Remington knew what he was doing when he set this rink up. I have a feeling it will only continue to grow in popularity."

Wilder was glad it had turned out to be a positive thing, but he wasn't sure it was beneficial for Lexi to be so busy working full time when she was also training.

"Were there any issues with people renting skates?" Lexi asked.

"Not really. A few people had to swap out the skates because they didn't fit the way they were used to their shoes fitting."

Soon, the lights blinked out in the café, and Luke waved a good-bye as he headed for the exit.

"I'm going to do the ice before I leave tonight," George said. "So it's ready for you to practice tomorrow morning."

"I feel badly that you have to stay late because of me."

"Don't you worry about it, Lexi. I'm happy to do it. I think my wife prefers I be home later in the morning, anyway. This way, I can stay with her until lunch."

"As long as you're sure it's not a problem."

"If you ever need someone to fill in, I've operated the machine before," Wilder said. "It's been a few years, but I think I could manage it."

"You've helped out at the rink in town, right?" George said.

"Yep. Back when I was playing some hockey."

"Looks like everyone has gone," George said. "So I'm gonna get to working on the ice."

Because of the size of the rink, they had to use a ride-on ice resurfacing machine. Wilder watched as George made his way to the far end of the rink, where he opened a large door. Once inside, he must have pressed another button because a portion of the boards on the far side swung open.

This place was truly a marvel considering how they'd set it up. The practical parts of operating a rink didn't interfere with the aesthetics of the place.

"I need to get home," Lexi said as they walked back to the office.

"Mik and your coach aren't giving you any hassles, are they?"

She sighed. "They don't understand why I'm continuing to work when they want me to be available to train all the time. The way it used to be."

"I'm sure that would be ideal," Wilder said.

"But not realistic at this point. Training before could be our sole focus because my dad was funding us, and we didn't need to work to pay for coaching or rink rentals. It's different now. We're more like other skaters who have to work to pay their bills while they train."

"It would probably be easier on your body if you only had to focus on training."

"True. But that's just not how things are this time around."

"Do you think you can still perform at the high level even if you're not able to focus on training as much?"

"I think we can, but only time will tell." Lexi sat on her chair with a sigh. "We just need to make sure that we're totally focused on the training when we're training. Mik needs to park his attitude at the door and focus on what Irina is telling us. We don't have the time for him to argue with Irina over stuff."

"Let me help you," Wilder said, going to a knee in front of her.

"You don't have to," Lexi said.

"I know. But you're tired. Just relax."

He was quick to loosen the laces, then he removed the skate. When she wriggled her toes once they were free of the boot, he took her socked foot in his hand and rubbed the bottom of it.

"Oh, you really shouldn't do that," Lexi said with a laugh. "It feels so good I'll insist you do it all the time."

"I don't mind."

He massaged one foot for a few minutes, then removed the skate from her other foot and massaged that one. Though he was willing to do it longer, he knew she needed to get home.

"Thank you," she said when he sat back. "That felt divine."

Wilder straightened to his feet. "You're very welcome."

After they put on their jackets, they waved at George as they left the rink. The snow had continued to fall steadily over the time he'd been inside, so Wilder walked with Lexi to her car and helped her clear the snow from it.

"You've done a lot for me today," Lexi said. "I have no idea why, but I sure appreciate it all."

"I'm happy to help, especially since my schedule isn't nearly as full as yours. I consider you a friend, and friends help each other out."

Lexi stared at him for a long moment, the falling snowflakes catching on her eyelashes as they stood in the snow. The light from the lamppost she'd parked in front of allowed him to see her face, but as usual, it was hard to decipher her expression.

"I haven't had a lot of friends in my life," Lexi said. "I don't really know how they usually act."

Truth be told, he was doing a lot more for her than he usually did for a friend. Not that he wouldn't help a friend out. Everyone knew that if they asked him for help, he'd definitely give it.

With family, he might periodically jump in to do stuff without being asked, but with Lexi, he was actively looking for ways to help her, knowing it meant he could see her more often.

It really wasn't what he should be doing, but he found himself fascinated by her, and he wanted to get to know her beyond the surface level she seemed to give to everyone else.

"Thanks again," she said. "For everything."

"I hope you rest well and have a good day tomorrow. I'll probably stop by at some point."

She smiled. "I look forward to it."

With that, they said goodnight, and Wilder made his way back to Serenity, following Lexi until he needed to turn toward the house.

He hadn't ever expected to find himself so entranced by a woman. But Lexi, with her guarded and sometimes icy demeanor, had definitely captured his attention. Wilder didn't think it was a passing curiosity, which probably wasn't a good thing.

Hopefully, they could build a friendship that was beneficial to both. That had to be enough, because he knew anything more would require too much compromise since their lives were so different.

# CHAPTER TWENTY-TWO

Lexi wearily headed for Kayleigh's office. The woman had phoned earlier and asked Lexi to come see her when she had a moment. George had told her he'd keep an eye on things, and if someone came asking for help on the ice, he'd tell them to come back later.

It had been a week of training and working, and just like Wilder had warned, she was burning the candle at both ends. She collapsed into bed each night, feeling like she had barely closed her eyes before her alarm went off. Even with the intense training they'd done before, it had never left her this exhausted.

As she stepped into the office, she greeted Andrea, Kayleigh's assistant, who sat at a desk in the small space.

"You can go on in," the woman said with a smile.

"Thank you."

Lexi felt decidedly underdressed for the meeting when Kayleigh stood from behind her desk, revealing a deep purple pantsuit with a cream silk blouse. Her hair was pulled back in a twist, and her makeup was impeccably done.

It left Lexi wishing she'd had a change of clothes. But since the call for the meeting had come after she'd left her apartment, she hadn't had a chance to bring anything.

"Thanks for coming," Kayleigh said with a friendly smile, gesturing to a small sitting area on the other side of the office. "Let's sit there."

Lexi sank down onto the couch, grateful for a chance to sit, even if it was for a meeting with her boss.

"How are things going at the rink?"

"It has been busy since Thanksgiving. It's like once people discovered it, they started talking about it."

"Do you need more help there?"

"I'm not sure. It seems to be working okay as it is. I'm not sure about the café and the skate rental, though. You'd have to talk to Luke and George about that."

"And how are you doing with training while also working?"

Lexi debated what to say. She didn't want to say anything that might jeopardize her job there. While she did have *some* savings, she needed the money she earned at the rink to cover her rent and her not-so-cheap meal prep.

"It's going pretty well."

"Tiring, I suppose." Kayleigh's look was sympathetic, and Lexi worried it was going to be leading up to Kayleigh letting her go under the guise of giving her a break.

"Training always is."

Kayleigh stared at her for a moment before nodding. "I have a proposal for you."

"A proposal?"

"Yep. We here at Remington wish to get behind you in your bid for the Olympics."

Lexi frowned. "What does that mean?"

"It means that Alexander wants to sponsor you. He wants you to be able to focus solely on your training, so he'll pay your expenses in exchange for you doing some promotion for the Remington hotel line."

"He wants to tie his company's name to me?" Lexi shook her head. "I'm not sure that's a good idea. Given the controversy in my past."

"He knows all about that and still wants it."

"What do you and Hudson think?"

"I understand your concern," Kayleigh said. "From a strictly business standpoint, I'm not sure it's the best decision. However, we know that sometimes things aren't so black and white. The bottom line is that the controversy was your father's, not yours. No one would likely even know your name had you not been a high-profile athlete."

That was true, and there had been lots of times Lexi had wished she'd had that anonymity.

"I think this is a good opportunity for you to separate yourself from your dad and his controversy. And if Alexander is throwing his support behind you, others will be less likely to come after you."

"Do I have to leave here?"

"Nope. You can still use the rink for your training, as long as you're willing to work around the hours there. We'll hire another skater to work your shifts. Maybe offer Talya additional shifts, so your afternoons will be free for whatever you need to do to train."

Lexi exhaled heavily, feeling a weight lift from her shoulders. Maybe she could do this after all.

It wasn't until that moment that she realized how overwhelmed she'd been feeling. "Thank you. Thank you."

"You can thank Alexander. He's the one that made the final decision."

"What's the best way to thank him?" she asked.

"You can do it in person this weekend. He's flying in with the family for a couple of days of skiing."

Some might be nervous about meeting someone of Alexander's caliber, but her dad had taught her from a very young age how to interact with the wealthy and famous. After all, until two years ago, they'd belonged to that world.

Her mom was still in it with her wealthy husband. But in all honesty, Lexi was glad she'd left it behind. Except she hadn't, not entirely.

"We'll arrange a dinner here at The Steakhouse on Saturday so that you can spend some time with him."

"Is this proposal just for me, or is it for Mik, too?"

"You're a team, so he'll obviously benefit," Kayleigh said. "But this time, I think it's best that it's just for you."

Lexi had no idea how Mik and Irina were paying their bills. She hadn't asked, and they hadn't volunteered any information. Mik probably had funding through the national skating organization, though it wouldn't be as much as they'd received during their time on the top of the podium.

She had some doubts that they were going to achieve the success Mik and Irina wanted, unless she and Mik could really solidify their partnership. There was still distance between them. She didn't trust him entirely, and that needed to change.

But that didn't mean romantically. That ship had truly sailed. Sailed and sank. Never to be heard from again.

"When does the new schedule start?"

"Next Monday. We'll need to find someone to replace you."

"Talya might have some ideas. I wouldn't be surprised if she knows other skaters around here."

"Okay. I'll give her a call and see what she thinks." Kayleigh smiled at her. "We'll get this worked out. No worries."

Lexi appreciated her confidence, and for the first time since she'd started training again, she felt a clear sense of hope. Maybe they really could pull this off.

Back at the rink a short time later, she put her skates back on, then got to work.

Just after four, Wilder showed up. That had been the case every day so far that week, and Lexi had no idea what to make of it. Not that she was wishing he'd leave her alone. The opposite was true. She enjoyed spending time with him.

"How's the ice?" he asked as he leaned up against the boards.

"Slippery," she told him with a grin. "I've been told that a few times today."

He stared at her for so long that Lexi wondered if she had something on her face. "Well, they're not wrong."

"How were the slopes?"

"Also slippery."

"No broken bones?"

Wilder grimaced. "Yeah. Actually, we had someone injure their arm. Not sure if it was broken or not, but they were in pain."

"That's a shame."

"It is," he said. "Unfortunately, it happens. Usually when people aren't paying attention to instructions given at the top of the slope."

"I talked to Kayleigh today," she said, glancing out over the rink, checking on the handful of skaters that were circling the ice. They appeared to just be enjoying skating laps to the music. A couple of them were even holding hands.

"What did she have to say?"

"She said Alexander was willing to sponsor us, freeing me up so I don't have to split my time between work and training."

That brought a wide smile to Wilder's face. "That's amazing. I'm glad you'll be able to just focus on the training. I think that's really what you need."

She narrowed her eyes at him. "Did you have anything to do with this?"

He hesitated for a moment before he said, "I may have mentioned to Kayleigh that you were probably burning the candle at both ends, having to work and train."

"I don't need you fighting my battles for me," Lexi said, trying to keep her indignation from her words. She appreciated that he wanted to do that for her, but she knew herself better than he did. "I am capable of knowing what my body can and can't handle."

She thought he might get uptight with her response, but he just nodded and gave her a small smile. "I know that. I was just stating a fact. I didn't go to Alexander about anything. He doesn't talk to me the way he talks to Kayleigh and Hudson. But what I do know about the man is that he makes his own decisions. He can't be talked into anything he doesn't want to do."

Lexi clenched her hands together. "I just don't want people to think I can't handle things."

"You've been to the Olympics and dealt with what happened with your dad," Wilder said. "I think we all know you can handle whatever comes your way. But things are different for you going into this. You had support back then, and we're going to give it to you now."

"I don't know why. You didn't even know me until a few weeks ago."

"What can I say? I'm a good judge of character."

Lexi gave a huff of laughter. "This still isn't about dating, right?"

Wilder hesitated a moment before he nodded. "You're my friend."

It was a bit of a left turn in their conversation, but the more time they spent together, the less it felt like just a friendship. She needed the reminder as much, if not more, than Wilder.

"Our lives are too different for anything but friendship." The words hurt to say, but she felt it was necessary. "I mean, if you'd even feel any sort of way... about... things."

"Don't sell yourself short," he told her. "If the circumstances were different..."

His words and the shrug that followed made her heart race.

No. She didn't want to think about that.

She couldn't compromise her goals in life to follow him traveling all over the world, and she doubted he wanted to change the way he lived his life just to be with her. His work with the orphanages was definitely an important thing to him, as were his travels.

Wilder cleared his throat. "Anyway, does this mean you'll have your evenings free?"

Lexi nodded. "We'll be training more during the day, but I'll have my evenings now."

"You can join us for our pizza nights," Wilder said. "And maybe come to church with us, if you want to."

"Pizza?" She shook her head. "That's not part of my meal prep."

"We usually have pizza night every Friday. It's family and some friends, and we get together for pizza and sometimes we play games."

"Sounds like fun."

"It usually is. You could bring your own food, as long as you can handle being around pizza without giving in to temptation."

"I'll have to see."

"Let me know if you want to come," he said. "Even if it's at the last minute, since you'll be bringing your own food."

"Well, I won't be able to come this Friday since the new schedule isn't taking effect until Monday."

"It's usually every Friday, unless there's an early basketball game."

"Basketball game?"

"Jay coaches the high school team, and they usually have a game on Friday or Saturday night."

Lexi marveled at the normalcy in Wilder's life. Pizza dinners. Church with family. Basketball games. It was a life she'd never experienced, but she knew that it was far more common than the life she'd lived as a professional athlete.

Did she want to become a part of that? To find out what it was like to live a normal life? Or would it lead to distractions that she didn't need as she trained for another crack at the Olympics?

The normal life had never appealed to her, simply because she'd never imagined a life different from what she'd had. Getting back to training with two big competitions looming was once again offering that life. But now, she wondered if she could find a way to balance the skating life with something more... normal.

"I'll have to see how my training goes," Lexi said, reluctant to commit to anything before she saw how the change in her schedule was going to play out.

"Fair enough." Wilder paused, then said, "Do you put up a Christmas tree?"

"I've never done it myself," Lexi said, grateful for the change of subject. "My mom always hired someone to come in and decorate our house for the holidays."

"A bunch of my family went to cut down trees on Friday."

"Cut down trees?"

"They went to a nearby Christmas tree farm, and they got a couple of trees. One for our house, and one for Jay and Misha's place. The kids had a blast, and they got to see Santa."

"I've never done that." Lexi had actually thought stuff like that only happened to Instagram people or in Hallmark movies.

"I used to love it as a kid, but my schedule hasn't worked out for me to go in recent years. I did get to decorate with them over the weekend, though. That was a blast."

Lexi really liked how much Wilder seemed to enjoy hanging out with his nieces and nephews. Her dad hadn't had anything to do with children that weren't his. Really, he hadn't had a whole lot to do with her, either. Even though he came to her competitions, when he was home, he was busy with work. Or stealing... whatever it was he did.

"Did I tell you that Janessa announced her pregnancy on Thanksgiving?"

"Oh wow. That's amazing."

"It is," he agreed. "It's great that my siblings are making sure the next generation is plentiful."

"Given how many people are in your family, even if each one only produced one kid, it would still be plentiful," Lexi pointed out.

Wilder laughed. "This is true. So far, Charli and Blake have three. Jay and Misha have two, and Gareth and Aria have one. Janessa and Will's baby will make grandbaby number seven for my parents."

"Have I met Gareth and Aria?"

"I don't think so, but you've probably seen Gareth. He plays the drums at church most Sundays."

Lexi had watched another livestream Sunday evening, but she couldn't recall what the drummer had looked like. She'd have to pay closer attention next time.

She still wasn't sure about going to church yet. The change in her schedule meant that work wouldn't keep her from attending, though training might.

This change would lead to a schedule similar to what they'd kept before, but Lexi sensed an impatience and intolerance in Mik and Irina this time. They weren't happy about her working and had tried to subtly get her to quit before moving on to more pointed suggestions that she was being selfish by continuing to work.

So far, she'd managed to ignore them, but no doubt they'd think they'd succeeded in wearing her down when she let them know that she wasn't needed at the rink anymore. But just because she wasn't working anymore, Lexi wasn't going to let them take over her life.

And maybe church should be the first stand she took with regards to that. She'd tell them that, just like before, she'd be taking off Sunday morning and early afternoon. Since they should have a day where they let their bodies rest a bit, it might as well be Sunday.

"I meant to ask you," Wilder said, shifting on his feet as he reached out to grasp the boards. "Is it still okay that I'm showing up to watch you guys rehearse?"

"It doesn't bother me." In fact, she rather liked that he was so interested in her skating that he kept showing up. "I have no idea—nor do I care—how Mik and Irina feel. Okay, that's not entirely true. They've asked why you keep showing up. However, it's none of their business."

"Good, because I've really enjoyed the glimpse behind the scenes. I can see how much the two of you are improving. It's like you're gelling. You're more in sync than you were at the start."

Lexi nodded. "I think we are, too. Mik had to adjust to skating with me again, and I think he's done that."

"Is it that difficult to switch partners?"

"Not for the singles elements. But his previous partner was a couple of inches taller and a little heavier, so he made adjustments for throws and spins with her. Now that he's back with me, he needs to make those adjustments again."

Wilder lifted his hand to the back of his neck before dropping it as he cleared his throat. "Is Mik... uh... trying to revive your personal relationship, too?"

"He made the suggestion once," she said. "But when I shot him down, he let it go."

"Shot him down with an ice arrow?"

Lexi couldn't help but laugh. "You know it."

Several people came into the rink, their laughter filling the space. Wilder turned to look at them, then said, "Looks like they're making the rounds. Some of them were on the slopes earlier."

Lexi thought about making a comment about spoiled rich kids, but then realized that to someone like Wilder, *she* was a spoiled rich kid. Or at least she had been.

"Guess I'd better be prepared for the influx onto the ice," she said, watching as the majority of the group headed for the skate rental. Only a couple of them went to the café.

"Have fun," Wilder said as he backed away from the boards. "Talk later."

She nodded, then watched as he strode toward the exit. Someone called out to him, however, so he veered in the direction of the group that were standing at the skate rental.

One of the women smiled and stepped closer to Wilder. Unfamiliar jealousy swirled through Lexi, making her frown.

She blinked, then turned away. Jealousy had no place in her life right then. Especially over a man she'd repeatedly shoved into the friend zone.

There was no reason she should get upset when other women paid attention to him, and when he paid attention to them. But it was there, nonetheless.

Interestingly enough, she'd never really felt jealousy over Mik. But then, they hadn't had the time to spend with other people. Their parents and coaches wouldn't have allowed it. Other female skaters might have been interested in Mik, but one look from Lexi had them keeping their distance.

Looking back now, she realized it hadn't been because she didn't want Mik paying attention to them. She just hadn't wanted him to be distracted from their skating. Distractions kept them from being able to perform at their highest level.

Wilder was different.

He'd offered her friendship and support that was completely separate and apart from her skating. Unfortunately, this time around, he was a distraction for her, and she wondered if she needed to shut down even their friendship.

She and Mik hadn't cultivated friendships before, and they'd been at the top of their game. Was that what she needed to do this time around, too? Would the sacrifice be worth it in the end?

The thought of not having Wilder in her life hurt Lexi's heart, which was probably a pretty good indicator that, yes, she should end their friendship. Continuing to hang around Wilder, even knowing the futility of hoping for something more, would only lead to heartache when he left again in the spring.

She couldn't end things yet, though, because she'd made a commitment to the Christmas fundraiser. Plus, she wasn't ready to not have Wilder in her life.

After Christmas, however... She'd need to focus completely on her programs.

Maybe it would have been better if she'd gone to Maine. Was it too late to suggest that?

# CHAPTER TWENTY-THREE

"Back off, Mik," Lexi said as she skated away from him, frustration bubbling in her stomach.

Conflict between them wasn't entirely new, although they definitely clashed more now than they had in the past.

"It's a waste of time," Mik yelled after her. "Everything here is a waste of time."

Lexi jerked around to face him. Narrowing her eyes, she headed straight for him, stopping in a spray of ice.

"This is my life now," she hissed at him. "The one I was forced to build after my dad torpedoed my life and you walked away from me. So you don't get to come in here and tell me that my life—the one I'm putting on hold to help you out, by the way—is a waste of time."

"You're overreacting."

"No. I'm done."

She skated for the exit where Irina greeted her with a frown, which deepened into a scowl when she looked past Lexi to Mik.

Good. Let him deal with her temper.

"The rink becomes unavailable in half an hour," Lexi muttered. "Be off it by then."

Lexi snatched her guards off the boards and shoved them on her blades before leaving the ice. She headed for her office, tuning out the yelling in Russian that was going on behind her. If she'd focused, she could have understood what was being said, but she just didn't care.

Mik had sometimes been selfish before. But then, so had she. Now, however...

He had gone past selfish to arrogant, telling Lexi that she should be thanking him for giving her a break and saving her from her pathetic life in a small town in Idaho. Like it hadn't been *him* who'd contacted *her,* begging Lexi to help him out.

The fight had just been stupid and, yes, a waste of time. She had told Mik and Irina that her time off for the fundraiser was non-negotiable. And yet, Mik persisted in bugging her about it. All because it meant a shortened training day followed by a day completely off the ice.

There was nothing that could be done about it, even if she'd wanted to. Which she didn't.

In about an hour, people would be arriving to begin decorating the space in preparation for the fundraiser the next day.

Lexi didn't have a lot to do with that part of things, but she'd let Mik and Irina believe she did. Otherwise, they would have insisted on meeting at the rink in town for more training. She hadn't wanted that. She'd wanted a break.

From the training. From Irina. And most definitely, from Mik.

"We're going."

Irina's harsh voice drew her attention. Lexi looked up and nodded.

"Be at the rink Sunday at two."

For a moment, Lexi hesitated, then she gave Irina a firm look. "You need to talk to Mik and make sure he understands that I am giving what I can. If that's not enough, he can walk away. And if his attitude doesn't improve, we're not going to be able to pull together enough to medal, let alone win."

The fact that Irina nodded and didn't argue was telling. She agreed with Lexi. At least to a certain extent.

"I'll talk to him." Irina turned and walked out the door without looking back.

Lexi blew out a long breath, her shoulders slumping. Not for the first time, she wondered if this had been a mistake. Where was the joy in winning if she did it with someone she couldn't stand?

Sure, the gold medal might give her the redemption she needed to attain the future she wanted. However, at moments like she'd just endured, she felt like the price might be too high.

Leaning forward, Lexi unlaced her skates and slipped them off, wiggling her toes as she recalled the time Wilder had rubbed her feet. She knew it had been a spur-of-the-moment thing and meant nothing more than someone realizing that she'd been on her feet all day.

However, she'd been careful not to let it happen again, regardless of how much she'd enjoyed it. She'd known it would be far too easy to get addicted to those foot rubs. And something told her it was best not to get addicted to anything tied to Wilder.

When she heard the door to the rink open, followed by the muffled sound of conversation, Lexi got up and slipped her feet into her comfortable shoes. As she left the office, she spotted a few familiar faces.

"Hey there," Charli said when she spotted Lexi. Behind her, Amelia and Janessa were removing their outerwear.

"Hi." She saw the little girl had her skate bag. "Are you planning to skate?"

"Is it okay if she does?" Charli asked.

"Yep. That's not a problem. I won't be joining her, though. I just took my skates off a little while ago, and I'm not keen to put them back on just yet."

"I'm sure that's true," Charli said as Lexi led them over to where a couple of tables had been pushed together so they could set the boxes and bags they carried.

Whoever the resort had hired to decorate the buildings for Christmas had done a great job. It was a very rustic décor, with lots of greenery, buffalo print ribbon, and pinecones, which suited the look of the resort very well.

Soon, jackets were piled up on a nearby chair, and the women were pulling stuff out of the boxes and bags. In another chair, Amelia took her skates out and shoved her feet into them. Lexi went to her and helped her tighten and tie them.

"How's the training been going?" Janessa asked.

"Good. How's the pregnancy going?" Lexi asked as she quickly finished the first skate.

It seemed that Janessa didn't care who knew about her pregnancy. In fact, according to Wilder, she had done everything but take an ad out in the paper to let people know.

"Wretched," Janessa said with a grimace. "At least until about two in the afternoon. Like, right about now, I finally start to feel better. They don't tell you that morning sickness can last well past morning."

Lexi got to her feet, watching as Amelia made her way over to the entrance to the ice. She slipped off her guards, then stepped on the ice, pushing away from the boards with more confidence than she'd had when she'd first started skating with Lexi.

"Oh sure we do," Charli said. "I remember telling you about that a lot."

"I know, but I didn't believe you."

"What?" Charli sounded indignant. "Why not?"

"Because I thought you were just saying that so I wouldn't go out and get pregnant before I was married."

"Oh, shut up," Charli said with a laugh. "You did not. And besides, I think Lexi would have a hard time believing that a nurse doesn't know about a lot of the more common aspects of pregnancy. Plus, Aria was sick during different parts of the day throughout the early part of her pregnancy. She's your best friend, so I know she told you, like she told me."

"Yeah, but mine is worse than either of your experiences."

Lexi lifted her eyebrows at Janessa. Sometimes the way the sisters interacted made her laugh. Having never had a sibling, she didn't have that type of relationship with anyone. They sniped at each other, but even she could tell that it came from a place of love.

"Regardless," Janessa said. "I'm surviving and praying that the second trimester will bring relief."

"When is that?"

"One more week, and I'll be in my second trimester."

"Hope you feel better."

"And then you can finally tell everybody you're pregnant," Charli said as she leaned to pull something out of the box.

Again, Lexi's eyes widened. She'd been sure Wilder had said Janessa had been telling everyone.

"It's not my fault that I'm not super good at keeping a secret," Janessa said. "I was excited. Plus, this is my secret to tell. I'd never tell someone else's."

"By the time you have this baby, you will be wishing that you'd kept it to yourself a little while longer."

"What do you mean?"

"By the end of your eighth month, people are going to see you coming into church with your belly and comment on the fact that you're *still* pregnant. Right about when you're feeling your worst, waddling around with swollen ankles, all the comments will make you feel like you're enormous."

"Well, it's too late to do anything about it now," Janessa remarked. "I'll keep that in mind for the next one."

"Speaking of babies, where's Shiloh?" Lexi asked.

"Denise was at the house to clean today," Janessa said. "And she offered to keep an eye on her."

"She has Ciara too," Charli added. "But Peyton and Layla still had school."

"No school for you and Amelia?" Lexi asked.

Charli shook her head. "Something happened to the heater overnight, so they cancelled school today."

"Since Mom already had Timmy for the morning, she offered to watch him for the whole day so Aria could cover for me at the clinic today," Janessa said. "She took pity on my sick, pregnant self."

The door to the rink swung open again, and this time it was a small group of ladies. While Janessa and Charli went to greet them, Lexi made her way to the boards. Amelia was in the middle of the ice, practicing a spin.

Watching the girl, Lexi was struck again by how at ease Amelia was on the ice. Layla still had some stiffness when she moved. Amelia, on the other hand, had really loosened up over the past few weeks. Like she was no longer afraid of falling. Of the ice hurting her.

"How is she doing?"

Lexi glanced at Charli, then looked back at Amelia, who'd just landed the jump she'd been practicing. She hadn't spoken to her and Blake yet about the girls beyond saying they were doing well. Because they were. She just wasn't sure how to tell them that their younger daughter was probably going to surpass their older one fairly soon.

"She's doing really well," Lexi said, then decided to test the water. "How does she feel about figure skating?"

"She loves it. I thought she might like ballet better, but she's definitely talked about figure skating more, especially since you started teaching her."

"Is Layla in ballet too?"

Charli nodded. "I think she probably prefers ballet, though she'll never actually say that since she really likes you."

"Do you make the girls take both?"

"No. We give them the choice. Should they only be in one?"

"Not from a teacher's perspective. In fact, ballet can be beneficial for figure skaters. Especially those who go on to compete."

"And do you think they could go on to compete?"

"I'm sure they could," Lexi said. "You'll just have to be prepared that one might do better than the other."

"Really?" Charli was silent for a moment, then she said, "Are you talking about Amelia?"

"I'm not saying that Layla can't achieve success with hard work, but it will likely come a lot easier for Amelia."

"Huh." Charli stared at the little girl.

Lexi had no clue how Charli felt about that revelation. Still, it felt wrong not to let Charli know about her younger daughter's potential, even if it might not be what Layla would want to hear.

Someone called Charli, drawing her attention from the ice. She glanced back at Amelia, then said, "Thanks for letting me know."

As the woman walked away, Lexi was left feeling that perhaps she *shouldn't* have let her know. Sometimes navigating these situations with people she didn't know well was a challenge she wasn't sure she wanted to take on.

For the next hour or so, she helped out where needed. They were setting up tables with Christmas tablecloths for the bake sale and other auction items. There were signs that someone had drawn that looked quite amazing. She'd never been to a fundraiser before, and though this didn't have the most polished presentation, everything was welcoming and cheerful.

When she had a free moment, Lexi wandered back over to the rink. She stood at the boards, watching Amelia again. The young girl seemed to be tireless. She hadn't come off the ice since first arriving.

Shortly before four, Will arrived with Layla and Peyton in tow. He greeted Janessa with a hug and a kiss, then stood with his arm around her, taking in what had been done so far.

"Are we going to practice tonight?" Layla asked as she joined Lexi at the boards.

"I'm not sure if your uncle is coming here after he's done work or not," Lexi said. "If he does and wants to skate, we can run through it a couple of times."

"I'm excited to do it," Layla told her. "It's almost like my ballet recital."

"Do you enjoy ballet?"

"Yep. I like it a lot."

"Better than skating?" Lexi asked.

Layla paused, her gaze on her sister. She gave Lexi a quick look, then said, "I like them both."

"It's okay to like dancing more than skating," Lexi told her. "I took ballet lessons as well, but I always preferred skating. For some people, ballet is what makes them happier."

Layla gave a slow nod. "I do like skating, but I really love ballet."

"How about Amelia?"

"Oh, she likes skating a lot better."

"Hey there, Elf number one and Mrs. Clause."

Lexi turned to see that Wilder had arrived while she'd been distracted by her conversation with Layla. His cheeks were reddened from the cold, and his hair looked disheveled, like he'd been running his hand through it.

"Hi, Uncle Wilder," Layla said with a grin. "Are you gonna skate?"

"We should probably do a run-through one more time if everyone is up to it."

"I'll go get my skates."

Layla darted away, but Wilder stayed at the boards with Lexi.

"How's it been going?"

"Pretty good, I think."

"From what I've heard, we're going to have a good turnout."

"I hope so."

Wilder turned to face her, leaning an arm along the boards. "How was your day?"

"It was fine," she said. "Mik wasn't happy about our training being interrupted, but he'll get over it."

"Do you want to come for pizza once we have everything ready to go here?"

Over the past couple of weeks, Wilder had extended the invitation each Friday, but Lexi had declined to go. She'd tried to offset that rejection by attending church with them.

Lexi just wasn't sure that she should spend more time with the Halversons. At least attending church involved other people, not just Wilder and his family.

But that day, she was finding it difficult to say no to him. Maybe it didn't matter. They'd both agreed that they were just friends.

"Sure."

Wilder's expression brightened as he raised his hands like he'd just won something. "Excellent!"

Layla returned with her skates, and while Wilder helped her, Lexi went to her office to get her and Wilder's skates.

By the time she got back, Layla was out on the ice with Amelia. Wilder sat down on the bench beside her and took his skates.

"Do you need help lacing *your* skates?" Wilder asked as they sat down on the bench.

"No, sir," Lexi said. "I've been lacing my own skates since I was about ten."

"How are you feeling about tomorrow?"

Lexi considered it for a moment, then said, "A little nervous."

Wilder paused mid-lacing, turning to look at her. "Nervous? I wouldn't expect that, given the experiences you've had."

Lexi shrugged. "What can I say? This is much more personal than any competition I've been in."

"It's going to be great," Wilder said with a grin. "Just have fun with it. People will be entertained by whatever we do. They don't really have any expectations. They're not going to mark you down if you do a double jump instead of a triple."

"You're right."

She just wasn't used to skating for something so casual. Even when they skated for the galas following competitions, there was still a high expectation of what she and Mik would perform. They might not have been judged officially, but people still liked to see perfect programs.

"Let's go have some fun," Wilder said as he stood up.

He offered her his hand, and after a moment's hesitation, she took it. Once she was on her feet, he let go, and Lexi missed the feel of his hand in hers.

Shaking it off, she went with him to the ice, took off her guards, and stepped out on the ice. There were still lots of people setting up for the next day's activities, but a few came to the boards to watch them.

They didn't go right into the program. Lexi did some stretches as she skated, feeling her muscles protesting being put to work again that day.

Wilder chased after the girls, who shrieked with laughter as they darted away from him. Even in this, Amelia showed herself to be a lot more at ease on her skates, as she evaded Wilder for much longer than Layla was able to.

Lexi pulled up their song on her phone, then connected it to the Bluetooth sound system. When Wilder and the girls joined her, she said, "Ready to go?"

"Yep!" Layla said, while Amelia nodded.

Seeing Janessa at the boards, Lexi gave her the phone to start the song when they were ready.

They got into position, with Wilder and the girls at the entrance to the ice. Wilder had his hockey stick, and as *Here Comes Santa Claus* began to play, he and the girls headed out first.

After they'd skated through the first verse, they circled back around, and Wilder dropped his stick on the ice by the boards and reached out to take Lexi's hand. Together, they executed some turns and spins, while Layla and Amelia followed them, also doing some jumps and spins.

It wasn't a complicated program, and they didn't even do it perfectly, but it was fun, and Lexi couldn't help but smile when they finished. She was perched on Wilder's knee and the girls were standing with them, their arms raised like Lexi and Wilder's.

The people who'd gathered at the boards applauded and cheered. Lexi stood up and turned to face Wilder as she skated backwards a few feet. He remained on his knee, watching her for a moment, then he gave a grin and got back up to his feet.

He held out his hands to the girls, and then the three of them were off around the ice again. Lexi skated over to where Janessa stood and took the phone back from her.

She pulled up the playlist she'd created with all kinds of upbeat Christmas music, both traditional and contemporary. When she clicked on the first song, the girls let go of Wilder's hands and skated to the music, using their own choreography.

Wilder skated over to her, leaning over the boards to hug Janessa. "What do you think, Nessa? Will tomorrow be a success?"

"It's going to be great," Janessa said. "I think it will be the best Christmas fundraiser ever."

Wilder chuckled. "Never mind that it's the first one we've ever done."

"You guys are so cute as Mr. and Mrs. Claus, with the girls as elves. I can't wait to see you in your costumes."

Lexi shared Janessa's excitement, though she wasn't as vocal about it.

"How close are we to being done here?" Wilder asked, waving his hand at the space.

Charli turned to look at the part of the building where most of the stuff had been set up. "We're probably done for tonight. We'll come back a few hours before the start tomorrow to set up the last few things. Most people will be dropping off their baking at our place, but some will be bringing it out here."

When Kayleigh and Hudson showed up, they had a familiar man with them. Wilder had said he hoped that Alexander would show up, and it appeared that he had.

The older man shook hands with those present, smiling and chatting. He was definitely good at making people feel at ease. His presence could be imposing—given the perfect cut of his suit, his perfectly styled hair, and his expensive watch and shoes—but his smile was warm and seemed genuine.

"Alexandra," he said as he held out his hand to her. His smile creased the corners of his eyes and seemed to grow from the smile he'd given others. "It's so wonderful to see you again."

"Please call me Lexi," Lexi requested as she shook his hand. "It's good to see you again, too."

"I hear you have a fun program planned for tomorrow."

"I think it is," she said. "You just missed our practice of it."

"I'm kind of glad I did because I'm looking forward to seeing the actual performance tomorrow."

"Layla, Amelia, and Wilder are part of it too," Hudson said. "So we're all looking forward to the antics."

"Are you two coming for pizza?" Charli asked.

"Nope," Kayleigh said. "We're going for dinner with Alexander."

"All the more pizza for us," Wilder told her.

"Like you aren't going to just order less pizza," Kayleigh retorted.

Most of the non-Halversons left as they stood talking to Alexander, calling out their goodbyes as they walked to the door. A few minutes later, Alexander headed off with Kayleigh and Hudson.

Will and Wilder helped the girls out of their skates while Lexi took hers off.

They put the skates and the hockey stick in her office, then they all left the rink. The others headed for their cars, but Wilder walked with Lexi to hers.

"So you're coming over?" he asked as she pressed the fob to unlock the doors.

"I guess so." She still wasn't sure it was the best idea, but she needed a break from her own company or that of Mik and Irina.

"What type of pizza do you want? Or will you bring your meal prep?"

She was so tempted by the idea of pizza, but in the end, she knew she couldn't take time off from training *and* eat badly. "I'll bring my meal prep."

"Sounds good." With a smile, he opened her door for her. "See you in a bit."

With a nod, she slid behind the wheel. He closed the door, then gave a wave and jogged to where he'd parked. Lexi watched him go, feeling a weird sense of happiness just from having been in his presence.

It wasn't something she'd experienced before, and as she glanced in her mirror to see his car behind hers as they pulled out of the parking lot, she wasn't sure she could be strong enough to put the distance between them that she knew she should.

For sure, she wasn't going to put that distance between them before the fundraiser. It wouldn't do if Santa and Mrs. Claus were estranged.

# CHAPTER TWENTY-FOUR

Wilder walked into the chaos of the kitchen back at the house and let out a sharp whistle. Everyone turned to look at him, their expressions ranging from annoyance to curiosity.

"If the baby starts crying because of that, you're sleeping in the garage," Charli said as she crossed her arms. "What are you making a racket for?"

"Lexi is coming to join us for dinner," he said.

"And you needed to make an announcement for that?" Janessa asked.

"Yes, because she's coming, but she's not going to eat anything here."

"She's eating special food," Layla said. "Right, Uncle Wilder?"

"Yep. She's going to bring her own food, so don't try to encourage her to eat the pizza and dessert."

"We won't," Amelia said quickly. "She has to give her body the fuel it needs to be able to train as hard as she needs it to."

"I'm impressed, Berry," Wilder told her, holding out his hand for her to slap. "That is very good, and I know Lexi appreciates your support."

Amelia beamed up at him as she gave his hand a hard slap. She'd been warming up to him, and he enjoyed their little interactions.

"We're behind her," Janessa said. "No talk about food tonight."

"Thank you."

Wilder was surprised and happy that she'd finally agreed to come for the evening. It wasn't that he didn't understand that her focus was on her training, but he thought maybe she needed a little break now and then.

She'd been attending church with them, and he'd counted that as a significant win. But as a friend, he also enjoyed spending social time with her. Hopefully, she felt the same way and that the evening would be a good break for her.

When the doorbell rang, the girls raced off to answer it before Wilder could even turn in that direction. Still, he followed them, getting there in time to see Lexi step into the foyer.

"I can take your jacket and hang it up," Amelia volunteered, holding out her hand.

Lexi gave her a smile as she unzipped it and shrugged out of the jacket. "Thank you."

When Amelia took the jacket and went into the closet to hang it up, Layla said, "You can leave your boots there." She pointed to the boot tray just inside the door.

After she'd done that, they all went back into the kitchen. Everyone greeted Lexi, and Wilder was glad to see that she didn't withdraw behind her polite smile. The smile she gave the people there was friendly and even a bit warm.

"We're just about ready to eat," Charli said. "Someone can go ahead and open up the pizza boxes."

While a couple of people moved to do that, Charli approached Lexi. "Wilder said you were bringing your own food tonight. Do you need it warmed up in the microwave?"

"Yes. That would be great." She handed over a container that didn't look like it held a whole lot of food. "I usually put it in for a minute and a half."

"Would you like water to drink? Or we have soda—diet and regular—milk, or apple and orange juice."

"Water is just fine," Lexi said. "Thank you."

As the microwave whirled, Blake said a prayer for the food. He'd just finished when it beeped. While the kids lined up to get their pizza, Charli went to the microwave and pulled Lexi's food out.

"Do you want a plate for this?"

"Nope. I usually just eat out of the container. No sense in dirtying more dishes."

"A woman after my own heart," Charli said with a smile. "Which is precisely why we're using paper plates for pizza."

Wilder went into the dining room with Lexi, letting her choose a seat, then he set his can of soda at the seat beside her to claim it as his. The girls hurried to take the seat on the other side of Lexi, and Amelia pouted when Layla beat her to it.

But instead of saying anything, Amelia just circled around them and took the seat beside the one Wilder had planned to sit on.

"Here, Berry," Wilder said, offering his chair. "You can sit here."

She smiled up at him again. "Thank you."

Though he might have liked to sit closer to Lexi so they could talk, he was fine sacrificing a little of the evening for the girls. Once they were done eating, they'd probably head downstairs with Peyton to watch a movie or play video games. For sure Layla would go, Amelia might stick around.

Wilder went to the kitchen to grab some pizza, and by the time he made it back to the dining room, most of the chairs were taken. He smiled when Amelia waved her hand at her dad when he went to sit beside her.

"Uncle Wilder is sitting there."

Blake's brows rose. "He is?"

"Yep. He let us swap seats, so that's his."

"Is this one okay?" Blake asked, pointing to the one on the other side of Wilder's seat.

"Yep. That one's yours."

"Thanks, Berry."

"You're welcome, Daddy."

The exchange was so cute, and Wilder couldn't help but smile as he took the seat between them. He glanced up as Charli walked in, Shiloh on her hip. She circled the table to give the baby to Blake.

"I'll be right back," she said.

Wilder sensed a sudden tension in his sister, but he had no idea why. What had happened in the last few minutes?

When she returned, she had Shiloh's high chair and a bowl of food, which she set on the table. Blake settled the baby in the seat while Charli disappeared again. Wilder glanced over to see Blake's gaze tracking his wife.

"Everything okay?" Wilder asked Blake, keeping his voice low.

Blake frowned as he put a few pieces of mushy carrot on the tray in front of Shiloh. At almost seven months, she was now eating people food and was practicing feeding herself.

"I don't... know. Everything was fine a few minutes ago."

Wilder knew Charli could be mercurial with her moods sometimes. He was as puzzled as Blake was. He hoped for Blake's sake that the guy hadn't upset her in some way and just hadn't figured out yet what he'd done. That was never fun with Charli.

Eventually, Charli returned with a plate and settled into the seat on the other side of Blake with the highchair between them. She was quieter than usual, but Wilder didn't stay focused on her. She'd snap out of whatever was bothering her soon enough.

Lexi was talking with Rori, which Wilder found interesting. From what he'd come to know of Rori, and what Lee had shared about her, the two women couldn't be more different. However, it appeared that Rori was either a figure skating fan, or she'd brushed up on Lexi's career because they were talking about skating.

He wasn't sure if Lexi enjoyed talking about her previous skating career. Perhaps if she wasn't attempting to revive her career, she might not want to revisit it. However, she seemed fine talking about past skating programs and her experiences as a high-performance athlete.

Though previous Friday nights had included games or singing, that night it ended up just being eating and talking. He hoped Lexi wasn't bored, but she didn't appear to be.

Wilder had a feeling that Lexi knew how to converse with people, even if she wasn't interested in what they were saying. She was a professional and a public figure, after all.

Finally, people began to leave, and Lexi said she needed to go as well.

"Can you come out to my car for a minute?" she asked as they walked to the foyer after saying goodbye to the others.

"Sure." Wilder opened the closet and pulled both their jackets out. "Is there something wrong with it?"

"No. I just want to talk to you about something."

"Oh?" That sounded promising... or ominous. He wasn't sure which.

The air was crisp as they stepped out of the house onto the porch. It had continued to snow off and on since the first snowfall that had stuck around. The slopes were in great condition and ready for the influx of skiers who would come in over the next several weeks.

He got into the passenger side seat while Lexi slid behind the wheel and started up the car. It didn't take long for warm air to flow from the vents. It definitely heated up more quickly than his car did, and apparently, it had heated seats.

"So, what's up?" he asked, angling himself toward her.

Though it was dark, the streetlight cast a bit of light into the car, allowing him to see her fairly clearly.

"I hope I didn't do something wrong," she said as she stared out the front windshield.

Wilder frowned. "What do you mean?"

"Well, earlier at the rink, I told Charli that I thought Amelia had good potential as a figure skater, probably even better than Layla." She paused, her brow furrowing. "Then when I was speaking with Amelia earlier, she referred to Charli as Layla's mom. And now I'm confused, especially because Charli seemed to not be happy while we ate."

Wilder mulled over her words. "It's true, Amelia isn't Charli's daughter in the biological sense. Not the way she is Layla's. Amelia is Blake's daughter from another relationship. However, he is Layla's father."

Lexi turned to look at him. "I'm confused."

Wilder gave a huff of laughter. "Yeah. It's a bit complicated. Blake and Charli dated back when they were in college, and she got pregnant. He didn't know because he'd left her and joined the military. Fast forward, he came back to town last year with Amelia, and somehow, they managed to sort things out and fell in love again."

"And Shiloh?"

"She's adopted. They got her just a couple of months after they were married earlier this year."

"So do you think Charli's upset that I said that Amelia was a better skater than Layla?"

Wilder shook his head. "If anything, I think she might be more upset that Amelia called her Layla's mom."

"Do they not have a good relationship?"

"I would say that it's... okay. It's not like they fight or anything like that. Amelia just always goes to Blake when she needs something. And she never calls Charli Mom."

"Does Layla call Blake Dad?"

"She didn't at first," Wilder said. "But Lee told me that a couple of months ago, she started referring to him more consistently as her dad."

"That's probably hard for Charli to see," Lexi said. "Especially since she seems to really love and care for Amelia."

"She does," Wilder agreed. "She loves and cares for all kids. It's why she's a teacher."

"I hope I didn't do anything to complicate the situation." Lexi sighed. "I don't always know how to approach people with stuff like this."

"You're doing just fine," Wilder assured her. "And this isn't of your making. Honestly, I think Charli was happy to hear that Amelia is excelling at skating, even if she's doing better than Layla."

"How do you navigate so many relationships?" Lexi asked. "Do you just go around like a bulldozer, not caring? Or do you have to walk around on eggshells?"

"A bit of both. As you get to know the people around you, you understand how to best deal with them. Most of all, I just try to approach things in a loving and caring manner. Adding in a little humor always helps."

"You kind of just pushed your way in with me."

Wilder grinned. "Oh yes. A little persistence helps too."

"Why did you persist?" she asked.

"You're fascinating," Wilder said. "And I enjoy getting to know fascinating people."

"Because I'm an Olympic gold medal winner?"

"That might be part of it," he said. "But you seemed to be holding yourself apart from everyone."

"And that didn't work for you?"

Wilder took a moment to figure out how to respond to that. "In my time of traveling around the world, meeting all kinds of people, I've learned that people who hold themselves apart usually are one of two things. They're hurt, and they're trying to protect themselves. Or they're shy or reserved, and just need someone to initiate conversation."

"And which am I?"

"I would have to say that I think you're a little bit of both."

She seemed to consider his words, then shrugged. "You're not wrong. But it seems like a lot of effort to go to for a stranger."

"You were only a stranger at the start," Wilder told her. "Now you're a friend."

Wilder thought she might deny it, but she didn't. That made him smile, even if was edged with a bit of sadness. He wished that their lives were more compatible overall, so that they could be more than friends.

At the moment, they had some compatibility. With them both being into winter sports, there were things they had in common. But even in the commonalities, there were things that were different.

Like her being a professional athlete, while he was simply a ski instructor. It was a small thing that was growing more significant as time went on. Her winter sport was going to take her away from Serenity. It might just be temporary at first, but Wilder didn't think it would be long before it was permanent.

But for the next twenty-four hours, she was simply Mrs. Claus to his Mr. Claus, and they had the joint goal of entertaining the kids and raising money for the orphanages.

"Sorry this wasn't as entertaining as I promised," Wilder said as he gestured to the house.

"It was fine."

"Hopefully tomorrow is as entertaining as I hope. If not, I give up promising entertainment!"

Lexi laughed, which was a sound Wilder hadn't heard nearly enough of. "Maybe people just needed a quiet evening before the main event."

"I hope so. It's important that it be a success."

"What time do you plan to be at the rink tomorrow?"

"The doors open at one, so I think I'll probably be there by eleven, if not earlier. I might get a call from someone who needs to be in there before eleven. In which case, I'll go whenever they need me."

"Just don't forget your costume," she said.

"I won't. I'm excited to wear it."

Lexi shook her head. "Most men wouldn't want to be caught dead in that outfit."

"True. But I'm not most men. I love stuff like this. The more fun, the better."

"You're popular with the kids, aren't you?"

"Yep." Wilder grinned at her. "But I'm also popular with the adults. Especially if I'm keeping their kids entertained."

That got another laugh out of Lexi. "Well, I'm sure that will be the case tomorrow."

"Yep. If they want to skate with Santa, maybe we'll have a round of crack the whip."

"Oh goodness," Lexi said the words in a huff of laughter. "I'm imagining Santa sending kids flying into the boards."

"It's gonna be a blast. You just wait and see."

"I'm curious to see how it all works out," she said. "Do you think Alexander will be there for the whole time?"

"I doubt it, but you never know."

"I should probably talk to him at some point," Lexi mused, running her hands over the steering wheel.

Wilder reached out to rest his hand over the one of hers that was closest to him, stilling her movement. "You don't have to be nervous about meeting with him. He's actually a pretty cool guy. Just like Hudson."

"Just like Hudson?"

Wilder realized then that maybe Lexi wasn't aware of the relationship between the two men. "Isn't Alexander your godfather?"

"Yep. Though I'm not sure how or why he is."

"But you don't know about him and Hudson?"

Lexi turned to face him. "What about him and Hudson?"

"I guess it's not really a huge secret. Alexander is Hudson's father."

"What?" she exclaimed.

"Yep. Bit of a story there, but he and Hudson are finally building a relationship."

"So Kayleigh is the daughter-in-law of the man who owns Remington?"

"She is. Although she was working for the company before she ever met Hudson."

"You have a very... interesting family."

"I do." Wilder would like to think he was the *most* interesting to Lexi, but he wasn't sure that was the case.

Wilder's phone rang, and he shifted to pull it out of his pocket. Seeing it was Janessa, he answered it. "What's up, sis?"

"Where are you?"

"I'm outside talking with Lexi," he said. "Do you need something?"

"You're outside?" The porch light flickered wildly.

"I'm not on the porch," he told her with a laugh. "It's too cold to be standing outside."

"Oh." The porch light stayed on. "Where are you then? You could see what I was doing so obviously not too far away."

"We're sitting in her car with the heat on."

"As long as you're not heating things up..."

Wilder scoffed. "That's not happening."

"Well, maybe it could in the future."

Rolling his eyes, even though she couldn't see him, he said, "I'll be in soon. Goodbye."

Wilder hung up the phone and slid it into his jacket pocket. "Janessa's looking for me."

"I should probably be going anyway. I need to get some sleep before our big day."

"It's going to be great," Wilder told her as he reached for the door handle. "But you're gonna need your rest so you can handle all the fun."

"For a minute there, I thought you were going to say I needed some beauty sleep."

"Nope." Wilder pulled the handle, opening the door and flooding the interior of the car with light. "You definitely don't need more of that."

Flashing her a smile and wink, Wilder climbed out of the car, then shut the door. With a wave, he turned and jogged toward the front porch. He probably shouldn't be flirting with her, but for the first time in a while, he was around someone he actually wanted to flirt with.

In fact, it was probably wrong of him to flirt with her because they'd defined their relationship to be strictly friendship. For him to agree to that and then flirt with her the way he did wasn't right and could be downright confusing to Lexi.

He didn't want to complicate things in a way that might lead to her backing away from even their friendship.

Sighing, Wilder opened the front door and slipped inside. He'd need to be more careful about that in the future.

"Is Charli still out here?" Wilder asked when he found Janessa and Will in the kitchen. "Or has she gone to their rooms?"

Janessa shook her head. "She, Blake, and the baby disappeared a few minutes ago. The girls are upstairs."

"Did Charli seem okay to you?"

"She seemed a bit off, but I don't know why." Janessa frowned. "Do you?"

Wilder shook his head. He didn't know for certain, but he wasn't going to speculate with Janessa. If Charli was struggling with something, Janessa was the most likely person she'd confide in.

"I'll check with her," Janessa said. "But it's possible Blake will be able to help her with whatever is bothering her."

If someone had told Wilder that one day he'd be living with his siblings, their spouses and children, he would have told them they were crazy. Wasn't the goal to grow up and move out on his own? Or maybe live with a roommate?

Though normally he had no problem staying with his parents when he returned each fall, he was actually glad he'd had to move into Charli and Janessa's this time around. Living with his siblings had actually turned into something he really enjoyed.

And a big bonus was also being able to get to know his brothers-in-law and his nieces in a way he wouldn't have been able to if he hadn't been living with them. Though he knew Will pretty well, he hadn't known Blake at all. And with Lee living there, he was also having a chance to get to know Rori.

With Janessa now pregnant, however, the house would soon be bursting at the seams. He had no idea if Janessa and Charli planned to live together indefinitely, but it was likely he'd have to live with his folks or find another place to stay when he returned next year.

"I'm going to bed," Janessa announced. "I'm exhausted, and I won't be able to just lay around tomorrow, so I'd better get my rest while I can."

"Thanks for all your help," Wilder said as Janessa got up from the bar stool.

"You're welcome. It's been fun, and I think tomorrow is going to be a blast."

"I hope so. A lot of people are putting in a significant effort for it."

Janessa came to give him a hug, then she left the kitchen with Will.

Wilder grabbed a couple of cookies, then sat down at the counter with his phone. Opening his email app, he found an email in his inbox from the director of one of the orphanages. He'd stayed in contact with them, and he'd let both orphanages know about the fundraiser they were doing. He'd also told them that he'd spoken at the church and shared about their ministries.

As he read the email, his thoughts turned from the fundraiser. The letter was basically to thank him for what he'd done so far, but they also wanted to know if he'd be interested in giving orphanage presentations at other churches in the area.

The woman said they'd be responsible for contacting the churches, and they'd get pamphlets and other information to him, if he'd be willing to present it all to different congregations.

A smile grew on Wilder's face as he considered what they were asking. As long as they weren't too far away, he'd be able to do it without having to take much, if any, time off work.

He wouldn't give them an answer right away. His focus needed to be on the fundraiser, but once that was over, he'd give it some serious thought.

It would give him something to do, because he was pretty sure that he wouldn't be spending much—if any—time with Lexi in the days and weeks ahead. The thought made him sad, but at the same time, it was probably for the best.

# CHAPTER TWENTY-FIVE

Lexi finished curling her hair, then checked to make sure the partial updo she'd created would hold for skating. She was used to securing her hair for competitions, but she usually put it all up. This time, though, she'd left part of it down, and she'd found a Christmassy headband, so she slipped that on and fastened it in place so it wouldn't fall off as she skated.

Her outfit was in a garment bag, ready to go. She planned to get dressed closer to the time of the fundraiser, just in case she needed to help out beforehand.

Once she had everything she needed, she left the apartment. As soon as she turned on the car, Christmas music poured out of the speakers. Even though she hadn't really been in the mood for Christmas, the fundraiser had helped shift her attitude. So now she had the music of the season playing whenever she was in the car.

She spotted Wilder's car when she pulled into the parking lot, and his parting words from the night before came to mind. Not that they'd ever really gone away.

It had been a moment that had left her speechless with her heart thudding heavily in her chest. This man...

He'd brought her so much joy that she'd never realized was missing in her life. He never took himself too seriously, which meant that even though he knew that she had a very talented skating partner in Mik, he had no problem partnering with her for the fundraiser.

Some men might have been intimidated by her and Mik's abilities, but Wilder had no problem accepting his own skill level and having fun with it. She wasn't sure she'd ever be able to be that carefree, but today would definitely be a step in that direction.

With butterflies of anticipation fluttering in her stomach, Lexi got out of the car and retrieved her stuff from the backseat. Snow crunched beneath her feet as she walked to the door of the rink. They had cleared most of the snow, but it looked like a bit more had fallen overnight.

Though the rink was usually kept a bit on the cold side, it still wrapped her in warmth as she stepped inside. Christmas music and conversation greeted her.

"Hey there," Wilder called out when he spotted her. He immediately walked in her direction, a broad smile on his face, making his warm brown eyes sparkle. "Ready for a great day?"

"I am." Her smile came more easily than it ever had before. It wasn't the smile that she gave when she was in the kiss and cry area or talking to reporters. This was the smile she gave her mom, and now, it was the one Wilder seemed to draw from her with little effort.

"So am I." He motioned to the tables that had been set up the day before. "We have a lot of baked goods to sell, and I think the auction items are going to bring in a lot of money."

"That's great."

Together, they walked toward the area where most of the things had been set up. Lexi briefly detoured to her office to drop off her bags.

"Good morning, Lexi," Wilder's mom said as they joined her and Wilder's dad at one of the tables.

"Good morning."

"This is going to be so exciting," she said, her smile rivaling her son's.

"We're in charge of the silent auction," her husband said. "I'm looking forward to seeing the generosity of everyone. I know they're going to come through."

Lexi could see where Wilder got his optimism. When she'd first met his parents, she'd been surprised at how friendly they'd been toward her. She was sure that Wilder had told them about her past, but it didn't seem to matter to them.

Mrs. Halverson's gaze moved past Lexi, and her smile grew. Turning, Lexi spotted Kayleigh coming towards them with Hudson and Alexander. Now that she knew they were father and son, she could see the similarity between them. It was so strong that she was surprised that she hadn't picked up on it herself.

She was used to seeing both men in suits, but that day, they were each wearing jeans and thick sweaters under their jackets. Kayleigh was also in jeans that she'd paired with an oversized sweater. Her hair was pulled back into a high ponytail. She didn't look like the polished manager of the resort.

Mrs. Halverson greeted them each with a smile and a hug—even Alexander. While Mr. Halverson shook hands with the men and hugged his daughter, pressing a kiss to the top of her head.

As she watched the two interact, Lexi felt a pulse of pain in her heart. She missed her dad. Not the man who had stolen from people. Not the arrogant businessman.

She missed the man who'd gone to all her competitions. Who, even though he'd been busy a lot of time, had hugged her and kissed her when he'd been around. He'd been the one to help make her dreams come true.

But it was all gone.

And she had to wonder if any of it had been real. He'd said that everything he'd done had been for her and her mom. As if placing the responsibility for his theft on them made it better. All it did was increase her guilt.

Thankfully, she'd had money of her own earned through endorsements so that she hadn't been left completely destitute. Her mom had had plenty of money because she'd inherited a large sum of money when her grandfather had passed away. So they'd been okay financially.

But Lexi had lost her dad, and her mom had lost her husband because of his actions.

Pushing aside those thoughts, she focused on the conversation going on around her. Kayleigh, Hudson, and Alexander walked with the Halversons to the silent auction and baked goods.

"You okay?"

Lexi turned to Wilder and forced herself to give him a smile. She was okay. And if she could get rid of the thoughts about her father, she'd be even better. "Yep. I'm fine."

Wilder looked like he didn't believe her, and for a moment, she thought he might push. But instead, he just gave a nod.

"Are we putting on our costumes before everything starts?"

"We probably should," she said. "I'll put my skates on as well since I'm used to walking around in them."

"Plus, they make you taller."

She chuckled, feeling some of her sad thoughts ease away. "Yeah. They do. But still not as tall as you."

Charli and Blake's arrival with the girls interrupted their conversation. Mrs. Halverson made a beeline for them. She greeted them all with hugs and kisses, even Blake, then she took the car seat and carried it over to one of the tables.

"How was Charli this morning?" Lexi asked as she watched the family follow Mrs. Halverson.

"She seemed better," Wilder said. "Janessa, on the other hand... She probably won't show up until this afternoon. She wasn't feeling so hot."

"I'm sorry to hear that."

Wilder shrugged. "All part of the joy of being pregnant, I guess."

"Are we getting changed, Uncle Wilder?" Layla asked as she came up and grabbed his arm.

"Do you want to spend the afternoon in your elf costume?"

She grinned. "Yep. That would be cool."

"Then go ahead and get changed."

"You can use the bathroom or my office," Lexi told her.

With a nod, Layla skipped over to where Amelia stood with her hand in Blake's. After a moment's conversation, Charli picked up a bag and followed the girls into the bathroom.

More of Wilder's family showed up, most of them carrying boxes which apparently held more baked goods and a few more things for the auction. There was also a table that held a stack of pamphlets, along with a display board with pictures and information about the orphanages.

The café was open, and George was there for the skate rentals. They'd agreed to let kids have skates for free, though adults had to pay, with the proceeds going to the fundraiser.

There was a spot on the far end of the rink that they'd decorated for Wilder to take pictures with the kids. It wasn't the conventional picture with Santa setup, but Lexi thought the kids would have fun with it.

As one o'clock neared, Lexi headed for her office to get changed. It didn't take too long to put on the pieces that made up her costume, then she sat down to put on her skates. She didn't have a mirror in her office, so she made her way to the bathroom to check that everything looked okay.

"You look so pretty!" Amelia exclaimed as she ran up to Lexi before she could reach the bathroom.

Lexi smiled down at her. "So do you."

"Should I put my skates on?" she asked.

"If you want. We're not skating until one-thirty, so you'll have to walk around in them."

"I can do it."

"Then ask your mom or dad to help you tie them," Lexi said, making sure to emphasize *your mom* so Amelia knew that's what she considered Charli.

As Amelia ran off, Lexi slipped into the bathroom and checked herself out in front of the mirror. She was used to wearing costumes, but this one was definitely a first. Not much sparkle, and it definitely covered more of her body than any of the other ones she'd worn.

When she left the bathroom a couple of minutes later, she saw immediately that people had already started to arrive. The Christmas playlist she'd set up on her tablet played over the sound system.

Looking around, she spotted Wilder. Or rather, she spotted Santa. If she hadn't known it was Wilder, she wouldn't have recognized him as he walked around with a bit of extra padding and a white wig and beard.

"Look at you!" Wilder exclaimed, spreading his arms wide. "Santa is one lucky man."

Lexi felt her cheeks flush with uncharacteristic heat as she gave an exasperated shake of her head. "The costumes seem to be working for you and the girls."

"Yep." He turned in a circle. "I think I could get some use out of this in the future."

"You could get a job as a mall Santa next year," she said.

"Maybe. But I think we should make this fundraiser a yearly thing."

Lexi hadn't thought much about where her future might take her, or if Wilder would continue to be in it. It made her feel a little sad to think that she might not be there in a year's time. Or that Wilder might not be in her life anymore.

Pushing aside the pain, she said, "That's probably a great idea because it already looks like people are excited to be here."

Wilder turned to view the rink and the groups of people milling around the area. Some had apparently taken advantage of the café and were already sitting at the tables on the far side of the rink.

"Santa!"

A little boy came running toward them, his arms spread wide. Wilder didn't falter at all. He dropped to one knee and allowed the little guy to hug him. The boy's parents quickly approached them, apologizing for their son's action.

"Don't worry about it," Wilder said as he got to his feet, still holding the boy's hand. "It's what I'm here for."

"Oh, thank you so much."

Somehow, the couple managed to pry their son away from Wilder. As they walked away, the little boy expressed his displeasure but didn't pull away from his parents.

"Maybe we should circulate before we get on the ice," Wilder suggested, offering her his arm.

After a moment's hesitation, Lexi slipped her hand into the crook of his elbow. Even though her skates added a couple of inches to her height, she still didn't match Wilder's height.

Alexander grinned when he spotted them, which Lexi took to mean he was pleased with the events of the afternoon so far. Layla and Amelia joined them, skipping alongside her and Wilder as they circled around the rink. They stopped frequently to talk to kids who wanted their attention.

The parents and other adults who'd shown up to support the event—many even appeared to be guests of the resort—lingered at the tables, checking out the auction items, the baked goods and other items that were offered for sale. They'd rented out a few tables for people to sell homemade items. Everything about the rink—from the decorations to the music—screamed Christmas.

Though she hadn't ever been a big fan of Christmas, it was clear that Wilder was, and she was catching his enthusiasm. As a skater, she was used to going into character for programs, so she easily slipped into the role of Mrs. Claus.

When it was time for them to get on the ice for their little program, she felt a new sort of excitement. She always had a level of nervous excitement when preparing to skate a program. But this time, it was more of a fun excitement.

Using the speaker system, Hudson let people know that Santa was going to be skating, and by the time the song started, people had gathered all around the edge of the rink.

Wilder picked up his hockey stick and then, with the girls on either side of him, he skated around the rink, the three of them performing the turns and jumps they'd practiced. When it was time for Lexi to join them, Wilder handed off the hockey stick to Layla and held out his hand to Lexi.

She took it without hesitation, then they got into the waltz position. As she faced Wilder, he smiled at her. Lexi relaxed as he guided her around the ice, trusting that even though the program wasn't being judged, he took it seriously. Still, they managed to have fun, and everyone watching seemed to enjoy it.

The program flew by, and soon it was over, and she was perched on Wilder's knee, their arms stretched wide with the girls standing beside them. People around the rink clapped and cheered, and soon, kids were joining them on the rink.

Rori also came onto the ice, carefully making her way around to where there was carpet and a decorated chair set up for pictures. After Wilder had skated with the kids for a bit, the four performers joined Rori, and the children whose parents had paid for pictures lined up to have them taken.

Kayleigh was standing on the other side of the rink, coordinating the line up of kids. She and Rori would work on emailing the pictures out in the next week.

It seemed to all be going smoothly, which made Lexi happy and grateful, considering the mess they'd had at the start. Where they'd ended up was sure to be a success for raising money for the orphanages, and that was the best they could hope for.

Halfway through the afternoon, just as they'd finished skating the program for the third time, she spotted Mik and Irina standing at the edge of the boards, watching them. Lexi narrowed her eyes at them, but then she decided she needed to just ignore them. She still had stuff to do.

She had no idea how long they'd been there, but they didn't appear to stay long after she'd seen them. By the time they were done with the pictures for that time around, the pair had disappeared.

As the day neared its end, Hudson wrapped up the silent auction. From the sounds of things, people had been generous with their bids. Lexi had never heard of a silent auction, and from the bids Hudson read out, it seemed that people were actually willing to pay more than what the item was worth. Significantly more.

It would have driven her dad mad. He always harped on about value for money. The last thing he'd have done would have been to bid more for something than it was worth. Although, if it would have made him look good, he might have considered it. Plus, he would have liked to look like he had money to spare.

Lexi hated when thoughts of her father crept into her mind. She wanted to get to the point where she didn't think about him at all, but something told her that wasn't ever going to happen.

Once it was only the volunteers left—which was made up significantly of the Halverson family—Alexander announced that he'd arranged for a meal to be served in one of the small convention halls at the hotel. With so many people helping out, it didn't take long before the rink was back to how it normally was, and people began to make their way to the hotel.

Charli and Blake had left earlier, but the girls were still there, apparently riding with Wilder. They'd wanted to keep their elf costumes on, but Wilder and Lexi had both changed out of their outfits.

"Want to ride with us to the hotel?" Wilder asked as he and the girls pulled on their jackets.

"I have my car," she reminded him.

"I can drop you back by here after we're done."

It seemed senseless for him to have to come back by the rink later when she could just take her car right then. However, it didn't stop her from accepting his offer.

After the rink was locked up, they piled into Wilder's car, with the girls getting into the back seat. It only took a few minutes to get to the hotel, where Wilder pulled around to the front door to let her and the girls out before going to find a parking spot.

"Are we waiting for him?" Layla asked.

"I want to look at the decorations," Amelia said.

"Why don't we do that while we wait for him to come back?" Lexi suggested.

The hotel lobby had been decked out with huge Christmas trees, and festive greenery covered every surface and hung in swags above the windows. Warm white lights twinkled from amongst the branches. The large stone fireplace was blazing, spilling warmth and the scent of burning wood out into the space.

The girls were exploring the trees, each of which had a different theme, though the color schemes were all the same. It was a very beautiful space. The people who'd been hired to decorate the resort had done a great job.

She'd already seen that in the decorating at the rink, but they had gone over and above in the hotel. It was beautiful.

Wilder appeared as she and the girls were looking at a tree with lots of red bows and pinecones on it. He smiled at her. "They did a great job in here, didn't they?"

"They really did."

"Well, I don't know about you, but I'm starving," Wilder said. "Let's go eat."

As they walked to the room where they were to eat, Lexi realized she should have just gone home. After a day of not training, she really shouldn't be eating anything but her meal prep.

However, it was too late to back out now. If she did, it would mean Wilder would have to take her back to her car, and she wasn't about to ask that of him.

Hopefully, there was some food there she could eat. If worse came to worst, she'd eat just a little, and then have her meal prep when she got home.

When they reached the room, Lexi saw a couple of long tables set up, along with a buffet. Wilder guided her to one of the tables where Kayleigh, Hudson, and Alexander stood.

"That was truly wonderful," Alexander said when he spotted them. "You two were the perfect Mr. and Mrs. Claus. Did you have fun?"

"I always have fun," Wilder said with a grin. "How about you, Lexi?"

"I had fun too. It was one of the least stressful programs I've ever skated."

"I'd like to talk to you more about your programs," Alexander said, then tipped his head toward the buffet. "Let's get some food first."

As they made their way through the buffet, most of the guys piled food on their plates, while the women took a little less. Lexi focused on protein and complex carbs, which, of the food there, included a grilled chicken breast, mixed vegetables, and a salad. She skipped the desserts altogether.

Back at the table, she set her plate on the table, then sat down, glad to be off her feet. When Alexander settled into the chair across from her, she was grateful that Wilder took the seat beside her. She'd already come to appreciate how comfortable he made situations and conversations that she found a little stressful.

And when a man of Alexander's stature wanted to talk to her, she was glad to have Wilder nearby. Thankfully, Kayleigh and Hudson joined them as well.

"So tell me how your training is going," Alexander said as they began to eat.

"I think it's going well," she told him. "Mikhail had to relearn to skate with me, since his last partner and I have different body types. Once he'd managed that, we were able to be much more in sync."

"Are you going to Nationals?" he asked, making it clear that he'd done some research on competitive figure skating.

"That's the plan." Irina had let them know that she'd notified the skating officials that Lexi and Mikhail were back together again. Now they were on their way to Nationals, and then hopefully, the Olympics.

"Are you training tomorrow?"

"For a few hours in the morning. We're usually there from five until the rink opens, but on Sundays, we go from five until ten. It's our lightest day."

"I might stop by, if that's okay."

"Yes. That would be fine."

"Also, I'd like to propose something for you," he said.

Lexi gripped her glass in both hands. "I'm listening."

"When you're back from the Olympics, if you're interested in pursuing a coaching career, I'm offering you the use of the rink here to do that."

"How would that work?"

"Don't worry about that yet. Just know that it's an option."

"Why would you do that for me?" she asked. "Why have you done any of this for me?"

"Your mom and my wife were friends, and your dad wanted me to be your godfather. When we heard what happened with your dad, Candace insisted that we step in to help you."

"I appreciate all you've done. It's made a world of difference for me."

Alexander's smile was genuine with warmth. "I'm glad we could help you, and I think staying here in Serenity will do you a world of good." He turned to clap Hudson on the shoulder. "After all, it's been great for Hudson."

"Can't argue at all with that," Hudson agreed.

Once they finished eating, they didn't linger, and soon Wilder was driving her back to her car.

"Do you have plans for Christmas?" he asked.

"I'm not sure. Mom wants me to go to France to be with her, but I'm not sure I want to deal with jetlag in the midst of training. We're limited on time as it is."

"Well, if you're here, you're welcome to join us," he said. "Our Christmas always includes a lot of people, so we'd be happy to have you."

She wasn't sure about spending Christmas with Wilder and his family. But if she didn't go to France, she would be completely on her own. Mikhail and Irina had already said they were going back to Maine for a couple of days over Christmas.

"And I'd like for you to be there, too," Wilder said. "So give it some thought."

Oh, she would. The question was, would she let logic or emotion lead her to a decision?

As she drove home, Lexi realized that she needed to embrace logic, and logic said that she needed to back away from Wilder and their friendship. It was a distraction that she didn't need right then, given that training was going to ramp up even more now that the program was over.

Her emotional response to him was something she'd never experienced before, and her feelings for him were even more intense than what she'd felt for Mik. Which shouldn't be the case.

But Wilder had drawn her in, and while he might be able to keep his feelings in check, she wasn't so confident about her own ability to do the same.

So it was best all around that she just back off and focus on her skating.

# CHAPTER TWENTY-SIX

With a winter storm closing in on them, Wilder left the ski shop by two on the Monday following the new year. With no one allowed on the ski slopes because of the weather, he decided to head home. He could have hung out at the ski shop for the last couple hours of his shift, but Trev assured him there was really no need to stay.

Once he reached his car, he slid behind the wheel and started the engine. He cranked the heat, hoping to chase away the chill in the air, then got back out and cleared the snow off the windows.

Hopefully, Kayleigh had left already because he could see the snow piling up in the parking lot. The road between the resort and Serenity would be impassable by nighttime if they didn't get the plows out quickly.

He also hoped that Lexi had left the rink. She was from Maine, so he would think that she'd dealt with winter storms in the past. Enough that she'd know that she needed to get home before it got too bad.

The temptation was there to go to the rink and make sure she'd left already, but he resisted. She'd made it clear that she needed him to back off.

In the days between the fundraiser and Christmas, something had changed with Lexi. At first, he'd thought it was just her being busy with training. But when he'd again issued the invitation to spend Christmas with them, she'd declined. But then she'd added that she thought it would be best if they didn't spend so much time together.

He'd pressed her for a reason, and when she'd given it, he couldn't argue with her. She was right. Their friendship had kept edging into territory that wasn't *just* friendship. And he knew that she was also right when she'd said their lives were just too different.

He hadn't thought seriously about switching up his plans and the way he lived his life. But he'd always assumed that when he decided to settle down, he'd be staying in Serenity.

If Lexi's return to competitive skating went well, and she was able to start coaching at a higher level, Serenity was probably not where she'd want to stay. Even though Alexander had offered her the use of the rink for that purpose. Or maybe she'd even decide to continue to skate with Mik if they had a successful run at Nationals and the Olympics.

It hurt to think of not having Lexi in his life. He'd had a girlfriend in high school, but no one since. However, his feelings for that girl didn't even come close to what he'd developed for Lexi. He had done his best to respect their "friendship only" relationship, but it had been a challenge.

It wasn't until she'd essentially cut him out of her life that Wilder had realized that in the back of his mind, he'd been hoping that somehow, they'd be able to figure something out to enable a romantic relationship. With her career in flux, he'd known it couldn't be something they worked out for a while, but now it didn't seem like it was likely at all. And in the process, he'd lost a friendship as well.

It hurt, and Wilder didn't know how to handle it.

Since Lexi didn't seem to want him checking on her, he sent a text to Kayleigh instead. Hudson was out of town, but he was probably aware of the weather.

*Hope you're at home. Hudson will kill me if anything happens to you.*

**Kayleigh:** *Hudson's been after me to leave, so I'm on my way now.*

*Good. Slopes are closed, so I'm headed home too.*

**Kayleigh:** *Drive safe. Love you.*

*You, too.*

Setting his phone in the cup holder, Wilder reversed out of his parking spot. He flicked on his wipers as he left the nearly empty parking lot at the ski shop, clearing the wet snow that kept gathering on his windshield.

He drove slowly along the road, watching for anyone who might need help. There were other cars on the road, but most were all-wheel drives, which meant that he'd need their help before they'd need his.

When he got home, everyone but Blake, Lee, and Janessa were there. The city appeared to be shutting down for the blizzard. All the kids, Will, and Charli were home since school had dismissed early because they didn't want to chance the buses getting stuck because of the increased snowfall and dipping temperatures.

"Hot chocolate, Uncle Wilder?" Amelia asked. "Layla's..." She paused and frowned for a moment. "Mom is making it for us."

"Sure. That sounds great." He peeled off all his outerwear and put everything in the closet before heading into the kitchen. There he found Will sitting at the counter with Shiloh, while Charli was at the stove stirring something in a pot.

"No Janessa?" he asked as he joined Will.

"Lee's picking her up. Both clinics are staying open a bit longer."

"Is school cancelled already for tomorrow?"

"Yep," Charli said as she turned to take several mugs off the wrought iron mug tree. "So an extra long weekend for us, with the exception of the few hours we had to go in this morning. They should've just let us have the whole day off when we knew we were getting snow."

"Is Blake still at work, too?"

"He's on his way," Charli said. "He's swinging by the store to pick up a few essentials."

"Essentials?" Wilder asked, reaching to take the baby from Will.

The man hesitated for a moment, then relinquished the little girl. "I want her back."

"Getting your practice in?"

"You know it."

"So, what essentials?"

"Let's see..." Charli began to ladle hot chocolate into mugs. "Chips. Frozen pizza. Chocolate. You know. All the necessities when we're snowed in."

"Do you need to cancel your presentation on Sunday?" Will asked.

"I shouldn't have to," Wilder said, thinking about the church in Spokane where he was scheduled to give an orphanage presentation. It would be the second one he'd given, and each one felt significant and like he was doing something important. Which he was. Thankfully, Trev had been willing to give him a little leeway in his start time on Sundays to make his presentation at the churches that weren't in town. "I think the plows will have gone through by then."

Charli slid a mug across the counter to him. "You should probably still contact them."

"Yes, Mom," he said with a laugh, then snuggled Shiloh's neck, making her giggle. "Right, Shi-Shi. Yes, Mama."

"Here you go, Will," Charli said as she handed him his mug.

It wasn't long before the front door opened. Amelia went to see who it was, and Wilder heard her greet Janessa. When she came into the kitchen, Lee followed her with Rori. The woman carried a duffle bag over her shoulder, so Wilder assumed she would be hunkering down with them for the blizzard.

Rori dropped the duffle bag on the floor by the entrance to the kitchen, then came to join them at the counter. Charli handed out more hot chocolate and offered them cookies.

Since there weren't enough stools at the counter, they shifted over to the breakfast nook. As she slid onto the bench across from Wilder, Rori said, "Looks like we'll see how Lexi and Mik do at Nationals this week."

"Yep." Lexi might have put distance between them, but that didn't mean he wasn't aware of what was going on with her professionally.

"Have you read the forums and stuff about Lexi and Mikhail being partners again?"

Rori was aware that Lexi had chosen to focus on her training instead of hanging out with them, but Wilder hadn't shared that it went deeper than that for him.

"I have, and it seems like people's opinions are all over the place."

"I wish we could see her again," Layla said. "I miss having her coach us."

"Once the Olympics are over, she'll be able to coach you again," Charli said as she sat down at the breakfast nook. She cast a questioning look at Wilder, but all he could do was shrug.

"Don't people like that they're competing again?" Layla asked Rori.

"Some are thrilled that they're back together. Those seem to be the people who've been big fans all along. I think the ones who don't want them competing again are fans of other pairs who will be negatively impacted by their return."

Layla was old enough to be aware of what had gone on previously with Lexi and Mik, and she didn't think it was fair what had happened to Lexi. So now, she was definitely a big fan of the couple. Well, a big fan of Lexi. She seemed to be reserving judgement on Mikhail as a person.

"There are lots of people who think they won't be able to rise to their former glory," Rori said. "I hope that how they perform at Nationals will shut a lot of those people up."

Wilder wished that he could text Lexi, but he was also trying to respect her wishes.

He knew that his siblings had experienced bumps in their quest for love. None of them had gone from point A to a committed relationship in a straight line. But he'd figured that was because they were more intense than he was.

Wilder was more easygoing, taking things as they came. His mom had always said to just live his life, doing what God led him to, and that he might end up meeting someone with similar interests. He'd thought that might have been the case with Miriam, but in the end, he'd only felt friendship for her.

But instead of falling for someone who had a similar outlook as him, he'd fallen for a woman who couldn't be more different from him. The only thing they had in common was their faith, but he didn't think that was enough.

"I wish we could go see her compete in person," Layla said.

Wilder definitely wished that, too. "I think we'll probably have a better view of them skating if we watch it on the big screen in the basement."

"That's true," Charli said as she reached over and took a fussing Shiloh from him. "And we can make a big deal of it with snacks and stuff."

"It starts Thursday, so we don't have much time to get ready."

Wilder couldn't help but wonder how Lexi was doing as she prepared. He wanted to talk to her. To assure her that she had their support.

But maybe that didn't matter to her. It seemed she'd had a fairly small team of support previously, so maybe she was fine not knowing that she had a bunch of people in her corner.

He wondered if her mom would attend, even though she'd said her mom didn't like going to her competitions. Maybe she'd make an exception since her ex-husband—her daughter's father—was in prison and couldn't make it to her competitions anymore.

Once the girls were done with their hot chocolate, Charli sent them up to their room to get their bedding since apparently they were going to have a sleepover with Rori in the basement.

"Have you talked to Lexi?" Charli asked once the girls had left.

"Nope." Wilder slowly spun the mug between his fingers. "I told you that she said she needed to focus. She doesn't want me bothering her."

Charli frowned. "You two seemed to get along so well together. I honestly thought it would become something more."

"It would never have been anything more than a friendship," he said, staring down at the mug. "Our lives are just too different."

"I'm sure you could have figured something out."

"Which one of us would have had to give up their way of life?" he asked.

"Definitely you," Janessa said without a moment of hesitation.

He lifted his brows. "What? Why me?" Wilder couldn't deny that there was a big part of him that would have loved to show Lexi the world. To travel to his favorite places with her.

"You're getting older, Wilder," she said. "It's time for you to move forward. Stop gallivanting all over the world. Settle down."

Those two words made Wilder cringe. Settle down? It sounded so boring, and definitely not what he thought he'd do until he was well into his thirties. He didn't have a plan in place to make that kind of transition yet.

But would he do it if Lexi would give him a chance?

The *yes* that echoed through his mind took him off-guard. It wasn't something he'd seriously considered because at first it had just been a friendship, and then they'd decided that was all it could be. And then... well, she'd shut down even that.

Still, he couldn't help but pick up his phone and tap out a message.

*Hope everything is going well for the competition this weekend. We'll be praying for you and cheering you on. Take care!*

He set his phone face down on the table, unwilling to sit there staring at it while he waited for her response. She'd get back to him when she was able to. Or maybe not at all.

"What would I do if I settled down?" Wilder asked.

His siblings were quick to rattle off a bunch of stuff. All of it was ludicrous to him. "I'm not going back to school, so doctor, nurse or accountant are out of the question. So is teacher."

"Just use the degree you have," Lee said. "I mean, you're able to work as you gallivant around the world, so you should be able to stay in one place to do it."

"True, but the view as I work while gallivanting is usually new and stunning."

"Seriously though, Wilder," Charli said. "You need to look a little further into the future."

"I *am* looking into the future. I have already started to plan for when I leave in April."

"But how about beyond that?" she pressed. "Do you have plans for *that?*"

He didn't, really. So much could happen before he made the decision to "settle down." What was the purpose of planning that far into the future, when his plans might not line up with where God wanted him?

That was why he didn't even plan a year into the future. It felt like a waste of time.

"You might lose out on an opportunity with someone or something if you're unwilling to consider that settling down might need to happen sooner."

Wilder felt unfamiliar irritation rise inside him. "You make it sound like Lexi wanted something with me, and I'm rejecting her to go gallivanting around the world. That's not the case."

"But if it was?"

"I would probably reconsider my immediate plans."

He wasn't sure what a future with Lexi might have looked like if she really was interested. It was hard to imagine living and raising a family anywhere but Serenity. No matter where he went, Serenity was always home for him. It was where he always came back to. And even in his nebulous future, it had always involved putting down roots in Serenity.

"Well, it's a moot point," Wilder said. "Unless Lexi changes her mind and wants to see if we could have something together, it really doesn't matter."

"But you need to open yourself up to the possibility of a plan for your future needing to come together sooner rather than later."

"Okay, well, it doesn't have to happen in the middle of a blizzard," Wilder said.

Thankfully, everyone was distracted by Blake's arrival with the "essentials" he'd picked up at the store. As they unpacked the bags, the discussion turned to what they would have for supper.

It wasn't much of a discussion because they all agreed pretty quickly that the day called for a warm, hearty dish, and that dish was going to be chili and cornbread.

While Blake went upstairs to take a shower, the rest of them tackled dinner prep. Wilder pitched in to help Janessa make the cornbread muffins, retrieving the ingredients as she read them out to him, choosing to take on the supervisory role as she sat at the counter.

The icy wind continued to blow, and the snow steadily fell in the dark beyond the windows. But inside the house, there was warmth and laughter. Wilder participated, but his thoughts were split between the cornbread he was making and Lexi.

She still hadn't replied, and he couldn't help but be a bit worried.

When the cornbread was divided into the muffin papers in the tin, Wilder carried them over to the oven and slid them in.

As he sat down on the stool beside Janessa, his text alert sounded. He pulled his phone out and felt a swirl of relief when he saw the message he'd been waiting for.

**Lexi:** *Thanks. We just arrived at our hotel and will have a couple of days to practice before our short on Thursday.*

After considering a variety of replies, he finally settled on *That's great. Hope all goes well!*

The sick pit in his stomach as he thought of her and Mik at the hotel took him off-guard. She'd made it clear she didn't want anything with him, so Wilder didn't know why he was so bothered.

Well, he did know why it bothered him. She might want distance from him, but he didn't want distance from her. He wanted to be there for her, supporting her as she reached for her dreams one more time.

Instead, Mik was going to be the one helping her achieve them. It would be easier for Wilder to accept that if he could be there for her, ready to celebrate with her if it went well or commiserate if it didn't.

"Stop moping around," Janessa said as she jabbed him in the ribs with her elbow. "If God wants you and Lexi to be together, He'll guide you in that direction."

"That only works if she's willing to be guided."

"Are you?" she asked.

"Am I what?"

"Willing to be guided?" She leaned on her arm on the counter and shifted to face him more fully, propping her cheek on her hand. "Are you willing to be guided?"

Wilder pondered her words. He'd always assumed he was. For years, he'd kept to the same schedule. Leave Serenity in April, travel outside of the US to produce videos, return to Serenity in October or November. Figuring if God wanted him to change up his schedule, He'd make that clear.

And it seemed that God had. When Wilder had encountered that situation in Thailand, it had sent him in a direction he'd been more than willing to embrace. And now the orphanage work was a part of his summer plans.

More recently, he'd taken on some responsibility for sharing information about the orphanages, and he was happy to do that too.

He realized that those two changes had fit into the life he already lived, so of course, it had been easy to accept God's guidance in those. But how would he react if God seemed to be leading him away from the life he'd planned to live for years to come?

Maybe he wasn't as willing to be guided as he'd always assumed he was. It was easy to accept God's guidance when it aligned with what he wanted. Now he realized it wasn't quite as easy when it might take him completely off the path he'd wanted to keep traveling.

Still, in this particular situation, if Lexi wasn't willing to consider God's guidance, it wouldn't matter much if he was.

# CHAPTER TWENTY-SEVEN

Lexi breathed heavily as she and Mikhail sat in the kiss and cry, waiting for the score of their long program. Irina was sitting next to Mik, while Lev—who'd joined them since he had other skaters in the competition—sat beside her, his presence a heavy weight on her.

They all knew that a gold medal might not be won in the short program, but it could definitely be lost. Their short program had left them in third, which, since they hadn't competed together in over a year, wasn't bad. At least in her mind.

Mikhail had been ticked, and Irina hadn't been happy either. Considering where Mik had been placing with his previous partner, she thought he should be happy that they were at least that high in the ranking.

In the past, third would have made her as ticked as Mik currently was. But given the journey they'd travelled to get there, they were actually sitting pretty well.

Lexi knew that Mik and the coaches were hoping for gold. She had slightly lower goals. She was just hoping to make the podium, even if that meant third.

Winning gold would pretty much guarantee that they would make the Olympic team. Silver or bronze would still mean they'd be considered. Anything less than that, it wasn't as likely they'd be given one of the coveted spots.

Lev continued to mutter to her about what they'd missed, as if she hadn't seen their stumbles just played out on the rerun. She kept herself perfectly still as she smiled, aware that the cameras were on them. There was no way she was going to let the world see the turmoil going on inside of her.

Other skaters and some fans might not want her there, but she belonged on the ice. These past few weeks had proven that she still had something to give. Whether that was as a skater or a coach, she couldn't walk away yet.

A roar sounded from the crowd as the scores came up. The knot of anxiety in her stomach unraveled. They were in first, which meant they were guaranteed at least third place, since only the pairs that were first and second after the short program were still left to skate.

They'd done their best. Now their future was in the hands of the two last pairs to skate. One of which was on the ice, skating a few more minutes of warmup while they waited for their turn.

Now that they had their scores, the four of them stood up and moved away from the kiss and cry area. There was another area set up for the current first, second and third place teams to wait. The pair that had been in third got up and left, while the other two pairs shifted down to give Lexi and Mik the first-place seats.

Lexi didn't want to be sitting there with the other skaters. She knew what they thought of her. A couple of them had been very vocal about her following her dad's arrest.

Weighty silence settled over the area, but Lexi kept a serene expression on her face. She was not going to let them see her sweat. Never had, never would.

As she sat there, she kept her gaze on the large monitor, but her thoughts were a million miles away. Or at least as many miles as it was to Serenity Point, Idaho.

The past few weeks had been hard. For the first time in her life, the training hadn't had her total focus.

She'd known that she'd made the right decision in putting distance between her and Wilder, but it hadn't been easy. There hadn't been a day where she hadn't thought about him. Wondered how he was doing. Wished she could see him.

It was only after he wasn't around that she became aware of how much he'd taken care of her. Making sure she was eating. Checking to see if she needed anything. Bringing lightness and laughter to her life when it had been at its darkest.

She hadn't known that laughter was such an important part of life until Wilder had befriended her. He'd shown her that even though she had to take certain parts of her life seriously, she didn't have to be serious all the time. She wished she'd taken the time to tell him how life-changing meeting him had been for her.

Instead, she'd told him that she didn't have a place for him in her life. It had been more important to protect herself than to maintain a friendship with him.

Was he watching? Had he seen her and Mik skate?

His text had said that they'd be supporting her, so Lexi hoped that meant he'd be watching. She probably should have worked out a signal to give the camera in the kiss and cry to let him know she was thinking of him. Her signal to her mom was touching the necklace her mom had given her, which she always wore.

She missed Wilder so much. More than she had thought possible, and her heart ached with the loss of him from her life.

Love at first sight wasn't something she believed in, but from their first conversation, something was there. She might not have recognized it for what it was initially, but soon enough, her heart was telling her that Wilder was someone special.

Though they'd become friends, her heart had wanted more, even though she'd known it wasn't going to work.

Come the snow melt, Wilder would be off on his world travels once again. And her life was going to keep her in the US.

It had taken her years to fall in love with Mikhail, but with Wilder, she'd fallen faster and deeper. She wished with all her heart that they had a chance.

When Mikhail let out a groan beside her, Lexi focused on the screen again. The pair in second place had just taken over first from them, with one pair left to skate.

As the pair came into the waiting area, the pair in third got up and left. She and Mikhail and the other pair shifted down to free up space for the new first-place team.

This was definitely not something she'd missed. Most of the time, she and Mikhail had been the last or second to last to skate. Being third meant sitting through two more programs before knowing their final placement. It was excruciating, especially since there was so much riding on their performance here.

Mik muttered in Russian about how all their training time would have been wasted if they ended up third. Since they were at an event with mostly English-speaking skaters, it was unlikely any of them understood what he was saying. But still, Lexi responded—also in Russian—telling him to shut up.

Russian was a strong second language for Lexi. Since very young, she'd been surrounded by people who spoke the language. Mikhail's parents both spoke it, which was why he did. Then to have coaches who were also Russian, it had just been inevitable that she'd pick up the language.

"*Just settle. It's not done yet.*" She continued to speak in Russian, keeping her expression placid so the others in the area didn't have even a clue to what she was saying to Mik.

"*But we needed to win.*"

"*We'll be fine.*"

He kept muttering in Russian, but Lexi tuned him out. Rather than space out to thoughts of Wilder and how much she missed the man, she watched the first-place team as they skated.

Inwardly, she winced as she watched them struggle. It wasn't that she wanted them to skate perfectly, but it was never easy to watch someone falter, knowing it could happen to her and Mik.

She knew the moment when Mik realized what was going on. His body went taut beside her, and out of the corner of her eye, she saw him focused on the monitor.

When the program ended, the pair skated dejectedly to the center to acknowledge the crowd.

"*I think we have a chance.*"

Lexi agreed, but she didn't say anything. All they could do now was wait for the scores and hope that they'd done enough to end up with silver.

"*If we don't get at least silver, they're biased against us.*"

All she could do was nod, because Lexi agreed. That performance should drop the pair down to at least third. But politics could still come into play. As much as they'd tried to make the sport objective over the years, it still had a subjective component to it.

A roar went up from the crowd, containing a mix of cheers and boos. Lexi's breath froze in her lungs for a moment as the realization sunk in that they'd managed to do it. They'd won silver.

That position was honestly more than she had allowed herself to hope for. It wasn't that she thought they hadn't skated well enough to earn it. She'd just been uncertain that people would actually give them a fair shot, considering her past.

The pair who ended up in first jumped to their feet, screaming and hugging. Lexi stood when Mik did and exchanged a hug with him, though they didn't react as vocally as the other team.

It was a relief to have this first competition over, and she could only hope that they'd done enough to get them a pass onto the Olympic team. If they were given a spot, they'd have about a month to prepare.

Once the medal ceremony was over, they gathered up their things and left the arena to return to the hotel where they were staying. They went to Irina and Lev's room to discuss the competition. Or rather, the other three talked, and Lexi listened.

"If they put you on the Olympic team, we need to move back to Maine," Irina said, pinning Lexi with her gaze. "You don't need to stay in Serenity anymore. You're not working."

Lexi crossed her arms. "Alexander Remington is sponsoring me. I need to be on his property."

Plus, she really didn't want to leave Serenity. She had a feeling that Alexander probably wouldn't care if she moved back to Maine. But for some reason, she didn't want to leave the area.

It had offered her a soft place to land when she'd needed to find some direction in her life. And she knew that even though she had asked him to back off, if she needed something—anything—Wilder would be there for her. She wouldn't have that in Maine. She'd be alone with people who had let her down when she'd needed them the most.

"And you need to reconsider Worlds if we make it to the Olympics." Lev crossed his arms over his barrel chest. "Move back to Maine."

Though Irina had been pressuring her, Lev ramped it up. He was used to calling all the shots. However, Lexi did have a backbone. One that had only grown stronger after they'd abandoned her when she'd needed them. She didn't feel like she had to cave to his demands anymore.

"I'm not moving to Maine." Lexi got to her feet. "So if that's a deal-breaker, feel free to call Amberlyn and ask her to partner with Mik again."

"You'd give up the opportunity to go to the Olympics over moving back to Maine?" Irina demanded.

Lexi put her hands on her hips. "You'd give up a chance to go back to the Olympics with a top performing team over a move back to Maine?"

It was a showdown, but Lexi wasn't going to back down. She'd come to realize that going to the Olympics for the second time wasn't the be-all and end-all. The result of this competition had been validating. She could still skate at a high level of performance.

But did she need a second Olympic medal?

Not if it meant leaving a place she'd come to think of as home. Maine had nothing to offer her but memories that ended in hurt and loss. She didn't want that.

"You need me more than I need you," she told Lev.

She could see the anger building in his eyes, but she didn't back down. It felt like she was at a crossroads. A monumental moment in her life.

Finally, Lev waved his hand dismissively in the air. "If you don't win gold, you can't blame us."

Lexi turned and left their room, eager to get back to hers and take a long, hot shower. Her muscles ached, but it was an ache that testified to all the hard work they'd done over the past weeks. And it had paid off.

After her shower, she dressed in a pair of cozy pajamas, then placed a room service order. Mik and the coaches would probably go down to the restaurant, but she had no interest in that.

She curled up in a chair by the window and unlocked her phone to see if she had any messages. Warmth spread through her as she saw Wilder's name on her screen. She went to her text app to read the whole thing.

**Wilder:** *Congrats on getting silver! We've been praying for you, and you did such a GREAT job. It was a beautiful program, and you looked beautiful as well. Look forward to seeing you skate at the Olympics.*

As she read the message, tears pricked her eyes. After the interactions with Mik, Irina, and Lev, it was a balm to her spirit, and it encouraged her in a way nothing else had.

Even though she'd put distance between them—pushed him away, if she was going to be honest—he was still in her corner. Still praying for her. Still wanting the best for her.

She pressed the edge of her phone to her forehead as she bent her head forward. After she'd lost her dad and Mik and the coaches had abandoned her, she was sure that the only person who would be there as a support for her would be her mom.

Her phone dinged and when she looked at it, her heart pulsed with an ache as she saw two more messages had come in. One from Layla and Amelia, and one from Charli.

Both messages were enthusiastic about her performance and the result of the competition. Even though she'd had to pull back from coaching for the time being, they still supported her.

It reinforced her feeling that she was meant to be in Serenity. She wanted to coach the girls, especially Amelia, and she wanted to work with others who might want to learn from her. She didn't need to coach top tier skaters, though she did feel she had plenty to offer them.

She would fulfill her commitment to skate through the Olympics and possibly Worlds. She hadn't made up her mind about that just yet. But then she was done with competitive skating.

No longer was her drive to be a better skater than everyone else. She wanted—needed—to find a new purpose in her life.

After reading through the messages, she sent replies to Layla and Charli, thanking them for their support. She'd just finished the message to Charli when there was a knock on the door.

Getting up, she went to answer it. The young man there gave her the order she'd placed with room service. After thanking and tipping him, she carried it to the small table in the corner of the room.

It was just a simple salad with grilled chicken breast, but it would be enough. She hadn't been able to bring her meal prep with her, so she had to make do with what she could find on the menu.

As she ate, she contemplated her reply to Wilder. There was so much she wanted to say to him, but she was still ever mindful of the fact that his life would be taking him away from Serenity. Until she was sure that her feelings for him were solidly in the friendship area, she couldn't interact with him the way she wanted to.

*Thanks. I wish we could have won it on our own merit, but a win is a win, and we did skate clean. Still don't know about the Olympics. Hopefully, we'll find out this week.*

After she hit send, she went to her bag and pulled out her tablet. She found a site that had streamed the event and located their short program. Now that the competition was over, she was curious what the commentators had said with regards to her and Mik's return to the ice.

She wasn't as interested in their comments about their actual skating, though she did want to view it to see their performance for herself. Sometimes she didn't remember the details since she didn't dwell on anything that happened in the program until afterward.

Taking the tablet to the table, she set it up to play while she ate. As she picked up her fork, she took a moment to thank God for the food and for where they'd placed in the competition.

She wasn't sure that God cared all that much about figure skating, but she was thankful for how well it had gone, so it felt right to thank Him for how it had unfolded.

During the short program warmup, the commentators touched on Lexi's "retirement" along with Mik's pairing with Amberlyn. They said nothing about what had led to their partnership dissolving almost two years ago and only seemed to have positive things to say about their return to competition.

She skipped the other pairs' programs to get to her and Mik's short program, then watched as they skated through it. The program wasn't completely new, but they'd made changes to it, so the judges were seeing that revised version for the first time.

There were definitely a few issues, which was why they'd ended up third after the program. Their score was a an accurate reflection of how they'd skated.

Once that was done, she found the stream for the long program and once again listened during the skate warm up. The commentators didn't say anything more than what they'd said during the short program warmup, and she had to say she really appreciated that they didn't dip into the gossipy stuff that was found in the online forums.

And thankfully, they didn't seem to feel that she didn't deserve to be on the ice again.

After watching the long program, she felt like perhaps they'd been underscored, but not significantly. Not enough that they had been robbed of the gold.

When she finished her salad, she got up and put the dishes outside the door. She really wished that she was heading home the next day, but they still had to get through the Gala.

Her phone's screen lit up with a message, and she wasn't surprised to see that Wilder had messaged her back.

**Wilder:** *I can't believe that they wouldn't give you a spot. You have a proven track record, and you also proved tonight that you still have the ability to put a top performance on the ice. We'll be praying that it works out for you to be on the team.*

It seemed like Wilder thought that God would be interested in her future in skating. So maybe she could pray about it as well.

*Thank you.*

**Wilder:** *You're welcome! Praying for you is an honor and a privilege. Be sure and let us know when you hear.*

*I will.*

She wished she could video chat with him. It felt like forever since she'd seen his face, even though she'd seen him at church a week ago. But they hadn't talked. She'd arrived right before the service started and left as soon as it ended. It had been an attempt to keep some distance between them.

Still, he had become so important to her, and she didn't know how to accept a friendship with someone she loved.

Did he know how she felt? Did he care?

She'd done her best to hide her growing feelings from him, despite the fact that she'd opened up more to him than pretty much anyone else she'd ever met. The last thing she'd wanted was for him to feel like he had to let her down easy. There had been no indication that staying in Serenity was even an option for him.

No, it was best to keep her distance for as long as it took to get over Wilder.

Still, two days later, she texted him when they received news that they were part of the US figure skating team going to the Olympics. His enthusiastic response gave her warm and fuzzy feelings that showed that she wasn't making a whole lot of progress getting over him.

The morning was dark and cold as she headed to the rink the day after they arrived back from Nationals. She opened the door, frowning when she noticed the lights over the ice were on.

When she stepped inside, her gaze went to the ice where there was a bunch of balloons. Holding them was Wilder. He also had a bouquet of roses and a big sign that said *Congratulations, Lexi! We love you!*

But it was seeing Wilder again that took her breath away. She had missed him more than she'd realized.

"What's all this?" she asked as she reached the boards.

"Are you kidding me?" Wilder lifted the flowers and balloons into the air. "It's not every day someone gets to go to the Olympics. That deserves to be celebrated! I know that you're going to be focused on that, so the girls and I decided we'd just give you a little celebration before you got down to work."

Lexi wanted to weep with the futility of her feelings as she went to where he stood. He was so amazing. So full of life and fun. So ready to celebrate others. So genuine in his actions and words. He'd lit up her life with his easygoing, carefree approach to life.

And it would be all of those things that would take him away from her in April.

"Thank you," she said, taking the flowers he held out to her. It took every ounce of the emotional control she'd learned over the years to keep all of that sadness from showing. "This is all so amazing."

Wilder beamed, his smile wide, his eyes sparkling. "You deserve it. You've worked hard, and I know you're going to keep working hard. I'm not here to distract you from that. We just wanted to let you know that we're in your corner, cheering for you. No matter the outcome at the Olympics, we know that you're great."

The emotion that rushed through her hit the wall she was trying to keep in place. But despite the cracks, it held. She needed it to hold.

When the door to the rink opened, their attention shifted to Mik as he walked in the door. He scowled when his gaze landed on them. Jerking his knit cap off, he stalked over to where they stood.

"We need to practice," he muttered, dropping his bag on the bench. "With no distractions."

"I'll leave," Wilder said. "When I'm finished talking to Lexi."

Mik's scowl deepened, but he busied himself with his bag.

"Let's take this to your office," Wilder said.

"It's not really my office anymore," Lexi told him. "But I can put everything there while I'm practicing."

In the office, Wilder put the vase of flowers on the desk, then tied the balloons around the narrowest part of the vase. He set the sign on the chair.

"I'd better go before your coach arrives and assassinates me with a look."

Lexi chuckled as they left the office. "Yep. She can do that."

At the main door, she said, "Thank you again."

He reached out his hand as if he was going to touch her, but then dropped it, giving her a soft, warm smile. "I know you need to focus on your training, but if you ever need anything, just give me a call."

"I will," she said, wishing he didn't have to go. "It's going to be pretty much nose to the grindstone time. We didn't skate perfectly, so we'll be having to make sure that doesn't happen at the Olympics. Head down, skates on the ice."

"You can do it." With one final smile, he pushed against the door and walked out into the cold, dark morning.

Lexi watched him leave, feeling like he was taking a part of her heart with him.

# CHAPTER TWENTY-EIGHT

With a tray in his hands, Wilder headed down the stairs to the basement. Amelia and Layla were down there already, emptying the tray Layla had carried down. All kinds of drinks and snacks covered the coffee table in front of the overstuffed couches.

They were getting ready to watch a playback of the long program of the figure skating competition at the Olympics. Since the games were taking place in Europe, the time difference meant that they were televised in the early afternoon in Serenity.

Because of school and work, they hadn't been able to watch the competition as it was actually happening, but everyone had promised not to check the results before they had a chance to watch the competition together. They were going to pretend they were watching it live.

"Do you think they're going to win?" Amelia asked as she moved the glasses from Wilder's tray onto the coffee table. "Even though they're in second coming into the final competition?"

"I think they can," Wilder said. "Last time, they came in third and ended up second. And this time, it's a lot closer."

The short program scores between them and the team that ended up first had been within tenths of a point. But even if they weren't first, they were definitely within striking distance. If they skated clean, he thought they'd take the gold. Their long program was incredible.

He hadn't been able to read much in Lexi's expression following the short program. She'd had a smile on her face as she sat with Mik and the coaches after they'd skated, but it was her professional smile.

The other three had been busy talking back and forth, while Lexi had sat there like a rock in a babbling brook. Calm in the midst of a storm. It was similar to how she'd been when she'd competed before. No matter how Mik and her coaches reacted, she kept her calm.

He and the girls planned to watch the whole competition, even though Lexi wouldn't be skating until near the end. The others planned to come downstairs as it neared the time for her to skate.

He'd watched her short program on his phone between handling ski groups, but he wanted to watch this one on the big screen they had in the basement. Even if it meant watching it after the fact. He'd sent a text to Lexi to let her know their plans, so she'd know why he didn't send a message right away if—when—she won.

"Let's start the stream," Amelia said, pointing at the television.

They were watching a playback of a livestream because sometimes the television stations didn't show all the skaters, and Amelia, especially, wanted to see them all.

After grabbing their snacks and drinks, they settled on the overstuffed couches. Layla and Amelia took the loveseat, while Wilder stretched out on the large couch. Normally, he would have just watched the last six skaters, but since he didn't have anything better to do, he decided to hang out with the girls.

At some point, Charli brought Shiloh down to hang out with them, and Wilder transferred to the floor to sit next to her.

"How many pairs have gone?" she asked as she stood for a moment watching the TV.

"Six."

"Only six?"

"The long programs take longer," Layla said.

"It's just lucky we can fast forward through the ice resurfacing or we'd be sitting at four pairs."

"Well, give us a head's up when it's almost time for Lexi," Charli said as she headed for the stairs.

"I really like that girl's costume," Amelia said, pointing at the screen.

The girls chatted about what they liked about the pair currently on the ice. Wilder kept one eye on the screen, one eye on Shiloh, who was happily chewing on a toy as she sat with a pillow behind her.

When they were cleaning the ice for the second time, the camera showed some footage from behind the scenes.

"Stop fast forwarding, Uncle Wilder," Amelia said. "Isn't that Lexi?"

Sure enough, on the screen, Lexi and Mik were walking through the building in their Team USA uniforms. Lexi was pulling a small suitcase. They walked with confidence, not interacting with anyone along the way. Lexi looked like she had ear buds in, totally blocking out everything.

Even though this wasn't live, and he wasn't seeing her in person, Wilder's breath caught in his lungs.

He was so proud of her. She had come back from a horrible set of circumstances to show the world that she still had it. He might not know if she had won, but that didn't matter to him. He still admired her for working hard and braving a potentially hostile environment to try for Olympic gold one more time.

He made a note to ask her what she listened to when she was trying to block out the world. If they ever talked again.

Aside from the flowers and balloons after she and Mik were named to the Olympic team, they'd had no real contact.

He'd seen her at church a couple of times, but she'd sat near the back and left as soon as the service was over. He had no idea if her commitment to her training was simply because of the Olympics, or if she'd always trained so hard.

Had she always trained to the exclusion of everything and everyone else in her life? Or was it just to cut him out?

That day would show if it all paid off. He didn't know how Lexi viewed it. But, in Wilder's mind, if they skated a clean program, he would consider it a success. Regardless of whether or not they won gold.

Something told him that Mik and the coaches—and possibly Lexi—wouldn't feel the same way.

By the time the second to last flight of skaters had finished, they'd seen a real assortment of programs. Some that had been well skated. Others, not so much.

"I'm gonna go tell Mom it's almost time," Layla said as she jumped to her feet.

Amelia scooted down onto the floor next to Wilder. "I hope Lexi does good and doesn't fall."

Wilder glanced down at her. "She's trained very hard, but sometimes, things happen."

"Maybe we should pray for her," Amelia said. "That she has a good skate. Do you think God would care about that?"

"I think He would." Wilder considered his niece, then said, "Did you want to pray now?"

Amelia nodded and reached for Wilder's hand. Smiling as her small fingers tightened over his, Wilder listened as she asked God to give Lexi a good skate and to help her win the gold medal.

Did God answer prayers retroactively? Hopefully He did so that Amelia could see that answer to prayer.

Soon, the ice cleaning was done, and the last flight of skaters was on the ice to warm up. Layla reappeared, followed soon after by Janessa and Will. The rest of them showed up a few minutes later.

Will sat down in one of the armchairs, and Janessa settled on his lap. Lee and Rori sat down on the loveseat, while Amelia and Layla stayed on the floor with Wilder. Charli and Blake sat on the couch with Shiloh, who was having a bottle.

Amelia continued to show her knowledge of the sport as she pointed things out during the warmup for Lexi, Mik, and the other pairs. It rankled a bit to see Lexi skate hand in hand with Mik, but Wilder knew it was all part of being a pairs skater.

They skated together around the rink, practicing a few jumps and a throw before they separated to warm up on their own. Wilder wished the camera would stay on Lexi, but he had to be content with glimpses of her as the warmup progressed.

Finally, the warmup period ended, and most of the skaters exited the rink, leaving only the fourth-place team on the ice since the teams skated in reverse order of how they placed after the short program.

Lexi took her guards from the coach, then slipped them on. She disappeared with the other skaters as the first team to skate took their position at center ice.

The fourth and third place pairs both skated, with the third-place team faltering and ending up in second after the fourth-place pair, who had skated a flawless program. It just showed how easily things could change with a simple two footed landing or a hand down on the ice.

"I'm so nervous," Amelia said as she clutched her hands under her chin, her wide-eyed gaze on the television.

Finally, Lexi and Mik circled the ice hand-in-hand, then stopped in the middle of the ice to get into their starting pose. None of the nerves Lexi was surely feeling showed on her face. Her expression was beautifully serene as she lifted her chin and waited for the music to begin.

"I love her costume," Layla said. "It's so beautiful."

Wilder had to agree. Lexi had mentioned changing her costume for this one, and though he wasn't sure why, it was clear that she'd made a good decision. It had a fitted top and a flowy skirt in shades of dark purple and blue, but it lacked the nude illusion that many of the other female skaters had chosen as part of their costumes.

Her dark hair was pulled back from her face in an intricate braid, showing her delicate features. There was determination on her face, and on Mik's as well. The camera zoomed in on her face just as her eyes closed.

Wilder thought that this was more than just a skate for a gold medal. At least for Lexi. This was her opportunity on a world stage to rise above the things that people wanted to pin on her because of her father's actions.

"Here we go," Wilder murmured as the music started and a hush fell over the room. When Lexi opened her eyes and began to move, Wilder wondered if she'd been praying or if it had just been part of the starting position.

There was no denying the chemistry on the ice between Lexi and Mik. It was an athletic chemistry that showed itself in how easily their movements flowed around each other. It was like they knew exactly where the other person was at all times. Their skill and athleticism were equal.

They both completed the difficult jumps without error and the jump combinations with ease and flow. And it was like the music had been written just for them.

"Oh, that was so beautiful," Amelia murmured when the program came to an end. "They have to win."

Wilder agreed. The end of their Romeo and Juliet program might have been tragic, but the program itself was a triumph for both Lexi and Mik. Wilder wasn't sure they could have skated it any better.

He thought the program deserved the gold, but the last team to skate had done a great job in the short program, so it stood to reason that they'd also do a great job in the long one too. These were the best of the best, after all.

The commentators had calculated how much was needed for them to temporarily take first place and maintain their silver position. The wait for the scores seemed to stretch on forever.

There was tension on the faces of Mik and the coaches. A lot was riding on this for them, too. Even Lexi showed some uncharacteristic tenseness as she waited. There was no smile on her face as she stared up at something, presumably the scoreboard.

"They're taking too long," Layla said. "Why is it taking so long?"

It did seem to take an eternity before a roar went up from the crowd, and the commentators shared the score, which well exceeded the amount they needed to retain their position.

"This team has had a limited season together, so this is a season's best," the man said. "But it's also not far off their personal best. I'm not sure they could have skated this program any better."

Wilder grinned at the commentator's words. He thought they'd skated it amazingly well, but he wasn't the professional. And he was a bit biased. So hearing someone who knew what they were talking about say that it was great was a good sign.

"I know I shouldn't wish for someone to fall," Amelia said, her voice soft. "But I really hope that they do. Sorry, Daddy."

Blake gave a huff of laughter. "I understand why you feel that way, Berry. However, sometimes even doing your absolute best doesn't guarantee winning. And their victory would mean more if they won against another program that was skated well."

"Yeah. I suppose."

It was probably a difficult concept for someone Amelia's age to grasp. However, it was a good learning experience, especially if she hoped to go into competitive skating herself.

The first placed team skated well, with no falls, but as far as Wilder was concerned, their program lacked the beauty of Lexi and Mik's. So, in his mind, there was still hope for Lexi and Mik.

"This team is going to need a season's best in order to beat the program by Alexandra Corbyn and Mikhail Andropov," the female commentator said. "Their personal best score would do it, but they haven't achieved that this season with this program."

Wilder said a prayer that all the hard work Lexi and Mik had put into their skating would pay off. Blake was right. As long as they skated a clean program—which they had—they should be pleased

with                                                        themselves.
But he had a much more laid-back approach to things, even sports.
Lexi and Mik's mindset was probably a lot different.

A roar went up from the crowd, but Wilder didn't know who
they were cheering for. But then Amelia jumped to her feet, punch-
ing the air with her fist.

"Alexandra Corbyn and Mikhail Andropov take the gold," the
commentator announced. "After a break in their partnership for a
year and a half, and Mikhail taking on a new partner for a season,
they've come back together and won the gold."

Lexi's smile had grown a bit as she hugged Mik and their
coaches. It was like she was finally letting her emotions show. And
for good reason.

As he watched them celebrate, Wilder wished he could be there
with Lexi to share her joy after what they'd accomplished. But was
there a place in her life for him? Was there a place in his life for
her?

Would she even want him in her life?

He stared at the screen, watching as someone interviewed Lexi
and Mik. Like previous interviews Wilder had seen of them, Mik
took control. Unlike those previous interviews, however, Lexi
didn't stand there looking up at Mik with a smile. Though she had
a smile on her face, her attention stayed on the interviewer.

"And how about Worlds?" the woman asked. "Will we see you
there?"

Wilder held his breath as he waited for Mik's response. He
glanced down at Lexi, then looked back at the interviewer with a
sly smile. "We'll have to see."

Wilder wasn't sure if he hoped that they'd go or not. But in the
end, he'd support Lexi either way. He just hoped that she didn't
get pressured into it by Mik and the coaches if she really didn't
want to go. However, maybe having had a taste of competing again,

she'd be tempted to return to that life... for more than just this season.

He'd been praying a lot lately about his feelings for Lexi. He knew that he couldn't just base his decisions on how he felt. Pursuing anything with her would be a major change in his life, and he couldn't just jump into it without seeking God's will.

They continued to watch as the winners were presented with their medals. Lexi shook hands with the other skaters as she and Mik made their way to the gold medal position on the platform that was set up for the ceremony.

Wilder felt tears prick his eyes as the American national anthem began to play.

When it finished, Charli cleared her throat and said, "Well, that was amazing."

"I want to skate in the Olympics," Amelia announced. "And I want Lexi to show me how to do it."

Wilder glanced at Charli in time to see her exchange a glance with Blake. Was that an *oh no* look, or an *I told you so* one? He'd heard a lot of stories about athletes who'd been motivated to go to the Olympics after being inspired by watching an athlete perform at the Olympics. Maybe this was Amelia's moment.

"Do you think I can do that, Daddy?" Amelia asked, looking over at Blake.

"You can do anything you want, Berry. As long as you're willing to do the hard work."

Amelia nodded. "I'll do the hard work."

"I don't think I want to go to the Olympics," Layla said. "Lexi has had to work so hard, she hasn't even been able to coach us. But I'll be there to cheer you on."

Amelia smiled at her sister. "Thanks, Layla."

Soon the broadcast of the Olympics pairs skating final ended. There was still one more skating event, which was the team finals, and then Lexi would be able to come home.

Or would she go to France to see her mom? Or would she go to Maine?

He had no idea what her next plans were.

Everyone got up and began to gather up the snacks to take everything back upstairs to the kitchen. Even the girls pitched in, picking up the garbage.

Once everything was cleaned up, Wilder jogged up the stairs to his bedroom, then dropped down on his back on the bed. Lifting his phone, he tapped out a message to Lexi.

*Congratulations! What an amazing accomplishment! All your hard work has paid off. It was an absolutely beautiful, strong performance!*

He didn't expect an answer, since it was likely she was asleep, given the time difference. After thinking it over, he composed another message.

*We'd love to throw you a party when you get back. Do you think you'd be up for it?*

*If not, that's fine. We were all just so excited to see you win!*

After he sent the messages, he groaned as he tossed the phone onto the bed beside him. He should have waited until she responded to his first message before sending off the second and third. His impatience had gotten the better of him.

He went downstairs a little while later to help with supper by entertaining Shiloh. Blake was flipping burgers on the stove, while Charli manned the French fries in the air fryer. The girls were in charge of setting the table in the breakfast nook. Janessa and Will were up in their room since Janessa wasn't feeling great. Lee and Rori were out on a date.

It was a simple meal, but Wilder wouldn't complain because it tasted great. The girls ate theirs quickly, then asked if they could take their dessert downstairs to eat while they watched some television.

Once it was just the three adults and Shiloh, Charli sat down across the table from Wilder, cupping her mug in her hands.

"What do you think about Amelia wanting to be an Olympic figure skater?" she asked.

"The dream has to start somewhere, right?" Wilder plucked a cookie off the plate in front of them. "And for someone hoping to rise to those levels of competition, it's probably best they start young."

"I'm not sure we can afford to have her train the way Lexi trains."

Wilder wanted to say that Lexi probably wouldn't charge them that much. However, it would mean going from one lesson a week to more. Many more. And he had no idea if Lexi was actually going to come back to Serenity to coach.

Blake reached out to cover Charli's hand. "If it seems that Amelia really has potential, we'll figure out how to make it work."

Charli nodded. "I want to make sure she can get the training she needs."

"We just have to pray for God's guidance as we talk with her and figure out if this is indeed her future."

"Do you know if Lexi is planning to come back here to coach?"

Wilder shook his head. "No clue. We haven't talked about her future or anything past the Olympics. At this point, I don't even know if she's going to Worlds."

"Haven't you guys been talking at all?"

"Not really," Wilder admitted. "She made it clear that her priority was her training, so we haven't talked much beyond just the odd text here or there."

"That's just so weird," Charli said. "Every time we've all been together, she's really seemed into you."

"I don't know." Wilder broke off a piece of cookie but didn't eat it. "We get along really well, but we both agreed that friendship was all we could have. Our lives are too different for anything else."

"So does that mean that if circumstances had been different, you'd date her?"

Wilder shrugged, then ate the piece of cookie to buy himself some time.

"Do you really like her?" Charli asked when he didn't respond.

He definitely did like her, but it went more than that. The connection they'd shared confused him because they were so different. But there was no denying that he loved her. He'd never really understood the saying *absence makes the heart grow fonder* until Lexi had put distance between them.

Each day they were apart made him realize that he wanted her in his life every day. He wanted to stop by the rink before his shift to say good morning. And once he was finished on the slopes, he wanted to be able to go to the rink to see how her day went.

But that only worked when they were both in the same place, which, given his current life, would only be for a few months out of the year.

"Have you prayed about this?" Blake asked.

Wilder nodded. Lexi was the first woman he'd really focused prayer on. Anytime she came to mind, he said a prayer for her, which meant that he was saying several prayers a day for her.

Charli looked at them over the rim of her mug. "And how do you feel God is leading you?"

"I don't know."

How was one supposed to know?

His feelings weren't leaving. If anything, they were getting stronger. Was that from God?

"Are you ready to make changes in your life?" Charli asked. "Because obviously that would be required if you were going to pursue something with Lexi."

He'd been thinking about that, trying to figure out if there was a way to keep part of his summer plans while still having a relationship.

"Don't run from love without giving it serious thought," Blake said as he wrapped his arm around Charli. "We were fortunate to have gotten a second chance, but that's not always the case. Don't let Lexi be your biggest regret."

"Try," Charli encouraged him. "You've only been looking at why it won't work. Take some time to think and pray about how to make it work."

Wilder nodded. He could do that, but Lexi had to want to do that too. It wouldn't make any difference if he was willing to consider a serious relationship with Lexi if she wasn't willing to do the same.

It was time for a real conversation with her. Hopefully she'd come back to Serenity once the Olympics were over, and she could spare him a few minutes for a talk, even if she was preparing to go to Worlds.

Maybe it was time for more balloons and flowers.

# CHAPTER TWENTY-NINE

Lexi glared at Mik, trying to keep her temper under control. However, the man was making it exceedingly difficult. After so many years together, he knew what buttons to push with her, and it was infuriating.

But they'd never fought as much as they had in the past few weeks. She tried to keep things calm, but the only time Mik stopped trying to antagonize her was when they were at a competition.

"I agreed to the Olympics," Lexi told him. "You're just lucky that I also decided to go to Nationals and Worlds. But that's it. Once Worlds is done, we're finished."

It seemed no matter how many times she told him that, he just wasn't hearing her. Well, he probably *did* hear her. He was just choosing to ignore what she was saying because it wasn't what he wanted to hear from her.

Mik crossed his arms and returned her glare. "You owe me."

"I what?" She mirrored his position, crossing her arms as they faced off. "You dropped me. How can you say I owe you anything?"

"If it weren't for your father stealing all of our money, we wouldn't have lost so much."

Lexi's stomach twisted at his words. She knew in her mind that she didn't bear the responsibility for what her father had done, and yet... the guilt was still there.

For a moment, she considered giving in to his demands. Maybe she *did* owe him. But how much did she owe him? Would he use this manipulation to gain control over her and her life for as long as it served his purposes?

She couldn't allow herself to be caught in that situation. Over the past few weeks, she'd come to understand what she did and didn't want in her life, and Mik and competitive skating were landing firmly in the "didn't" column.

"I don't owe you anything, Mikhail," she told him, keeping her voice as calm as possible. "I am not responsible for my father's actions. He—and he alone—bears that."

"If it weren't for your father, my family would be in a much better position."

"You benefited from what he did as much as I did," Lexi reminded him. "You didn't have to pay for ice time, the coaches, or the costumes. If you hadn't been partnered with me, you would have had to lay out money for all of that stuff. You were happy enough to take all those freebies along the way."

Mik spat a curse in her direction. "I probably would have been better off without you as a partner."

That statement was laughable, but Lexi knew that if she laughed, it would make the situation worse. There was no way he could have found a better partner. They had been a perfect pair, and they had the gold medals to prove it.

"I should have found someone else and paid for all those things. At least my family would have something."

Lexi didn't believe that they were quite as destitute as Mik was making them out to be. His parents were highly sought after research scientists who—according to Mik—the US government had helped escape from Russia in order for them to work for the States.

Had they lost money to her dad? Undoubtedly, but from what Mik had said over the years, they'd been well compensated for the information and skills they brought to the government lab where they both worked. They'd had a gorgeous home, several cars, a big boat, and always took expensive vacations.

322 · KIMBERLY RAE JORDAN

"So your family had to move?" she asked. "Did they sell the boat and the cars?"

Mik's expression hardened, and when he didn't answer her questions, she figured none of that had happened. Meanwhile, she and her mom had lost their home in Maine and their vacation home in Colorado.

And Mik had still had his reputation. Meanwhile, Lexi had been blackballed, and she was done with it all. She'd shown the world that she still had the ability to skate and win, so she had nothing left to prove.

"I'm done skating competitively," Lexi reiterated. "It was always the plan for us to retire after this Olympics anyway, even before everything happened with my dad."

"But we were supposed to have started up a skating school. That's not going to happen now that we don't have the rink."

Even if they still had the rink, there was no way Lexi would work alongside Mik. They'd managed to keep the cracks from showing while they'd competed, but it wasn't sustainable long-term.

Mik clearly disliked her, and Lexi couldn't say that she held any fondness for the man she'd once planned to marry. If they continued to work together, it would be far from an ideal arrangement.

"You wanted one more Olympic medal so you could end your career on a high note instead of the low note it would have been with Amberlyn," Lexi reminded him. "You got what you wanted, so just let it go. If you keep pushing, we can just go ahead and pull out of Worlds, because I can't see skating together with so much tension and anger between us."

"We are *not* canceling Worlds," Mik said with a shake of his finger in her face.

"Enough," Irina exclaimed with a clap of her hands. "Get to work."

The fact that the woman had stood silent until the moment Lexi threatened to pull out of Worlds told her that Irina was hoping that

Mik might succeed in convincing her to reconsider her retirement. All of it irked Lexi and made her not want to set one blade on the ice.

But still, she jerked off her guards and stepped onto the ice, moving away from the boards with long smooth strokes. She took off, heading for the far end of the ice, eager to work out some of her tension.

It was no surprise when the practice was an abysmal failure. Her individual jumps were wobbly, with her even falling on a couple of them. The pairs elements were outright disastrous.

Lexi wasn't on board for doing throw jumps, but she also knew better than to voice that objection to Irina. But as Mik flung her into the air, Lexi realized she was in for a rough landing and tried to not tense up too much. Still, after falling on the landing, she slid backward into the boards, knocking the wind out of her.

She sat there for a moment, taking deep breaths. It wasn't the first time she'd experienced such a fall, but it had been awhile since it had last happened. With an inward groan, she got to her feet, refusing to allow Mik or Irina to see how much it had jarred her. She was going to have some bruises after this practice.

When their training time finally came to an end, Lexi couldn't have been happier.

"Same time tomorrow," Irina said, as if Lexi would forget.

Or maybe she was making sure that Lexi didn't change her mind about Worlds.

"I'm retiring after Worlds, Irina. You and Mik need to understand that."

Irina gave a single nod of her head, then sailed out of the arena, wrapped in her precious fur coat. Mik wasn't far behind her.

Lexi let out a long breath, her cheeks puffing with the effort. Since the rink was still quiet, she slumped down on the bench but didn't remove her skates right away.

She was exhausted. Between the training, the flights, jetlag, and competing, her body had taken a beating. Previously, she hadn't had as hard a time dealing with all of that, but this time, it was a struggle.

Was it because her body and her mind weren't in sync? Before, she'd been totally focused on training and competing. Her mind had been committed, and so had her body.

This time around, however, her mind wasn't one hundred percent on board with the training and competitions. While she'd been at the Olympics, she'd been thinking a lot about her mom, about Wilder and Serenity, about the life she wanted to build outside of competitive skating.

She missed her mom and the hugs she always gave her. She missed coaching the girls. She missed seeing Wilder walk through the door of the rink, his eyes twinkling as he smiled.

She hadn't wanted to be so far away from everyone. Now she was back in Serenity, and it still wasn't enough. She hadn't seen Wilder since her return, and she wondered when she might. It was possible it wouldn't be until she went to church.

They'd shared a few messages, which had been nice, but it wasn't the same as talking to him face to face. But it was her own fault that wasn't happening. She'd pushed him away.

Training had been a convenient excuse. In reality, there had still been time for her to spend with him and the others if she'd allowed herself to.

"Everything okay?"

Lexi straightened and looked up to see Talya standing beside the bench.

"Yep." Lexi gave her a smile. "How've things been here?"

"We've had some busy days, but not like we had over the holidays."

"That's good."

"Congrats on winning gold at the Olympics. It was a beautiful free skate."

Lexi had to force her smile. Her competitions were still a touchy subject, given the argument she and Mik had just had.

"Thanks."

"Are you going to Worlds?"

"That's the plan."

"I hope you get gold again."

"We're certainly going to try for it." Lexi leaned over and unlaced her skates. "But one never knows how it's going to go."

Thankfully, Luke arrived then and distracted Talya from their conversation. Lexi finished taking off her skates, then got up and went to the office to get her boots and jacket. She planned to head home and take a long hot bath before falling into bed for a nap.

Somehow, she needed to get her mind and body back on the same track. Hopefully, pampering her body a bit might help.

The ringing of her phone woke Lexi later that night. Though she'd had a nap, she had still gone to bed at her normal time, knowing that she needed all the rest she could get. But apparently, someone was determined to keep her from sleeping undisturbed.

Blinking, she squinted at the phone, then frowned when she saw Irina's name on the screen.

"Hello?"

"Alexandra, Mikhail has been in a car accident."

The words hit her hard in her half-dazed state. "What?"

"He was in a car accident and is in the hospital."

"Is he okay?"

"I don't know yet. They won't tell me anything because I'm not family. His parents are on their way. They phoned them but couldn't give them much information either. Just that he'd been taken to the hospital."

Lexi sat up, running a hand through her hair and dragging the elastic out. Leaning forward, she said, "Are you at the hospital?"

"No. There's no hospital here."

"He's in Coeur d'Alene?"

"Yes."

Lexi wanted to pepper her with questions, but it seemed pretty clear that the woman didn't know anything. "Do you need me to do anything?"

"*Nyet.*"

"Well, call me as soon as you have an update, please."

"I will." She paused, then said, "You made him very upset with your conversation earlier today."

Irina's words left her speechless. For a moment. "Are you telling me it's my fault that Mik had an accident?"

The non-committal noise Irina made said more than any words could have what the woman thought.

"No, Irina," Lexi said, coming wide awake. "I done taking responsibility for the actions of others. Not my father and not Mik. If Mik was upset, he had no one but himself to blame. He knew what we agreed to and shouldn't have tried to convince me to change my mind."

Rather than respond, Irina hung up, leaving Lexi to deal with a mixture of anger, frustration, and worry. She might not be getting along with Mik, but she didn't wish him any ill will.

Lexi looked at the time on her phone. 11:04 She'd only been asleep for about an hour, but now she wasn't sure she'd be able to fall back to sleep.

The urge to call Wilder was strong, and she knew without a doubt that he'd answer her, even though it was late. Just talking to him would make her feel better, she was sure of it.

She didn't really know how she felt about the situation with Mik beyond worry, especially when she had no details. Was it a concussion? A broken arm? Bumps and bruises? Something worse? How had it happened?

Lexi hated questions with no answers.

She tapped the screen to bring up Wilder's contact information. Taking a deep breath, she made the call.

"Hello?" His voice was rough, like he'd been asleep already.

"Wilder, it's me. Lexi."

"Lexi?" She could hear movement, and then he cleared his throat. "Is something wrong?"

How she wished that she could just call him because she wanted to talk to him. But they didn't have that sort of relationship, so of course he'd know that her calling him meant something was wrong.

"Lexi?" he prompted.

"Sorry. Irina just called to let me know that Mik has been in a car accident."

"Really? Is he okay?"

"I don't know. No one will give us details because we're not his family."

"Did they take him to the hospital in Coeur d'Alene?" he asked.

"Yes."

"I know my brother has contacts there and could probably find out how he is, but I don't think he'd do it because he's constrained by privacy laws. Is Mik's family coming?"

"Irina said they were on their way, which makes me think it might be serious."

"I'm so sorry to hear that."

"I probably shouldn't have called," she said with a sigh. "I'm just worried and needed to talk to someone."

"I'm glad you decided that someone was me," Wilder assured her, his voice gentle. "I told you if you ever needed something to call me."

"I thought that was for things like a flat tire or getting stuck in a snowbank."

"Well, it was definitely for those things, but also for other things too. Like this situation."

Lexi sighed. "Mik and I had a fight earlier today."

"What about?"

"He doesn't want to retire after Worlds, and he's trying to get me to continue competing next season."

"And you don't want to?" Wilder asked. "You did so well at the Olympics. I thought you might want to."

"It's different now." Lexi plucked at the fabric of her comforter where it was bunched in her lap. "Whatever connection Mik and I had that made skating with him easy, is now gone. There's a lot of anger and tension between us."

"It's not showing when you skate."

"That's good. I work hard to not let it show, and I'm sure Mik does as well."

"So he didn't want to take no for an answer?"

Lexi shook her head, even though he couldn't see the movement. "He said that I owed him."

"What?" The outrage in Wilder's voice validated Lexi's own feelings about Mik's assumption. "That is ridiculous."

"His family lost a good chunk of their savings because of my dad," Lexi told him. "So he says I owe him and need to continue to skate with him because of that."

"Like I said... ridiculous."

"I know what my dad did to them wasn't right, but for the majority of our skating career, my dad covered all the expenses. We had a private rink. Devoted coaches. Tutors, so we didn't have to attend school. So, in their case at least, the money my dad took was actually going to support their son's career."

"So you told him no, and he got mad?"

"Yeah. He was really ticked off at me. I think Irina was hoping that he'd succeed in convincing me because she didn't tell him to back off."

"It might all be a moot point now," Wilder said.

"That's true. Depending on how injured he is, he might not be able to skate at Worlds."

"I hope that's not the case."

"You think I should skate at Worlds?"

"The thing is, Lexi, I think you belong on the ice. Your skating is absolutely breathtaking. So if you want to go to Worlds, and Mik is okay to skate, then I think you should. Beyond that? I think you should choreograph a singles program and let me video it and put it up on your YouTube channel."

"I don't have a YouTube channel," she said.

"Not yet, you don't. But you could, and it would be a way for you to continue to share the beauty of your skating without having to travel or compete. You could also do some coaching videos."

"You've thought this through," Lexi said, pleased that he'd been thinking about her even though they hadn't been talking.

"I have," he agreed. "You have a talent that you should share with the world, and I have the ability to help you make that happen."

Lexi slid down against her pillow, pulling her comforter up over her shoulders. All the strain of the day—of the past few weeks, actually—slid away. She couldn't do anything for Mik right then, but maybe she could figure out a piece of her future.

"So you're proposing we collaborate on YouTube?" she asked.

"Yep. I think we'd make a great team."

She wondered what he meant exactly. Was he strictly talking about doing videos together? Or was there something more? Could there be something more?

"How would you video me if you're not here?" she asked. "Would I have to find someone to take the videos, and then you'd edit them?"

There was a pause on the other end of the line, then Wilder said, "Actually, I'm probably going to be spending more time here now."

"You're going to quit traveling?" Her heart leapt at the thought of him being around more than just the winter months.

"Not entirely. I'm still going to try to spend three or four weeks at the orphanages during the summer, but I think maybe it's time to scale back on my traveling around the world for the other months."

"Wow. I didn't think you'd want to do that."

"I think it's what God wants me to do," Wilder said. "It's funny how something that was once so important to a person can fade when something of more importance comes along."

"I sort of understand that," Lexi said. "That's how I feel about competing. It was once my world. My total focus. But I just don't want to do it anymore. I've reached the pinnacle, so I don't have anything more to prove. I still want to skate, but competing is just not that important now."

"Are you going to coach?"

"I'd like to continue to coach the girls, if they want that, and possibly pick up a few more students. Right now, I'm not looking for anything too intense. Maybe I'll see if Kayleigh will give me my job back."

Wilder chuckled. "I'm sure she will if that's really what you want to do."

"To be honest, it's not my favorite thing, but it gives me access to good ice, and it pays the bills."

"That it does."

Silence stretched between them, but Lexi didn't find it awkward. She was just happy to know that there was someone who cared on the other end of the line.

"I hope Mik isn't too badly injured," she said as her thoughts circled back around to him. "He's been so upset and angry since we started skating together again."

"Given how his programs were going with his previous partner, I'd wager a guess that he was already upset and angry. He brought his bad attitude with him into your partnership."

"If he's not able to skate at Worlds, he's going to be livid."

"If that's what happens, I guess it puts to rest the question of whether you should continue to skate or not."

Lexi didn't think that Mik would give up on trying to convince her to go another season, especially if they didn't make Worlds because of his accident. He'd say he had time to recover from his injuries and would be ready to go by the next season.

Lexi just couldn't see it working out for the two of them, and if he was badly injured, he would need to focus on recovery rather than on her. Because she knew with confidence and peace that her path was leading her away from competition.

# CHAPTER THIRTY

Wilder left the house earlier than he needed to in order to make his shift at the ski shop, but it was necessary. When he pulled into the parking lot of the rink, he wasn't surprised to see Lexi's Audi there already. In fact, he'd counted on her being there.

He'd had a feeling that even if Mik was still in the hospital, Lexi would be at the rink. He was pretty sure that she found solace on the ice when things were unsettled in her life.

Pushing open his car door, he stepped out into the cold, wintry morning. Plumes of frosty air appeared as he exhaled. Even with gloves on his hands were cold, so he shoved them into the pockets of his jacket.

It wasn't the greatest weather for skiing. However, the die-hards would be out, regardless of how cold it was. They'd dress in layers and be ready to endure the cold for the sake of the thrill of a run down the slopes.

The more casual skier, though, would most likely hole up in front of a fireplace somewhere in the resort. Probably with a hot drink in hand.

Wilder hurried across the parking lot to the front door, eager to be out of the cold. Gripping the large door handle, he let himself into the rink.

He was immediately greeted by the sound of music drifting through the air. He didn't recognize the singer, but then, he didn't really listen to a lot of that style of music.

The song had a bluesy tone to it, and Wilder wondered if it meant something to Lexi.

He thought he'd see her skating, but there was no movement on the ice. It wasn't until he neared the boards that he spotted her. She sat on the ice against one of the wooden posts that joined the boards together, legs straight in front of her, with skates on her feet.

Her head was tipped back as if she was staring at something on the ceiling, although there was nothing there. But then he realized that her eyes were closed.

For a moment, Wilder paused, taking in the sight of her. She looked beautiful, sitting there on the ice. The place that was her element. He hated to interrupt her, so he carefully braced his arms on the upper rail of the boards and waited.

He would have paid good money to know what was going through her mind. After their conversation the night before, he was encouraged. It was possible that Lexi felt the same way about a relationship that he did.

The very idea made him want to charge ahead, but Wilder didn't move any closer to her. He was content to watch her from a distance for the moment.

He'd continued to pray about a relationship with Lexi and what his future might look like if she wanted that, too. Obviously, the biggest change had to be how much time he spent traveling in the summer.

It would be easiest to consider cutting the time he spent traveling to places like New Zealand or Iceland. Those trips added no significant value to his life beyond giving him enjoyment of the beauty of God's creation. He was starting to revisit some of the places he'd already been to, so deciding not to do that sort of traveling anymore wouldn't be a big loss.

Over the years he had made some interesting connections with fellow travelers in hostels, which he'd miss doing. But the most important part of his travels of late had been the time he spent at the orphanages, and that wouldn't change. Even if he made other changes in his life, that could—and would—stay the same.

Once he'd decided that he could make the change necessary in his life to support a relationship, he'd actually gotten excited about the possibility.

He'd never been overly resistant to change in his life. He just needed a good reason for it. And he thought that making room in his life for a relationship was a very good reason.

Of course, it would all be for naught if he'd misread his interactions with Lexi. If Lexi wasn't interested, the changes wouldn't be necessary. At least not yet.

Another song started once that one ended, but it was in the same style. Lexi didn't move, so Wilder went to the entrance of the ice and stepped out onto it. He felt more confidence moving on ice when he was wearing skates, but he managed to make it to where Lexi sat.

Turning, he lowered himself onto the ice next to her, propping his back against the boards.

As she turned her head towards him, she opened her eyes. When he smiled at her, she smiled in return, and he felt some of the worry he'd had for her ease.

"Hey," he said, realizing that up this close, he could see there were dark grey flecks in her light blue eyes. They truly were beautiful, just like her.

"Hi. What are you doing here?"

"I was worried about you," he said. "Wanted to make sure that you were doing okay." He paused. "Are you?"

She turned her head, looking back at the ice as she shrugged. "I haven't heard anything more about Mik. I'm scared to contact anyone to get information because I assume they're all blaming me."

As the cold seeped into his legs and butt, Wilder reached for her hand. She tightened her fingers around his and clung to him.

"It's not your fault," he assured her. "Mik is responsible for his own actions, and if people are blaming you for what's happened to him, they're wrong."

"I just want to live my life free of this guilt everyone keeps trying to heap on me."

Wilder rubbed his thumb over the back of her hand. "I wish there was something I could do to help you with that. But in the end, you're the only one who can let go of it. I can tell you that you shouldn't feel guilty, but you need to work that through yourself."

She didn't say anything, but he felt her shift some of her weight to lean against his arm. It made Wilder want to gather her close.

"Do you think you played a role in what happened with your dad or Mik?"

"My dad said he stole in order to provide me and my mom with a life of wealth. He said he needed the money to help cover the expenses of my career. So yeah, I do feel like I played a role in it. Like I built my career on the backs of the people who gave my dad their money."

"Do you think that you wouldn't have excelled the way you did if you had to do it the way other skaters do?"

"I think I still would have been a great skater. I was willing to work hard. My dad could have created an outdoor rink for me to practice on in winter and paid a rental fee at a local rink. My mom could have homeschooled me instead of hiring a tutor. We could have done it."

"So the fact that your dad chose to do it the way he did is not your fault. You were a kid when he began making those decisions."

"I know."

"This is something you need to pray about," Wilder said. "God can help you with your guilt. And maybe talking to a counsellor might help, too."

Wilder thought she might laugh at the suggestion, but instead, she nodded. "My mom suggested that when everything happened, but I told her I was fine."

"Sometimes our parents know best," Wilder said, then chuckled. "But don't tell my parents I said that."

"I won't."

"Thanks. I appreciate you having my back."

"Anytime."

Wilder liked the sound of that. "I've got yours too."

"We should move to the bench," Lexi said. "My legs are frozen."

"So's my butt."

Wilder let go of Lexi's hand and got to his feet, reaching out to grab onto the boards to steady himself. He held out his hand to Lexi to help her up. She grabbed on tight and came up to her feet more easily than Wilder had.

Together, they left the ice and went to the bench, which was infinitely more comfortable. The music kept playing as they settled on the bench.

"I had another reason for coming to look for you today," Wilder said.

She glanced over at him. "What's that?"

"I wanted to ask you out on a date."

Lexi froze for a moment, then shifted to face him more fully. "What?"

"I discovered that I really, really like you, and I want to spend more time with you, with the hope of being in a serious relationship one day. I mean, if that's what you want."

"But... I thought our lives didn't mesh well together."

"Are you planning to stay here in Serenity?"

She nodded. "I hope to. I like it here, and it's been good to me."

"Well, I'm willing to make some changes to my life,too," Wilder told her, relishing the sense of peace he had as he said those words.

Instead of smiling, though, Lexi frowned. "Why?"

"Because I care about you. A lot."

"I don't want to be the reason that you regret making a change to the way you've lived your life," she said. "I don't need even more guilt to add to what I'm already carrying."

Wilder understood why she would feel that way, given what she'd been dealing with. But he didn't want her to think that every man would create situations that would heap guilt on her.

"I won't regret it," Wilder said. "I promise. If I really want to travel, there's nothing to say I couldn't do short trips instead of being gone for several months at a time. And you could come with me. Maybe we could spend some time at the orphanages too."

He wouldn't have thought he'd be as excited about his future without the traveling as he was. It wasn't as if he couldn't go back to traveling if things didn't work out with Lexi.

Not that that was how he thought things would go. He was going to do his best to make a relationship work because he loved her and wanted her in his life.

"It's just hard," Lexi said. "Two men who said they loved me have blamed me for their actions, and that hurts so bad." She glanced at him and cleared her throat before looking back down at her hands. "Uh... Not that I'm saying that you, uh... love me."

"Oh, but I do."

There was a moment of silence before she looked at him again, shock on her face. "What?"

"I do love you," Wilder said. "That's why I want to be with you."

"How could you love me already?"

"How could I not?" Wilder countered. "You're amazing, and I admire your strength and determination."

Lexi took a deep breath. "We're so different."

"Does that mean you don't like me?" Wilder hoped that wasn't the case, but he knew that someone with her type of personality might have a hard time dealing with his relaxed, easygoing approach to life.

338 · KIMBERLY RAE JORDAN

Obviously, it wasn't an issue for him. He could adapt to how she liked to have things done, and maybe she would come to see value in having a life with a little more flexibility. But even if she didn't, he thought they could still work it out.

"I do like you," she said, wrapping her arms across her waist. "A lot. It's why I put distance between us after the Christmas program. I didn't want my feelings to get even more involved because I figured there was no chance for us."

Wilder felt a glimmer of hope at her words. It was a start, and he could work with that. Hopefully, the fact she liked him meant that one day she could love him. But the only way that would happen was if she was willing to give them a chance.

"You've been there for me in ways no one but my mom has," Lexi continued. "I have been thankful for that. In the midst of such a tumultuous time, you've been a constant source of support, even when we weren't really talking. Whenever I thought about you during those times, though, I was encouraged by the knowledge that you were in my corner."

"I am definitely in your corner," Wilder assured her. "I'll always cheer for you."

She looked at him with a smile. "And that's something I really appreciate about you."

It wasn't quite the declaration of feelings he hoped for, but it was a step in the right direction.

"So... A date?"

"If you're sure you don't mind that my life is still a bit of a mess."

"Do I strike you as someone who is scared by a mess?" Wilder asked.

"No. Not really."

"I'm not scared by a mess. Truth be told, I'm probably more scared by perfection because I know the effort it takes to attain that in life. Plus, no one can maintain that for any length of time without it negatively affecting them."

Lexi nodded. "Perfection does take a lot of time and effort."

"I don't need you to be perfect," Wilder told her. "Just genuine. Be your wonderful self. And that means the good and the bad."

"I've never really let many people see that side of me." She gave him a small smile. "You're probably the only one, other than my family, coaches and Mik."

"And I'm honored you've shown it to me." Wilder took her hand again. "It's that side of you that I've fallen for. Not the beautiful, talented ice queen, but the woman who works hard, who shares her knowledge, and is willing to help others."

Lexi lowered her head. "I haven't always been that way."

"But you're that way now," Wilder said. "And that's what matters most."

Before she could respond, her phone rang. Letting go of his hand, she fished it out of the pocket of her jacket. After a moment's hesitation, she answered it.

"Irina?" She paused for a moment, then said, "How is he?"

Wilder wished that he could hear both sides of the conversation. He watched Lexi as she listened to whatever Irina was telling her. Her expression didn't reveal a lot, but he could tell she wasn't happy.

"Okay. I'll stay away." There was another stretch of silence as she listened to more of what Irina was saying. "It was good working with you again. I hope all goes well with you."

Lexi's expression saddened, then she said goodbye and lowered the phone to her lap.

When Wilder slipped an arm around her waist, Lexi sank against him. He held her close but didn't force her to talk.

"Mik is okay," she said when she finally spoke. "I mean, he was injured, but he should be okay in time."

"Did she tell you what his injuries are?"

"He has a concussion," she said. "And his lower left leg and ankle were crushed."

"Oh." Wilder realized exactly what that meant. "So, no Worlds?"

Lexi shook her head and let out a sigh. "No Worlds. And no next season. It's over."

That sounded so final, and even though she hadn't wanted to skate for another season, Wilder was sure that this wasn't the way she'd wanted to end her professional skating career.

"Is Irina leaving?"

"Yep. She's heading back to Maine since there won't be any more training."

"Wow. That's quick."

"Mik is going back too. As soon as he's able to travel."

"Is his family here?"

"She said his parents arrived a couple of hours ago." She paused. "And they told her to let me know that I'm not welcome to see him."

Wilder tightened his hold on her, and Lexi rested her head on his shoulder. "I'm sorry. I know that's not how you would have wanted things to end."

"Honestly, this ending feels worse than the first time around. Last time, I knew he was mad at me. This time, however, I think he truly hates me. And that's hard to accept."

"You were so close once that I'm sure it's hard to reconcile what you had years ago with what's happened in the past couple of years."

"He loved me once," she whispered. "How did it get to hate? What did I do to deserve that?"

"You didn't do anything," Wilder told her. "Your dad did something, and Mik chose to go after you because you're the easy target."

"It's over now," she said with a sigh. "Officially over."

"Do you think another guy will approach you about a partner-ship?" Wilder asked. "Now that you've reappeared on the competitive scene?"

"They might, but I'm not interested in continuing with a new partner. It's time to truly move forward."

Wilder liked the sound of that because he really thought it was best for her to be focused on the future instead of the past. He just hoped that he would be part of her future.

But he couldn't be selfish.

"I know life is probably going to be a bit uncertain for you over the next little while, so if you can't consider a relationship right now, I completely understand. I will still be there to support you, whatever you decide to do with your life."

Lexi straightened and turned to face him. Her blue gaze was intense as she stared at him. With heart pounding, Wilder waited for her to share what was on her mind.

"If you can deal with the mess my life is currently, I want you in it with me."

Relief rushed through Wilder, and he smiled. "Then that's where I'll be. And we can sort out our futures together."

"I like the sound of that."

Wilder did too.

# CHAPTER THIRTY-ONE

Lexi circled the rink, taking long strokes, then positioned herself for a jump. As soon as she took off, she knew she wasn't going to be able to do the number of rotations she was aiming for. Instead, she popped the jump into a single and focused on landing safely, then bent over to brace her hands on her thighs.

Anxiety plagued her, as it had since she'd woken that morning. Straightening, she shook her hands out as she took short strokes over to the boards, not certain she wanted to chance another jump when her focus was just not there.

It had been just over four weeks since she and Wilder had started dating, and for the most part, it had been a wonderful time. That day, however, felt like it was a test of their relationship.

She was back to working at the rink, although it was only part-time, and she was still a spokesperson for Remington, having done a couple of commercials for them. The money from both of those was good, but she'd recently decided to move out of her fancy furnished apartment.

Wilder and his family had helped her find an apartment that was in a nice part of town and, though smaller, the space had felt like home the first time she'd taken a tour of it. So, on the weekend, she'd be making the move to her place, which was unfurnished.

At least she had a mattress, and the rest of the furniture she'd bought would be delivered early the next week. While she was excited about her new place, her mom was less so.

She thought that Lexi should stay where she was, and she'd offered to cover the cost of the rent. However, Lexi had turned her down. The building she was moving to was nice, even if it wasn't as posh as the current one. It had a decent gym and good security, which was important, and it wasn't too far from Charli and Janessa's, which was a nice bonus.

Slowly but surely, her life in Serenity was taking root.

Lexi continued to skate while she waited for Wilder to show up. She'd hoped skating would serve as a distraction and ease her anxiety, but it really wasn't working. And sadly, the rink hadn't been very busy that day, which didn't help to keep her mind off things.

Kayleigh had agreed for Lexi to continue to work at the rink, though only part-time. She basically had the same schedule as Wilder, working Thursday to Monday. She didn't start as early as he did, though, and she worked only until five.

Her Saturday mornings were spent coaching. She coached Amelia and Layla together, and then she had a group of five students that she worked with when she was finished with the girls. It wasn't the coaching she'd envisioned doing in her future, but it was still satisfying.

When Wilder showed up, he walked in with Amelia, Layla and a slender young woman. The girls ran over to the ice and carefully stepped out on it to hug Lexi.

"Hi, babe," Wilder said as he reached them. He gave her a smile that held a wealth of affection. "How was your day?"

"It's been good." Aside from the anxiety over meeting a woman who had known Wilder longer and was a part of something that was super important to him.

"I want you to meet Miriam," he said, angling himself to gesture to the woman who had come in with him.

Lexi mustered up her professional smile for Miriam. It was all her anxiety would allow. The one the woman gave her in return was friendly.

"And Miriam, this is my girlfriend, Lexi."

"Nice to meet you," Miriam said as she held out her hand.

Lexi reached out to shake it. "Nice to meet you, too."

She wasn't sure how to converse with this woman, who was even more different from her than Wilder had been. Thankfully, she had overcome her reluctance to deal with those differences with Wilder, and if necessary, hopefully, she could do the same with Miriam.

Wilder seemed more than happy to carry the conversation, telling Miriam about the rink and the resort. Amelia and Layla stuck close to Lexi, pushing each other back and forth on the ice, even though they were wearing street shoes.

"Are you still coming for dinner at Mom and Dad's?" Wilder asked.

More than anything, Lexi wanted to say no. It was far out of her comfort zone, and she'd rather hole up by herself in her apartment. But Wilder had said that he wanted her to be there, so she would go for his sake.

"Yes."

"I'll swing by and pick you up," he said.

"Are you sure?"

"Yep. I'm going to drop Miriam off and take the girls home, then I'll come get you."

Lexi appreciated that he wasn't spending time alone with Miriam. There were moments when she still felt a bit uncertain about her relationship with Wilder. Not that he ever made her feel that way. It was all her own thoughts making her feel that way.

After everything she'd been through, she had a hard time believing that he wouldn't come to regret giving up his life of travel. His life of freedom to be tied to Serenity for her sake.

"Why don't you girls go out to the car with Miriam?" Wilder said, holding out his keys to Layla. "I'll be out in a minute."

Layla grinned at her uncle as she took the keys. "Sure thing."

Once they had left, Wilder turned back to Lexi. "Are you sure you're up for dinner?"

Did he not want her to be there? Lexi was uncertain what to say. "Would you prefer I not be there?"

Wilder's eyes widened as he stared at her. "What?"

"I don't mind going, but if you'd rather I not be there..."

"Why would I want that?" Wilder asked, his tone incredulous. "I always want you to be where I am."

"I don't know." Lexi shrugged. "It seems that this is a dinner for your friends."

"It is, but I want you there."

She stared at him for a long moment, then nodded. "Then I'll be there."

Wilder's smile grew at that pronouncement. He leaned forward and pressed a kiss to her forehead. They hadn't officially kissed yet, and though some might say the delay was ridiculous, Lexi appreciated that he wasn't rushing things.

Given that she was still feeling like he was going to regret changing his life, Lexi was leery of moving too quickly.

"I'll text you when I've dropped off the girls."

"Okay. I'll be waiting."

Propping her arms on the boards, Lexi watched Wilder walk to the doors. His long, easy strides ate up the distance, and all too soon, he was gone.

With a sigh, she grabbed her guards and slipped them on her blades, then went to the office. She switched her skates for her boots and dried off the blades before putting the skates in her bag.

She had fifteen minutes left in her shift, so she went back out to the ice. Wandering over to the café, she chatted for a few minutes with Luke, then greeted Talya when she came in. Soon, it was time to leave, so she grabbed her stuff and hurried home, wanting a little time to freshen up before Wilder came to pick her up.

By the time the message arrived that Wilder was leaving the house, Lexi had changed her clothes and was fixing her hair. She had plenty of experience doing different hairstyles, and that day, she'd done her hair up in a partial twist that left the top part in a cascade of curls. She'd freshened up her makeup, adding a bit more eyeshadow and some lipstick.

With a final look in the mirror, Lexi grabbed her purse, phone, and keys and headed down to the entrance to wait for Wilder. As soon as she spotted his car, Lexi pushed open the door and headed over to where the car idled by the curb.

As she approached, Wilder got out and came around to greet her. He wrapped his arms around her and, as was his habit, kissed her forehead.

As he stepped back from her, his gaze went from the top of her head to her feet. "You look beautiful."

The man never failed to give her compliments, and they always made Lexi feel warm and fuzzy. He always told her she was beautiful, even when she was wearing jeans and a T-shirt.

"Then we make a good pair because you're looking pretty handsome."

Wilder chuckled as he opened the door for her. He waited for Lexi to settle in the seat before closing the door.

"It sounds like Jay and Misha are going to be there tonight too," Wilder said.

"That will be nice," Lexi said. She hadn't spent a lot of time with the couple, but from the little she knew of them, they seemed as nice as the rest of the family.

"I think they're hoping to spend some time at the orphanage."

"Will the kids go with them?"

"I'm not sure about Ciara, but I think it would be good for Peyton to go."

"It would probably be an interesting experience for him."

Wilder nodded. "Would you be interested in going?"

"Maybe? I'm not sure what I could do. It's not like I can teach skating there. What else do I have to offer?"

"You have plenty to offer. They need people to help with practical stuff too. I've helped build things and paint walls. If you don't mind getting a little dirty, there's lots to do."

Lexi hadn't thought about the more practical side of operating a setup like the orphanage. "I've never done anything like that. But if someone will teach me, I'll do my best."

Wilder glanced over at her with a grin that brought butterflies to life in her stomach. "I'll be happy to teach you."

Lexi considered what it might be like to go to a place like Thailand with Wilder and to work alongside him for the good of the orphaned children who were rescued off the streets. As she'd taken on more children to coach, she'd discovered she actually enjoyed working with them.

Until she'd started coaching Amelia and Layla, she'd had very little contact with kids. Even when she'd been one herself, her dad had already decided that she needed to be homeschooled, so the only kid she was around at that age had been Mikhail.

"So you said that Miriam is a nurse?"

"Yes. She came back to the States after graduating high school in Thailand and got her nursing degree."

"Has she lived at the orphanage her whole life?"

Wilder shook his head. "Her parents worked planting churches first, then about ten years ago, they started the orphanage."

"Does she plan to stay in Thailand with them?"

"Yes. She feels that's where God is leading her to minister."

From how Wilder answered the questions, Lexi figured he must have spent a lot of time talking with her. Did Miriam have knowledge of Wilder that Lexi didn't have yet?

"Did you two... date?"

The way Wilder hesitated made her stomach clench, and sudden nausea made her throat tighten.

"No. We didn't," he said after what felt like an eternity. "However, we did spend a lot of time together. We talked about trying a relationship, but there was just something missing for us. We decided that we were better off as friends."

Lexi felt herself get bogged down in a maelstrom of emotion. On one hand, she was relieved that there had never been anything between them. However, it was hard to accept that he'd wanted a relationship with the pretty nurse.

What right did she have to be jealous when they hadn't even dated? She had an *engagement* in her past, so she had no right to be jealous of a *friendship.*

The problem was that she wasn't sure she was worthy of Wilder or the sacrifice he was making. And she didn't know how to make herself worthy. Miriam had a career that ministered to people. Lexi's greatest talent was no longer relevant in this new phase of her life.

Aside from playing Mrs. Claus to Wilder's Mr. Claus, Wilder had no use for her ability to skate well enough to earn gold medals. It was hard and conflicting to feel like she'd had so much to offer in her previous life, and yet now she had so little to offer in this new chapter. A chapter that was becoming so important to her.

She wanted to give Wilder and their relationship so much, but what did she have beyond her love for him? A love she hadn't shared with him yet, even though he'd told her he loved her already. He hadn't said it again since then, though, so she was a little bit confused.

"You don't have to worry about Miriam," Wilder said. "There's nothing between us."

"Okay." She tried to push as much nonchalance into the word as possible, needing it not to seem like such a big deal.

Thankfully, they pulled up to his parents' house, so the conversation ended. Now she needed to pull out her professional persona in order to hide the awkwardness that came with being in an uncomfortable situation.

"Looks like Gareth and Aria are here too," Wilder commented as he pointed to another vehicle parked there, along with a couple of others.

At that point, she was taking the viewpoint the more the merrier. More people meant less chance of the focus falling on her. Less need for her to participate in conversations.

After they got out of the car, Wilder took her hand as they walked up the steps to the front door. He opened it without knocking, and they stepped into a wide foyer.

The house had looked big from the outside, and the inside revealed that to be true. The wall of the foyer was covered with framed pictures. Many of them were of the family, capturing them throughout the years.

Lexi would have liked to look at them more closely, but before she could do that, Wilder's mom came into the foyer.

"Welcome," she said, a wide welcoming smile on her face. She hugged them both, then led them into the kitchen where several people were standing around. "Let me introduce you to Miriam and her parents."

Wilder let his mom know that she'd already met Miriam, so Mrs. Halverson introduced the one couple in the room that Lexi didn't know. The woman's smile was friendly enough, but her gaze dropped to where Lexi and Wilder held hands and a small frown crossed her face.

Lexi couldn't blame her for not being happy that Wilder was with someone other than her daughter. Wilder was a catch, and any woman would want him to be with their daughter.

Miriam's mom moved off to speak with Mrs. Halverson while Miriam stood talking to Misha. Wilder led Lexi over to Gareth and Aria, who had Timmy in her arms.

"Peyton didn't come?" Wilder asked Gareth after they greeted them.

"Jay said they left the kids with Denise, since it's a school night."

"How are you doing, Lexi?" Aria asked.

Aria and Misha were the two women in the family that Lexi hadn't spent as much time with, but they'd always been friendly.

Letting Timothy go, when he reached for his father, Aria said, "How is the coaching going?"

"Very well. Layla and Amelia are doing great."

"Charli said that you think Amelia will do well in competitions."

Lexi nodded. "She's got some natural skill, and as long as she works hard, I think she'd excel in competitions."

"I hope some of them are close by," Gareth said. "We'd like to be able to go support her. It's been a while since we've had someone to cheer for, since Cole's games are all too far for us to travel to."

"Why don't we all go to the table?" Mrs. Halverson said, interrupting their conversation.

The large table was beautifully set, and the food smelled delicious. Wilder held a chair for Lexi, then sat down beside her. Aria was seated on her other side.

After Mr. Halverson said a prayer for the meal, Mrs. Halverson said, "Just so I'm not being deceptive, I want to say that I had help preparing this meal. Misha's mother, Denise, was gracious enough to lend me her skills because I'm nowhere near the cook that she is."

"Mom would have stayed for the meal, but she offered to watch the kids for us instead," Misha told them.

"It smells delicious," Miriam's mom said as they passed the bowls of food around.

The conversation as they ate centered mainly on the orphanage ministry, which, in spite of her feelings about Miriam, Lexi found interesting.

"Wilder, when you come to visit us next time, we'd like to have you do a video of the orphanage," Miriam's dad said. "I think it would be useful for presentations at churches here."

"I'd be happy to do that," Wilder said, excitement in his voice. "I've missed doing videos and have been trying to come up with ideas."

Lexi felt a little sick at his words. Already, he was missing something that was tied to his traveling. Was it the start of him resenting her for taking him away from that life?

She pushed the food around on her plate, trying to look like she was paying attention to the conversation as she took small bites of food. In fact, her mind was spinning through options of what she should do.

Did she love Wilder enough to step back from him? To let him go back to the life he'd happily been living until he met her?

She felt him lean against her arm and looked over to find him watching her with concern.

"Everything okay?" He kept his voice low as the conversation continued around them.

She gave him a quick smile. "It's all good."

It was clear he wasn't convinced, but he didn't push further.

When they'd finished eating, she got up and helped clear the table before they had dessert. When they sat down again to have pie and coffee, Wilder made sure his chair was close to hers, and he rested his arm on the back of her chair.

Lexi couldn't help but lean into him a bit as they ate their pieces of pie. Denise had made two types—apple and chocolate—and Lexi had chosen the chocolate, which was amazing.

From the conversation, it sounded like several members of the Halverson family would be making their way to the orphanage in the coming months.

"Wilder, how much time do you think you'll be able to spend with us?" Miriam's mom asked. "We sure enjoy having you around."

"I'm not sure yet. I'd like Lexi to come with me, so we'll have to talk and see how our schedules work out."

"Oh?" Her gaze went to Lexi. "Have you ever done any ministry work?"

Before she could say anything, Wilder said, "Lexi played a huge role in the fundraiser at Christmas. We couldn't have done it without her."

"It was such a fun afternoon," Aria added. "The kids really enjoyed having the two of them as Mr. and Mrs. Claus. I hope that they can do it again this year."

"I'd love to do it again," Wilder told her. "It was a lot of fun, and doing it with Lexi made it that much more special."

When he looked at her with affection, Lexi felt a bit of the uncertainty in her heart ease. She smiled back at him. "I enjoyed it too."

"Well, we sure appreciate all the money you raised for our orphanage," Miriam's dad said.

"We were thinking of doing a fundraiser for school supplies," Misha said. "Is that something that might be doable?"

After she finished her pie, Lexi leaned more fully against Wilder's side as she listened to them talk about another fundraiser. Wilder dropped his arm from the back of the chair to her shoulders, cupping her upper arm with his hand.

The conversation wound down when Timmy began to fuss. That seemed to be the cue for several of them—including her and Wilder—to leave. Miriam and her parents were staying with the Halversons, so they didn't follow the rest of them out to their cars.

As they drove back to her place, Wilder talked about the video they'd asked him to do. But when they got to her apartment, he didn't get out of the car right away.

"Can we talk for a minute?"

Lexi's heart sank. After spending time with Miriam and her parents, had he realized that a relationship with her was going to hold him back from what he really wanted?

Shifting to face her, he said, "How are you feeling about us?"

"What?"

"I got the feeling when I first asked you out that you had some hesitation about a relationship between us working," he said. "Do you still feel that way?"

There were times she still wondered about how real her relationship with Mik had been, and she didn't want that with Wilder. She had to be honest with him, and she hoped that he'd be honest with her.

"I'm still struggling to understand why you're willing to give up your way of life for me."

"I'm not just giving it up for you," he told her. "I'm giving it up for us. I'm giving it up for me because you make me happy, and I want that happiness in my life. I'm at peace about this decision, which tells me that this is where God wants me now. Not just dating you, but spreading the word about the orphanages. I'm excited about the change. I'm excited about being with you."

"Really?"

"You need to understand your value outside of skating. For most of your life, you've found your worth in your talent for skating. That's what people have valued most about you. And while I do appreciate and admire that talent of yours, that's not what I value most about you. I know that's also not what God values most about you."

It was hard to admit that there were times she didn't know why God would care about her, particularly because her talent was so useless.

"Do you doubt that God wants us to be together?" Wilder asked.

And that was one more struggle she had. How did she know what God wanted? She'd never actively sought God's will in her life before. Though that was obviously something she wanted now, how was she supposed to know how to do it?

Did she want God's will to be for them to be together? For sure.

"You're confident that He does?" She turned the question back on him.

"I am," he said. "I've prayed about something between us ever since I started having feelings for you. Even when we weren't talking, I prayed for you, and asked God to work things out between us."

"I've prayed about it too, but I just don't know how to know what God's will is."

Wilder reached for her hand, and Lexi found comfort in his firm grip.

"I think we need to start praying together for our relationship," Wilder said. "So we can know as a couple that we're following God's will."

A sense of relief and peace filled her, knowing that she wouldn't be alone in praying about their relationship.

Wilder squeezed her fingers as he cleared his throat. "Also, I know you were uneasy with Miriam today, and I'm sorry for the role I played in that. I should have realized that was a possibility and taken steps to protect you from feeling that way. If I ever say or do anything else that makes you feel uneasy like that, please tell me. I don't want to do that again."

Lexi felt the unease Wilder had referenced fade away at his words. She'd like to think she would have confronted him about how he'd made her feel, but she wasn't totally confident she would have.

She wasn't as confrontational as she'd once been. Her father's conviction and what had followed had broken her apart. Coming to Serenity had helped put her back together, mentally and spiritually. But she was different now. And while she hadn't lost her backbone completely—especially where Mik and her coaches were concerned—she was having to learn how and when to use it in other settings.

"Will you promise me that?" Wilder prompted.

"I will."

"I love you," he said. "I know that I haven't said it since that first time, but I don't want you to think that's changed."

"Why haven't you said it?"

"I thought maybe you'd feel pressured to say it back. I didn't want that."

His explanation just reinforced what a good guy he was and validated how she felt about him. "Well, I don't know if I would have felt pressured then or not. But I know that I don't feel pressured to say it now, and I still want to."

"Go ahead. Don't keep me in suspense." A smile grew on Wilder's face as he winked at her. "Say it."

Lexi laughed, her heart feeling lighter. "I love you, Wilder Halverson."

His smile softened as he leaned toward her.

At one time, she might have said that sitting in a car wouldn't be the most romantic place to share a first kiss. But that night? It was the most perfect place because it was just her and Wilder taking a small—but significant—step forward in their relationship.

The soft press of Wilder's lips to hers held a wealth of emotion for Lexi. It solidified the seriousness of their relationship and the love they had for each other.

She was glad that they had waited to have their first kiss. It made it feel that much more significant, and she knew in that moment that they both were going to work hard every day to make their relationship a success.

# EPILOGUE

The late August sun beat down on Lexi as she waited for Miriam to finish speaking with Misha. It was still early in the morning, but already the heat was taking hold. The temperature in Thailand was higher and more humid than in Serenity, and it had taken some getting used to the lack of air conditioning. But it had been worth it to experience what she had for the past month.

If someone had told her back in the spring, when they'd first met, that she'd come to consider Miriam a good friend, Lexi would have thought they were crazy. But over the time they'd been at the orphanage, she and the woman had gotten to know each other quite well. Lexi now considered her a good friend.

"It's been so great having you here," Miriam said to Lexi as Misha turned to talk to Miriam's mom. "I'm going to miss you."

"I've really enjoyed getting a chance to spend some time here," Lexi told her as they hugged. "And look forward to doing it again."

"We've got to go," Miriam's dad called over to them from the vehicle he was using to drive them to the airport. "I want to make sure we've got some time to spare, since I don't know what the traffic is going to be like."

All their bags were already loaded up in the back of it, so after a final wave, they climbed inside. Peyton sat in the front between Miriam's dad and Jay, while Lexi sat in the back with Wilder and Misha.

Lexi and Wilder had come to Thailand a month ago, then two weeks ago, Misha and Jay had arrived with Peyton.

She'd been very nervous about the trip and had almost backed out at the last minute. Wilder hadn't pressured her, though. He'd told her that if she really didn't want to go, he wouldn't force her and that it wouldn't change anything between them. But he still planned to go. With or without her.

It might have been the thought of Wilder spending an entire month with Miriam that had gotten Lexi on that plane out of Spokane. But now that they were preparing to leave Thailand, she was sad that their time was over. The only thing that made the goodbyes easier was knowing that they would be back. Of that, she was certain.

"Doing okay?" Wilder asked as he took her hand once the vehicle had started to move, heading for the large, guarded gate that led out of the compound.

"I am," she assured him. He'd made a point to check in on her frequently, and his care and concern had drawn them even closer together. Her love for this man was beyond anything she'd ever experienced before.

As Miriam's dad drove, Lexi leaned against Wilder and looked out the window. Thailand was a beautiful country, but she'd also come to know the beauty of the Thai people. Their culture and their resilience had been a joy to experience.

The orphanage was part of a compound. An expansive piece of land that was fenced in with several buildings, along with a large garden and a fruit tree orchard. In addition to the dormitories for the children, there was a large house with several bedrooms, which was where Miriam and her folks lived, and where they had stayed.

A couple of years ago, volunteers had come from the US and built a school, and one of the projects they'd helped with over the past month they'd been there had been a new building for women who needed a safe place to live. Wilder had taken videos of a lot of the work they did, as well as interviewing Miriam's parents about their vision for the ministry, hoping to use the video to share more about the work there with churches in the US.

The one thing that had taken some getting used to for Lexi was the presence of armed security guards that patrolled the perimeter and the gate of the compound twenty-four/seven. Wilder had explained why it was necessary, and once again, it was such a foreign thing to her. But taking children off the street and helping women escape abuse drew the attention of people who didn't want them to be safe and out of their sinister reach.

She had also worked alongside Misha and Miriam in the small clinic that served not just the compound, but the surrounding area. The poverty and physical suffering she'd seen had left an indelible mark on her heart. There had been difficult moments, but she would be back. If God allowed her to return, she would be back.

When they reached the airport, it didn't take long to unload their bags, say goodbye to Miriam's dad, and head into the terminal. Wilder and Jay took charge of guiding them to where they needed to be, making sure everything was in order for check in.

Once that was done, they headed for the security checkpoint. As they walked through the airport, Lexi marveled at the beauty of the space. It was a mix of glass and steel, with décor and stores that featured the cultures of the east and the west.

"Ready to go home?" Wilder asked as they settled onto padded seats near their gate.

"I wasn't when we were still at the compound, but now that we're here, I wish we were home already."

"Yeah. The twenty-four hours it takes to get home can be a killer. The first stretch is short. Just five hours to Seoul, South Korea, but then there's an almost eleven hour flight from there to Sea-Tac."

"Can you go with me to get a drink, Uncle Wilder?" Peyton asked from where he sat beside Wilder.

"Sure thing, buddy." Wilder turned to Lexi. "Want something?"

"Iced coffee if they have it, please."

After asking Jay and Misha what they wanted, Lexi watched the pair walk away, Wilder with his arm around Peyton's shoulders. In that moment, she knew with one hundred percent certainty that she wanted to marry that man.

Over the past several months, her love for him had only grown, as had his for her. She knew that, because he told her all the time how much he loved her.

When she spotted the pair coming back, it was clear from the expression on Peyton's face how much he adored Wilder. Over the past two weeks, Peyton had shadowed Wilder even more than his own dad. And Wilder had had so much patience as he showed him what to do so that he could help at the orphanage.

She hoped that it was God's will for this man to be her husband and the father of her children.

When he handed her an iced coffee, she smiled up at him. "Thank you."

"You're very welcome."

Peyton had handed Misha the drink she'd asked for, but before she could take a drink, Jay, who hadn't ordered a drink, covered her hand with his and lifted it to take a sip. "That's perfect."

"Uncle Wilder said we needed to get a large because you were probably going to make Mom share," Peyton said with a grin.

"I appreciate that, sweetie," Misha told him.

Lexi took a sip, humming in appreciation. "This is perfect."

It wasn't a surprise since Wilder was very familiar with how she liked her drink.

Wilder sat down beside her again, stretching out his legs as he took a sip of his own drink. He put his free arm around the back of Lexi's seat. Lexi leaned into him as she continued to drink her iced coffee.

"Are you excited to get back to the rink?" Wilder asked.

"I am, especially to coaching Amelia and Layla. With Amelia's first competition coming up soon, we'll need to focus on polishing up her program."

She'd found a rink in Coeur d'Alene that had opportunities for beginner skaters to compete. It wasn't tied to the bigger events sponsored by the national organization, which wasn't an issue. This was just to get Amelia's feet wet in the world of competitive figure skating. If she did well and enjoyed it, then Lexi would look at what steps were necessary to get her into competitions that were part of the national organization.

When the airline attendant called for their row to board, they dropped their empty cups into the garbage, then lined up to get onto the plane. After they found their seats, Wilder put their bags into the overhead compartment, then sat down beside her.

Though they weren't traveling first class, they'd decided that for the comfort of the guys—especially Jay—they would lay out the extra money to get premium seats. Their seat configuration meant there were only the two of them next to the window, and there was no one in front of them. Jay, Misha, and Peyton were in the middle section of the same row.

As the plane backed away from the terminal, Wilder took Lexi's hand, then together, they prayed for the trip that lay ahead. Lexi continued to hold Wilder's hand through take-off. She wasn't necessarily scared of flying, but the take-offs and landings were always a little nerve-wracking for her.

She hoped that this was just the first of many trips that they took together. After spending time immersed in the culture and beauty of another country, Lexi thought she might be more interested in traveling with Wilder, as long as her budget and schedule allowed it.

He handled all the aspects of traveling with ease because he'd done so much of it. That made things less stressful for Lexi, which meant she was willing to do more of it.

Throughout the flight to Seoul, they chatted about their plans for the next few months. It wasn't unusual for them to seek input from each other on things that might impact their future as a couple. How he sought her input and offered his was just one more thing she loved about him.

She'd received an email while in Thailand from the parents of a girl who had been taking skating lessons for four years, but now they wanted to get more serious with her training. They happened to live in Spokane, so at least they wouldn't have to uproot their entire life to accommodate training, as long as they didn't mind commuting for a little over an hour one way.

"Are you going to take her on?" Wilder asked.

"I want to meet with her first and see how she handles her skating ability."

"Do you rely on chemistry at all?" he asked. "Like if you get along?"

"We don't necessarily have to get along, but I need to know she respects our roles and is willing to listen and do what I ask of her. I didn't get along with my coaches all the time, but I respected their knowledge and did what they wanted."

"How are you feeling about it? Optimistic? Wary? Excited?"

Lexi considered his question for a moment, then said, "All of the above? Can I claim that?"

"You certainly can." Wilder gave her hand a squeeze. "Also, I think we need to seriously consider doing a skating video to upload to your channel."

Lexi still wasn't sure if that would be something that people would actually want to watch. But she had the time to do it and was willing to give it a try. Plus, being able to do something with Wilder always made her feel good. She thought they made a good team.

She might not be making plans for the Olympics or a World Championship, but these plans with Wilder still felt significant. They were working together for their future.

Two years ago, her world had fallen apart. She'd tried putting it back together herself, but had continued to struggle. Her mom had moved forward so quickly after the upheaval of their lives and had expected Lexi to do the same, but she just hadn't been able to.

It wasn't until she'd come to Serenity that she'd met people who'd showed her the importance of God in her life and had offered friendship and acceptance that had nothing to do with how many medals she had or what her father had done.

God had placed Wilder and his family in her life, and he had helped her figure out a way to put the shattered pieces of her life back together. And in the process, he'd taught her about love and how God intended it to be lived out in one's life.

Lexi leaned against Wilder's arm as she smiled up at him. "I love you."

Wilder's eyes shone as he smiled back, then he gave her a kiss. "I love you too."

~ * ~

"This looks even better than last year," Kayleigh said as she stood beside Wilder, taking in the transformed rink. "The community support is amazing."

Wilder couldn't help but agree, and it made him so happy. The more people that turned out, the more word of the orphanages spread. And the more money they were able to raise.

His gaze skipped over the crowd in search of one person. His person. The one he'd come to love above all others in his life.

No surprise, he found Lexi on the ice, and she wasn't alone. Over the past few months, the number of students she coached had grown. It was amazing to see how she'd blossomed as she found her footing in her new life.

Even her mom had come around and accepted that Serenity was where her daughter wanted to be, and that she was truly happy there. At that moment, Eileen stood at the boards with her husband, Leland, watching Lexi skate with some of her students.

Eileen and Leland were in town for the fundraiser, but they planned to stay through the new year, so they'd be there for Christmas. When his mom had heard that they were going to be in town, she'd extended an invitation for them to stay at the big family house. Lexi had been surprised, but happy, when her mom had accepted.

Alexander and his family were going to be there as well, and this year, Hudson and Kayleigh had invited them to also be part of the Halverson Christmas celebration. It was going to be chaos—as usual. And Wilder couldn't wait. The wilder the better.

"Santa!" Ciara came running over to Wilder, and, without hesitation, he scooped her up.

"How's Princess Ci?" Wilder asked her. "Have you been a good girl?"

"Yep!"

"How about when you punched Peyton?"

The little girl's light brown eyes grew wide. "How do you *know* that?"

He winked at her. "I'm Santa."

She stared at him for a long moment, then narrowed her eyes at him, looking well beyond her four years. "Are you really?"

Kayleigh started laughing, then reached out to take Ciara before Wilder had to reveal the truth. "Why don't we get your skates on?"

Ciara looked at Wilder, then over at Lexi. She had started to take lessons with Lexi too, and seemed to love it. "Yep. I want to skate."

As they moved off to find Jay or Misha to get her skates, Wilder headed over to where Janessa and Will stood next to the tables that held all the goodies for the bake sale. "Where's Slugger?"

Janessa rolled her eyes at him. "Stop calling Liam Slugger."

"Why? It's a special nickname between him and me." It seemed whenever Wilder held Liam, the baby took a swing at Wilder's face. He bopped Wilder on the nose or cheek with amazing accuracy. "I love my little slugger."

"Mom has him," Janessa told him with a shake of her head. "So if you're looking to get knocked out, you can go fight her for him."

"Thanks. I will."

Wilder found his mom with Liam in her arms, talking to some people by the large display that was set up for the orphanages. She and his dad had taken on the role of spokespeople for the fundraiser since they were as familiar with the orphan ministry now as Wilder. Maybe even more so.

When the person moved on, Wilder stepped up to her. His mom greeted him with a wide, knowing smile.

"Nervous, sweetheart?" she asked.

"A little," he admitted. "Though I don't know why. I'm positive she's going to say yes."

"I'm positive she's going to say yes too," his mom said. "Eileen and I are very excited about planning a wedding."

Wilder tried not to frown as he had a vision of what the pair might come up with. If Lexi got too overwhelmed, he'd have a word with his mom. Lexi, though, would have to handle her mom.

That was crossing the bridge before he got to it, however. Even though he was pretty sure that bridge was ready and waiting for him.

After giving his mom a hug and dropping a kiss on Liam's dark curls, he moved on, continuing his journey around the rink. Lots of kids wanted to talk to him, which he happily did, until he found himself back at the entrance to the ice.

It was almost time for him and Lexi to skate together again. He'd decided to propose during one of their programs in the middle of the afternoon. It was the time when all of his local family was going to be present. Most of them were already standing at the boards, making sure they had a good view of what was to come.

Wilder stood for a moment, watching Lexi skate with the kids. When they'd first met, she'd always had such an intensity around her when she skated. But now, it seemed like she had a real joy in skating. More often than not, she had a smile on her face when she was on the ice. Her genuine one, not her professional one.

As she turned on the ice, their gazes met, and immediately, her smile grew, lighting up her beautiful face. She left the kids to continue their skating and came over to where Wilder waited.

"Hello, Santa," she said with a flirtatious smile.

"Well, hello there, Mrs. Claus." He gave her a wink. "Are you ready for another whirl on the ice?"

"With you? Always."

For a moment, Wilder had a glimpse of them in the future. Hopefully, they'd still be skating hand in hand, sporting actual gray hair—not just wigs—and a few more wrinkles, but still as much in love as they were at that moment. Or maybe more. Already, his love for Lexi had grown well beyond what he'd felt initially.

It took a few minutes for them to clear the ice and get things set up for the programs. This year, Amelia, Layla, and one other girl that Lexi had been training had a little program that they performed first. Skating to the music of *Up on the Housetop*, the girls garnered lots of applause and cheers from the people gathered around the boards.

When they finished their program, Lexi and Wilder took their positions. They were still skating to *Here Comes Santa Claus*, but Lexi had updated the choreography a bit. However, Wilder had insisted that they still have the same ending pose that they'd had the previous year. He had an ulterior motive for wanting that, but Lexi hadn't protested at all.

Amelia and Layla were on the ice with them, and they skated their parts perfectly. When Wilder took Lexi into his arms to guide her around the ice, he couldn't help but smile. His heart felt like it was going to explode with the love he had for her.

"You are the most beautiful Mrs. Claus ever," Wilder told her as they skated. They'd performed the program enough that they didn't need to focus too much on it.

"And you're the most handsome Santa."

The joy on her face matched what he felt in his heart. They might have two different approaches to life, but they'd learned to compromise and to talk through situations to come up with the best way to move forward. Having to do that had brought them closer together.

"Ciara didn't recognize me earlier," Wilder said. "So I'm not sure how I can be the most handsome Santa when I don't look like myself."

Lexi tipped her head back in laughter. "And your humility is just so amazing."

"I know, right?"

They completed a lap around the rink, then they each skated with one of the girls before coming back for the last part. As they settled into their final pose, with Wilder on one knee and Lexi perched on his other, he reached into the pocket and pulled out the ring he'd chosen for her.

The clapping and cheering immediately died down as people realized what was going on. Lexi glanced around, then looked down at Wilder, her eyes going wide. Her mouth dropped down as she stared at him.

"Lexi, my love, since we officially started dating, I have known that you were the one I wanted to spend the rest of my life with. You've brought joy to my life and love to my heart in amounts I didn't know were possible. I want us to share that love and joy forever. Will you marry me?"

Lexi reached out and stroked her fingers along his cheek. "You met me at one of the lowest points in my life, and when I wasn't the nicest person. However, you stuck around and offered me support and understanding while I tried to find a new direction for my life. I'm just so glad that that direction has aligned with yours. I'd love nothing more than to be your wife and to continue our journey together. I love you."

"I love you too." Emotion choked Wilder, but he still managed to get the words out.

Cheers and applause echoed around the rink as he slid the ring on her finger. As they shared their first kiss as an engaged couple, Wilder thanked God for bringing Lexi into his life and for filling his heart with a willingness to change the way he'd been living.

She might have been queen of the ice when they'd met, but now, she was queen of his heart. Though they might only rarely be partners on the ice, off the ice, they were going to be partners for life, and nothing could bring him more joy.

# ABOUT THE AUTHOR

Kimberly Rae Jordan is a USA Today bestselling author of Christian romances. Many years ago, her love of reading Christian romance morphed into a desire to write stories of love, faith, and family, and thus began a journey that would lead her to places Kimberly never imagined she'd go.

In addition to being a writer, she is also a wife and mother, which means Kimberly spends her days straddling the line between real life in a house on the prairies of Canada and the imaginary world her characters live in. Though caring for her husband and four kids and working on her stories takes up a large portion of her day, Kimberly also enjoys reading and looking at craft ideas that she will likely never attempt to make.

As she continues to pen heartwarming stories of love, faith, and family, Kimberly hopes that readers of all ages will enjoy the journeys her characters take in each book. She has no plan to stop writing the stories God places on her heart and looks forward to where her journey will take her in the years to come.

www.ingramcontent.com/pod-product-compliance
Lightning Source LLC
Chambersburg PA
CBHW051943240626
47153CB00005B/1607